The Primrose Railway Children

JACQUELINE WILSON

Illustrated by Rachael Dean

PUFFIN

PUFFIN BOOKS

UK | USA | Canada | Ireland | Australia
India | New Zealand | South Africa

Puffin Books is part of the Penguin Random House group of companies
whose addresses can be found at global.penguinrandomhouse.com.

www.penguin.co.uk
www.puffin.co.uk
www.ladybird.co.uk

First hardback edition published 2021
This paperback edition published 2022
001

Text copyright © Jacqueline Wilson, 2021
Illustrations copyright © Rachael Dean, 2021

The moral right of the author and illustrator has been asserted

Text design by Janene Spencer
Printed and bound in Great Britain by Clays Ltd, Elcograf S.p.A.

The authorized representative in the EEA is Penguin Random House Ireland,
Morrison Chambers, 32 Nassau Street, Dublin D02 YH68

A CIP catalogue record for this book is available from the British Library

ISBN: 978–0–241–53763–3

All correspondence to:
Puffin Books
Penguin Random House Children's
One Embassy Gardens, 8 Viaduct Gardens, London SW11 7BW

For Naomi, with love.
Thanks so much for being such a star.

I knew something was the matter. Mum and Dad kept having these arguments. They didn't shout or yell – they whispered in another room so we couldn't hear properly. Somehow the hissing sounds were worse, even though we couldn't make sense of the words.

I woke up once and heard them downstairs in the kitchen. I looked at my watch. It was half past two in the morning! They always went to bed at half past ten, after the news. I usually heard them go to bed because I took ages to fall asleep.

I couldn't sleep because I was having trouble at school. My best friend, Amelie, was suddenly acting really weirdly. We'd been friends ever since we started in Reception when we were four and a half. We were devoted to each other from the first day, when I made Amelie a pink bead necklace and she made me a blue one. We used to wander around hand in hand, and pretended we were

sisters. We did look quite alike in those days actually, both of us a bit podgy, with fair plaits down to our shoulders and brown eyes. We liked doing exactly the same things too: we dressed up in our Disney Princess costumes and drew pictures with the sky right up at the top and stick people floating above the grass and played elaborate imaginary games with our teddies.

But now we were nearly ten we were totally different. Amelie's hair fell all the way to her waist, smooth and shining. Mine was curly and still wouldn't grow much past my shoulders. Amelie wore tiny skirts and tight tops and sparkly shoes. I'd have liked to wear them too, but Mum said I looked better in my dungarees and canvas boots. Amelie's felt tips had all dried up because she preferred playing on her iPad, but I still liked art. I drew lines of girls with their sparkly shoes firmly on the grass and I gave them all names and made up stories about them. I didn't play with my teddies any more, but I still acted out all sorts of imaginary dramas, when I knew I could be strictly private.

Amelie went to a real drama school on Saturdays now, and gymnastics and ballet after school. I didn't want to go to gymnastics because I found it difficult even doing a forward roll. I tried ballet too, but if I'm honest I was a bit rubbish at it, and got stuck in the elementary class with the babies. Dad and I danced together to old rock music instead, and he said I did a mean jive.

I *did* want to go to Amelie's drama class, but Saturdays were

Family Days. Mum went off to work before we got up on weekdays, and she generally didn't get home till I was in bed, but on Saturdays we all went swimming at her gym and then went to Pizza Express, and spent the afternoons going to the cinema or a museum or a stately house.

It was especially good going with Dad. He'd act out scenes from the film with me afterwards, and he'd tell me stories about the things in the exhibition and he'd show me around the stately house as if he was Lord Dad and I was his little Lady.

Mum and Dad and Perry and I still went on these Family Days. But nowadays my big sister Becks saw all her friends on Saturdays and hung out at the shopping centre instead. Perry didn't really want to come on Family Days either, but he didn't *have* many friends, and Mum and Dad said he was too young to stay at home by himself.

I'd always had lots of friends, thank goodness, but Amelie was always my best-ever friend – only now she seemed to have gone off me. We still sat next to each other at school but we didn't whisper together or pass each other little notes. She was forever craning round to send a scribbled note or whisper to Kate. They went to the same gymnastics class – and now Kate had started ballet too. She went straight into the intermediate class because apparently the ballet teacher said she had natural talent. Amelie and Kate started doing little dance routines together in the playground.

I tried to join in at first. They didn't actually say anything horrid, but they kept looking at each other, their lips twitching, as if they were laughing at me.

Amelie and I still went home together. Dad and Amelie's mum took it in turns to collect us in the car, but I found out Kate sometimes had a sleepover at Amelie's house after gymnastics or ballet. Amelie hadn't asked me to come for a sleepover for ages.

'Well, we'll ask Amelie to sleep over at ours,' said Dad.

So I did, but Amelie just shrugged and looked awkward, and said she wasn't really allowed to on school nights any more – which was a downright lie. That wasn't the worst of it though. I heard them whispering together in the playground, and Amelie said to Kate, 'If I tell you something awful about Phoebe, will you swear not to tell anyone else ever?'

I'm Phoebe. I felt like she'd set me on fire. I burned all over. What was she going to say that was so awful? She knew all my secrets. Would she tell Kate about the time in Year Two when I wet myself? It was shameful and even my tights got sopping, but I was only little after all. Would she tell Kate about how I tore up Perry's precious *1,001 Facts about Amazing Animals* notebook last week? It was very mean of me, but he'd only compiled twenty-three facts so far, and he was being so annoying, singing the same song over and over again until I wanted to scream. Would she tell Kate that I'd copied a little poem out of an old book and pretended

I'd written it myself, because I wanted to show off to Dad? He thought it was marvellous, and even Mum was impressed at first – but then she Googled the first line and found me out. That was truly awful, and when I told Amelie I made *her* swear not to tell anyone else ever.

I listened hard, my heart thudding, waiting for her to betray me. But she didn't mention that poem.

'I heard my mum talking. It's about Phoebe's dad,' Amelie said. Then she put her mouth right up to Kate's ear and whispered.

I couldn't hear a single word, but Kate gasped and put her hand to her mouth in a silly affected manner.

'No!' she said. 'You're joking me!'

'You two are the jokes!' I burst out, confronting them. 'What lies are you spreading about my dad?'

Amelie blushed. She's very fair, but when she blushes she goes tomato red and looks almost ugly.

'I don't tell lies!' she said, which was clearly a lie in itself.

'Is it really true that—' Kate started, but Amelie shoved her quite hard to shut her up.

'Ouch!' Kate protested.

'I was just telling Kate that your dad used to be quite famous,' Amelie blurted out.

'Really?' I said, disconcerted. Because this wasn't a lie; it was true. In fact, Dad used to be *very* famous. He was on television for

years and years before I was born. Becks says she can remember watching him when she was really little. You can still find his programme on YouTube. It was for little children, on CBeebies, and it was called *Robinson*. That's our surname. Dad's first name is Michael, though Mum and everyone else call him Rob.

There's this old book called *Robinson Crusoe*. Dad's got a much-thumbed Penguin classic copy. He's going to read it to me some time, but says it's rather old for me at the moment. He's told me a bit about the story though. The Robinson in the book is shipwrecked onto a desert island. So my dad made this pretend island, all sand, with pebbles for rocks. He created a little dough Robinson figure who lived all alone in a mud hut in the middle of the island. At the beginning of every programme he made little Robinson come out of his hut and Dad said: 'Here's Robinson. Who is he going to meet today?'

He didn't ever meet any people, but he met monkeys and pigs and wildcats and dogs and turtles and dolphins and jellyfish and even a woolly mammoth. If there was no one about he had a chat with the vegetables in his garden patch. He once had races with his runner beans. It's a bit weird, but it *was* for very little children.

There were *Robinson* books too. My mum published them – that's how they met. You used to be able to get toy Robinson islands as well. We've got a big one up in our attic. Dad and I used to play with it lots, just the two of us. I think Becks did too once

upon a time. Perry never saw the point. He used to get irritated with Dad.

'It's all wrong! Woolly mammoths were prehistoric creatures, so they're extinct now. Monkeys and pigs and turtles and all the others can't *talk*. Potatoes and carrots can't either. And those runner beans are silly – beans can't *run*.'

But maybe other children also thought Robinson silly, because the programmes went out of fashion – and Dad did too. He tried out all kinds of other ideas but the children's television people didn't like them. He tried adult television as well, science fantasy scripts. They were meant to be funny but no one laughed and they didn't get made. He got as far as a pilot half-hour for radio called *Cats in Space*, but it was never made into a series. Mum tried to persuade her editorial department to publish a *Cats in Space* book, but without any success.

Dad never gave up trying. He's not a quitter. He started writing a detective story and then a historical novel, but they didn't work out either. People said he wasn't really that sort of writer. So he went back to writing *Robinson*. He wrote *Robinson Rhymes*, and a sequel to *Robinson* called *Mrs Robinson and all the little Robinsons* but they were all turned down. Dad even had this idea of being a real-life Robinson on an actual desert island, filming himself. I was glad that idea got rejected because we would have missed him too much. Well, *I* would. *And* Perry.

Eventually Mum got him a job with Melissa Harris, adapting all her Puggy-Wuggy books for television. We can't stand Puggy-Wuggy. He's this goofy little dog who does daft things and wears a selection of awful outfits. He's always getting into trouble, but nobody minds because they think he's so cute. He isn't cute, he's revolting. Even Mum thinks that, but Melissa Harris is her bestselling author, and so she has to act as if Puggy-Wuggy is adorable.

Melissa Harris used to be on television a lot in some soap or other. Then she was in *Strictly*, dancing with Anton, and then she won *I'm a Celebrity* because people thought her hilarious – goodness knows why. She started her own YouTube channel, dressing up her weird little pug in ridiculous outfits, and she got thousands of followers.

Melissa Harris looks rather like a very ancient Puggy-Wuggy. I'm not sure how old she really is, but she looks about a hundred and one. She's got this silly squashed-up face with a button nose and big bulgy eyes, and her clothes are awful too, generally pink. Dad took me to meet her once. She called me a dear little poppet and patted me on the head as if *I* was a pug. She gave me a big pink cupcake and signed copies of all ten of her Puggy-Wuggy books, though they were much too young for me. Still, I suppose it was kind of her.

She was kind to Dad too. In fact, she totally adored him,

fluttering her eyelashes at him and acting coy. She wanted him to do everything for her, insisting he went shopping with her, and acting like he was a genius if he mended a plug for her. She said his scripts were absolutely wonderful, though she wasn't sure he'd captured Puggy-Wuggy's true spirit. She made him do them again and again. Perhaps it was a way of keeping him coming to see her. She'd even started calling him Robbie-Wobbie. *Really.*

I don't know how Dad could bear it. Well, I do. She paid him a lot of money for five mornings a week. Though I think they've fallen out now, because Dad doesn't go there any more. He doesn't do any kind of work just at the moment. He's still hoping that the animation firm making the Puggy-Wuggy series might make a programme of Robinson too.

'The head of the firm grew up watching *Robinson*. He told me he absolutely adored him. He'd much sooner work on a Robinson series rather than piddly Puggy-Wuggy,' Dad said.

Mum sighed. So did Becks, and Perry joined in. They've had enough of Robinson. But I just know they're going to be proved wrong. I bet Dad will get that film made somehow and Robinson will be a big hit all over again. Then *Dad* will be properly famous all over again.

'My dad's still famous,' I said to Amelie now.

'But—' said Kate.

'You look him up on Wikipedia,' I said fiercely. 'And his Robinson Island toy costs a fortune on eBay.'

Kate screwed up her face, looking remarkably like Puggy-Wuggy, but Amelie nodded.

'She's right,' she said. 'Come on, the bell's gone – we'll be late for lessons.'

I thought Amelie might have gone off Kate a little bit. I hoped she'd go back to being properly best friends with me again. But she hasn't yet.

So I had enough to worry about, without this new problem of Mum and Dad having these weird whispery rows all the time.

I asked Becks after we got home from school and had eaten our tea if she had any idea what they were rowing *about*.

'*I* don't know,' she said. 'Don't look so worried, Phoebes. Parents row sometimes. They get on each other's nerves. Like we do.'

We were in her bedroom and she was staring at herself in the mirror, practising selfie faces. She pursed her lips in a simpering pout.

'Do you think I look sexy like this?' she mumbled, trying not to move her mouth.

'No, I think you look ridiculous,' I said. 'Becks—'

'What?' She tried piling her hair on the top of her head, her chin tilted. 'Do you think I look better like this?'

'Worse. You look totally ludicrous. Becks, do you think they might be splitting up?' I whispered the last sentence because it was so worrying.

'No!' Becks let her hair fall round her shoulders again and shook her head vigorously. 'Well, I don't think so. Maybe Mum's getting a bit fed up, though. I think she's an absolute saint working so hard to support us while Dad faffs around doing nothing very much. He didn't even manage to keep that part-time job with the Puggy-Wuggy woman.'

I was thinking. The arguments with Mum had started up around the time Dad stopped working for her.

'Becks, you don't think . . . ?'

'What?'

'You don't think Melissa Harris tried to get off with Dad, do you?' I asked.

'Are you *crazy*? She's ancient. Years and years older than Dad. And why would she fancy him anyway? He's so untidy and his hair is all over the place – he shambles about like an old scarecrow half the time,' said Becks.

'He does not! He's ever so good-looking! And old women like that Melissa often want younger men, don't they?' I said uncertainly, trying to sound like a grown-up. 'Maybe Mum found out and that's why Dad doesn't work there any more. And they're having all these arguments because Mum's upset and blaming Dad,

though I don't see how it was *his* fault if Melissa Harris fell in love with him,' I said.

'You've been watching too many rubbish shows about people having affairs,' Becks said loftily. 'Real people just get a bit fed up with each other, that's all.' She was peering at her eyebrows now, reaching for her tweezers. 'Do you think they're getting a bit too bushy now?'

'No, they're way too thin. You make them look seriously weird,' I said.

'They're *groomed*, that's all. I don't want to go round looking like Frida Kahlo, thanks very much,' said Becks.

Dad and I looked at art books together sometimes. I knew all about Frida Kahlo. I loved her self-portraits, even the gory ones. I thought she looked beautiful in her bright dresses and jewellery. I even liked her big eyebrows.

'She's *artistic*,' I said. 'Dad and I think she's marvellous, so there.'

'You and Dad! You totally hero-worship him. You're pathetic,' said Becks, plucking away.

'So are you,' I said. 'You won't have any eyebrows left in a minute.'

I flounced out of the room. I went along the landing to the bathroom to try out selfie faces myself, tripped over four empty bottles of mineral water, grabbed hold of the side of the bath – and

then screamed. There was a baby crocodile swimming inside it!

I charged out, yelling for Dad.

Perry rushed out of his bedroom. 'Shut *up*, Phoebe!' he ordered.

'There's a crocodile in the bathroom!'

'Don't be so stupid! It's not a crocodile – it's a newt. Stop screaming like that, you'll frighten it,' said Perry.

'*It* frightened me! What's it *doing* there?'

'I found it in the garden. I think someone's tried to pick it up and now it's lost part of its tail,' said Perry. 'Look!'

'I don't want to look!'

'Don't be silly. It's very interesting. You wait. It will regenerate another tail in a few weeks. I want to watch it do that,' said Perry.

'You can't keep it in the bath for a few weeks!' I protested.

'I don't see why not. We can use the shower instead, or the bath in Mum and Dad's room.'

'Oh yeah, I'm sure they'll be very happy to have us trailing in and out of their bedroom every day,' I said.

'Well, they might not be *happy*,' said Perry, who doesn't really get sarcasm. 'But I don't think they'll mind too much when they understand.'

I peered down at the creature in the shallow water. It didn't look so scary now I knew it wasn't a crocodile. In fact, it looked quite sweet. Perry had piled up part of his mineral collection at one end of the bath and it crawled out onto it for a change of scenery.

'Why don't we give it a little waterfall?' I said, reaching for the cold tap.

'No! You absolutely mustn't pollute its environment with chlorinated water,' said Perry.

'Ah!' I said, looking at the empty mineral water containers. 'Mum's not going to be too happy about that.'

'It *needs* spring water. Well, ideally it needs a proper aquarium with a filter and a little dry deck at the top, but I haven't got enough pocket money, obviously,' said Perry. 'Though I suppose Dad might lend me some.'

Dad was in a funny mood today. Well, he'd been acting a bit oddly for a while now. He sometimes made a huge fuss of us and told daft jokes and mucked about to make us laugh. Other times he sloped off by himself and ignored us completely. He acted extra-fond of us when we came out of the school gate today, as if he hadn't seen us for weeks. He gave me a huge great hug and Perry a big grin and a thumbs-up sign. Perry doesn't like hugs, they make him feel weird.

Dad held back on hugs when we picked up Becks, because even a head-in-the-clouds guy like Dad knows you don't go hugging your fourteen-year-old daughter in front of all her friends. He complimented her instead.

'You're looking great, Becks. I like your hair like that,' he said.

She shook her head pityingly. 'What are you on about, Dad?

It looks a total mess today,' she said.

It *did* look a bit of a mess actually, because she'd tried sticking it up in a topknot, but there were long strands hanging down around her ears so she looked a bit like an Afghan hound. But she could have smiled at Dad, even so.

I suppose I love my brother and sister, but it's hard to like them sometimes. And Mum. We don't always get on. She always swears she doesn't have favourites but it's clear she does, and it's not me. She loves Becks best, because she's her eldest, and they're very alike. They act like they're best friends sometimes, chatting away, watching the same box sets together on Friday nights when Becks is allowed to stay up really late, and they have endless discussions about hair and make-up.

Mum loves Perry next. Because he's her boy? Because he's top of the class at school? Goodness knows.

I come last, as I'm not pretty and I'm not clever. I'm not particularly anything, apart from being good at making things up. And I'm quite good at art. I'm the one who takes after Dad. He says he doesn't have favourites either and he does try really hard to be a special dad to Becks and Perry. He doesn't have to try hard with me. He's my favourite person in the whole world – and I know I'm his.

Perry was looking at me appraisingly now.

'I don't suppose *you* could say you need an aquarium, Phoebe?

I'm sure Dad would get you one if you made out the newt was your new pet. You could pretend you're making up a story about it,' he said, trying to be encouraging.

'*The Amazing Adventures of Nigel Newt*?' I said.

'Yes!' said Perry, though I was just making a stupid joke. 'Go on, Phoebe. Please.'

'If I get you an actual aquarium, will you let me have your marbles?' I bargained.

They're not any old marbles – they're the beautiful old glass kind, with swirls of blue and green and yellow and red inside. They look breathtaking when you hold them up to the light and I wanted to keep them as treasure.

'You could have one of them, I suppose,' said Perry.

'For goodness' sake! One marble in exchange for an entire aquarium?' I said, exasperated.

'All right. One of every colour,' said Perry. He has to be the meanest boy in existence.

'*All* of them,' I said. 'Plus your fossil and your piece of amber and that pretty purple crystal thing.'

'That's real amethyst, Phoebe. You're not getting that. It's the star piece of my gem collection,' said Perry.

'Look, do you want a proper home for this weirdo little creature or not?' I said.

I dangled one finger in the water, touching it to see if I was

really scared of it. The little newt seemed more scared of me, actually, and swam faster.

'Stop it, you'll contaminate the water,' Perry said sternly. 'And you'll have to wash your hands thoroughly too, because they'll have little newt germs on them now.'

It must be so strange living in Perryworld, seeing everything in scientific terms. But he only wanted what's best for this little newt. He's my big brother and I wanted to please him. I wanted his glass marbles even more.

I went looking for Dad. I thought he'd still be in the kitchen, loading the dishwasher after tea, having a cup of coffee, doodling ideas in his Moleskine notebook, doing all his usual Dad things. But he wasn't there, he wasn't in the living room, he wasn't in the television den, he wasn't in his bedroom, he wasn't in the spare bedroom or either of the bathrooms or the upstairs or downstairs loo. He wasn't out in the garden or in the shed or in the front porch. He wasn't in his car or in the garage. He wasn't anywhere.

I peered up and down the street, though I knew Dad wouldn't go out and leave us, not when Mum wasn't back from work yet. I went back into the house and called for him as loudly as I could. I rechecked every room. I was starting to panic. Where on earth had he gone?

I started to think the most terrible things had happened. That's the worst part of having a vivid imagination. It veers out of control when you're worried and runs a little horror film inside your head. I kept seeing images of Dad slumped in a dark corner, clutching his chest; Dad opening a window and falling out of it; Dad seized by robbers, bound and gagged and stuffed in a trunk.

I knew these were silly fantasies and couldn't possibly have happened, and yet I still looked in every corner, peered out of every window, and climbed the steep steps to the attic where we kept several battered trunks of our old toys and books and baby clothes.

The light was on – and there was Dad, sitting in the middle of the floor staring at a model of Robinson's island.

'Dad! Oh, Dad, I've been looking for you everywhere!' I burst out, running to him.

'Hey, darling,' said Dad. He'd been looking so sad and thoughtful, but now he had a smile on his face and he held out his arms to me. 'What's up, lovie?'

'I just panicked a bit when I couldn't find you,' I said, sitting down beside him.

He gave me a big hug and didn't let me go. His head rested on top of mine, and his arms held me so tightly I could hardly breathe.

'Silly girl,' he said, his voice sounding funny.

'Are you all right, Dad?' I asked.

'Of course I am,' he said.

'So what are you doing, up here all by yourself?'

'Just . . . thinking,' said Dad. 'Mum's not home, is she?'

'No, it's not even seven yet.'

'Oh well, I'd better start getting her supper ready all the same,' said Dad. 'I've got her a special treat.'

I wasn't sure this was a good idea. Mum never really wanted a proper meal like us, though Dad's a good cook. She only ever wants a bowl of soup or scrambled eggs nowadays. No wonder she's as thin as a pin.

Dad didn't move, in spite of his words. He stayed hugging me.

'You are all right, Dad, aren't you?' I asked.

'Of course I am. Right as rain,' he said.

I reached out and picked up the toy Robinson. 'Do you know something? We've never played that it's rained on Robinson's island. Maybe there could be a real tempest one day? How would Robinson cope if his mud hut blew right away and half the palm trees came crashing down?' I said.

'He'd have to cope,' said Dad. 'You know our Robinson. He's equal to anything.' He gave an odd laugh.

'Dad, can I ask you something?'

Dad stiffened. 'What?'

'I know it's probably very expensive, but could you possibly buy an aquarium?'

Dad stared at me and then laughed properly. 'An aquarium?'

he said. 'You want to keep fish, Phoebes?'

'Well, I don't, I'm not too keen on the idea. No, it's for Perry. He's found a newt that's lost its tail and he's desperate to see if it really can grow back. The newt's in the bath at the moment, so it's going to be very inconvenient. I know it sounds ridiculous, but Perry really, really wants to keep it. You know what he's like,' I said earnestly. 'And I've got this story idea about a little newt, you see, so it would be very helpful for inspiration.'

'All right!' Dad said, jumping up, pulling me with him. 'Do you think Pets at Home will still be open? Let's give it a go. We'll all make a little trip there. See if we can make it before Mum gets home. Come on, call Perry and Becks!'

Perry gave a great whoop when he heard the plan. Becks was less enthusiastic.

'Have you all gone crazy? You want to buy an aquarium for a *newt*? And it's way too late anyway – Pets at Home will be shut,' she said.

'I think that retail park stays open till eight, Becks. I want to buy Perry a pet. In fact, I want to buy *all* of you a pet,' said Dad. He looked at me. 'Would you like a rabbit or a guinea pig, Phoebes?'

'Oh, I would absolutely love one!' I said, thrilled.

'This newt isn't a pet, it's an experiment,' said Perry. 'That's why I really need an aquarium. But I won't waste it. I expect I can find lots of small amphibians and do a proper study on them.'

'Well, thanks very much, but count me out,' said Becks. 'I'm staying here.'

'There's a TK Maxx right next to Pets at Home, isn't there?' said Dad. 'Fancy a new dress?'

'Dad? What's going on?' asked Becks.

'I just fancy a wild spending spree with my three favourite kids,' said Dad. 'Let's go mad with the credit card.'

'All right then!' said Becks.

So we piled into the car and drove to the retail park. Dad and Perry and I went into Pets at Home and Becks went into TK Maxx to choose an outfit. Perry cast his eye over the aquariums and selected one in seconds. I took much longer, squatting down and peering through the glass at all the rabbits and guinea pigs playing inside. I thought I'd like the rabbits best, and they were very lovely with their floppy ears and fluffy tails – but I felt much more attracted to the guinea pigs. They were so small and tubby and timid, and they had such woffly noses.

'I'm guessing it's a guinea pig, Phoebes?' said Dad, squatting down beside me.

'Yes please! I just love them, I don't know why,' I said, trying to choose which I liked best.

'It's because they look just like you,' said Perry.

'You shut up! How can you be so mean, when I've sweet-talked Dad into getting you the aquarium!' I said indignantly.

'I wasn't trying to be mean,' said Perry.

I stared at the guinea pigs, breathing deeply in concentration.

'There, you're even twitching your nose like them!' said Perry.

I elbowed him hard and whispered a very rude word to him. Dad hardly ever tells us off, but he hates it if we use bad language.

'So which little guinea pig's coming home with us?' Dad said.

There was a small white-and-tan one curled up in a corner, but it suddenly bobbed up and trotted to the glass, staring straight at me.

'Oh, that one! It's chosen me! Do you think it's a boy or a girl?' I asked eagerly.

It wasn't obvious, even to the assistant who came to help us, but she thought my guinea pig was probably female.

'Then I shall call her . . . What shall I call her, Dad?'

'How about Daisy?' Dad suggested.

'Oh yes, that's perfect! She's my little Daisy. Oh, I love her to bits already,' I said. 'Why don't you get Dad to name your newt, Perry?'

'The newt isn't a *pet* – how many more times do I have to tell you?' said Perry. 'You like to name *everything*, Phoebe! Look at Wiffle!'

I blushed. I'd been given a turquoise furry pencil case when I started school. It wasn't in the shape of any animal, but it had bug eyes that swivelled round and round. The eyes made it – *him* –

seem like a little person. I carried him everywhere with me, even at home, and sat stroking Wiffle on my lap when I was watching television.

Wiffle was too grubby and matted now to use at school, but I kept him with my collection of teddies and secretly took him into bed for a cuddle at nights.

'Do you think Daisy would like to have Wiffle in her cage for company?' I asked Dad. 'She might like to sit on him – or use him as a little duvet? Oh, she'd look so sweet!'

'Well, you'd better pull Wiffle's eyes off first, in case she chews them off and swallows them,' said Dad.

I could see the sense in that, so I decided to keep Wiffle for myself. Dad paid at the desk and the assistant helped us out to the car with the aquarium and Daisy in her cage, plus a sack of hay and a bag of guinea pig nuggets and a water bottle. It seemed bizarre that two tiny creatures needed such cumbersome equipment, but Dad didn't seem to mind.

We left everything in the car, with the window open a crack, and went to find Becks in TK Maxx. I had to go into the changing rooms looking for her. She was prancing about in front of the mirror wearing a purple sparkly crop top and small black satin shorts.

'Becks!' I said.

'Don't they look great?' said Becks, posing, her hand on her hip.

'You can't wear them *out*!' I said. 'Mum would never let you walk down the street like that.'

'They're party clothes for when you go clubbing,' said Becks.

'But you're much too young to go clubbing,' I said.

'That's all you know. Practically all the girls in my class go clubbing,' said Becks. 'And I'm going too. I'll just make out I'm having a sleepover with Jas or Emily and then we'll go together. I'll need proper heels as well. Do you think Dad will buy me some shoes too?'

'Maybe. You'd better hurry up though. We've already been ages in the pet shop. Becks, I've got the most adorable little guinea pig called Daisy – you'll absolutely love her. How can you want boring old clothes when you could have a furry little guinea pig?' I said. 'Do you know what – I'm going to write a picture book about her. I can do all the drawings. She'll look so sweet!' I added.

'Each to their own,' said Becks, changing back into her school uniform.

She hovered by the shoes when we came out of the changing rooms. 'What do you think of those ones – the strappy silver ones with the amazing heels?'

'Mum would never let you wear them in a million years,' I said.

'I could always change into them when I'm out of the house. Look, they've got them in my size!' Becks whipped her school shoe

off and slipped her foot into one of the astonishing shoes. 'Oh, wow! Look how good it makes my leg look!'

She was actually right. I kicked one of my school shoes off too and stuck my foot in the other shoe. Sadly it didn't have the same effect on my own leg, and the shoe was so big for me I looked like Minnie Mouse. I stood on tiptoe in my socked foot and attempted walking. It was seriously impossible, like teetering on a tightrope.

'You look ridiculous, Phoebes,' said Becks. My face must have fallen, because she added, 'It's just because you're too young. You'll look fine when you're my age. Hey, do you think Dad really will buy them for me? And the top and the shorts? I mean, they're so reduced it's a total bargain, but even so I think money's tight at the moment. And Perry's aquarium must have cost a lot. We'll probably get home and find the wretched newt has climbed out of the bath and escaped anyway.'

'Daisy hardly cost anything, though I suppose her hutch was expensive,' I said. 'Still, she's got to have somewhere to live, hasn't she? Becks, do you think Mum and Dad keep arguing because of money? I thought we had heaps,' I said.

'We did when the whole Robinson Island thing was on the television, and the books and toys sold masses too, but they don't any more, do they?' said Becks.

'Mum must earn a lot, though. She's head of her whole department,' I said.

'Yes, I suppose,' said Becks. 'Poor Mum. I wish she didn't have to work so hard. She looks so tired all the time.'

'She *likes* working hard,' I said. I didn't want to feel sorry for Mum. I used up all my energy feeling sorry for Dad.

He was waiting patiently for us. Perry was yawning his head off and cracking his knuckles, but Dad beamed as we approached.

'Found something pretty, Becks?' he asked eagerly. 'Let's see!'

Becks flashed her outfit and shoes at him for half a second.

Dad looked a bit puzzled. 'Are you sure you've got the right size, darling? They look much too tiny,' he said.

'They fit perfectly, Dad. I've tried them on. They look fantastic, don't they, Phoebes?'

'Mm,' I said.

'Great,' said Dad, reaching for his wallet. He didn't even notice the heels on the shoes. He seemed in a daze, but he happily zapped the credit card in the machine. I noticed it actually had Mum's name on it. He did sometimes use it when he was doing a big shop at the supermarket, so I hoped it didn't really matter.

'Dad, are you sure we can afford it?' I whispered.

'Of course we can, little worrypot,' said Dad, giving me a hug. 'Now, let's get back to the car. Daisy will be feeling lonely.'

I insisted on having her cage on my knee. She squeaked anxiously when the car started moving so I opened the cage just enough to slip my hand inside to soothe her.

'She'll escape if you don't watch out!' said Perry. 'You're only making her more anxious by stroking her.'

'You're just saying that because *you* can't stand being stroked,' I said, but I saw he had a point. Daisy didn't know me yet and couldn't be sure I wasn't going to hurt her. If I was in a cage and a giant hand almost as big as me started touching me I'd be terrified.

I eased my hand out again, closed the cage very carefully, and whispered through the wire netting instead.

'Don't be scared, little Daisy. Everything's going to be all right. That strange juddering is just our car. And this whispery voice is me, Phoebe, and I'm going to look after you and make you the happiest little guinea pig ever. And that horrible vomiting sound is only my stupid brother, Perry, making fun of me. The sigh is my big sister, Becks, who thinks she's so cool and yet *I* think she's silly. The little chuckle is from my dad who's the best father in the whole world.'

Dad chuckled again. At least I think it was a chuckle. It sounded a bit odd.

Mum's car was on the drive when we got back. I suppose we'd been quite a long time. The front door opened, and there she was, still not changed out of her smart work suit, her long hair tangled as if she'd been running her hands through it. Her make-up was smudged, though she usually looked china-doll perfect for work.

'Oh God, where have you *been*? I was so worried! Didn't you get my texts?' she demanded.

'What? Sorry, Petra, I don't think I took my phone with me,' Dad said, patting his jeans pocket and shaking his head apologetically.

'Why didn't *you* answer, Becks?' Mum said. 'You send me a text saying *Dad's acting weird* and then when I text back, again and again, and then *call* you, you don't reply! I've been so worried!'

'Oh, sorry, Mum, there can't have been any signal,' said Becks, getting out of the car.

'You're so thoughtless!' said Mum, almost in tears.

We climbed out of the car, looking at her uneasily. Why was *Mum* acting so weird?

She saw the bags Becks was holding. 'TK Maxx?' she said. Then she saw Perry struggling to lift the aquarium from the boot, and me clutching Daisy's cage. 'You've been on some wild shopping spree?' Her voice was louder now, so she was almost shouting.

'Let's all go indoors. I was just buying the kids a few things, making a fuss of them. And I've got you a present too, Petra,' said Dad. He handed her another TK Maxx bag. He must have bought her something when he was waiting with Perry.

Mum just let the bag slip to the floor. 'I don't want your present,' she said, and went back indoors.

Why did she have to spoil such a lovely evening, when Dad

was trying so hard to give us all wonderful treats?

'Don't be like that, darling,' said Dad, and followed her into the kitchen. 'We didn't mean to worry you.'

'Of course I was out of my mind with worrying! I couldn't believe it when your car was missing and the house was in darkness. You were missing, the kids were missing too. I thought – well, I thought anything could have happened. Why didn't you at least leave me a note to tell me what you were doing? That's just so typical of you, Rob. You don't tell me anything and then it all goes so desperately *wrong*.'

'Petra!' Dad's voice was sharp. 'The kids will hear you!'

Becks had gone straight upstairs, smuggling her new outfit and shoes into her bedroom before Mum could take a look at them. Perry had gone upstairs too, checking on the newt. But I was lurking anxiously outside the kitchen, and Dad sensed I was there, even though he couldn't see me.

'You sit down, Petra, and have some supper. I've made you a little asparagus tart,' said Dad proudly. 'And there's a tomato salad all mixed in the fridge, and a little lemon mousse for after. Plus a beautiful bottle of Chablis, nicely chilled.'

'I'm not hungry,' said Mum ungraciously, but she let him pour her a glass of wine.

She drank it rapidly – and then suddenly reached out and took hold of Dad's hand.

'I'm sorry,' she said quietly. 'I just—'

'I know,' said Dad.

She just *what*? He knew *what*?

I was about to rush to them and demand they tell me exactly what was going on. But then Dad bent his head and kissed Mum and she put her arms round his neck and I went hot with embarrassment and relief. I'd been so scared they might be splitting up – and yet it was clear that they still loved each other.

I crept away, trying to puzzle it all out. I couldn't mope too long though. I had Daisy to think about now. I swept all my old teddies off the top of my chest of drawers, tucked Wiffle under my pillowcase, and carefully arranged Daisy's cage on top. I very gently took her out of the cage and sat on my bed with Daisy on my lap. She huddled into my school skirt, trying to hide.

'It's all right, Daisy. I know it feels really strange and scary now, but you'll get used to it soon. This is your new home. I'll make it as comfy for you as I can. You're my first-ever pet and I love you so much,' I whispered.

Of course she couldn't understand what I was saying, but after a while she calmed down. In fact, she seemed to be asleep. I laid her in the middle of my bed and stood up so I could start making her a cosy nest of hay in her cage – but immediately she shot off and I only caught her just in time, at the very edge of the bed.

'Oh my goodness, Daisy! You're a guinea pig, not a lemming!

Please don't do that!' I said.

I checked my bedroom door was tightly shut and then put her on the floor. She was very cautious for a minute or so, scarcely moving, but then she started scurrying around. I'm not very tidy, so she had to run an obstacle race, zigzagging between my slippers and pyjamas and school bag and swimming kit. Then she darted under my bed, where she busily started scrabbling together a tissue and fluff with her paws, trying to make her own nest.

'Oh, you dear little thing,' I said. 'OK, you make your nest down there while I make you a special deluxe one in your cage.'

We both worked busily, and then I crawled under the bed and hooked Daisy out, covered in fluff and little tissue strips, and popped her into the hay. She burrowed right into it, making herself comfortable.

I went to the bathroom to fill her water bottle. The newt and its swimming pool had vanished, so Perry was clearly busy with the aquarium in his bedroom. Becks was in her room too, dressed up in her new outfit, shoes and all, taking photos of herself and sending them to her friends.

I went downstairs to forage in the fridge for greens for Daisy in case she fancied some supper. I saw that Mum had eaten her own supper after all. She was sitting on the sofa in the living room with Dad, their heads close together. I breathed a great sigh of relief. Perhaps they'd stopped quarrelling about the mystery thing,

and had now gone back to being proper friends again.

They came up to say goodnight, when Daisy and I were both in our separate beds.

'I'm not really sure your bedroom is the best place to keep a guinea pig,' said Mum. 'It's not exactly hygienic, is it? And she's going to get a bit whiffy.'

'No she's not – I'm going to clean out her cage every day,' I said. 'I have to have her in with me, so I can reassure her if she gets lonely.'

Mum sighed, but for once she didn't persist. Dad gave me a big kiss and a huge hug and then tucked me in, with Wiffle beside me.

'Night-night, little Phoebes,' he said, and then he whispered in my ear, 'Never forget your old dad loves you all the way to the moon and back.'

We never saw Mum on a weekday morning. She set off to work before we'd even got up. But she was there the next morning, sipping coffee, wearing her best grey suit and her black heels with the bright red soles. And even more surprising, Dad was wearing a suit too, with a new white shirt and a navy striped tie. He never, ever dressed in smart clothes. He always wore jeans and T-shirts, mostly advertising long ago music tours, apart from one that was his Manchester United top. They were our favourite team. He'd bought me a matching T-shirt in a kid's size too.

'*Dad?*' I said.

'Hi, sweetheart,' he said. 'Sit down and eat your rabbit droppings.'

It was Dad's silly nickname for muesli. It wasn't especially accurate either, if guinea pig droppings were something similar –

I had been dealing with them this morning, determined to keep Daisy fresh and clean.

'You look so different!' I said. I usually thought of Dad as a bit of a roly-poly, but he looked much slimmer out of his baggy T-shirts and loose sweaters.

'No need to look so startled. I just thought I'd smarten up my act a bit,' said Dad.

Becks came into the kitchen, busy texting, and nearly dropped her phone when she looked up. 'Dad! What's up? You look weird!' she said.

'Thank you for the compliments, girls,' said Dad, holding out the sides of his trousers and pretending a curtsy.

'And why aren't you at work, Mum?' Becks's voice wobbled. 'Oh God, you're going to a solicitor's, aren't you?'

'What?' They both stared at us anxiously.

'You're getting a divorce!' said Becks.

'Of course we're not,' said Dad. 'I love your mum to bits. Where would I be without her?'

'Yes, where?' Mum muttered. She took another sip of coffee. 'I'm simply going to a meeting this morning, and it doesn't start till nine.'

'And Dad?' said Becks, staring at him.

'I've got a sort of meeting too,' said Dad. 'It's – it's about a new job.'

The tightness in my chest eased a little. I started cutting a banana in a ring round my muesli, and then made a little heart of blueberries in the middle. I always made a pretty pattern for good luck.

'What kind of new job? Oh, Dad, it's not with the animation company, is it? Is Robinson going to be a cartoon?' I asked eagerly.

'Let's hope it will be one day. But no, this is a bit different. I'll tell you all about it if I get it,' said Dad. He smiled at me, looking me straight in the eyes – but the tightness came back and I knew something was wrong.

Perry came barging into the kitchen talking non-stop about amphibians and their preferred diet. He started on his toast and jam – he won't eat anything else for breakfast. It has to be expensive French strawberry jam too. It's not specially for him and yet he creates a huge fuss if any of us want a spoonful.

It wasn't until he'd gobbled his two slices, talking with his mouth full, that he actually focused on Mum and Dad. He looked very startled.

'What's up?' he asked, taking a drink of milk. He always leaves a white moustache above his lip. He's a pretty revolting specimen of boyhood, all told. I wouldn't be able to stick him if he weren't my brother.

'Nothing's up,' said Mum. 'Now go and clean your teeth. And

have a good wipe round your mouth. We're all leaving in five minutes.'

'What do you think is really going on?' I whispered to Becks as we went upstairs to gather our school things.

'I don't know,' said Becks. She looked worried, and that made me feel even more worried myself.

'They said they're definitely not getting a divorce,' I reminded her.

'Yes, I know – but something's really seriously odd,' said Becks.

'What do you think Dad's new job is?'

'Goodness knows. Mum's maybe found him another PA position for some mad old writer like the Puggy-Wuggy woman?'

'But he hated doing that,' I said.

'Yes, but it's about time he did *something*, rather than loafing round the house all day,' said Becks.

'He doesn't *loaf*. There are all sorts of things always going on in his head,' I said. I absolutely hated it when anyone criticized Dad – especially if I had a sneaking suspicion they were right.

Perry didn't join in our discussion. He gave his teeth the most cursory brush ever, swiped a towel over his mouth (my towel!) and then charged downstairs to the garden.

'Perry! We're leaving in *three* minutes now!' Mum shouted after him.

I looked out of my bedroom window and saw Perry zooming

round the garden, clutching an old flowerpot. His head was bent and every few seconds he ducked down and snatched something from the grass.

I passed him on the stairs as Mum was shouting for us again, counting down the seconds. He had a disturbing collection of beetles, slugs and worms at the bottom of the flowerpot, clearly the newt's breakfast.

'. . . five, four, three, two—'

'One!' said Perry, reappearing triumphantly. He put the dirty flowerpot on the coffee table and picked up his school bag. It was this weird trick he had. He left everything to the last possible moment, and yet was never actually more than a minute or two late.

'Right then,' said Mum. 'We'll all go in my car today. Then I'll drive off for my meeting and Dad will . . . see about this job.'

'Wish me luck!' said Dad.

We dropped Becks off at her school first. Dad craned round from his front seat and gave her a kiss.

'*Dad!*' said Becks, wiping her cheek, but she gave him a kiss back.

When we got to Blatchford Juniors Perry was out of the car like a shot, but he yelled over his shoulder, 'Bye, Dad. Bye, Mum.'

Dad got right out of the car then, so he could give me a proper hug.

'I'm wishing you luck, Dad. All the luck in the world,' I said, reaching up to kiss him.

'Bless you, my Phoebes,' Dad said, and he laid his cheek on the top of my head. I felt him draw breath as if he wanted to say more, but then he just murmured, 'Love you to the moon and back,' the way he always does.

He got back in the car and Mum drove off. I stared after them, telling myself that everything was absolutely fine. There was nothing to worry about. Nothing at all.

A familiar grey Range Rover drew up near the school entrance, and Amelie jumped out. Her mum wound the window down.

'Are you all right, Phoebe?' she asked.

'Yes!' I said, a bit startled.

'That's good. Well, I hope everything goes OK today. Bye-bye then. Bye, Amelie. You be nice to Phoebe today!' she said, and drove off.

I felt myself flushing. Of course I wanted Amelie to be nice to me, but not because her mother ordered her to be so.

Amelie gave me an awkward smile.

'You don't have to be nice to me,' I said. 'I know you're really Kate's best friend now.'

'I'm your friend too,' said Amelie. 'My mum's made Millionaire's Shortbread. I've got some in a little plastic box.

You can have a piece now if you like.'

Amelie's mum made the most mouth-watering Millionaire's Shortbread ever. I wished my mum made cakes and biscuits, especially extra-yummy sweet ones. I wasn't supposed to eat them – Mum said they would spoil my teeth – but I absolutely adored Millionaire's Shortbread. It would be rude to refuse, seeing as Amelie was offering it.

'Yes please!'

'I'll have one too,' said Amelie.

We went behind the art studio because our school has a Healthy Eating policy, and the Food Police check our lunch boxes every day to make sure we haven't smuggled in anything ultra-sweet and sugary. Millionaire's Shortbread ticks every box you could think of, which is why it tastes so fantastic.

It felt deliciously wicked to be munching it in school only half an hour after we'd eaten breakfast. Especially because it was just the two of us. I thought I heard Kate's voice calling for Amelie. She blinked guiltily, but didn't make any attempt to go to her.

'Are you going to give a slice to Kate?' I asked.

'Maybe later. Not now. She's such a blabbermouth,' said Amelie.

I felt a stab of sheer joy.

'Yes, she is a bit,' I said, as casually as I could.

'So. How are you doing?' Amelie said.

'OK,' I said warily.

'How's your dad?' Amelie went on, not quite meeting my eyes.

'What do you mean?' I asked.

'I don't mean . . . I just . . . I was simply chatting, that's all,' said Amelie.

'You don't think he's ill, do you?' I asked, suddenly reeling. Was that it? Dad had lost weight recently, quite a lot, though I hadn't noticed until today. And he'd been acting so oddly too, sad and dreamy one moment, then wildly over the top the next. Was he all dressed up because he was going into hospital today for an operation? Had he only pretended he had an interview so we wouldn't worry? But why had Mum and Dad been secretly quarrelling? She wouldn't be angry with him if he was really ill, would she?

'No, of course I don't think he's ill,' Amelie said quickly. 'Well, not like he's got an *ill* illness.'

I peered at her, the last chunk of Millionaire's Shortbread staying in my mouth, suddenly tasting too sweet.

'You don't think my dad's got a *mental* illness, do you?' I asked.

'No! Anyway, it's nothing to be ashamed of, as lots of people have mental health issues. My gran got so depressed she had a nervous breakdown and had to go to hospital for a while,' said Amelie.

That bothered me. I knew deep down that Dad *was* depressed,

even though he tried to hide it. He was only pretending to be happy, even last night when he had taken us to the retail park.

'Well, my dad's happy, happy, happy,' I said, pretending myself. 'And guess what he did last night! He bought me a guinea pig!'

'Seriously? Oh, you lucky thing, I *love* guinea pigs!' said Amelie.

'She's called Daisy and she's brown and white, with the cutest little face, and she goes like this–' I gave a fair imitation of Daisy's squeaks.

Amelie laughed delightedly, acting like her proper self again.

'You must come round and see her,' I said.

'Oh, I'd love to! Did he buy guinea pigs for all of you?'

'No, he bought an aquarium for Perry because he's doing these crazy newt experiments,' I explained.

'Your brother! He's such a geek!' said Amelie.

'Tell me about it!'

'So what did he get Becks?'

'He let her choose anything she wanted in TK Maxx, so she picked out this teeny tiny top and really short shorts and mad shoes that are much too high to walk in.' I snorted.

'*Really?* What did your mum say?' Amelie asked. 'I bet she thinks the heels are too high!'

'She hasn't seen them. Becks has got them hidden in her room,' I said.

'I bet she looks fantastic in them,' said Amelie. She's always been a bit in awe of Becks, goodness knows why. 'Do you think she'd let me try her high heels on when I come round?'

She said *when* I come round, not *if.*

'Yes, of course,' I said. 'Becks likes you a lot.'

'Does she really?' said Amelie, delighted.

I wondered about saying *I* liked her a lot, but thought that might sound a bit slushy. But I was so happy. I still didn't know why she was going on about Dad in that weird way, but at least she was back to being my proper friend.

Kate made a fuss when lessons started, thinking Amelie and I had been hiding from her deliberately. Amelie did her best to calm her down, wanting us to go round in a threesome at break, but Kate was still in a bit of a sulk.

'She can't half be moody at times,' said Amelie.

'Yeah,' I replied.

'Oh well, she'll get over it,' said Amelie. 'What shall we play?'

I longed to play one of our old pretend games. I loved it way back in Reception when we played Mermaids every day. I called myself Pearl and Amelie called herself Coral, and we both had long shining green tails and swam through the ocean that flooded the playground whenever we snapped our fingers.

However, I knew Amelie would think me babyish if I suggested playing that kind of game nowadays. I thought quickly. 'Let's play

that we're both on YouTube and we have massive followings. You can tell everyone about hairstyles and make-up, and I'll play pranks. You can go first if you like,' I said.

Amelie *did* like. She was actually quite good at it, quick with her patter and smiling all the while. I didn't have a chance to do any pranking until lunchtime, and then it didn't quite work out, because I got a bit carried away. A large stray cat had stalked round the edge of the playground, so I made out that it was a wildcat on the attack. It was just a silly joke but a little bunch of Year Three girls took me seriously and ran away from it, screaming.

Mrs Morrison, our form teacher, was on playground duty. I thought I was going to be in Big Trouble as she's generally very strict – but after she'd calmed all the little ones, she simply shook her head at me. She didn't even tell me off.

She was nice to me in art that afternoon too. She talked about the Dutch artist Van Gogh and showed us his Sunflowers painting. Then she asked us to paint a vase of flowers. Amelie and Kate painted neat little yellow bouquets right in the middle of their papers. I decided to be bold and bright and splashy, just like Van Gogh, and painted enormous red and purple tulips that filled the page.

'Um, you've done it wrong. We're meant to be doing yellow sunflowers,' said Kate.

'Mrs Morrison just said flowers, so we can choose any kind,' I said, hoping I was right.

'Everyone else has done sunflowers,' said Kate smugly.

'Never mind, Phoebe, yours is still good,' said Amelie.

'I think it looks a right mess,' said Kate.

I was beginning to think she was right, and felt worried, but Mrs Morrison seemed delighted when she walked around looking at our paintings.

'Well done, Phoebe! What a lovely picture. I love the way you've filled your page. And how clever to have chosen tulips!' she said.

It was my turn to feel smug, though I just ducked my head modestly, not wanting Amelie to think I was being a show-off.

When the bell went for home time I had to spend quite a while in the cloakroom, as I had red and purple paint up to my elbows. I'd worn an apron but I'd somehow managed to get purple on my school uniform too. I soaped my hands and scrubbed at my skirt while Amelie waited with me.

When I was relatively paint-free at last, though very damp, we went out into the playground together. Perry was standing at the gate, his arms folded, looking impatient. Mum was talking to Amelie's mother. But where was Dad?

'There you are!' said Mum. 'What on earth have you been doing? And why are you soaking wet? Honestly, Phoebe!' She sighed in exasperation, but not as if she was really irritated. She was just reciting words as if they were lines in a play.

'Where's Dad?' I asked.

Amelie's mother looked at Mum.

'Let's get in the car,' said Mum. This time she said it firmly. Even Perry jerked into action.

'Bye, Amelie,' I said. I could see it definitely wasn't the right time to ask her round to my place.

'Bye, Phoebe,' she said.

Then, bizarrely, Amelie's mum gave my mum a hug. They'd known each other ages, and were friends, but it was mostly because Amelie and I were close. They weren't really on hugging terms at all. They didn't even see each other that often because Mum was always at work.

'Why were you and Amelie's mum hugging?' I asked as I got into the back of the car beside Perry. Becks was in the front seat, peering at her phone. 'Are you best friends now, like Amelie and me?'

'No, we're not,' said Mum.

'I thought you and Amelie weren't friends any more though,' said Becks, looking round.

'Yes, well, we've made it up. She was lovely today. I think she's gone off Kate, thank goodness,' I said. 'Amelie and I made up this fantastic game – we pretended we were both on YouTube. She talked about make-up and I played pranks—'

I realized no one was listening. Becks was messaging again

and Perry was deep in a school library book called *Our Native Amphibians*. Mum was trying to reverse out of her parking space. When she turned round to check for cars I saw she had tears in her eyes.

'Mum?' I said, alarmed. 'Mum, what's the matter? Why aren't you at work? What's happened? *And where's Dad?*'

Mum tried to drive off, but a car hooted at her furiously.

'Watch out! You nearly went straight into me!' another parent shouted.

'*Mum!*'

'Be quiet, Phoebe,' Mum snapped. 'I've got to concentrate on the road or I'll get us all killed. Not another word till we get home!'

'And then you'll tell us—'

'Shut *up!*' Mum shouted.

I pressed my lips together, startled. Becks turned round from the passenger seat and shrugged her shoulders sympathetically. Perry looked up from his book, his hands over his ears.

'It takes two to three weeks,' he said.

I stared at him blankly.

'What?' I whispered.

'For newts to grow a new tail,' he said impatiently.

'Stop talking. All of you,' said Mum.

So we were silent all the way home. The worries inside my head buzzed like angry bees. Mum stayed in the car when we got

to our house. She still gripped the steering wheel, her head bent.

'Mum?' said Becks gently.

Mum looked up at her. Tears were running down her cheeks. We all stared at her, scared. Becks helped her out of the car and we went up the path together. Old Mrs Sutton next door was peering at us out of her window. We didn't like her much, because she was so nosy. She was tapping on the glass now, beckoning to us.

'Mum, Mrs Sutton wants to say something,' I said.

Mum just shook her head and put the key in the door. 'Phoebe, come inside. We're not talking to that old busybody,' she said.

I went in, surprised. Mum didn't like Mrs Sutton any more than we did, but she usually made us be polite to her because she was old and lonely. I started thudding up the stairs, desperate to see how Daisy was getting on. Perry was already in his bedroom to see if the newt had produced a millimetre of new tail yet.

'Perry! Phoebe! Come back downstairs,' said Mum. 'I need to talk to you.'

'In a minute,' I called. I'd bombarded her with questions when we were getting in the car, but now I was suddenly too scared to hear any answers. I just wanted to stroke Daisy and feel pleased that Amelie and I were friends again.

Perry didn't even answer.

Becks came up the stairs. 'Come on, you two. Mum wants us. Stop messing about,' she said. She looked very pale. 'Don't you

realize, something awful's happened?'

'Not to Dad?' I said, and then I hurtled back down the stairs, though I could hear Daisy squeaking in anticipation.

'I'm conducting my experiment,' Perry protested behind me, but when he reluctantly put in an appearance he was white too, his freckles very noticeable.

'Come here, children,' said Mum in the kitchen. She stood beside the island, pouring herself a glass of wine.

We sat down at the table, staring at her.

'Is Dad all right?' I asked, my voice croaky. 'Promise he's not ill!'

Mum shook her head and took a gulp of wine.

'He's not *dead*, is he?' I whispered.

'No, of course he's not dead, Phoebe,' said Mum. 'He's just . . . got a new job, that's all.'

'Well, that's great, isn't it? So he'll be home soon?' I asked hopefully.

'Well. No. That's the sad bit,' said Mum. 'He can't come home because his new job is too far away.'

'Has he been having an affair?' Becks asked. 'He hasn't left us, has he?'

'Of course he's not been having an affair! But he has had to leave us for a while, I'm afraid,' said Mum.

'For how long?' I asked. 'Days? A week?'

'Longer than that. Maybe months,' said Mum. She swallowed.

'He's not coming home for *months*?' I gasped.

'Oh no!' said Becks. She touched her cheek. 'Why didn't he *tell* us? I didn't even let him kiss me goodbye properly!' She started texting rapidly.

'Are you trying to text him?' Mum asked. 'It's no use. He hasn't got his phone with him.'

'He hasn't got his *phone*?' Becks repeated.

'I know, it's bizarre – it's all to do with this new job. It's started straight away. Poor Dad's so upset he couldn't say goodbye. He's not allowed to tell us anything about it,' said Mum. '*I* don't even know where he is exactly or what he's doing.'

'You mean he's like a *secret agent* or something? Our *dad*?' Becks asked incredulously.

'I know! I've guessed! Oh my goodness!' I said, suddenly jumping up. 'It's OK! Well, it's not OK, as it's going to be utterly dreadful without him, but I know what he's doing. It's *Robinson*!'

'Don't be silly, Phoebe, that telly thing finished years ago,' said Becks.

'This is Dad *being* Robinson, on a real desert island! He kept trying to get people interested in the idea, remember? He'll be filming himself on this island, keeping a record, showing how he's getting on, and then when he comes back he'll turn it into a documentary feature and it'll be a big success – I just know

it will!' I said, dancing up and down.

'Oh, Phoebe, don't be so naive!' said Becks, sighing at me.

'No, Phoebe's spot on,' Mum said quickly. 'You've guessed it, you clever girl! But you mustn't tell anyone. It's meant to be a deadly secret.'

'I won't breathe a word,' I said dramatically.

'Are you *serious*, Mum? Why on earth couldn't he tell us?' Becks asked. She frowned at me. 'Did he tell you, Phoebe?'

I didn't say anything. I just wanted her to think for one glorious moment that Dad had confided in me.

'Dad barely told *me* anything,' said Mum.

'But look at Phoebe, looking so smug and mysterious!' Becks cried. 'You know she's totally Dad's favourite. It's not fair!'

Becks suddenly sounded like a four-year-old, rather than fourteen. It was thrilling that she was so sure I was Dad's favourite. I suppose he did make a big fuss of me. He'd have made a fuss of Becks too, but she was always so impatient with him. 'Oh, *Dad*!' she was forever saying. He took lots of notice of Perry too, but Perry couldn't stand being fussed over by anyone.

'Can I go back to my experiment now?' Perry said over his shoulder, halfway to the kitchen door.

'Perry!' said Mum, but then she sighed and nodded, refilling her glass. Her hand shook, and wine splashed on the kitchen table.

'Mum, you're not getting drunk, are you?' I asked anxiously.

'No, I'm not!' said Mum. 'For goodness' sake, Phoebe!' She took a deep breath. 'Well, I suppose I'd better make you all some supper.' She looked in the fridge, poking in the vegetable drawer.

'Or we could get pizza?' I suggested. 'Dad always lets us have a pizza when he can't think what to cook.'

It wasn't a serious suggestion, because Mum is always totally against any kind of takeaway – but to my astonishment she reached for her phone.

'OK. What sort would you all like?' she asked.

I liked extra cheese with pineapple. Becks had the veggie special, and Perry had the totally plain basic pizza – he wouldn't eat anything else. Dad liked cheese and pineapple too, but he wasn't here. He wasn't going to be here for ages.

It hadn't felt real before. I suddenly wondered if I really wanted pizza after all. I wasn't hungry any more, though I felt empty inside. I ate my pizza, and a left-over quarter of Becks's pizza too. I even had strawberry ice cream afterwards, seeing how far I could push Mum. Somehow I still felt empty, though I felt sick too. I kept yawning, and didn't protest when Mum sent me up to bed really early.

I spent a long time stroking Daisy, whispering in her tiny ear. She was such a comfort that I wondered about taking her into bed with me – but I was worried about turning over in the night and accidentally squashing her. I didn't much like the thought of her

little poos on my sheets either, so I popped her back in her own bed in the cage.

I usually read for half an hour or so before settling down. I was halfway through a great story about four children lost in the Amazon after a plane crash, but I started reading one of my old *Robinson* picture books instead. I could hear Dad's voice in my head as I read. It was a comfort – but it made me cry.

'Oh, Phoebe,' said Mum, coming in to say goodnight.

'I miss Dad so much already!' I sniffed.

'I know. I do too. But he hasn't gone away for ever,' said Mum, tucking me up.

'It feels like it!' I said.

'We're all going to miss him terribly, but I suppose we'll get used to it. Everything will get back to normal,' said Mum.

But it didn't.

I woke up very early and heard Daisy rummaging away in the hay. Perhaps she was looking for some breakfast. I thought she might fancy some fresh greens. I went running downstairs in my pyjamas to ask Dad whether he thought she'd like dandelions. I actually got as far as the kitchen, thinking he'd be having his usual coffee while he laid the breakfast table – and then I remembered.

Dad wasn't here. Mum was having coffee, her hair tied up in a neat topknot. She was wearing her weekend clothes, jeans and a crisp blue shirt and snow-white trainers – Mum was always immaculate even when she dressed casually.

'Why aren't you at work, Mum?' I asked.

'I thought I'd work from home for a few days so I can take you to school. When I go back to the office, Becks will have to walk

you and Perry there, though I'm not sure how she'll feel about it,' said Mum.

'She'll hate it,' I said. 'Perry and I can walk ourselves. It's not like we're babies.'

'It's a long walk though, with so many roads to cross. I'm not sure it would be allowed,' said Mum. 'Do you want breakfast now?'

'Actually, I'm on a hunt for Daisy's breakfast first. Do you think she'd like dandelions?' I asked.

'Probably,' said Mum. 'There are several big clumps by the hedge. Your dad always seems to miss them when he mows the front lawn. Oh God, that's another thing. Another job for me to do.'

She started tapping away at a to-do list on her phone. I went into the hall.

'Phoebe! Put some clothes on before you go out in the front garden!' Mum called.

I couldn't be bothered to trail all the way upstairs. My pyjamas covered much more of me than my school uniform, so I didn't see any problem. I opened the door, went to the hedge to pick some dandelions – and saw a strange man waiting at the gate.

'Hello?' I said uncertainly.

'Ah, you must be one of the Robinson children. How are you, dear? Can I have a few words with your mum?' he said.

'Who are you?' I asked.

'Just fetch her, there's a good girl,' he said.

I sighed, and went back to the door. 'Mum! *Mum!* This man wants to talk to you!' I shouted.

Mrs Sutton bobbed up at her window, looking out eagerly. Mum came to the front door. The man suddenly whipped out a camera and took a photo of her.

'Phoebe, get back inside!' Mum said, rushing to get me indoors. 'How dare you speak to my daughter! Get away from my property!' she shouted at the strange man.

Mrs Sutton was goggling at the window, her mouth open.

'And you can stop spying on us, you nosy old trout!' Mum yelled.

I was astonished. Mum never, ever shouted in public or called people rude names. She was always icily polite, even when she didn't like someone.

'Phoebe!' Mum tugged me sharply.

We saw the strange man walk up Mrs Sutton's garden path as we retreated indoors.

'Mum! You called Mrs Sutton a nosy old trout!' I said, sniggering.

'Oh God!' said Mum. She started laughing too – or perhaps she was crying. She massaged her forehead, her eyes shut. 'What am I going to do?' she muttered.

'Come and sit down, Mum. Don't worry, I think you frightened that weird man away. Who *is* he?' I gabbled, as I steered her back

into the kitchen and sat her down at the table.

'I don't know. But how *dare* he come here and start accosting you!' said Mum.

'Well, he didn't exactly *accost* me,' I said. 'He just asked to talk to you. Why did he take your photo?'

'Goodness knows,' she said. 'Come and have some breakfast.'

'But I didn't get a chance to pick Daisy's dandelions!' I wailed.

'You're not going out there again, Phoebe,' Mum said firmly.

'But he's gone to talk to the nosy old trout now,' I said.

'Don't *you* start calling her that! Though she *is*,' said Mum. 'What do you have for breakfast nowadays? Still muesli with fruit?'

I hesitated. 'Dad sometimes makes us pancakes,' I said. Actually Dad rarely made pancakes, just on days when he felt we needed cheering up: when Becks had a maths test or I had to face the horror of Sports Day. Perry always wanted toast with strawberry jam for breakfast, no matter what.

'I used to make your dad pancakes when we first got married,' said Mum, her voice going wobbly. She cracked eggs into a bowl and started making a batter.

'Mum, do you think that horrid man knows about Dad?' I said, winding an end of my hair round my finger.

'What?' said Mum, stopping still and staring at me.

'Maybe he's a reporter and he's found out that Dad's gone off to this island,' I said. 'Mum, which island *is* it? Is it like a

real desert island, with coconut palms and white sandy beaches?'

'I don't know, darling. Dad wouldn't even tell me. I'm not supposed to talk about it. And you mustn't either. Not to anyone.'

'I won't.'

'It's a total secret,' said Mum. 'Nobody else must know.'

I nodded. I opened the fridge door, looking for greens in there. I was in luck. Kale! I couldn't stand it myself, but I hoped Daisy would think it a gourmet treat. I felt very hot. I kept my head in the fridge, trying to cool off.

'Phoebe?' said Mum. 'It's all right – I know you're helping yourself to greens for Daisy. I don't mind.'

'You're being ever so kind today, Mum,' I said.

I meant it as a compliment, but her face crumpled. 'Am I mostly so horrible then?' she asked.

'No! You're usually just a bit . . . snappy,' I said.

'Snappy?' Mum asked, looking devastated.

'Just a bit. Mum, I've got to tell you something else. Please don't be cross, but I think Amelie knows about Dad too. And she's told Kate.'

Mum stopped beating the eggs. 'What did Amelie say?'

'She was just whispering stuff to Kate. She said things like, *you'll never, ever guess about Phoebe's dad.*'

'And then what did she say?' Mum asked.

'I couldn't hear properly. I just told her to stop talking about my dad like that,' I said.

'Wretched little girl,' Mum muttered.

'Who? Me or her? But it's OK, Mum, she hasn't said anything since, and yesterday she was absolutely lovely to me and we're best friends all over again. In fact, I was going to ask, can I have her over for a sleepover some time?'

'No,' said Mum, and she beat the batter so hard it started splashing out of the bowl.

'There you are. Snappy,' I said, and went upstairs to feed Daisy.

She was extremely appreciative, greeting me with lovely little squeaks. She started gobbling her greens enthusiastically. Guinea pigs must have very weird taste buds if they love kale.

Becks came into my room. She was very pale and she had dark circles under her eyes, as if she'd been up all night.

'You look a bit rubbish,' I said.

'Thanks!' said Becks. 'Well, you *always* look rubbish.'

I was hurt. I hadn't meant to be rude; I'd simply been concerned about her.

'The oddest thing happened just now,' I said. 'This man standing at our gate talked to me, and then took a photo of Mum, and Mrs Sutton was peering at us and you'll never, ever guess what – Mum called her a nosy old trout! To her face! Can you imagine!'

Becks took hold of me by the shoulders. 'What man?' she demanded.

'It's OK, he wasn't a weirdo. I think he could have been a reporter,' I said. 'Did you take it in? Mum called Mrs Sutton a *nosy old trout!*'

'Why would a reporter be hanging round our house?' Becks asked.

'Well, maybe someone's found out about Dad's island adventure and they've gone to the papers and now they want to do a story on it. They'll try and find Dad and spoil all his plans,' I said.

'Oh, Phoebe,' said Becks, shaking her head at me. 'You don't really believe all that stuff, do you?'

'Yes! Dad used to talk it over with me but I never thought he'd actually go through with it,' I said.

'It's just make-believe, Phoebes. Mum was just going along with you. She doesn't want us to know what's really happened. I've been thinking about it all night long. I think they *have* split up. Or they're giving each other space while they decide what they want to do,' she said.

My heart began thudding. 'But they were all lovey-dovey with each other the other night.'

'Because they're both upset about it,' Becks said.

'Shut up! You're making *me* upset now,' I said.

'I think Dad might really have been having an affair,' said Becks. 'He's been acting kind of guilty recently.'

'No he *hasn't*!' I said – though I knew what she meant.

'That's why he's the one who's got to go. Maybe he's gone to live with this other woman.'

'How could you possibly say such a thing about our dad?' I said furiously. 'Dad wouldn't ever, ever, *ever* leave us!'

He wouldn't ever, ever, ever leave *me*!

'There's no need to get so angry with me! I'm just trying to be rational, that's all. I can't think of any other explanation,' said Becks.

'Then you've got a warped, twisted, horrible mind and I hate you for thinking it!' I shouted, and I started hitting her.

'Stop it! Have you gone crazy? You're hurting me!' Becks said, pinioning my arms to my side.

'Let me go!' I said. When she wouldn't I tried to spit at her, but it just dribbled down my own chin.

'Stop being so disgusting!' said Becks.

'You're the one who's disgusting, daring to suggest such an awful thing! You don't really think that at all – you're just jealous because Dad told me all about the island and not you!'

'You're pathetic, stuck in your little dream world, hero-worshipping Dad,' said Becks.

I wriggled one arm free and tugged her hair as hard as I could.

She let me go, shrieking and holding her head.

Perry came into my room, staring at us. 'Are you two having a *fight*?' he asked. 'I could hear you even through my headphones!'

'No, of course not. Phoebe's just getting into one of her states,' said Becks. 'Oh my God, look!' She snatched one or two long hairs from my hand. Maybe a few more. 'Look what you've *done*! Oh my God, have I got a bald patch now?' She ran to my mirror to examine the side of her head.

'Of course you haven't!' I said, but I felt sick with fear. Had I really torn a hunk of my sister's hair out?

'There *is* a tiny little bald patch, look!' Becks cried, parting her hair.

'Only if you pull your hair back like that. It's about the size of a pin. You don't have to make such a fuss!' I said tearfully.

'It'll grow back anyway, like my newt's tail,' said Perry. 'What's that funny smell from downstairs?'

'Mum's making pancakes for a treat,' I said.

'Not for me?' said Perry, alarmed. 'I just want toast and strawberry jam.' He ran out of my room and started thumping downstairs, calling to Mum.

Becks and I were left glaring at each other. I wiped my eyes. My hands were shaking. Becks and I had had fights before, but we just pushed each other. I'd never really *hurt* her.

'I'm sorry, Becks,' I mumbled. 'You shouldn't have said that – but I shouldn't have pulled your hair out. It doesn't show, I absolutely promise. Does it hurt a lot?'

'Let me pull a lock of your hair out and then you'll see,' said Becks, rubbing her head. 'Look, I didn't mean to make you so upset. Maybe you're right. Perhaps Dad *is* making a Robinson documentary.'

'Yes, of course he is,' I said firmly.

We went downstairs. Perry was sitting at the breakfast table munching his boring old toast and jam. Mum had a plateful of pancakes waiting for Becks and me, decorated with blueberries and whirls of maple syrup, with whipped cream in a bowl.

'Oh, yum!' I said.

They tasted really good too, though I actually preferred them with sugar and lemon juice, the way Dad made them. Still, I knew it wouldn't be tactful to say so.

'You don't know what you're missing, Perry,' I said. 'Try one.'

I offered him the plate of pancakes but he veered away.

'No thanks!' he said. 'Not for my breakfast.'

'Perry said you girls were fighting,' said Mum. She wasn't eating the pancakes either. She just sipped her black coffee.

I glanced at Becks, scared she was going to tell on me. She shook her head slightly and went on eating. Her hair looked perfectly normal, long and silky – it was a great relief.

'Mum?' I said, munching. 'About Dad – ? What if we *need* him for any reason?'

'I told you, darling, I don't know exactly where he is, and I haven't got any way of getting in touch,' said Mum.

'But he *is* on this island, isn't he?' I asked.

'Well, I don't know whether he's got there yet.'

'Yes, but he *definitely* is doing a Robinson film, isn't he?' I persisted. 'You solemnly swear?'

'Oh, Phoebe. Give it a rest. *Yes*, I solemnly swear,' said Mum.

I nodded at Becks triumphantly. 'There!' I licked my finger and wiped it round the creamy pancake crumbs.

'Phoebe, for goodness' sake!' Mum snapped, almost like normal.

'And Dad will be all right, won't he? He'll manage on the island? He'll find enough to eat? What if there's no fresh water? Could he crack open a coconut and drink the water inside?' I asked.

'Yes, I'm sure he could.'

'But what if he couldn't? What if he can't find enough to eat and drink? What if he falls out of a tree when he's climbed up it for coconuts?' I went on, little disaster scenes playing inside my head.

'I'm sure he'll have some way of summoning help,' said Mum. 'Stop getting so worked up and *stop* wiping your finger round your

plate. You'll be licking the plate itself next.'

'I've finished my breakfast. I'm just going to make an entry in my newt diary,' said Perry. He glanced at the clock, then added, sounding a bit panicked, 'We're actually late for school.'

'Well, I was wondering . . . Perhaps you can all skip school today,' said Mum.

We stared at her.

'Are you serious, Mum?' Becks asked. 'I've got a drama rehearsal at lunchtime.'

'I need to see Amelie, otherwise she'll be Kate's friend again,' I said.

'We *have* to go to school. It's not a holiday,' Perry insisted.

'What's the matter with you? Most children would be thrilled at the chance of missing school,' said Mum.

'But you're the one always going on about our education,' said Becks.

'*Dad* never, ever let us stay off school, even if we begged him,' I said.

'I've got a maths test today,' said Perry. 'And I bet I'll come top again.'

'Will you all just be quiet!' said Mum. She shook her head helplessly, little strands escaping from her topknot. 'I don't know what to *do*.'

We fidgeted uncomfortably. Mum *always* knew what to do.

What was the matter with her now? I slid off my chair and went over to her.

'You're missing Dad, aren't you?' I said.

'Of course I am,' said Mum.

'I wish he hadn't gone,' I said, the misery of it washing over me again. 'I know it all has to be secret, but I do wish he'd have told us before he went. Do you think he's missing us as much too?'

'Of course he will be,' said Mum, putting her arm round me.

'Then maybe he'll change his mind and come back!' I said.

'I don't think he can,' said Mum.

'I just love him so,' I whispered.

Mum held me tight. 'I know you do, darling,' she said.

There was a knock at the door.

'Now what?' said Mum.

'It's Dad!' I said. 'He's changed his mind and come back to us!'

'Don't be silly, he'd use his key,' said Perry.

'It's probably that hateful Mrs Sutton. We won't answer it,' said Mum.

There was another knock: *rat-a-tat-tat, rat-a-tat-tat.*

'That's Amelie's special knock! She's come calling for me,' I said.

I leaped up and ran out into the hall, though Mum tried to keep hold of me. Then I stopped. The letter box was open and someone was peering through.

'Hello! Can I just have a few words?' said a man's voice.

'Oh my God!' said Mum behind me. She grabbed my arm and pulled me back into the kitchen, breathing hard.

'Who was that, Mum? Another reporter?' I asked, scared.

'I don't know. Maybe. But we're not going out there. We're staying put until they clear off. All right? Do you all understand?' Mum said urgently.

'This is weird,' said Perry. 'I don't like it.'

'Well, go and play with your newt for a bit,' said Mum.

'I don't *play* with it,' said Perry, offended, but he stalked off all the same.

Becks was tapping away on her phone. Mum looked at her sharply.

'Who are you texting? Look, I don't want you to send any messages to any of your friends, not just now. Switch the phone off altogether,' she said.

'Mum! I'm just telling—'

'Listen to me. I don't want you messaging anyone. Give it here!' Mum snatched the phone from her.

'You can't take away my *phone*!' said Becks.

'I can do what I like. I'm your mother,' said Mum.

'And I'm your daughter and I have rights too. My phone's my property. And I need to get in touch with Jas and Emily because we're all in this play and I'll be badly letting them down if

I suddenly don't turn up,' said Becks. 'This is a ridiculous idea. We can't stay away from school for ever!'

'Of course it won't be for ever. Just a few weeks. Then it will be the summer holidays,' said Mum.

'What?' said Becks. 'Mum, you've gone crazy! You're making this up as you go along! I know you're in a state because of Dad, whatever he's done. I know you're keeping something secret from us and it's so stupid, because obviously we're going to find out whatever it is sooner or later.'

Mum pursed her lips, then opened her laptop and started Googling something. I craned my neck so I could see. It was the Quirky Cottages website. We went on holidays with them every year. We stayed in a converted chapel in North Norfolk. Dad used to pretend to be a man of the Church and speak in a solemn up-and-down vicary voice.

'*Remember the eleventh commandment, young Phoebe. Thou must never forget to take thy swimming costume to the beach, because thy father will smite you if he has to trail back to the dwelling place to fetch it,*' he'd say.

It was going to be so strange and sad and lonely without him this summer. Still, we'd got to know the Rowlands family who stayed at the big flint cottage next door, and we could still go on the beach with them and have picnics and go swimming together. Georgia Rowlands was a bit younger than me, but I quite liked making fairy palace sandcastles with her.

Mum phoned the number and started speaking to the booking agency.

'It's Petra Robinson here,' she said. 'We've booked the Old Chapel for a month this summer as usual, but I wonder if it's possible to change to another cottage, even at this late date?'

'Oh, Mum! We love the Old Chapel!' I protested.

Mum raised her eyebrows at me furiously. I subsided.

'We're fully paid up, and that's fine, but I'd actually like to downsize. I was wondering if you have any really remote cottages on your books, ideally available right away?'

Mum waited while we looked at her, horrified.

'*Remote?*' Becks mouthed at me.

That meant in the middle of nowhere, with a long boring trek to the beach or the village shop.

'Oh dear,' said Mum, sighing. 'You haven't got anything at all?'

We sighed too, with relief.

Mum was listening. 'Really? No, no, it doesn't matter if it's pretty dilapidated,' she said.

'Yes it does!' Becks whispered.

'She's gone a bit nuts!' I whispered back.

Mum had been moaning about the Old Chapel for several years, feeling it should be redecorated, with new beds – and maybe a whole new kitchen too. She was always so ultra-fussy. Why

wouldn't she mind somewhere dilapidated now?

'No, truly, it doesn't matter a bit if it's very basic. Just so long as it's got a roof and some beds it'll be fine,' said Mum. 'And we can go there today? I'm not sure how long we'll be staying. Shall we say up till the first week in September? So how much extra will that be? You're sure? Well, that's marvellous. And the address and key code?'

She wrote down the details for this tumbling-down cottage in her Moleskine diary – and rang off. She looked at us triumphantly.

'There! All done! Now, you girls had better go and pack. We're going to have a lovely long holiday.'

'Like Dad, in a way,' I said.

'I suppose. Now, first I have to talk to Perry about all this – and then I've got to have a long think about everything we need. Off you go,' said Mum, wandering round the kitchen, picking up coffee and tea and kitchen roll and a bunch of bananas almost at random.

'You mean I should do my own packing?' I said.

'Yes. So you have a good think too, Phoebe. Don't just tip any old thing into a suitcase. No use arriving with every single T-shirt you possess and no knickers,' said Mum.

'I'm not sure how to fold stuff properly,' I said anxiously.

'Well, *try*,' said Mum.

'Come on. I'll show you,' said Becks, and she pulled me out of

the room. 'Don't worry, Phoebe. She'll have probably changed her mind again by the time we've got packed.'

'She's not acting anything like Mum,' I muttered.

'I think she's having a bit of a breakdown,' Becks whispered.

'This is all so scary,' I said.

'I know,' said Becks.

'I wish Dad was here,' I mumbled.

'Yes, but that's the whole point. He's not,' said Becks. She looked as if she might say more, so I rushed into Perry's room – before Mum could come up and talk to him.

'Get out!' he said curtly. It's his usual form of greeting so I didn't take any notice.

'Perry, you've got to start packing your things,' I said. 'Mum's booked us into some grotty-sounding cottage and we're going there straight away, on holiday.'

Perry blinked at me. He used to wear glasses until some boys started picking on him, and now he's experimenting to see if regular eye exercises will improve his eyesight instead. His face looked oddly naked without his glasses, though he still had shiny pink dents either side of his nose where they used to rest. He was squinting at me now, his face contorted, because he was bewildered.

'Don't pull that face, it makes you look weird,' I said. 'We'd better get our suitcases from the attic and get started because Mum isn't half in a mood.'

'I don't want to go on holiday,' said Perry, sounding anxious.

'I know,' I said. 'Becks and I don't either. But Mum says we've got to go. So come on.'

'I'm in the middle of my newt experiment!' said Perry. 'I can't transport the newt. It's highly unlikely it would survive. So I'll just stay here.'

'All by yourself?' I said.

Perry thought for a moment. 'Mrs Sutton could check up on me,' he said. 'I can show her the newt. And I can eat toast and jam for breakfast and lunch and have baked beans for supper. I can fix all that myself.'

'You'd get terribly lonely,' I said.

'No I wouldn't. I'd go to school as usual.' Now he sounded calm again. 'And I could play video games whenever I wanted and stay up really late every night. It would be wicked!' Perry's face glowed at the thought.

'Come on, you two, stop nattering,' Becks called, coming down from the attic with her own silver suitcase. 'Get the clothes you want to take spread out on your beds and gather up your washing stuff and shoes. Put your shoes in your case first, so they don't crush your clothes. And Perry, you can't pack newts or worms or any of the other revolting creepy crawlies in your smelly old room, OK?' said Becks, sounding very much like Mum.

I could see she was very proud of herself for being so grown-up, but when I looked in her bedroom I saw she'd already dumped a mountain of clothes all over her bed, the sparkly crop top and tiny shorts right at the top. Her shoes were all lined up two by two on her rug, the new high heels the most prominent. She started sorting through the clutter of make-up and hair stuff and jewellery on her dressing table.

I went back to my own bedroom and opened my wardrobe, but I got distracted by Daisy. She came right up close to the mesh on her cage, her nose twitching, squeaking hopefully.

'Are you saying you want *more* kale?' I said, astonished. 'I don't think I'd better give you any more, Daisy. It looks like we've got a long car journey ahead of us, and you might be sick.'

I loved Daisy passionately but I didn't want green gloop seeping out of her cage and dampening my lap. She was going to take up quite a lot of room, plus her bag of dry food and her sack of hay. I decided I'd better cut down on everything else. I wouldn't need many clothes in the country. I dressed in my jeans and my Manchester United T-shirt to match my red Converse boots and red-and-black stripy socks. I dug out two more T-shirts and a big navy sweatshirt in case it got cold, and shorts if it was sunny, plus my wellies because it often seemed to be wet and muddy when we were on holiday. I added pyjamas, knickers, more socks, and my

best dress in case I made a new friend and they invited me to a party.

I fetched my sponge bag from the bathroom and shoved my hairbrush into it. I didn't have any make-up or jewellery like Becks. I tipped out all my homework stuff from my school bag and packed it with felt-tip pens and crayons and drawing pads and several paperbacks. There! I was done!

I went upstairs to the attic to find my suitcase. It was an embarrassingly babyish *Frozen* one but it couldn't be helped. It was easy enough to find, but I got distracted by the Robinson game laid out on the floor.

'Oh, Dad!' I said, and I knelt down beside it, starting to cry. After five minutes or so I managed to stop and mopped my face with the hem of some old curtains. Then I picked up the little Robinson figure and gave him a kiss goodbye.

I took my own six *Robinson* picture books off my shelf when I was back in my bedroom. They were all signed *To darling Phoebe, Love you to the moon and back, Dad xxxxx*

They were too young for me now, like my suitcase, but I packed them at the bottom of it nevertheless, with my washing things and wellington boots. Then I sprinkled knickers and pyjamas and the rest of my clothes on top. I tried folding my T-shirts but they went a bit wonky, and they were going to get horribly squashed anyway, because I'd got so much stuff now and

the *Frozen* suitcase was nowhere near big enough.

Still, I'd got packed all by myself. I wasn't sure how I was going to squash me, my suitcase, my school bag, and Daisy in her hutch with all her food and bedding into the car – but I was ready.

There were no sign of any strange men hanging about outside when we were all ready, but we couldn't just get in the car and make a quick getaway. We didn't fit. There were too many suitcases and bags, too many cardboard boxes, and too many animal containers. Mum conceded that I couldn't just abandon Daisy, but she drew the line at the newt in its big aquarium still half-filled with water.

'It's not a proper pet, Perry,' she said.

'I know. It's an experiment,' he said.

'Well, we'll find you something else to experiment on when we get to the cottage. Now, set the newt free in the garden where you found it and put that huge aquarium back in your bedroom,' Mum said firmly.

'I can't possible abandon my experiment now,' said Perry, equally firm.

There was a long and pointless argument. Occasionally Dad can talk Perry round when he's made up his mind. Mum isn't so good at it. She tries various strategies but Perry becomes more and more obstinate. He's autistic so his brain is wired differently.

We all knew what was going to happen, even Mum. Perry had a meltdown and howled. We had to wait ages for him to calm down.

I knelt down beside Daisy's hutch in the hall and whispered soothingly to her in case she found the upheaval upsetting. The aquarium was in the hall too. I peered at the newt.

'Perry, your newt's looking pretty agitated because you're making such a row. Maybe he'll be so upset he won't grow a new tail after all,' I said loudly, bending over him.

Perry went into a little huddle, his knees up by his chin.

'In what way agitated?' he asked, hiccupping.

'He's dashing about, trying to escape,' I said, exaggerating a little.

Perry swallowed hard and sat up, silent now, though tears were still streaming down his scarlet face. He got to his knees, stood, and went to see for himself.

'Thank you, Phoebe,' Mum whispered, shaking her head. 'Well, that was a waste of time. Let's try getting in the car again. With the wretched aquarium.' Actually she didn't say wretched.

She used another word entirely.

Perry reassured himself that his experiment was still alive and sat in the back of the car with the aquarium on his lap. I sat beside him with Daisy in her hutch, all her equipment leaning on my legs. My school bag and Perry's ancient Thomas the Tank Engine duvet were squashed between us.

'Why am I lumbered with you two twerps as siblings?' said Becks, as she sat in the front seat – though she had *two* suitcases *and* an enormous shoulder bag stowed in the boot.

Mum's big suitcase was wedged in the boot too, along with all the provisions and utensils.

'It looks as if we're moving house, not just going on holiday,' I said.

Perhaps Mrs Sutton thought that too, because she suddenly appeared at her window, struggling to open it.

'Oh God, what's she going to say?' said Becks.

'What's *Mum* going to say!' I said expectantly.

But Mrs Sutton simply called, 'Goodbye! Goodbye and good luck! I shall miss you!'

'She'll miss snooping on us,' Mum muttered, but she wound down her window and called goodbye back, and waved.

We waved too and then we drove off. I tried craning round to peer out of the back window, though it was very difficult with Daisy's cage pinioning my knees. Mrs Sutton went on waving

until Mum turned the car at the end of the road.

'Well, well,' said Mum. She didn't say any more, just kept steadily driving. We didn't say anything either. We didn't quite know how to react. Whenever we went on holiday in the past, Dad always started singing straight away, starting with 'We're All Going on a Summer Holiday!' and then taking us through an ancient medley of summery songs. He pretended we were tuned into a radio station called 'Dad Gold', and sometimes broke into wacky commentary: *The Robinson family are twenty minutes into their summer holiday. If you spot their navy Audi with the slightly bashed bumper – tut tut, bad driving, Mr Robinson! – toot your horn and give them a cheery acknowledgement!*

But Dad wasn't here and we weren't going on a proper holiday. We drove right past Blatchford Juniors and I screwed up my eyes to have a good stare through my classroom window. The day had turned so topsy-turvy I almost expected to see my own self sitting at my desk, head bent over my maths work. I was hopeless at sums so it was good to be missing it – and yet I felt I'd give anything to be sitting next to Amelie in that classroom, with everything back to normal.

Perry wanted everything to be normal too. 'I was going to get the Form Prize again,' he said mournfully.

We went past Becks's school too. She sighed. 'I know it was only a little end-of-term play, and I don't want to sound as if I'm

boasting, but everyone said I was really good in it. Mr White was going to film it and put it on YouTube. You never know who might have seen it,' she complained.

'I'm sorry, darling,' said Mum. 'But I'm sure you'll have a chance to be in some other play.'

'I was already word-perfect. I've wasted hours and hours learning my lines,' said Becks.

'Yes, I can see it's upsetting. But please don't go *on* about it, Rebecca,' said Mum. Becks was Mum's favourite but it was always a warning sign if she used her proper name.

'It could have been the start of a whole new acting career,' Becks continued relentlessly.

Mum slowed the car. 'All right,' she said. 'Out you get. Take your many suitcases out of the boot and go into school. Be the little star of your school play. You've got your own key to the house. I'm sure you can fend for yourself during the summer.'

We all stared at Mum. She was joking, wasn't she?

'Oh, ha ha, very funny,' Becks muttered.

'So, you're coming with us, are you?' said Mum.

'Well, yes. I haven't got any choice, have I?' said Becks.

'Exactly. And sometimes we have to do things we don't want. So will you *all* just stop moaning. I'm doing my best,' said Mum.

I felt indignant. *I* hadn't moaned – but I could see this wasn't the time to point this out. We sat in silence. Mum switched on the

car radio. She fiddled with the stations until she found one with pop tunes, which was a mistake. We were all painfully reminded of Dad. Mum switched to Radio Four and Woman's Hour. They were talking about periods.

'Mum!' said Becks, agonized, and Perry put his hands over his ears. Mum changed stations again, to some swirly piano music. I quite liked it, and pretended the top of Daisy's cage was my own instrument. I splayed my fingers and tapped each note. Perry snorted scornfully.

It seemed like the longest car journey ever, and yet we'd only been on the road fifteen minutes. There was a clothes brochure scrumpled in the netting on the back of Mum's seat, the sort you get inside the Sunday newspapers. I flipped through it, pretending I had all the money in the world.

What sort of clothes would I choose when I was grown up? I fancied one of the long swirly dresses with bold bright patterns. I'd wear it with coloured tights and big boots and look dead artistic. What could I buy for Dad? There were various men's T-shirts, striped or plain, but Dad liked the old rock star kind. There were trousers too, cream with a crease, but Dad lived in jeans, apart from when he wore his suit . . . I tried to concentrate on the jerseys, wondering if Dad would prefer a grey cable knit or a navy V-neck, but I'd started to feel sick.

I dropped the brochure on the floor and lay back as best I

could, eyes shut. The sick feeling started to get overwhelming.

'Mum, I think I'm going to be sick,' I told her.

'You can't be feeling sick already,' said Mum.

'I *am*,' I protested.

'Well, wind your window down a bit. And don't think about it. You'll feel better in a minute, I promise,' said Mum firmly.

I didn't feel better. I started to feel a lot worse.

'Mum! I can't stop it!'

'Ew, stop the car quick, Mum, I can't stand the smell of sick,' said Becks.

'Oh God!' Mum drew up in a lay-by.

Perry looked at me as if I was one of his experiments, and made no attempt to help me wriggle out from under Daisy's cage. Mum had to hold the cage herself while I turned my back on everyone and was horribly sick. I felt sure I would never, ever want to eat a pancake again in my life. Luckily I had my hair tied in a scraggy ponytail and I managed not to stain my red T-shirt. There was just a tiny splash on one of my Converses but I rubbed my boot along the grass bank to clean it.

'Are you OK now, Phoebe?' Mum asked.

'Sort of,' I said weakly.

'Dear heavens, this cage weighs a ton! I wish you didn't have to rest it on your knees,' said Mum.

'I don't mind. Is Daisy all right? She's not too upset, is she?'

Dad would have made out Daisy was worried seeing me being sick. He'd have probably pretended to *be* Daisy, talking in a little squeaky voice, and maybe he'd have twitched his nose and twiddled with imaginary whiskers.

Mum did peer in the cage, but shook her head. 'I don't think she's even noticed,' she said.

I clambered back in, slotting my feet into the small space on the floor, and Mum lowered Daisy and her cage onto my lap again.

'Phoebes, you're such a baby! Most kids have grown out of being travel-sick at your age,' said Becks.

'I can't help having a sensitive stomach,' I retorted.

'Well, so have I, and I think you've been a bit sick on yourself,

you messy thing,' said Becks, sniffing. 'Honestly, it's smelly enough in the car with those two creatures in the back.'

'The newt doesn't smell in the slightest!' said Perry indignantly.

'And neither does Daisy. She's clean as clean and her hay just smells lovely and summery,' I protested. 'And so do I!'

We squabbled in a half-hearted sort of way for half an hour or so. I'd started to want to go to the loo now, but I was a bit shy of saying so in case they all rounded on me again. Luckily Perry felt the need too.

'Mum, I need the toilet!' he said.

'All right,' said Mum. 'I'll stop at the next service station.'

'You two babies,' said Becks, but when we stopped ten minutes later she was just as keen to go as we were.

I washed my hands extra-carefully afterwards, and then my face, and sluiced all round my mouth at the water fountain.

'Careful, you're splashing all down your front,' said Mum. 'Why did you have to choose that tacky Manchester United shirt? You know I hate it.'

'Dad bought it for me,' I said. I turned my back on Mum and stalked out of the ladies' room. Perry was waiting for us, by one of those machines full of brightly coloured teddies. They had googly eyes just like my pencil case. *Wiffle!* He was still tucked under my pillow. I'd forgotten to pack him!

Perry was staring at me. 'What is it?' he asked. 'You've gone a

funny colour. Are you going to be sick *again*?'

'I've left Wiffle behind!' I whispered.

'Oh, goodness!' said Perry. 'How awful!' He wasn't mocking me. He understood the need for the same comforting friend at bedtime. He'd insisted on keeping the same duvet cover he'd had since he was little.

'I don't know how I could have been so stupid,' I said. 'I took all my clothes and underwear and washing things and goodness knows what – but I left Wiffle behind.'

'Well, we'll simply have to go back and get him,' said Perry.

'Do you think Mum will do that?' I asked.

'Of course! She'd drive back if she realized she'd left one of us behind, because we're family. So she'll drive back for Wiffle because he's part of your family,' said Perry.

'She's already cross with me,' I said mournfully.

'That's just the sort of person she is,' said Perry.

'Dad would have understood,' I murmured. He would drive back without hesitating. He wouldn't even go on about it. He might even pretend he'd forgotten something important himself, just to make me feel better.

Perry sighed. He turned to stare at the lurid teddies inside the glass window of the machine.

'Isn't it awful without him?' I said.

Perry said nothing. He pressed his forehead against the glass.

'Still, he's doing his very best for us,' I said earnestly. 'I bet this Robinson true-life documentary will be an enormous hit. Dad will manage on that island, easy-peasy. He'll make a shack and a garden and tame the animals and be absolutely ace at everything, won't he?'

I badly wanted Perry to agree with me, but he simply shrugged.

'If he *is* on an island,' he mumbled.

'Well, of course he is,' I said fiercely. 'What's the matter with you? He's been planning this for ages. He couldn't tell us because we might have let it out to people by accident. You do understand, don't you?'

'Just shut up,' said Perry.

Then Mum and Becks came out, in deep conversation, all pals again. They looked at Perry and me.

'*Now* what is it?' Mum asked.

I took a deep breath.

'Mum, I'm ever so sorry, and I know this is going to be very annoying, but all these teddies have got googly eyes and made me realize I've left Wiffle behind,' I said.

'Is that all? Don't worry, darling, we'll get you one of those weird little creatures if you really want one. Shall we all give it a go and see if we can scoop one up?' said Mum.

'But I don't want another one of these teddies. I want *Wiffle*!' I said.

'Oh, Phoebe, why do you have to make such a fuss about everything? You're like a toddler! Lighten up, for goodness' sake.'

'It's not a lightening-up matter! It's totally devastating!' I insisted.

'Stop being so melodramatic. You don't expect me to drive fifty miles home again to get a wretched *pencil case*, do you?' said Mum.

'Yes!' I felt tears come to my eyes. 'Dad would drive five hundred miles to get Wiffle,' I said.

Mum ignored this. She searched in her purse for cash, put a pound in the slot, and started operating the crane. I had my head lowered, but I watched through my eyelashes. She was surprisingly deft at it, managing to scoop up a magenta bear with googly eyes in just three goes. She wound it smoothly towards the hole and dropped it through neatly.

'There!' she said triumphantly, picking it up. 'One brand-new little teddy. It's quite sweet actually. I rather like its little dress. Matching knickers too, see!'

'Thank you, Mum,' I said faintly. She was doing her best, but I hated the magenta bear. It was surprisingly hard, and had a simpering expression and an odd bubblegum smell. It wasn't remotely a substitute for dear old Wiffle, but I could see there was no point saying so.

Mum decided we might as well have a very early lunch as we

were already parked here at the service station. She even let us have McDonald's, though she just had a coffee herself. She bought a couple of cheap CDs in Smith's too, *Rock Songs For the Road* and *Songs to Sing Along To*.

She played them both twice over as the journey went on and on and on. I laid back limply, still feeling vaguely sick, wondering if the burger and chips had been a good idea after all. There wasn't anything to look at out of the window, just endless motorway.

But at long last there were suddenly proper trees and fields and hills in the distance.

'How long until we get there?' Perry asked, for the fifteenth time. He'd been increasingly anxious about his newt. He covered the aquarium with a corner of his duvet to try to make it go to sleep.

'We're nearly there,' said Mum. She tapped the postcode she'd been given into the satnav. 'Ah! Ten miles. About twenty minutes at most.'

'Not long now,' I whispered into Daisy's cage. She'd behaved impeccably throughout the journey, sensibly sleeping most of the time. Every so often I eased a finger into her cage and touched her very gently to check she was still breathing. I marvelled at how small and soft she felt. 'I do love you, Daisy,' I whispered.

'Per-lease!' said Perry. 'Daisy is a little rodent. She can't possibly understand what you're saying.'

'*You're* a great fat ugly rodent and you understand,' I retorted.

'Stop bickering,' said Mum. 'Come on, let's sing along with the music.'

'Mum, these songs are *ancient*,' Becks said.

They were, but we knew a lot of the words because Dad sang this sort of stuff frequently, especially when he was vacuuming or cooking.

I love you, Dad, I said inside my head. *I love you to the moon and back. To the sun and all the planets and through all the black holes, whatever they are, but I'll always come back, and you must come back as soon as you possibly can because I miss you sooooo much.*

We were in real countryside now, with narrow twisty lanes, an occasional pub and a few straggling cottages.

'We seem to be in the back of beyond,' Becks said, sighing. 'I can't imagine there's many shopping centres or clubs around here.'

'You've wasted too many hours shopping already, and you're too young for clubs,' said Mum. 'It's time we all learned to appreciate a bit of peace and quiet. We'll get in touch with nature!'

'What, listening to the birds and smelling the roses and all that rubbish?' said Becks. 'Come *on*, Mum. You've always hated the idea of the country, all the mud and muck.'

'Well, maybe it's time I gave it a try,' said Mum. 'Keep your eyes peeled for a likely pub or little restaurant. I thought we'd eat out tonight. I'm too whacked to do any cooking.'

There didn't seem to be anywhere likely at all, though we were all looking now. The lanes were getting so twisty I started to feel sick again, and had to open the window.

'Oh, Phoebes! What's that disgusting smell? Wind that window *up*!' Becks commanded.

'It's just cow sh–,' said Perry.

'Perry!' said Mum, who's always very strict about us swearing, though she does it herself.

'Well, it *is*. It's quite an interesting smell, actually. And no wonder. Ruminants have four compartments to their stomachs, and as they digest they produce volatile fatty acids—'

'Shut up, Perry,' Becks and I said in unison.

Mum was twiddling with the satnav map. 'Ah yes, here's the little flag!' she said triumphantly.

'Mum, it's miles from anywhere!' said Becks.

'Good, that's exactly what we want,' said Mum.

Becks turned round to look at Perry and me. '*No we don't!*' she mouthed.

The trees were so dense now they formed a tall arch over our heads. I still couldn't see any pubs. I felt queasy and yet somehow ravenously hungry at the same time. And I needed to go to the loo again, badly. Where *was* this wretched cottage?

I knew holiday homes came in all shapes and sizes. The converted chapel had been beautiful, with a stained-glass window

that made the beige carpet glow yellow and red and blue when the sun shone. We'd stayed in a converted barn once too, but that had been just like a proper house, not a cow in sight.

'Mum, what does this cottage look like?' I asked, feeling worried.

'I don't know. They haven't got a proper picture of it on their website. Just a view of fields and a river. We can go for lots of walks and maybe we could hire some canoes – that would be fun, wouldn't it?' said Mum.

'If they haven't got a picture of it then it must look awful,' said Becks. 'And I heard that woman on the phone say it was dilapidated.'

'Yes, well, beggars can't be choosers,' said Mum.

'Are we beggars now?' I asked, shocked. 'Surely we've got lots of money. You earn a lot, don't you, Mum?'

'I suppose so, though I might have to take a drop in salary if I'm going to be working less hours this summer. And there are various bills and things we have to pay. And other stuff,' said Mum, as she drove up a hill.

'What other stuff?' I asked. 'Surely there'll be more money to go round if Dad isn't with us?'

'Well, actually we've got a big debt to pay off,' said Mum. 'So we'll have to pull our horns in a little.'

'Where does that expression come from? What sort of horns?

Cow's horns?' I asked, puzzled.

'Snails,' said Perry. 'The garden snail has retractable eyes and it pulls them in if it feels threatened.'

'Mr Know-it-all,' I muttered.

We got to the top of the hill and then coasted downwards.

'You've got debts?' said Becks.

'We'll manage. Don't worry about it! Now, here we go, Wildbriar Lane! That sounds very romantic, doesn't it? According to the satnav the cottage should be just down here, on the right,' said Mum.

We peered hard. There was nothing on the right. Just trees and an old red telephone box with the phone torn out.

'Well, it's going to be a tight squeeze, all of us living in the telephone box. We'll have to go to sleep standing up,' I said. I thought it was quite a funny joke, but no one laughed.

'Perhaps it's on the left,' said Mum, but there was no sign of a cottage there either. 'Oh well, satnavs are notoriously dodgy in the countryside. We'll carry on down the lane. That woman on the phone definitely said that the cottage was in Wildbriar Lane.'

We drove very slowly down the entire length of the lane. There were no cottages at all, no outbuildings of any kind, not even a dog kennel.

'Do you suppose there's *another* Wildbriar Lane?' Mum wondered. 'Or are we in the right village?'

'There *isn't* a village,' said Becks. 'There isn't anything at all. What's this cottage called, Mum?'

'They didn't actually give me a name. They just said "the cottage". Hang on, I'll phone them, and ask for proper directions. This is ridiculous.'

Mum drew up by the side of the road and got out her mobile. She tried the number. Then she looked at her phone.

'Oh God, there's no signal,' she said, sighing.

'No signal!' said Becks. She peered at her own phone. 'Oh my God! We can't stay here!'

'Calm down! I'm sure there'll be a signal at the wretched cottage, if we ever find it,' said Mum, peering at the map on the satnav again.

'*What if there's no Wi-Fi either?*' Becks said. 'Mum, this is ridiculous! Why can't we just go *home*?'

'Because we can't,' Mum snapped. 'We're here now. And we'll drive on until we see a house or a pub or a village store and we'll ask for directions there.'

She started up the car and we drove off, slowly, just in case we'd somehow missed seeing the cottage before. We drove and drove. Out of Wildbriar Lane, up another hill, down a road that didn't have a proper name at all, just The Road.

'This is like one of those creepy films,' I said. 'People get completely lost in a place that doesn't seem real at all, and then

they *think* they're getting to a proper village at last, and see some buildings, and they go rushing up to this pub thankfully and fling open the doors and then scream, because there are all these zombies sitting there, grinning at them.'

'You and your imagination,' said Mum.

'I'm like Dad,' I said.

Perry didn't comment. He'd gone very quiet. We peered at the signs.

'Look, it says Primrose Railway,' I said.

'Well, there has to be a little town or village if there's a railway,' said Becks, sighing with relief.

'I don't think it can be a proper one. Maybe it's one of those little trains for children. Remember how you loved going on the Thomas the Tank Engine ride when you were little, Perry?' said Mum. 'Aha! Look down there – houses! At last!'

There were six terraced houses in a row, called Railway Cuttings. They were tiny, with a little patch of garden in front of each one. Mum got out and knocked at the first. No one answered. She went to the second. No answer again.

Becks, Perry and I watched from the car. 'I bet they're all empty,' said Becks.

'Because they're all in the pub. Zombies get thirsty,' I said.

'Shut *up*, Phoebe,' said Becks.

The door opened at the third house and a middle-aged

woman in an apron came to the door. The woman nodded.

'Look! I think she knows where it is!' I said.

'Worse luck,' said Becks. 'This is madness. I don't want to be stuck in the middle of nowhere for weeks and weeks!'

'Do you think Mum *has* lost her mind?' I asked.

'You'd think so. *And* Dad,' Becks said bitterly. 'Just our luck, both our parents going off their heads.'

I wanted to poke her hard, but I was trapped underneath Daisy's cage. Mum was hurrying back to the car now, smiling.

'That lady was ever so nice. She knew the cottage! We were in the exact right place! Hey ho, back to Wildbriar Lane,' she said, starting up the car and doing a complicated three-point turn.

'But Mum!' I protested. 'There wasn't a single cottage there. We looked and looked,' I said.

'Yes, but we weren't looking properly,' said Mum. She breathed a sigh of relief as she got the car pointed in the right direction.

Becks turned round and pulled a face.

'There wasn't a cottage anywhere, was there, Perry?' I whispered.

He shrugged his shoulders. He was looking very tense. I realized this was really hard for him. He hates it when his routine is changed. He was clutching the edge of his Thomas duvet, as if it was a cuddle blanket.

'Don't worry,' I said softly.

He didn't reply. Mum drove back steadily until we got to the brow of the hill. Then she parked the car.

'*Here?*' said Becks.

'Look out of the window. See Wildbriar Lane, twisting about down there? And see that little blob of red?' said Mum.

'That's the telephone box,' I said.

'Yes! Exactly. Now follow directly along from the telephone box, through the trees, out the other side, over that field – what's that!'

'A cottage!' I said. 'But it doesn't have a road going to it!'

'I think you're right. We'll have to park by the telephone box and hope for the best. Still, we've found it!' said Mum.

'You mean we'll have to hump all our luggage through the trees?' Becks asked.

'Yes, it's a bit of nuisance, isn't it? But we'll manage. Come on, chin up, everyone, this is an adventure,' said Mum. She sounded as if she was trying very hard to convince herself as well as us.

We drove back down to the telephone box and Mum parked the car. 'Right! Hang on, let's have a little recce,' she said, jumping out. 'There doesn't seem to be any footpath at all. We'll just have to make our way through the trees as best we can. We'll leave the suitcases in the car for the moment. Becks, you help Phoebe with the guinea-pig cage. I'll sort out Perry and his aquarium.'

Becks jumped out, came round to my side of the car, opened the door and started trying to edge Daisy's cage out.

'Careful! Do it ever so gently! She'll get upset if you tug like that,' I protested, as we pushed and pulled.

'It's so heavy!' said Becks, having to hold the cage herself as I wriggled out. 'Feels like you've got a real pig inside, not just the guinea sort!'

'You're the real pig,' I said. 'Don't tip the cage like that! Poor little Daisy!'

Mum and Perry were making even less progress. Perry was refusing to budge, his aquarium still swathed in his duvet.

'Come *on*, Perry,' said Mum, pulling at the duvet.

'No!' said Perry, as the aquarium was exposed. 'No, no, no, no!'

I peered. The newt was lying on its back. It wasn't moving. It looked as if Perry's experiment was over and done with.

'Nigel Newt!' Perry cried, to our astonishment. 'Oh, Nigel!'

He put his head on the glass of the aquarium and wept.

It took Mum a good ten minutes to coax Perry out of the car, leaving the aquarium behind. Becks and I put Daisy's cage down and waited.

'*Nigel* Newt?' Becks whispered.

'Sweet!' I murmured.

We were touched that our fierce brother had obviously loved the newt. It wasn't just an experiment. He was Nigel, a beloved pet.

Even Mum had the sense not to remind Perry that he could probably find a dozen replacements if he went looking. He didn't want another newt; he wanted Nigel. If anything happened to Daisy I wouldn't be consoled by a new little guinea pig. Well, not for a while.

Mum offered to give Perry a cuddle, though he rarely lets any of us give him a hug. He reared away, but she managed to wipe his face with a tissue.

'Leave off, Mum,' he mumbled, sniffing.

'Right. Let's find the cottage,' she said. 'I suppose we just walk through the trees and then we'll come across it.'

I wasn't really used to wandering through trees. It was like a little wood and I had to keep reminding myself there weren't any wild wolves in England any more. It was all so eerily quiet and I jumped every time a bird squawked. Daisy's cage was also so big that I couldn't really see where I was going. Even so, I spotted dandelions out of the corner of my eye.

'Becks, can we put the cage down a minute? I must pick those dandelions for Daisy's supper,' I said.

'For goodness' sake, there's bound to be heaps more dandelions nearer the cottage,' said Becks. 'Let's just get there, OK? My arms are really aching.'

'Do you think we're going the right way? We won't get lost, will we?' I asked. I wondered if there were woods like this on Dad's island, as well as palm trees on the beach. 'What are all these trees anyway? They're all so big and knobbly.'

'Oaks,' Perry mumbled up ahead, still sniffling. 'And very old.'

'I wonder if any of them are hollow? I read a book once about some runaway children and they hid inside a hollow oak,' I said eagerly. 'That would be so cool.'

Dad could perhaps sleep inside a huge oak until he had time to build himself a proper shelter. It would keep him safe from . . .

Well, it wouldn't be other people, because the whole point was that he was all alone. The Robinson in Dad's books chatted to all the animals on the island, but they were mostly friendly, though the woolly mammoth could get irritable at times.

'Perry, woolly mammoths are totally extinct now, aren't they?' I called.

'Don't be ridiculous! They were around in the Ice Age. Everyone knows they're extinct now,' said Perry witheringly.

I was hurt. I hated it that Perry always knew so much more than me. It was because he read so much. Perry liked encyclopaedias and manuals, any book full of facts. I loved reading too, but I liked stories.

Becks was clever, though she tried to hide it. She skipped her homework and spent ages doing dumb stuff with her friends – and yet she nearly always came top in exams.

I had never been top of anything in my life. Well, Dad said I was his Top Girl. He always encouraged me to show him my stories. He said they were brilliant and that I'd grow up to be a writer like him. My teachers never gave me high marks for my stories at school. They fussed about things like paragraphs and punctuation and handwriting and spelling. They did say I had a vivid imagination though. And I loved to draw too, so I always got good marks in art.

It wasn't always a great thing to have a vivid imagination,

especially trekking through a forest burdened with a great cage so you couldn't run away quickly if a wildcat or a rabid bat suddenly flew at you. It was a relief when the trees started thinning and we found ourselves at the edge of a field covered in great tufts of grass. I took a step and nearly twisted my ankle.

'Whoops! Watch out, it's full of potholes,' I said, struggling to keep a firm hold of my end of Daisy's cage.

'They're not potholes, they're rabbit holes!' said Perry.

'All these holes are made by rabbits?' I said. 'It's like *Watership Down*! Oh, I do hope we see lots of rabbits. Do you hear that, Daisy. Lots and lots of friends!'

'You mustn't ever try to let her out of the cage, or you'll lose her in seconds,' said Mum.

'Especially as some of them are badger holes!' said Perry. 'Look at this huge one.'

'It could just be made by a huge fat rabbit,' I said.

'No, the hole is in a D shape so that means it's definitely a badger,' said Perry. His face lit up. 'Oh, how wonderful! Badger setts! I'll come out here after dark and see if I can spot any!' Perhaps he was starting on a brand-new Badger Project now.

'Not alone, matey,' said Mum firmly. 'Perhaps we'll all come and watch, once we're settled. So where's the cottage, then? We saw it, didn't we? Right behind the field. It must be *this* field, mustn't it?'

I screwed up my eyes against the sun and squinted at the hedge

in the distance. I saw something browny-red sticking up above the tangle of leaves and brambles.

'Is that a chimney?' I said, pointing.

'Oh, you clever girl!' said Mum.

I glowed, happy I'd spotted it first. We had to skirt all round the field because it was too difficult to wade through the tufty grass. It was heavy going even so, especially for Becks and me carrying Daisy in her cage. It looked at first as if we were going to have to burst through the bramble bushes, but when we got much nearer we saw that a bit had been hacked back, showing an old wooden fence and a rickety gate.

We had to fiddle and tug at the rusty latch, but at last eased it open. Mum and Perry went first, then Becks backed through with her end of the cage, so I was the last to see the cottage.

It was truly the storybook cottage of my dreams. It had a thatched roof and roses and honeysuckle climbing up the white-washed walls! Well, the thatch was threadbare in places, and the flowers grew in a wild tangle, plus the walls badly needed a fresh coat of paint – but that just made it look more picturesque.

'Isn't it *lovely*?' I said.

As I spoke there was a rustle from the thatched roof, and a little blue bird flew out above our heads.

'Oh, look! It's a bluebird! A bluebird of happiness, like in the fairy tale!' I breathed.

'It's not a bluebird, you fool, it's a blue *tit*,' said Perry the pedant, but he couldn't help sniggering when he said the word 'tit'.

'I wonder if it's nesting in the thatch,' said Mum. Now, where's this key hidden away? I think the woman on the phone said it was round the back.'

Becks and I put Daisy's cage on the doorstep and we all went round the side of the cottage to the back. There was a little miniature wooden house there, with a long run beside it.

'Is that a doll's house?' I asked eagerly.

'No, it's a chicken coop,' said Mum. 'Only no chickens, thank goodness.'

'Oh, chickens would have been fantastic. Fresh eggs for breakfast!' I said. 'So what's that other little house thing?'

'Oh God, no! Please don't let it be an outside loo!' said Mum, looking horrified. She pushed the door open gingerly and then gasped 'It *is*!'

We took turns peering. Becks held her nose. It didn't exactly smell of toilets, more a strange dank earthy reek. It didn't seem to have a light inside, but we could see a weird wooden seat with a hole in it.

'I'm not using that!' said Becks resolutely.

I was about to tell her she was being silly when I saw a spider scuttle across the floor away from the sudden sunlight.

'I'm not either!' I said quickly.

Perry was squatting down, looking interested. 'I wonder what kind of spider it was?' he muttered.

'We don't want you to identify it *or* keep it in a cage,' said Becks. 'Mum, we *can't* stay here, in the back of beyond, without a proper toilet!'

Mum looked as if she might agree. But she found the key cage beside the back door, punched in the number, and pulled out two keys.

'Let's just see inside,' she said.

She tried the back door. She had to try the key several times, and then give the door a big shove, but she managed it and we stepped inside.

We were in a kitchen, but it didn't remotely resemble our one at home, though they were both green. Ours was a muted shade called Breakfast Room Green – we'd had it done two years ago when Mum had a new kitchen installed to celebrate a promotion. We also had a big shiny cooker and a special Belfast sink and a kitchen island and so many cupboards I could never remember where anything was kept. There was an enormous table with six carefully chosen chairs, none of them properly matching, but somehow blending together. At least, that's what Mum said. She

liked the kitchen to look totally unused, with a striped jug of flowers on the table and a big bowl of oranges and lemons to add a bit of colour to the kitchen island.

This kitchen had colour everywhere. The walls were a bold apple green and covered with pictures. Some were proper paintings of countryside things – birds and butterflies and sheep and cows and flowers, all brighter than usual. They were all painted in a big bold way. Mrs Morrison would have approved. And so did I!

There were quaint old ornaments everywhere, on the windowsill and above the old range and all over the big dresser that reached right up to the low wooden-beamed ceiling: toby jugs and china dogs and shell boxes and teapots in the shape of cats and cottages. There were plates on the dresser too, deep green ones like cabbages, and a set patterned in blue and orange.

The round table had a pattern too, diamond shapes in different shades of yellow and brown painted onto the wood, so that it played tricks with your eyes. The chairs didn't match, but they didn't blend together: there was a big wooden chair with a carved back, a rocking chair, a squat yellow chair with a cushion featuring a cross-stitch cat, and several old-fashioned canvas beach chairs.

'It's too crowded! I don't like it,' said Perry, screwing up his eyes.

'Well, *I* think it's amazingly lovely!' I said, whirling round, picking up a toby jug to examine it.

'Put it down!' Mum said sharply. 'For God's sake, it could be valuable! I can't make this out. I've seen plates like that in antique shops – and yet some of this stuff is just old junk. And how on earth do you cook on *this*?' she said, backing away from the old range.

'Weird,' Becks agreed, but she wasn't having a proper look at anything. She was staring at her mobile instead. 'Still no signal! And there's no *Wi-Fi*! Mum, did you hear? How am I going to keep in touch with all my friends?'

'Perhaps you could write a letter?' I suggested. I think I'm the only person in the world who *likes* writing letters. I space them out neatly, and then I do a decorative border all round the edge in different colours. The only trouble is I haven't usually got anyone to write to. But now I could write to Amelie! We could be proper pen pals, and I'd sign off *Your best friend for ever* and hope she'd write the same back to me.

Perry was pacing round the kitchen, frowning. 'This kitchen is hurting my head. And there's no toaster!' he said.

'I expect I might be able to toast things on the range,' Mum said doubtfully, picking up a pair of kitchen utensils that looked like wire tennis rackets.

'But it won't taste the same,' Perry wailed.

'It might taste *better*,' I said. 'Mum, can I have the rocking chair? I've *always* wanted to sit in a rocking chair. And I think

Daisy would absolutely love sitting on my lap and being gently rocked to sleep, just like a little furry baby.'

'Not in the kitchen, Phoebe. I don't think that would be very hygienic,' said Mum.

'Well, can I take the rocking chair into the living room then?' I said.

I went out into the narrow corridor, looking for it. I peered round a door.

'Is this it?' I said, not sure.

In some ways it was like the most sumptuous little living room ever, with dusky rose walls and deep crimson velvet curtains, still very grand even though they were faded. There were two sofas too, covered in big bright shawls and huge blue and green and red cushions, some embroidered, some patterned with tiny rounds of glass. There was an old threadbare rug too, just like a magic carpet in fairy tales. But the other half of the living room was bare floorboards, with a big easel and a table covered with a clutter of dried-up paints and stubby chalks. A half-finished painting was propped on the easel, and several further canvases were stacked against the wall: pictures of wild flowers, an apple tree, a bowl of fruit and a rabbit, all very large.

'An artist must live here! He's painted all these pictures, and the ones in the kitchen. I like the rabbit best! Oh, do you think he'd paint Daisy?' I said excitedly.

'It could be a woman artist,' said Mum, peering round. 'And she should have tidied all her clutter away!'

'Unless she's dead,' I said.

'Don't be morbid, darling,' said Mum.

'Well, she's not living here now, is she?' I said. I went back into the corridor and peered up the dark narrow stairs. 'Unless she's up there? Lying in her bed.'

'Don't be silly,' Mum snapped, but she went up the stairs cautiously. I felt a bit scared of what we might find myself, even though I'd just been joking. But there was no one upstairs, male or female, just two bedrooms, a big wide cupboard with double doors – empty – and a tiny bathroom with a hip bath and a very old-fashioned toilet.

'Thank God,' said Mum.

More paintings hung on the corridor wall. There was a jolly one of two people having a dance. The man had a quiff and a sharp suit and blue suede shoes and the woman had a ponytail and a crimson skirt that whirled about her hips. It was the sort of dancing Dad and I did!

'This is a crazy house,' said Perry. 'I don't like it one bit. Too many pictures and patterns. It's too bright!'

'Well, it'll be pitch dark tonight. There's hardly any light switches!' said Becks. 'And there aren't even enough bedrooms. How can we possibly stay here? We can't all squash in together!'

'I'll sleep in the cupboard thing,' said Perry. 'I like the shelves.'

'But it hasn't got a bed,' said Mum.

'I don't need a bed. I've got Thomas,' said Perry. 'I like sleeping on the floor, because then I know I can't fall off it.'

'I suppose we could sort you out with some cushions from downstairs,' said Mum. 'Then you could have your Thomas duvet on top of you.' She went backwards and forwards to the proper bedrooms.

The big one was blue and white, with a patchwork cover on the double bed. The low ceiling was blue too, with white painted birds flying across it. The little bedroom was purple and white, and very plain, though I liked the painting of violets hanging on the wall.

'Tell you what, I'll have this purple one,' said Mum. 'You two girls can have the big room.'

'Oh, Mum, thank you, thank you! I just love the birds! And look, Daisy's cage will fit beautifully on that little table,' I said happily.

'I'm not sharing with Phoebe! She's far too messy and she snorts in her sleep,' said Becks.

'I do not!' I retorted indignantly.

'And I am *definitely* not sleeping in the same room as a rodent,' said Becks. 'That guinea pig smells.'

'She does not! How dare you! *You're* the one who smells of

yucky make-up and hair products and all those different sickly perfumes,' I cried.

'Oh, for goodness' sake!' Mum shouted. 'What's the matter with you? All this squabbling and moaning and sniping! Why are you *all* so difficult *all* the time?'

She was yelling at us as if she couldn't stand us. I felt tears pricking my eyes. *Mum* was the difficult one! Why couldn't she act like a proper mum and make a fuss of us and help us feel special? Why did she keep snapping and shouting at us? Why didn't she know how to look after us properly? Why couldn't she be fun? Why couldn't she be like *Dad*?

I felt the tears spilling down my cheeks.

Mum sighed impatiently and went downstairs, leaving the three of us standing there, looking at each other.

Becks put her arm round me. 'Don't, Phoebes. It's OK, we'll share the blue room – and I suppose I'll have to put up with Daisy too.'

'I'll keep her as clean as clean. As clean as . . . a fluffy cloud,' I said.

'You sound like that stupid advert for toilet paper,' said Perry, poking his head round the door. He looked like he might cry again himself. 'It's my fault,' he murmured.

'What's your fault?' I asked.

'That it died. The newt,' said Perry.

'You looked after him ever so carefully. You even gave him proper mineral water to have a little swim in, and he had the best aquarium ever,' I said.

'I should never have taken it away from its natural habitat. It's an elementary mistake,' said Perry.

'Well, you won't make it again. Maybe you can keep something else in the aquarium. Goldfish?' Becks suggested.

'But they wouldn't be an experiment, would they?' said Perry. 'Not like—'

He was clearly going to say Nigel, but he clamped his lips together, embarrassed.

'Perry, say no if you like, but do you think we could maybe have a little funeral for Nigel?' I asked. 'We could find some kind of box for a coffin and dig a hole in the garden and we could all say a few words . . . what's it called, oh yes, a eulogy!'

When we went to Granny's funeral Dad did a lovely eulogy for his mum, gently funny, making everyone laugh as well as cry. I think Perry was remembering too, because he gave a little smile.

'We could do that tomorrow,' he said.

'You two!' said Becks, shaking her head.

Mum came back upstairs. She'd given her face a wash, presumably at the kitchen sink. She took a deep breath.

'Sorry, sorry, sorry,' she said awkwardly. 'The water's stone cold. I'll see if I can find the boiler and get it switched on. And

then we'd better make the trek all the way back to the car for our cases. This is a bit ridiculous. I know they said the cottage was pretty basic, but it hasn't even got a proper bathroom. I'll get in touch with Quirky Cottages and we'll find somewhere else to stay. This is way too quirky.'

'Yay!' said Becks. 'With proper WiFi? And a bedroom each?'

'I'll do my best,' said Mum.

It took us another half-hour to go to the car and then struggle all the way back laden with suitcases and boxes. We left the aquarium with its sad small contents in the back seat. Perry sniffed a little but didn't cry again. I worried about Daisy, still on the doorstep in her hutch. I was scared she might suddenly have keeled over with the shock of the long journey and the jolting ride to the cottage, but when we got back to the cottage at last Daisy seemed fine. I knelt beside her and she squeaked eagerly.

'Yes, Daisy! I bet you feel really hungry and thirsty. I'll fetch you a bowl of water and a bowl of your food, and the biggest juiciest clump of dandelions I can find, OK?' I said.

I tended to all Daisy's needs and cleaned up her cage so that Becks couldn't possibly say she smelled. Mum and Becks bustled around inside the cottage. Perry unpacked his suitcase, and arranged everything with neat precision in the cupboard: clothes on one shelf, pyjamas and washbag on another, and books and special possessions on a third.

'Some of those marbles are mine,' I said, reaching for his big glass jar. 'One of every colour, you promised!'

'No I didn't! And anyway, the aquarium is useless now,' said Perry miserably, snatching the jar back.

I scowled at him as he spread out his duvet on the floor on top of two big sofa cushions.

'I don't think that looks very comfortable,' said Mum. 'Maybe you'd better have the purple room.'

'No! I *want* to sleep in the cupboard. It's totally cool,' said Perry.

'But there are no windows,' I pointed out. 'If you close the doors it'll be totally dark. There's no light switch!'

'I *like* the dark,' said Perry. 'And I've got my torch with me. I can curl up and read a book, easy-peasy.'

'Fancy liking the dark!' I said, but I was glad he'd cheered up.

Perhaps it hadn't been a wise move to tend to Daisy before doing my own unpacking. Becks had totally commandeered the blue room, spreading her stuff around everywhere, and taking up nine-tenths of the wardrobe. She'd spread her make-up and brushes and bottles all over the little table underneath the mirror, and she'd even lit one of her candles so that the whole room reeked of some odd rosy smell.

'Becks! You're making the room pong!' I coughed, waving my arms in the air to disperse the smell.

'It's lovely,' said Becks.

'No, it's not, it's disgusting. Imagine what it's like for Daisy with her sensitive little nostrils. And move all that junk off the table, that's where her hutch is going,' I said.

We bickered about it for a long time. When we trailed downstairs we found Mum sitting in the kitchen, with a glass of wine.

I frowned at it. 'Mum, you're always drinking wine now. Are you *sure* you're not turning into an alcoholic?' I asked.

'Don't be silly, Phoebe. Of course I'm not. I just think I deserve a glass of wine after that nightmare journey and this bizarre set-up here. I've looked everywhere for the boiler but I can't find the wretched thing anywhere. I'd give anything for a proper hot bath,' she said, taking another gulp of wine.

'But you can't drink now, not if you're going to drive us to a pub for supper,' I said.

'Well, I'm not sure I can face getting in that car again, not this evening. And we've been all round the moon and haven't seen a pub anywhere,' said Mum. 'We'll have a scratch supper here. I brought a few bits and pieces from home.'

It was actually a lovely supper. We had baked beans on toast, a really big portion each with two slices of toast. Mum let us have crisps too, and then a Tunnocks teacake each. They're Dad's favourite. He eats them like a little boy, nibbling the chocolate

dome off with his teeth, then biting tiny pieces from the biscuit base, leaving the glossy sweet white marshmallow till last. I eat them that way too.

'What do you think Dad's eating right this minute?' I asked.

Mum closed her eyes for a moment. 'I'm not sure,' she said eventually.

'I know he'll be catching fish and snaring animals and all that, but will he have some kind of starter pack?' I wondered. 'Just for the first day or two, before he gets himself organized. You know, like a picnic? Wouldn't it be funny if he was eating a Tunnocks teacake too, right this minute?'

Mum gave a tight little smile. 'Maybe he is,' she said.

We all went a bit quiet after that. Mum looked at her lap. Becks and I exchanged glances. Perry slumped in his chair, biting his lip. We became very aware of the grandfather clock in the corner. I found I was nodding my head in time to the ticks and tocks.

'Stop *doing* that!' said Becks. 'Come and help me with the dishes, Phoebe, if we're all finished.'

We cleared the table and washed the plates in cold water. 'Careful! They're so beautiful we don't want to chip them,' I said.

Mum took Perry to look for the boiler, as he was often good at finding things.

'Try not to keep going on about Dad, Phoebes,' said Becks. 'It just upsets everyone.'

'But that's ridiculous! I want to talk about Dad! I'm missing him so much,' I protested.

'We all are,' said Becks.

'Not as much as me,' I said. 'Most of the time you act as if you've forgotten all about him. Imagine how *lonely* he'll be feeling now, on his desert island. He'd like to think we were all talking about him and sending him little messages. I bet he's filming himself on his laptop right now, looking really sad.'

Then I went quiet.

'Phoebe?'

'I've just thought. Could there possibly be electricity on the island? Otherwise how could he charge his computer?' I said, nibbling at my knuckles. 'It doesn't make sense.' I was starting to worry.

'It's OK, Phoebe,' Becks said quickly. 'I expect he'll have a special camera. He'll set it up and film himself on that. And he'll have a big case of batteries for it.'

'Oh yes! Of course! And maybe he'll have another big case full of snacks, and mineral water in case it takes him a while to find a stream, because you can't drink seawater, can you? Unless you're a fish or a dolphin. Oh, Becks, do you think Dad might be able to swim with dolphins – he'd absolutely love that!'

I burbled on and on, making it seem real in my head. I even saw Dad shinning up a coconut tree and waving like mad as he

looked out to sea. I went out of the back door and stood on tiptoe and waved back. I knew this was an incredibly pointless thing to do, and that Dad couldn't possibly see me even if I grew as tall as the cottage – no, taller, the tallest building ever.

I wondered if Perry would know the name of the tallest building in the world. He loved poring over the *Guinness Book of World Records*.

I went back into the cottage to ask him.

'It's the Burj Khalifa in Dubai,' he said at once.

'You should go on one of those television quiz shows,' I said. Then I looked all around. 'There isn't a television!' I said.

'We can stream stuff on my computer,' said Mum.

'Not without Wi-Fi,' said Becks.

'Oh yes. Well, it won't hurt us for one night to go without television,' said Mum. She yawned. 'I'm actually tired out already. God knows where this stupid boiler is hiding. We'll have to boil up the kettle so we can have a little wash.'

'I'm not going to bother with a wash. I'm going to bed in my cupboard right this minute,' said Perry.

So we all went to bed. The sheets were clean, though very cold, and the pillows were a bit lumpy. Becks and I huddled together to get warm, but after a while she turned over, and within a few seconds she was snoring. There! She had the cheek to accuse *me* of making snorty noises.

Daisy rustled about for a while, checking out her cage, but then she went quiet. I wondered if Perry was asleep in his dark cupboard wrapped up in Thomas the Tank Engine. And was Mum asleep too, all alone in a double bed?

I badly wanted Wiffle, but he was still squashed under my pillow at home. I stared up at the white birds flying across the ceiling. It grew too dark to see them, but I knew they were there, circling above me. I imagined them calling softly, over and over and over . . .

I woke up very early, instantly wide awake. I wondered if Dad was too. He'd have so much to do. Perhaps he was already combing the beach for driftwood to help him make a shelter? Or was he wading in the water with a home-made rod, trying to catch a fish for his breakfast? He wouldn't have to eat it raw. Robinson had rubbed some sticks together and made a fire. And he'd climbed a tree for a coconut, smashed it open and drunk the water inside. I was sure Dad could do that too.

I wondered what we'd be having for breakfast. There wasn't much food left so we'd need to go to the shops. Only we didn't know where they were.

I wished there were still hens in the coop, then maybe we could have fresh eggs. Perhaps there was a farm somewhere? That's what children in books did when they went to the country.

They bought cans of milk too, and freshly churned butter, and there was always a friendly farmer's wife who gave them a cottage loaf still warm from her oven.

I slid out of bed and lifted a corner of the curtain to see if I could make out a likely farmhouse on the horizon. I was so dazzled by the sunrise that I simply stared at the sky, transfixed. I'd seen sunrises before, obviously, but there were always buildings in the way. Out here the sky was enormous, and totally flooded with colour. It was intensely red, edged with flaming orange, and then it spread out all around, turning the clouds a dusky pink.

I could scarcely breathe, my heart beating hard with the beauty of it. I opened the curtains properly.

'Don't!' Becks protested sleepily, rolling over and pulling the quilt over her head.

'No, Becks, look, there's the most beautiful sunrise ever!' I said.

'What?' Becks stuck one arm out of the covers and grabbed her phone. 'For God's sake, Phoebe, it's only just gone five! Close those curtains and come back to bed!'

'I can't sleep!'

'Well, I can,' said Becks. She hunched up small and within a few seconds she was snoring.

I sighed. I checked on Daisy, but she was asleep too, and didn't stir, even when I whispered, *'Dandelions!'* It seemed mean to wake her up when she'd had such a long strange journey yesterday.

I pulled on some clothes, and padded along the landing. I had a peep in Perry's cupboard. I could just make out his face. He was fast asleep, with the corner of his duvet over his nose for comfort. He looked so peaceful that I felt it would be mean to wake him too.

I checked on Mum instead. She was breathing heavily, curled round something big and navy. I caught my breath. *Dad!* Had he given up on his island scheme and come to find us? Oh, Dad, Dad, Dad . . .

No, it wasn't Dad. It was just Dad's jumper, his dear familiar fisherman's sweater. He wore it all winter and on cool days in summer. I loved it when Dad gave me a hug and I could breathe in its safe warm woolly smell and trace the raised patterns of the knitting with my finger.

Mum had fast hold of it now. She was obviously missing Dad terribly too. I stared at her, at her clutching hands, and felt the oddest twist in my stomach. It was as if *I* was the mother and she were the child.

'Dad will come back as soon as he can,' I whispered, and then tiptoed away.

I visited the tiny bathroom. The water was still stone cold so I gave myself the quickest wash ever. I opened the velvet curtains downstairs and looked at the sky again. It was softer and pinker now, but still beautiful. I went to look at the many stubby pastel crayons on the old table, then glanced at the unused canvases

stacked against the wall. I wondered if I dared have a go at drawing my own sunrise. I could make it big and bold, like the paintings in the cottage. I could fill a whole canvas with red sky. It would look glorious!

I got as far as propping a new canvas on the easel and taking a red pastel in my hand, but didn't quite dare to have a go. The art things didn't belong to me. Mum was renting this cottage but it didn't mean we were free to use anything in the house. When we stayed in the Old Chapel the owners left us a complimentary hamper containing tea and coffee and long-life milk and a packet of cookies and sometimes even a big bar of chocolate – but they left a little message, making it clear these were free.

I put the pastel down and stacked the canvas back in the corner. Thinking about the cookies and chocolate made me hungry, even though it was too early for breakfast. I went into the kitchen and checked on the cardboard box of provisions, but we'd eaten nearly all of it. There was still half a packet of Perry's sliced bread though, and butter and strawberry jam.

I quickly made myself a jam sandwich and gobbled it down fast. It tasted so good I couldn't stop myself making another. I felt guilty, but I could always go without my fair share at breakfast time if there wasn't quite enough left. I just had to make sure Perry could still have his usual two slices. Dad had explained to me over

and over how Perry's brain was wired up a bit differently from mine, and he sometimes couldn't help making a fuss, so I didn't want to do anything to upset him.

But why was Becks allowed to get away with being cheeky and sulky nowadays? She was always answering back and sighing and having a flounce. It was as if *her* brain had changed its wiring now she was a teenager. In fact, her brain seemed to have shrunk somehow, because she was just interested in things like TikTok and Instagram and make-up and hairstyles and clothes and boys. Especially boys. I'd peeped at her diary and she'd made all these lists of the boys at her school, writing down which ones she fancied most, and marking them out of ten. I knew some of these boys, and they were all *awful*.

I pondered the oddness of my brother and sister while idly digging my finger into the strawberry jam jar and licking up the luscious sweetness. I tried doing it with my eyes shut to see if I could find a lump of strawberry just by touch. That was the sort of experiment *I* enjoyed.

Then I wiped my sticky hand on my jeans, unlatched the kitchen door and went in search of a fresh clump of dandelions so that Daisy could have a tasty breakfast too. The garden didn't seem to have any left, just a lot of daisies in the long grass, and I wasn't sure Daisy would like them as much.

There was an apple tree with small green fruit, but when I

tried to take a mouthful it was like trying to bite a block of wood. Daisy had big teeth for her size, but I was sure it would still be much too hard for her.

I tried the field instead. It was like stepping into a different world. The ground changed to anthills and burrows, more daisies – and little yellow splashes of dandelions everywhere! I picked a great big bunch and then wandered up to the top of the field, peering around at everything properly now I wasn't lugging Daisy in her cage.

Fierce brambles surrounded the field on all sides and I had to watch out for nettles, but somehow it looked weirdly beautiful in the fresh sunlight.

I saw a small flash of white in the distance, then another. Rabbits! I crept nearer, watching the little brown creatures dart about, wondering why Nature gave them such obvious fluffy tails. I hoped there weren't any foxes nearby!

There was a huge brown bird of prey hovering high above the rabbits. I clapped my hands to make it go away, but I frightened the rabbits back to their burrows, and set a pair of pheasants squawking across the field. Big black rooks flapped out of their nests in the trees at the side and cawed at me.

I was out of breath so I stopped right in the middle of the field and sat down on a tussock of grass. I could see for miles across the meadows, though I couldn't spot any farmhouse or shops or pubs,

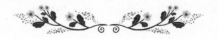

not even a church spire. We really were in the middle of nowhere.

In the middle of nowhere. That was the way all the Robinson programmes started. Dad said: *In the middle of nowhere, far across the seven seas, there was a small desert island . . .* Then the camera would focus on little Robinson. He'd be waving, a big smile on his face. *Robinson lives here all alone – but he isn't the slightest bit lonely. He has lots of friends . . .*

Would Dad make friends with the animals on *his* island and have adventures too? Was he missing us as much as we were missing him? Why hadn't he told us where he was going?

I rolled onto my tummy and howled, letting it all out at last.

Dad, Dad, Dad!

I didn't know if I was shouting it out loud or just screaming it inside my head.

Phoebe!

I stiffened. I listened so hard my ears throbbed. I heard it again.

Phoebe!

It was Dad's voice! Not near me, not in the field, far away – but I could still hear him perfectly.

'Oh, Dad! It *is* you, isn't it?' I whispered.

Of course it is! Do you think I wouldn't keep in touch with my best girl?

'Are you all right, Dad? How are you getting on? What's it like?'

It's . . . lonely.

'You're not ever meant to get lonely! You're supposed to have lots of friends, like in the books!'

I'll make friends – don't you worry. But I'll always feel a little bit lonely without you and Perry and Becks and Mum. I'm missing you so much already.

'We're missing you too, Dad. Ever so, ever so. Especially me.'

Well, you hang on in there, little darling.

'Will you talk to me again, Dad?'

Of course I will.

'You promise?'

Absolutely. Now, you'd better scoot back to bed, darling. Mum will be so worried if she goes into your room and finds you missing!

'Can we talk tomorrow?'

If you wake up early.

'If? You bet I will!'

I love you to the moon and back.

'I love you too, Dad! I love you, love you, love you . . .'

I went on saying it long after I knew he was gone. Then I picked myself up, wiped my face and walked slowly back to the house, holding the bunch of dandelions like a bouquet. I let myself in the door as quietly as I could, and made my way cautiously upstairs, pausing every time the old wood creaked.

The house was silent. I slipped into the blue bedroom. Becks was flat on her back now, her mouth slightly open, snoring softly.

I didn't want to tell her about Dad just yet – I wanted to keep it all to myself for a little while. Daisy was asleep too, not ready for her breakfast. I took off my clothes, wriggled into my pyjamas and got back into the bed. I stretched out, going over every word Dad said.

It was going to be all right. No matter how long he was away he would keep in touch. He was watching over me. He loved me to the moon and back.

I fell asleep and didn't wake up until Becks shook me.

'Come on, lazybones. Mum's making breakfast,' she said.

'I'm not a lazybones! I was up ever so early. I saw the sunrise! Oh, Becks, it was so beautiful,' I said, sitting up and hugging myself.

She was brushing her hair now, not really paying attention.

'I went out into the field,' I said.

'What? This morning? You went out all alone into that scrubby field?' Becks asked.

'It's not scrubby! Well, it *is*, but it's lovely too, all the wild flowers and the nature. I saw some rabbits!'

'Well, you were lucky not to put your foot down one of those rabbit holes and break your leg,' said Becks, bending down and brushing her hair over her face so it looked as if her head was screwed on backwards.

'And you'll never, ever guess what happened in the field,' I said. 'Someone came!'

Becks flipped her hair back and stared at me. 'Who came?'

'No, you've got to guess!'

'Look, stop messing about. You met some stranger in the field?' She was looking worried.

'Not a stranger. Oh, Becks, it was Dad!'

'*Dad? He came here?*' Becks said, gripping me by the shoulders.

'Well, not actually *here* here,' I said. 'But he spoke to me, he really did. I heard his voice as clear as anything.'

'Oh, Phoebe,' said Becks, letting me go. She sighed. 'Stop playing your silly pretend games.'

'No, this wasn't pretend. I swear it's true. Dad spoke, and he told me he was feeling a bit lonely but he'd be all right, though he was missing me so,' I said proudly.

'Honestly, Phoebe! It must have been a dream!' said Becks.

'No it wasn't! I was in the field and—'

'You *dreamed* you were in the field, silly,' Becks repeated. 'Look, I know it probably seemed real – lots of dreams are like that, but obviously you didn't get up and get dressed and everything. I'd have heard you.'

'You didn't hear me because you were snoring your head off,' I snapped. 'You're just jealous because Dad spoke to me and not you.'

'You're being ridiculous now,' said Becks, in a superior voice. 'Come on, let's go and have breakfast.'

I got out of bed in a sulk, feeling she was ruining my beautiful experience. Daisy was awake now, and squeaked excitedly when I slipped a dandelion into her cage.

'Aha!' I said triumphantly. 'Look, Becks. Dandelions! I picked them this morning *in the field.*'

'Those are the dandelions you picked last night,' she said.

'No, *these* are,' I said, picking up a few withered remnants. 'But these are the fresh ones, picked at dawn. See!'

I brandished them in her face and then got dressed all over again and skipped off down the corridor to fetch Perry. I peeped in the cupboard but Thomas the Tank Engine didn't have any passengers.

Mum was making a pot of tea, dressed in a pink shirt, white jeans, and her snowy-white sneakers. She looked very pink and white herself, as if she'd just had a hot bath, although I knew that was impossible.

'Morning, Phoebe,' she said briskly. 'Dear goodness, you look as if you've been pulled through a hedge backwards. And very grubby too. Go and have a wash!'

'I've *had* a wash already, Mum. Honestly!' I said, but she wouldn't believe me. She got quite cross, actually.

I wondered whether to tell her about Dad, but felt she'd say I'd been dreaming, like Becks. Perry would probably scoff too, and give me some long boring scientific reason for it being

impossible to hear someone if they were hundreds and thousands of miles away. I *knew* it was impossible, but I also knew it had really happened. I decided to keep it a secret. Dad had chosen to speak to me, not the whole family. He knew I loved him the most.

'Drink your tea while I make the toast,' said Mum. She looked in the bag of bread. 'Oh goodness, we really tucked in last night! There's not very much left.'

'There's enough for my two slices, isn't there?' said Perry, sounding alarmed. He was practising his eye exercises, holding a finger in front of his nose and slowly drawing it away from his face, focusing fiercely. It made him look very strange.

'Just about,' said Mum, counting slices. 'Did any of you have a midnight snack, by any chance?'

I busied myself fetching plates, carefully not meeting her eyes. I nobly only had one slice of toast, pretending I wasn't really hungry. Mum looked at me suspiciously, but didn't say anything. I was actually still starving.

'Oh dear, that wasn't much of a breakfast, was it?' said Mum. 'Look, I've had an idea. Let's go and find that railway station, Primrose. It'll probably have some kind of cafe, and we can have another breakfast there to set ourselves up for the day. I'm hoping we'll get a proper phone signal there too, so I can phone up the cottage agency and see if they can find us an alternative property.'

My heart started thumping. 'Oh, Mum, we've got to stay here!' I said. 'This is a lovely cottage!'

'Don't be daft, Phoebes, it's too small and there's no hot water and there's no Wi-Fi and no signal so I can't use my phone!' said Becks. 'We can't possibly stay.'

'It's a perfect size and it's supposed to be very healthy to wash in cold water, and who needs a boring old phone,' I said. *And it has a magic field where I can talk to Dad!*

'And it's got my cupboard,' said Perry.

'You two are the weirdest children ever,' said Becks, as if she was already an adult.

'I'm sure we'll find another cottage you'll like just as much – with a cupboard!' said Mum.

But it wouldn't have a field next door, and even if it did, it wouldn't be *this* field. Dad would be calling and calling and only the rooks and the rabbits would hear. Perry looked pretty desperate too. I suddenly wondered if Dad might be talking to him too.

'Does anyone talk to you in the cupboard?' I whispered in his ear, as we went out of the cottage.

Perry stared at me. 'What, like Mum calling me through the door to tell me to get up for breakfast?'

'No, not Mum.' I lowered my voice even more. 'Dad.'

'But Dad's not here.'

'I know. But he might still talk. If he tried really hard he

might be able to project his voice miles and miles and miles,' I murmured.

'That's impossible,' said Perry. 'I'd be really worried if I thought I heard Dad talking to me,' he added.

'Worried?' It was my turn to be puzzled. 'Wouldn't you be absolutely thrilled to know that Dad loved you so much he could communicate with you like that?'

'No, I'd be very anxious because I'd realize I was hallucinating, and generally that only happens if you're seriously ill,' said Perry.

'You mean . . . mentally ill?'

'Well, it can happen if you have the wrong medication, or after an anaesthetic . . .' Perry explained, but I'd stopped listening.

He'd made me anxious now. We'd had a lesson at school about how it was OK to say if you thought you had mental health issues – the school even had a counsellor we could talk to. Was *I* developing mental health issues? But I'd heard Dad's voice so clearly . . .

Perry stopped acting like a professor and gave a howl when we got to the car door. The aquarium was still in the back of the car, with poor Nigel on his back looking very dead indeed.

'We'd better have a funeral straight away,' I said.

'We'll deal with it when we get back from breakfast,' Mum said, hauling the aquarium out and putting it behind the telephone box. 'Come on, off we go.'

Perry managed to clamp his lips together and keep quiet.

'Good boy,' said Mum.

'I'm not a dog,' Perry muttered, sniffing.

We drove up to the top of the hill, and paused for a moment to peer at the cottage. It really was magic, hidden away like that.

'I was wondering if there was another road to it the other side, so we wouldn't have all the performance of trekking our luggage back to the car, but it's just fields and woods going on for ever,' said Mum. 'I know I told the agency I wanted somewhere remote – but I didn't mean somewhere off the road altogether. Thank goodness it's a lovely sunny day again. Imagine tramping over that awful field in the pouring rain.'

'I think it's a beautiful field,' I said tensely. 'And maybe this is such a magic place that it's sunny all the time.'

Perry rolled his eyes and started telling me why this would be impossible in England. He was still giving us all this information when we got to the crossroads with the sign to the Primrose Railway. It seemed much quicker getting there this time. It was as if it was our place already.

We turned down the road to the railway. There were more cars here, backed up, so we had to go quite slowly.

'I suppose lots of people are catching a train,' said Mum.

'I don't blame them,' said Becks. 'They can't wait to get out of here.'

I peered out of the window. There still weren't any shops or pubs, just the odd cottage. None were as interesting as ours. They didn't even have thatched roofs.

'Do you think this is Primrose village then?' I said. 'It's very small.'

'I suppose it is. I wonder why it's got its own railway station?' said Mum. We were crawling along now. 'And a very busy one too,' she said.

'Everywhere round here is called a flowery name. Primrose village, Wildbriar Lane. It's all so twee and cutsie-pie,' said Becks.

'Maybe Puggy-Wuggy lives here,' I said.

Mum went very still. Her hands gripped the steering wheel so hard her knuckles showed white. She kept on driving, though the car in front of her had stopped.

'*Mum!*' Becks shouted, and Mum braked just in time.

'Sorry, sorry,' said Mum. 'Can we all stop talking nonsense please so I can concentrate.'

'I was just joking, Mum,' I said, hurt.

'Well, don't!' she snapped.

I sighed loudly but kept quiet after that. Why did Mum always have to be so touchy? You could never quite relax with her in case you accidentally said something that annoyed her. We'd all giggled at those dreadful Puggy-Wuggy books before. Had I hit on the truth when I'd suggested Dad had had an affair with

Melissa Harris? No, that was nonsense. Dad was on a desert island, valiantly making a Robinson film to make money for all of us.

I stared out of the window again. There was an elaborate placard saying *Primrose Railway* in big italic writing, and some big metal advertising signs attached to the picket fence. They were very old-fashioned adverts for things I'd only vaguely heard of, Bovril and Ovaltine. They were drinks of some kind, but I'd never seen them for sale in Sainsbury's.

The cars were all turning into the station car park. It was a tight turning, so each family had to take their time. We all held our breath when it was Mum's turn because she wasn't that great a driver, though no one dared to say that.

We just made it through and edged along the parked cars, looking for a space.

'*Look!*' said Perry, pointing to an amazing car.

It was an ancient vintage vehicle, open-topped, painted shiny red, with gleaming hub lamps. A family of four jumped out, dressed in astonishing clothes. The mother wore an elaborate bonnet swathed with a chiffon scarf, and a pale grey costume with a skirt right down to the ground. The father wore a bowler hat and a strangely cut suit with a high-collared shirt. The girl wore a cream frilly pinafore over her dress, and a straw hat perched on top of her ringlets. The boy wore a little suit with the

oddest trousers that stopped at the knee. I'd seen them before in illustrations in old books.

'Knickerbockers!' I said.

Perry snorted as if I'd said something uproariously funny.

'What on earth do they look like?' said Becks. 'Is it fancy dress?'

'They're all dressed as Edwardians,' said Mum. 'You know, people from the early 1900s. And look, there's another family over there dressed up too!'

They were getting out of a perfectly ordinary minivan, but they were all in elaborate costumes too. There was even a granny with a patterned shawl and a nurse wearing a cap with streamers and a starched white apron, carrying a baby in a long trailing gown.

'Is it a time warp?' I said in awe.

'Oh, Phoebe, you're priceless!' said Mum. 'There's no such thing as time warps.'

I'd watched enough old episodes of *Doctor Who* with Dad to know that she was wrong. These people could easily be from way back in the past – though the minivan was puzzling. I peered round towards the station entrance. There were some families dressed like us, in jeans and T-shirts, but another group of Edwardians were greeting each other – young men in straw boaters and stripy blazers, and girls in floaty dresses and white

stockings. The station looked Edwardian too, with posters of people wearing bizarre bathing costumes at the seaside. There were framed sepia photographs of trains in the entrance hall, the big old-fashioned kind with great funnels.

Perry stood stock-still. He quivered with excitement.

'They're like Thomas,' he breathed. 'Steam engines!'

We peered through the ticket hall to the platform and saw an ancient brown and gold train standing there in all its glory.

'Oh, Mum! We have to go on it! It's a *Pullman*! We have to, we have to, we have to!' Perry said, rocking backwards and forwards in time to his words.

'It's very exciting, isn't it? This must be one of those vintage railway lines! It's not a proper railway station at all,' said Mum.

'I'm afraid I have to disagree with you, madam,' said an elderly gentleman in a navy uniform, a peaked cap on his silver hair. He gave her a little salute. 'The Primrose Railway is authentic in every single way. This small branch line was opened in 1906. It was closed down by the infamous Dr Beeching in 1964 but twenty-five years later a group of railway enthusiasts got together and worked tirelessly to get the branch open again. We close during the winter months, admittedly, but open with a fanfare over Easter. I've been working here voluntarily for over ten years, since I retired, and I'm proud to be a member of the Primrose Railway staff.' He thumped his chest as he said the last

few words. It was obviously a speech he'd learned by heart, and it
was clear it meant a great deal to him.

'My goodness,' said Mum. 'I apologize! It looks a wonderful
railway.'

'Are you travelling with us today, madam?' he asked.

'Well . . .' said Mum.

'*Yes!*' said Perry.

'Yes, please!' I said.

Becks rolled her eyes but she looked quite keen all the same.

'I thought we were here for breakfast?' said Mum.

'We've had toast and jam! We don't need any more breakfast!' said Perry. 'Buy us tickets for the Pullman train! Now!'

Perry forgot to be polite when he wanted something desperately. We were used to this, but the elderly gentleman looked shocked.

'Now now, lad, that's no way to talk to your mother,' he said, shaking his head. 'And I'm afraid the ten o'clock luxury Pullman trip is fully booked for a champagne breakfast birthday celebration. Did you see some of the passengers in period costume? Folks love to dress up for the Pullman experience. But you could relax over a very tasty breakfast in our Junction Cafe, and take a trip on the Sir Thomas Browning at eleven o'clock – *if* you ask politely.'

He furrowed his brow at Perry, his bushy silver eyebrows meeting over his nose.

Perry was intrigued. 'Sir Thomas – like Thomas the Tank Engine . . . sir?' he asked.

'Ah! So you're a devotee of the Reverend Awdry, are you, lad? I loved those books when I was a kiddie. And you'll never guess what *my* name is!' the old man chuckled.

'You're not actually called Thomas, are you?' said Perry.

'I am indeed. Mr Thomas Brown at your service. I like to kid that the train's named after me, but it was actually named after one of our major benefactors long ago. We need a few more benefactors now as a matter of fact. Do any of you children fancy lobbing a little of your pocket money into our funding bucket? A few thousand pounds from each of you would do nicely.'

'We don't have that kind of money, sir,' said Perry.

'He's joking, Perry,' said Becks.

'If my dad were with us I think he'd give you a thousand pennies,' I said. 'He'd love it here.'

'*I* love it here,' said Perry. 'We *must* stay, Mum.'

So of course she said yes.

We had our second breakfast in the Junction Cafe. It was very old-fashioned, with a glass dome over the cakes and floral china crockery. There were two jolly ladies doing the cooking, both wearing white caps and large aprons. The station special was a plate of eggs, bacon, sausages, tomatoes, mushrooms, hash browns and baked beans, with toast on the side and a pot of tea.

Mum was very much a bircher muesli and black coffee person, but she surprised us. 'Come on then, kids. Let's go for it! Four specials all round?' she suggested.

'A fry-up?' said Becks.

'I only ever have toast and strawberry jam for breakfast,' said Perry.

'I'd like the special breakfast, Mum! Yes please!' I said quickly.

'Good for you, Phoebe,' said Mum. 'Becks, I know it's not that healthy, but it's a special treat for the first day of our holiday. In fact, let's call it lunch, so you can eat it too, Perry.'

The plates of breakfast/lunch were even bigger and better than I'd imagined. Becks and Perry and I cleared our plates. I ate Mum's sausage and hash browns from her plate too, gobbling it down quickly before she could protest.

Then we bought four tickets for the eleven o'clock train. It wasn't quite as special as the Pullman, but it was still pretty exciting, with its gleaming paint and many carriages, each with their own number painted in gold. We selected our own carriage up at the engine end. It had lovely upholstered seats and a picture hanging on the wall as if it was a little living room. There was a splendid luggage rack and a sliding door that shut you off from the corridor. Perry and I went exploring and discovered a special old-fashioned lavatory at the end of the corridor, with a wooden seat and a pull chain, rather like the one back at the cottage.

There was a sudden loud rushing sound that startled us all.

'Oh, wow, that's the steam!' said Perry, rushing out into the corridor and sticking his head out of the open window. 'I can see it, I can see it!'

Mr Thomas Brown blew a whistle and another old gentleman up the platform waved a flag, and then we chugged off on our way.

'Oh, I love this! I wish all train journeys were like it. I'd love to go back to olden times,' I said.

It was like living in the past. There was countryside all around us, with an occasional old cottage, and farmland. We weren't near any roads so we couldn't see any modern cars. There weren't even any telegraph wires. We couldn't hear any planes up above, just the steady rhythm of the wheels beneath us.

Every so often there was a wonderful *whoop* as the steam gushed out – we could see wisps of it wafting past our window. Perry hung out of the corridor window, craning his neck to try to see the engine.

'Get your head back in! You could get it knocked off, or fall right out if you're not careful!' said Mum, rushing out of our carriage to stand near. We saw glimpses of Perry's face, distorted by the speed, his mouth a huge gape of happiness.

'He's loving it,' said Becks.

'So am I,' I said. 'It's absolutely fantastic! Don't you think so, Becks?'

'It's OK,' said Becks. 'It's really for little kids though – and old men that like to dress up in fancy-dress uniform and play trains, like Mr Thomas Brown.'

'Oh, don't be mean. Mr Thomas Brown's lovely. And so is this whole railway. Becks, we have to stay at the cottage. I can go to the field every day, and Perry can ride on the train,

and you can . . .' I tried to think of something that Becks would enjoy.

'Yes?' said Becks. She checked her phone. 'There's *still* not any signal. It's like we're on the *moon*. How come I could text home on the top of a mountain in Switzerland on my school skiing trip and yet I can't get any signal at all in this dreary old bit of England?'

'It's not the slightest bit dreary!' I said indignantly.

'For pity's sake, Phoebes, there's nothing here!' said Becks. 'No shops, no cinemas, no McDonald's. And no working phones!'

'Hey, maybe someone will mend the telephone near our cottage!' I said.

'Oh, very funny. I don't think anyone actually uses those old red phone boxes any more – and anyway, you couldn't message anyone. I've got nobody my age to talk to!' Becks gave a huge sigh and flung herself back in her seat, arms folded. Then I saw her expression change. Her eyes widened.

A young train attendant in an old-fashioned navy uniform had stopped to talk to Mum and Perry in the corridor. He was incredibly good-looking, with clean-cut features, blue eyes and thick wavy hair a little too long for his regulation cap, which he wore at a jaunty angle. He was smiling at Perry, probably telling him all sorts of train facts, and Perry was gazing up at him, ultra-impressed. Mum was looking amused and grateful.

'How old do you think he is?' Becks asked.

'Perhaps eighteen?' I said.

Becks nodded. 'Yes, I think you're right.' She breathed a sigh. 'He's gorgeous.'

'I suppose.'

'He keeps glancing over at us,' said Becks.

'No he doesn't! He's talking to Perry,' I pointed out.

'Yes, but he's looking at us. Well, me, actually,' said Becks.

'Kid yourself,' I said. 'Anyway, he's way too old for you.'

'Shut up,' said Becks. She swallowed. 'Oh God, he's coming in here!'

He gave a polite little knock on the window and then opened up our door. 'Hello, ladies,' he said, smiling.

We both giggled foolishly.

'Are you enjoying the journey?' he asked.

'It's amazing!' I said.

'Yeah, it's OK,' said Becks, desperately trying to act cool.

'Only OK?' he said, laughing. 'That's a bit lukewarm, isn't it? Come on, your sister's right – it *is* amazing. I was only a little kid when my grandad first took me here, and I was so excited I was awake half the night, burbling about it.'

'I expect our brother Perry's been having a burble,' said Becks.

'He's been asking all kinds of questions. He's very bright, isn't he?'

'I hope he hasn't been bothering you,' said Becks.

'Well, that's what I'm here for. To answer questions and make sure everyone's having a good time,' he said. 'And to check you've got your tickets.'

'So do you work here on a regular basis, or is this just a Saturday job?' Becks asked. This was a cunning ploy to find out how old he was, but he didn't seem to mind.

'It's a holiday job. I've just done my A-levels, so I've broken up early,' he said.

'Ah!' said Becks airily, as if she had too.

'So do you live round here, or are you on holiday yourselves?' he asked.

'Kind of,' said Becks.

'We're here for the summer,' I said determinedly.

'Great,' he said. 'Where are you staying then? In an Airbnb?'

'I wish,' said Becks. 'We spent last night in this weird little cottage without any hot water or proper facilities. You have to tramp across this field to even get to it!'

'But it's lovely, like a fairy-tale cottage,' I said. 'Honestly, you'd never know it was there if you were just driving along the lane.'

'I know which lane that is. Wildbriar Lane,' he said. 'You're staying in the artist's cottage!'

'That's right!' I said. 'So do you know her? It is a lady artist,

isn't it? She paints such lovely things.'

'That's right. Nina Cresswell. She lived there all by herself for donkey's years. My grandad used to know her. But then she got really old and fell and broke her hip. She had to go into a nursing home and never came out. She might even have died, for all I know.'

'Oh no!' I cried. 'Poor Nina!'

'Don't be so melodramatic, Phoebe! You don't even know her,' said Becks.

'I *feel* as if I know her!' I retorted.

'So you're Phoebe. And your brother's Perry. And what's your name?' he asked, looking at Becks.

'Rebecca,' she said. She was looking at him in a flirty way, her eyes big. She brushed her hair back over her shoulder so that he'd notice how long and shiny it was. She was acting so obvious I felt embarrassed – and yet he was smiling back at her.

'I do hope Nina isn't dead,' I said. 'I'd love to meet her one day.'

They weren't listening to me. He was telling Becks all about the railway, and the special novelty trips, and she was nodding eagerly as if she really cared about the Easter Bunny egg hunt and the Santa special rides at Christmas.

'These all sound lovely for little kids,' she said at last. 'But what about people our age?'

Our age!

'The railway's for all ages,' he said. 'But I don't suppose many of my friends ever take a trip.'

'So where do you all hang out?' she went on. 'You know, in the evenings?'

'We mostly go to Orlington – it's about five miles away. There are cafes and clubs, and the Cat and Dog sometimes has live music there,' he said.

'Oh, great,' said Becks. 'If you can *get* there. No wheels!' she said comically, though she couldn't legally drive anything more than a bike for several years.

'I could take you if you like. I've just got my own car. It's a bit of an old banger, but quite reliable,' he said.

'Oh, that would be great!' said Becks.

'OK then. Shall I come to the cottage tonight, around half seven or eight?'

'Could we make it later? About nine – and let's meet at the telephone box, save you having to push your way through all those trees.'

'Fine. I'll look forward to it – Rebecca.'

She dimpled at him. She was practically fluttering her eyelashes.

'Anyway, I'd better make my way down the train, doing my "Tickets, please!" spiel. Hey, better show me *your* tickets.'

153

They were very old-fashioned little rectangles, green for adults, blue for children. Children were counted as fourteen and under, so Becks had a blue ticket. She fished it out of her pocket, and then went bright red.

He raised his eyebrows, though he was grinning.

'I'm so sorry,' said Becks, totally flustered. 'It's my mother's fault. She will try to pass me off as a child.'

This was such an unfair lie! Mum was always scrupulously honest about prices.

'Don't worry,' he said.

'No, let me pay full fare,' Becks said, fumbling in her jeans pocket, though I'm not sure she even had any coins in it.

'It's fine. I won't tell,' he said. He opened the sliding door into the corridor and gave us a little wave of his hand.

'See you tonight,' Becks breathed. As soon as he'd shut the door she gave a little squeal. '*Wow!*'

'Becks, you're so dreadful! Telling such lies! And flirting like anything with an eighteen-year-old! Mum would die if she knew!' I said.

'I was simply chatting, that's all. And Mum's right over there. She probably saw us talking. I'm not doing anything behind her back,' said Becks, still pink in the face.

'You've only arranged to go on a date with him – in a pub! You can't go in a pub with someone you don't know anything about. You don't even know his name!' I said.

'Yes, I do. He's called Jake. Jake Brown. Didn't you see? He had a name badge pinned to his chest,' said Becks.

'Jake Brown!'

'Yes. Jake's a cool name, isn't it?' said Becks, murmuring it to herself.

'Jake *Brown*! Do you think he could be Mr Thomas Brown's grandson?' I asked.

'Who cares? Isn't he good-looking! It was so amazing – he

looked at me and I looked at him and it was like instant Romeo and Juliet!'

She'd been studying that play at school, forever floating about proclaiming Juliet's lines.

'Look what happened to them. They ended up dead!' I declared.

Becks scoffed at me. I suddenly changed tack, my heart thudding with excitement.

'Anyway, we're not staying here now, are we? Isn't Mum going to try to change cottages?' I said, testing the ground.

'I don't know. Our one's kind of fun,' said Becks.

She was on my side now, just because she'd met this Jake! And there was no doubt Perry wanted to stay here too. He gave a great whoop whenever the train whistled. Then we approached a tunnel, and he had to pull his head back in quickly. His hair was standing on end, he had black smuts all over his face, and his eyes were watering, but he still looked ecstatic as he came back into the compartment.

'Isn't this great!' he said. 'Steam trains are magic! Can we go on the train again tomorrow, and the next day, and the next, and the next and—'

'Perry! We can't go *every* day,' said Mum. 'And we're going to try to find somewhere else to stay anyway.'

'No, we want to stay in the artist's cottage,' I said. 'Don't we, Becks?'

'Well, at least for another week or so,' she said. 'Seeing as we're here.'

Mum shook her head at us. 'Honestly, make up your minds! The cottage is ridiculously inconvenient. We can't manage without hot water!'

'Oh, Mum, I'm sure there *must* be a boiler hidden in the attic somewhere. We could get a plumber in to sort it out for us,' Becks said breezily.

'Cold dips are meant to be good for you, anyway,' said Perry.

The three of us were united for once!

When we were through the tunnel we started to see a few more houses. The train came to a halt at a little station called Forest Lake. It was wonderfully old-fashioned too, with hanging baskets and bunting, and a porter in uniform standing on the platform with a whistle and a flag. Some families got off the train with hampers and cool bags, obviously going for a picnic in the forest or by the lake, but we stayed on board.

There was a whistle and a burst of steam and the train moved on. The rocking movement was so soothing that I nearly fell asleep. When I opened my eyes I saw we were on the outskirts of a little town.

'I've got some signal at last!' Becks cried, and started flicking through her messages.

Mum looked at her phone too.

'Has Dad sent a message?' I asked.

'No, darling. I've told you. He can't,' said Mum.

Well, not by phone, I thought. I shut my eyes, imagining myself back in the field, somehow hearing a faint echo of Dad's voice, even here in a jiggling railway carriage.

'Don't go to sleep, Phoebe! You mustn't waste a single moment! This is incredible,' said Perry, his nose pressed against the window. 'And Mum, don't start phoning people!'

'I'm checking with the Quirky Cottages agency. Maybe they've got another property in this area that would be more suitable,' said Mum.

She managed to get through, and started complaining about the cottage, though I kept interrupting her, unable to bear her criticizing it. The woman on the end of the phone agreed that it wasn't up to their usual standards, but said she had warned Mum about the lack of facilities. She was afraid they didn't have another property on their books anywhere nearby. She carefully didn't respond when Mum said there was no hot water, but promised that she'd already got in touch with a local lady to come in to clean the cottage weekly and change the sheets.

'So let's stay, Mum, please!' I begged.

'It's not really *that* inconvenient,' said Becks.

'It's the most convenient cottage in the entire world because it's near the Primrose Railway,' said Perry.

'All right, all right, I give in,' said Mum, and told the Quirky Cottages lady we were staying after all.

We reached the end of the line ten minutes later: Orlington Junction.

'Oh, *Orlington*!' said Becks.

As if on cue, Jake Brown was waiting outside our carriage, handing us down one at a time.

'We don't start the return trip for half an hour,' he said. 'We have to run the engine into a siding to get it in place for the return journey and check everything. I was wondering, perhaps you'd like to come and watch, Perry? Maybe hop up into the cabin beside the driver for a minute or two?'

'Oh *yes*!' said Perry, blushing with excitement.

'Well, that's so kind of you, but I really think I need to nip to the nearest supermarket to buy some food,' said Mum.

'Oh, Mum! You can go shopping any old time!' Perry wailed.

'Tell you what, Mum – I'll stay and look after Perry,' said Becks. 'Phoebe can go with you and help carry the shopping.'

'That's not fair! I want to see the engine too!' I said.

'Oh, for goodness' sake, Phoebe, when did you suddenly get interested in railway engines?' said Mum.

'When did Becks, for that matter?' I said, glaring at her.

'Don't worry – I promise I'll look after them,' said Jake Brown. 'They'll all be safe with me. There's a Tesco Express just over the

road so it's not far to go. But don't miss the train back, will you?'

So Mum went shopping and we stayed with Jake. He took us to meet the engine driver. We were allowed to climb onto the footplate and into the little cabin. It felt quite crowded, because the fireman was there too. A fireman had the hot and tiring job of shovelling coal into the firebox – only she was actually a fire*woman*, a lady called Ann, who said she'd been doing this job for the last twenty years.

'Wouldn't you sooner be the engine driver?' Perry asked bluntly. Ann just laughed and told him how much she enjoyed the work she was doing.

Alf, the actual engine driver, looked quite gruff, with a red fierce face, but he turned out to be a very friendly man.

'So what do you know about railway engines then, you two?'

'Not much,' I admitted.

'What about you, young man?' Alf asked Perry.

'I don't know much either, but I'm really interested,' said Perry.

Alf nodded kindly. 'Well, any questions, I'm your man,' he said.

'All right. Well, I know that the big Pullmans were very grand, much posher than our one,' said Perry seriously. 'They were built to be long-distance trains with restaurants.'

'That's right,' said Alf. 'That's more than most people know,

lad. Pullmans were built so that posh folk could travel in style. Ordinary folk like us can treat themselves to a trip on one now for special occasions – like that birthday party earlier. We like to keep up that tradition here at the Primrose Railway.'

'I think I shall have my birthday party on the Pullman,' I said.

Ann laughed again. 'Then I hope your mum and dad have got lots of money, young lady,' she said.

'But what's this sort of train called?' Perry asked.

'This is an express passenger, looking lovely in her green livery. We've got a couple of goods trains too, which we demonstrate on special days,' said Alf.

'That's how everything got delivered before there were lorries,' said Ann. 'No Amazon vans in the old days.'

'Then the little terriers without tenders are Tank engines,' said Alf.

'Like Thomas!' I said. Perry wasn't the only person in our family who had enjoyed the books when he was little – Dad used to read them out to us and use special voices for each of the engines. 'Did *you* read the Thomas the Tank Engine books when you were a little boy, Alf?' I asked.

'You bet I did,' Alf said. 'I was desperate to be a train driver when I grew up. I was actually an engineer most of my working life – I had to wait till I retired to achieve my big ambition.'

'I'm pretty certain *I* want to be a steam engine driver when I retire, though I think I'll be some kind of scientist first,' said Perry. 'I might be an anthropologist. Or a nuclear physicist.'

I always squirmed when he made statements like that, because he sounds like such an incredible show off, though I know he doesn't mean to be. But luckily Alf just nodded and said, 'Good for you, lad.'

He turned to me. 'Do you want to be a scientist too?' he asked.

'Oh no,' I said. 'I want to write *stories*. Or maybe illustrate them.' I thought about drawing these engines in my sketchbook. 'Why are the engines all painted different colours?' I asked, peering at another train in a siding.

'It's to distinguish where they come from. That tank has got the British Railway carmine and cream livery – we call it blood and custard,' said Ann.

'So where does our green one come from?' I asked.

'It's an LBSCR Bogie. It's called a Bogie so the leading wheels can swing, adapting themselves to the curves of the line. LBSCR stands for London, Brighton and South Coast Railway,' Ann explained.

'Each class of railway engine is divided into a number of distinct types – it's not just the livery,' said Alf. 'Think what other differences there might be.'

I tried hard, but Perry got there first.

'Wheels – they're different sizes and arrangements!' he said.

'Bright kid!' said Alf. 'You've got it. At first all engines were fitted with just one pair of driving wheels, but – well, what do you think happened?'

'I know! To get greater power they made two or maybe more pairs of wheels,' said Perry.

'Exactly. They passed on the driving force from the principal pair to the others by means of coupling rods. Train enthusiasts always distinguish the different engines by the number and type of wheels,' said Alf.

'Oh, let me see what this one's got,' said Perry, leaping out of the cabin. 'I bet I can identify *all* your engines now!'

I followed, wishing that Alf had called *me* a bright kid. Still, I was pleased to see how happy Perry was with this new passion. Becks was standing further along the platform, chatting to Jake Brown. *Her* new interest. She sighed when we joined them, but Jake smiled at us. He managed to stay smiling when Perry recounted every single fact he'd learned about steam engines, talking so fast and enthusiastically that a little bit of spit sprayed out of his mouth.

It was good to see Perry so excited, but it made me realize how sad and closed in he'd been looking ever since Thursday night. He had barely mentioned Dad, but he must have been be missing him terribly. Not as much as me, of course. No one could possibly miss Dad the way I did.

He'd have loved the Primrose Railway. He *might* even have let us all dress up as Edwardians for a special champagne breakfast on the Pullman. He'd have let me have a few sips of champagne just for the experience. Maybe he'd pretend I was a grown-up lady, and sweep me a bow and help me up into the railway carriage. I'd have a dress down to the ground with big puffy sleeves and a tight waist . . . But Edwardian ladies wore corsets, so it would be pretty uncomfortable. No, I would be an *arty* lady, wearing a long loose embroidered smock, with beads round my neck and bangles up and down my arms.

I twirled round, moving my arms up and down, shaking my imaginary bangles.

'Phoebe?' Jake said gently. 'Are you all right?'

'Oh, she's just making something up in her head,' said Becks. 'She's always doing that.'

'Excuse me, but I was talking,' said Perry. 'There's all sorts of things *I* want to know! How many steam engines are there here? How long does it take to train to be an engine driver? Do you have boy volunteers working for the Primrose Railway? And why *Primrose*?'

'The answer's obvious,' said Becks. 'Didn't you see all the countryside? I bet it's smothered with primroses in the spring.'

'It is too – and cowslips and bluebells,' said Jake.

'It must look so pretty,' said Becks.

'Never mind the flowers, *please* can you tell me about the engines?' Perry begged.

Jake started describing each one, though he kept glancing at Becks, his mind not really on engines at all.

I wondered what it would be like to be a teenager and have someone look at me in that way. Becks was pretty and I wasn't, so maybe it wouldn't happen to me. I didn't think I cared that much. Perhaps I'd end up like Nina Cresswell, living in a little cottage and painting all day long. I'd have a dog and a cat to keep me company, and a whole herd of guinea pigs that I'd keep in a big pen in my garden, with a huge dandelion patch and buttercups and daisies to vary their diet.

Then Mum came hurrying along the platform, red in the face, a big carrier bag in each hand, and another tucked under her arm, and I felt bad that I hadn't gone with her to help carry all the stuff.

'You weren't waiting in the same place! I thought you'd maybe got on the train and gone without me,' she puffed.

'Here, do let me carry something for you,' said Jake, instantly helpful.

Mum seemed almost as charmed as Becks. When he had settled us back in our carriage and hurried off to check there weren't any stray passengers who still hadn't boarded the train, she shook her head fondly.

'What a lovely polite young man,' she said.

'Yes, *isn't* he?' Becks said quickly.

'He knows a lot about steam engines,' said Perry. 'But I'll know just as much soon. Probably a lot more. Mum, there's a gift shop back at the main station. I need a guide book to the Primrose Railway, and any other books about steam engines.'

Mum sighed – but when we got back to the main station she bought Perry the guide book, and two others all about steam engines.

He clutched them to his chest and said thank you more than once. I roamed about the gift shop, hoping there might be something I wanted too, but all the books were either for very little kids, or they were closely printed technical tomes full of facts, and I didn't fancy a steam engine T-shirt or mug.

Becks just gave everything a cursory glance and went back onto the platform to have another chat with Jake. I peered in the window of the Junction Cafe, looking longingly at the cakes under the glass dome. They were selling lovely iced buns with a cherry on the top.

'They look very tempting, don't they?' Mr Thomas Brown was standing beside me, licking his lips.

'Tremendously,' I said, sighing. 'But there's zero chance of Mum buying me one, seeing as I had such a big breakfast – and it was technically a second breakfast too.'

'You're a girl after my own heart,' he said, chuckling. 'I believe in a good hearty meal. And a plate of cakes is always very tempting.' He patted the rather large tummy under his uniform. 'I daresay I should go on a diet but I can't stick that sort of food. I ask you, who would ever eat a plate of lettuce with relish?'

'I expect my guinea pig would,' I said. 'She certainly gobbles up her dandelions.'

'Exactly. Little furry rodents like salads. And sensible human beings like iced buns,' said Mr Thomas Brown.

'Not my sister!' I said, nodding at Becks.

'I see we're not the only ones looking at her. My grandson seems to have taken a fancy to her too,' he said.

'There, I guessed you were his grandad! You were the one who got him interested in trains!' I said triumphantly.

'That's what grandads are for,' said Mr Thomas Brown. 'Do you have a grandad?'

'No, they both died before I was born,' I said. I sighed. 'I've got the loveliest dad ever though. But he's away at the moment. And I do miss him,' I said. 'I miss him terribly.' My eyes went misty.

'Oh, you poor little mite. I'm so sorry!' Mr Thomas Brown looked appalled.

'It's not your fault. I'll stop in a minute,' I promised, sniffing. My nose had started running too.

'Here!' He fished in his uniform pocket, brought out an immaculate white handkerchief and handed it to me.

I dabbed at my face tentatively, not liking to give my nose a proper blow. I didn't know anyone else who used handkerchiefs any more. It was so much nicer than a crumpled tissue.

'I'll be back in a minute,' said Mr Thomas Brown, and darted away.

I thought he was being tactful, leaving me to have a private cry. I turned my face to the wall and tried hard to stop, but each time I thought I'd mastered it another sob burst out. There was really only one person who could stop me crying once I'd got started – and that was Dad.

I hid my face in Mr Thomas Brown's large handkerchief and howled.

'Now then. Try a bite of this. It's very difficult to cry and eat at the same time,' said Mr Thomas Brown.

He pressed one of the white iced buns into my hand and gave me a wink.

Mum told me off royally in the car going back to the cottage.

'For goodness' sake, Phoebe, you shouldn't ever take food from a stranger,' she said.

'But Mr Thomas Brown isn't a stranger! He's our friend now,' I protested.

'Stop calling him that! It's very irritating! He's Mr Brown; you don't need to keep saying the Thomas part. And of course he's not a friend. We don't know anything about him,' said Mum.

'I know heaps about him,' I said, licking the icing from my fingers. 'He's Jake's grandad and he once did odd jobs for the artist lady who lived in our cottage. Mr Thomas Brown – OK, Mr Brown – was just trying to cheer me up with the iced bun because he knew they're my favourite. I'd started crying, because of missing Dad.'

'What?' said Mum. 'Oh, Phoebe, you're shameless! And very greedy, asking for an iced bun when you had that enormous breakfast!'

'I didn't *ask*. I didn't know he'd gone to get it. Stop being horrible, Mum, you're spoiling everything,' I said, and I started crying again.

It wasn't fair. Perry was so absorbed in his steam engine books that he didn't notice I was in tears. Becks turned round and looked at me sympathetically, but didn't say anything. Mum just carried on driving, ignoring me. Someone had parked an old Vauxhall beside the telephone box but there was no sign of anyone.

'Perhaps we've got a visitor!' I said, sniffing.

'Don't be silly, Phoebe. No one knows we're here,' said Mum. 'And do stop being such a crybaby. Here, carry one of these bags for me.'

She gave another to Becks and carried the third herself.

'Why doesn't Perry have to carry one? He's older than me,' I protested sulkily.

'Perry's carrying his books,' said Mum.

'You always make excuses for him. It's not fair. And he cries much more than me. He positively screams sometimes,' I said.

'You know perfectly well that Perry can't help it. His brain's wired differently from yours,' said Mum.

'Yes. I'm much, much brainier,' said Perry smugly. He was

trying to read as he crossed the field, even though he kept stumbling.

Becks tried taking my hand to be comforting, but recoiled in disgust because it was still rather sticky. Still, at least she was trying to be nice.

'Do you really fancy Jake?' I whispered.

'Sh! You bet I do!' she whispered back.

'Did you tell him how old you are?'

'Of course not!' she said.

'Didn't he ask?' I persisted. 'He can't possibly think you're his age – you look much younger.'

'No I don't! But anyway, I said I was sixteen,' she whispered.

'You total fibber! What are you going to do when he finds out?' I asked.

'He won't. No one knows me round here, do they? Apart from you. And you won't tell on me, Phoebes, will you?' said Becks.

For a second I felt a wicked sense of power – but she *was* my sister.

'Of course I won't tell,' I promised.

'You're a pal,' said Becks, swinging her carrier bag.

'But I don't think Mum will let you go out with him tonight,' I said.

'Well, I won't tell her, will I?' said Becks.

'You can't just walk out of the cottage and disappear for the entire evening!' I said.

'I'll make up some excuse,' said Becks.

'Oh, Becks, you're going to get in so much trouble!' I said anxiously.

'See if I care,' said Becks.

I stared at her. She was smiling, jumping up and down on the anthills now we were in the field, practically whirling her carrier bag about her head. She really *didn't* seem to care.

I was walking past the spot where Dad had talked to me. I hung back, pretending I needed to do up my bootlace, and then when the others were right over the other side of the field, approaching the cottage, I flung myself on the grass and called Dad's name.

He didn't get a chance to answer. Mum glanced round and saw me.

'Phoebe? For God's sake, what are you doing? Get up at once, you'll get grass stains all over your T-shirt!' she called.

I hauled myself up and trudged across the field, angrily banging the carrier bag against my legs.

'And stop doing that, you'll smash all the eggs!' Mum shouted.

'I wish you'd gone away and left us instead of Dad!' I said, but I only dared mutter it, knowing she couldn't hear from that distance.

I went to the cottage in a sulk, clattering into the kitchen.

Then I stopped, astonished. There was a large blonde woman in a big pink shirt and trackie bottoms arranging a big plate of scones on the table. Mum and Becks and Perry were staring at her, looking dazed.

'Hello, dear!' she said. 'I'm Maureen. Well, Mo to all my friends. So are you the youngest then?'

'Yes, I'm Phoebe. So who are you, Mo?'

'Phoebe!' Mum said sharply.

Mo reached in her big shopping bag and put more things on the table: a pack of butter, a pot of red jam and a tub of double cream.

'I'm sorry, I think there's some mistake,' said Mum hastily. 'Are you staying here now? I've just rented this cottage for the summer!'

'I know you have, dear. From Quirky Cottages or some such silly title – though this one's certainly quirky, I'll say that. I'm amazed it's being rented out. It's been up for sale for a year or so now, but who would buy it in this state? I was astonished when the Cottages people got in touch. I've been keeping the place clean and aired, and the sheets are all freshly laundered, but no one's told me what to do with all Nina's *stuff*. I've no way of getting in touch with her—'

'So she's not dead?' I said.

'Well, not as far as I know. But she's poorly enough to need a

nursing home, though they haven't told me which one. Some nephew is trying to rent out the cottage, presumably needing help with the nursing home fees, but he hasn't left any instructions, and I haven't a clue where he is either. It's a rum state of affairs – but anyway you're here now, and *I'm* here to make you welcome. I've given the cottage a quick clean, made all the beds and popped a few necessities in the larder,' said Mo.

'Well, it's extremely kind of you, Maureen,' said Mum. 'But you didn't need to. I've just bought a whole load of shopping earlier on'

'Very sensible,' said Mo, looking at the logo on the shopping bags. 'But my butter and cream are fresh from the farm. I made the strawberry jam myself, and I baked the batch of scones this morning.'

'For us?' I said eagerly.

'Of course they're for you, lovie,' said Mo. 'I hope you like them.'

'I'm sure we will!' I said.

'We especially like strawberry jam,' said Perry.

'I made six,' said Mo. 'So there's one for all of us, and one going spare – unless we're being joined by anyone else?'

Mum flushed faintly. 'My husband's away on business,' she said, in the cool tone she uses when she wants to put you in your place.

Mo wasn't the slightest bit flustered. 'Just us then, dear, I'm sure you and the kids will still have a lovely time around here. Why don't you sit down and take the weight off your feet – you're looking a bit fragile,' she said.

We all looked fragile next to Mo, even me. She nodded at Becks. 'You pop the kettle on, love, and you two younger ones set the table. I know a cream tea is an odd lunch, but fresh scones go down well any time, I always say.'

'Well, it's such a kind thought, but we've already eaten at the railway station. Perhaps we'll have the scones later,' said Mum. She was ultra-polite but her tone was icy now.

'They'll be stone cold by then!' Mo protested. 'These golden beauties are still warm from the oven. Mmm, perfect,' she said, smiling at the scones on the plate.

'They look positively beautiful. And very yummy,' I said, quickly putting plates on the table.

Perry already had the lid off the jar of strawberry jam and was sniffing it appreciatively.

Becks obediently put the kettle on the old range, holding it at arm's length and then retreating rapidly.

'Oh dear, it's not playing up, is it?' said Mo. 'I've kept it on over the winter to ward off the damp.'

'The range works – but unfortunately the boiler doesn't,' said Mum. 'Well, it might, but I can't find where the wretched thing's

installed. I'm going to have to get a plumber in. We can't possibly stay here without hot water.'

'You couldn't find it?' said Mo, looking incredulous. 'It's right here!' She opened one of the kitchen cupboard doors and there was a boiler of sorts.

'Oh, dear lord! I thought that was just a storage cupboard,' said Mum. 'Surely a boiler should be bigger than that?'

'Certainly it's on the small size, even for a titchy cottage like this,' said Mo, switching it on. 'You'll have to have a rota for your baths!'

'I won't bother with one then,' said Perry.

'Don't be silly, Perry,' said Mum, glaring at him. 'Why on earth didn't this Nina get a proper boiler installed? And modern bathroom facilities!'

'Search me,' said Mo. 'She was quite posh by all accounts, but maybe she was strapped for cash. I don't think her artwork paid very handsomely. Not to everyone's taste, but it's colourful, isn't it?'

'I thought you said you'd already looked for the boiler in the kitchen?' Perry said to Mum in an accusing tone.

'Hey, hey, your mum's just not used to funny old cottages, that's all,' said Mo. She smiled at Mum sympathetically. 'Kids, eh? They don't half let you down at times, don't they?'

'Perry can't help being very . . . forthright at times,' Mum said

weakly. 'He's on the autistic spectrum.'

'Oh yes, they're very quick to give kiddies special names nowadays, aren't they?' said Mo.

She was so determined to be friendly to Mum that she didn't seem to notice her tepid response. Becks made the tea and we all sat round the kitchen table and ate Mo's scones. They were absolutely heavenly, especially thickly spread with cream and strawberry jam. Becks cut hers in two, but it was so delicious she gobbled up the other half too. Perry and I wolfed ours down and eyed the one remaining scone hopefully. Even Mum ate a couple of mouthfuls.

'Don't you like it?' said Mo.

'I'm just still rather full from breakfast,' said Mum. 'But it's delicious.'

'There! I pride myself on my light touch when it comes to baking,' said Mo. She'd eaten hers already, washing it down with her cup of tea. 'What would we do without a cuppa, eh?' she said to Mum.

Mum rarely drank ordinary tea. She might have a cup of that weirdly perfumed sort occasionally, but mostly stuck to black coffee. She gave Mo a tight little smile without nodding.

'So why aren't you kids at school then?' Mo asked. 'Tim and Alysha and Holly, my grandchildren, don't break up for several weeks.'

'There are special circumstances,' said Mum. 'Now! I think we'd better get on.' She stood up, brushing scone crumbs from her shirt, making it plain that she wanted Mo to go. I felt myself blushing, hating Mum for being so rude – but Mo didn't seem the sort of woman to take offence.

'Right, my dears. I'll leave you to it. I'll pop in again next Saturday then, do a bit of housework and change your towels and bedding,' she said, hauling herself to her feet. 'I've just popped a fresh set of sheets on the beds this morning.'

'Well, there's really no need,' said Mum. 'Thank you very much, but I'm perfectly capable of doing the laundry.'

'I don't think you are, dear, not in this cottage. There's no washing machine. I don't think you're really the type to be giving the sheets a scrub in the kitchen sink. Besides, Quirky Cottages are paying me. Every little helps. I don't earn much down at the railway,' Mo said cheerfully.

'You work at the railway!' said Perry. 'You're so lucky! I don't suppose you ever get to drive one of the trains, do you?'

Mo burst out laughing. 'I'd quite like to give it a go – but those old gentlemen prancing about in their fancy uniforms would go puce at the thought,' said Mo.

'Maybe Mr Thomas Brown would let you have a go – he's ever so nice,' I said.

'Oh, you know old Tom, do you? I agree, he's a total sweetie.

And he's still a fine figure of a man even now. But even *he* doesn't get to drive one of the engines,' said Mo.

'So what *do* you do there?' Perry asked.

'A bit of cleaning, and polishing all that brass, and I work several shifts at the cafe. Whatever needs attention. And if there's a big do – a wedding or a big birthday celebration – I set the tables in the Pullman, ready for proper silver service,' she replied.

'There was a birthday celebration this morning!' I said.

'Yes, and when those guests raise a glass to the birthday boy they won't see a smear on them, because I polished them up a treat!' said Mo. 'So you were down at the railway this morning, were you?'

'Yes, and we're going to go there every single day!' said Perry.

'Now, now,' said Mum.

'We *are*,' said Perry.

'Don't be silly, darling,' said Mum.

'We all want to. I want to go there because of the steam engines, and Phoebe wants to go there because she likes Mr Thomas Brown and Becks wants to go there because she likes Jake,' said Perry, his chin jutting.

Perry usually lived in a little world of his own, oblivious to everyone else, but it was surprising how much he noticed even so. It was Becks's turn to blush. Mum turned to her.

'Becks? Who's this Jake?' she asked.

'Oh, he's the ticket collector,' she said. 'He wore a name badge.'

'And you were talking to him?' Mum asked.

'Of course she was!' said Mo, gathering up her laundry bags of our barely used sheets and towels. 'That young man's a catch if ever there was one. My youngest daughter Yvonne is truly gone on him. She's devastated that he'll be off to uni after the summer.'

'Oh! So they're an item, are they?' Becks asked as casually as she could.

'Just friends, much to Yvonne's regret. I think he's fancy-free at the moment – so you could be in luck!' said Mo.

'For goodness' sake – Rebecca's only fourteen, much too young for boys!' Mum snapped. 'Well, goodbye, Maureen.'

Mo raised her eyebrows at Becks and took herself off, waving the heavy bags about as if they were totally empty. I ran after her, though Mum tried to call me back.

'Mo! Mo, can I ask you something?'

'What's that, lovie?' she said.

'The artist lady, Nina Cresswell, does she still paint?' I asked.

'Mm, I shouldn't think so, dear,' said Mo. 'Doubt she'd have the opportunity in a nursing home anyway.'

'Do you think she'd mind if I used her pastels?' I said.

'Of course you can! I'm sure she'd like to think they were being used. So you're a little artist, are you?'

'Well, not really. But my dad always liked my pictures. I wish you could meet him,' I said.

'Do you, dear?'

'He's not a bit like my mum,' I said. 'He's lovely and jolly and funny. But now he's had to go away and we don't know when he's coming back,' I said. Saying it out loud to someone who wasn't part of the family made it seem much more real. My voice wobbled.

'There now,' said Mo, and she put a laundry bag down and patted me on the shoulder. 'Don't you take it to heart.'

'He is coming back, though. I know he is,' I said determinedly.

Mo nodded, though she didn't look as if she believed me.

'We're not a proper family without him,' I said.

'Phoebe? *Phoebe!*' Mum was calling me from the cottage door.

'I'm sorry Mum was horrid to you,' I muttered.

'She was just a bit offhand,

that's all. Don't you fret. I daresay she's missing your dad as much as you are,' said Mo. 'You'd better run back to your mum now. But come looking for me next time you come to the station, right?'

'Definitely!' I said.

Then she went off across the field, swinging her bags again, and I went back to the cottage.

'I don't really want you talking to that lady,' said Mum. 'She means well, but you can tell she's a real busybody, wanting to know all about us. I'm sure she's the type who'll start gossiping about us behind our backs.'

'No, she's not! She was just being friendly and you were rude to her,' I said.

'Well, you are being extremely rude to me, Phoebe. You must learn to do as you're told and stop answering back,' said Mum, infuriatingly calm. 'And for goodness' sake, wash your face and hands – you've got jam smears all round your mouth.'

I gave myself a quick swill at the kitchen sink and then peered at my reflection in the shiny kettle. I looked like a gargoyle, but I hoped that was because the kettle was distorting my image. My fringe was sticking up oddly because I'd tossed and turned in the night, missing Wiffle. I knew perfectly well he wasn't real, he was just a few worn scraps of fake fur, yet I couldn't help imagining him all on his own back at home, wondering why I'd abandoned him.

I gave Daisy a cuddle instead. Mo had not only changed my

bed, she'd also changed Daisy's bedding too, and given her fresh water and food pellets. She was a very lucky little guinea pig getting such frequent room service.

'There now, Daisy,' I said, cradling her. 'Here I am! Did you miss me?'

She didn't try to make a bolt for it, but she didn't snuggle and make her little squeaky noises. I wished I knew what she was thinking. It must be strange for her to be shut up in a cage all the time. I certainly wouldn't like it. She must get very bored and lonely. What had happened to her family? Was she missing her brothers and sisters? What about her mother? Perhaps she was missing her father most of all.

I settled her back in her cage very gently. I wished I knew more about guinea pigs. Perhaps Perry knew a few facts about them? I went to find him. He wasn't in his cupboard. He was lying on the floor of the living room, reading one of his new steam train books. His nose was practically brushing the page.

'Why don't you wear your glasses?'

Perry rubbed the bridge of his nose. 'The print's very small, that's all,' he said. 'Push off, Phoebe, I'm trying to concentrate.'

'I just want to ask you things about guinea pigs.'

Perry squinted up at me. 'Boring!'

'I want to find out if they're brought up with their mothers and fathers like a proper family,' I said. 'You know all about newts

after all. Oh! We haven't had a funeral for Nigel yet!'

'I thought that was rather a silly idea,' said Perry.

'But you were terribly upset! You secretly *liked* Nigel. He must have a funeral!' I insisted.

'Why? It won't know anything about it because it's dead,' he said.

'How can you be so *sensible*? If I died all of a sudden, would you just let me moulder?' I cried.

'No, because you'd start to pong,' said Perry.

'You are revolting,' I said, prodding him with my toe because I knew he wouldn't like it.

'Ouch! Stop poking me! I'll tell Mum,' said Perry.

'Where is she anyway?'

'She went for a little walk to calm down. That's what she said.'

'And Becks?' I asked.

'She's climbing a tree,' said Perry.

'*Becks* is?'

'I know. The whole world's upside down,' said Perry. 'Now go away and leave me alone.'

'But I want to find out if guinea pigs feel lonely in their cages,' I said.

'Oh, Phoebe, why do you have to keep fuss-fuss-fussing about *feelings* all the time?' said Perry. 'You're doing my head in.'

But he scrambled to his feet, clutching his forehead melodramatically, but still willing to help.

'I can't Google it because we haven't got any internet connection, but I've brought my *Big Book of Living Creatures* with me,' he said.

I followed him upstairs to the cupboard. It was an enormous fat book that must have made his suitcase weigh a ton. He'd had it for several years and I wondered why he didn't think it too babyish now. I looked inside the cover and saw Dad's squiggly handwriting.

To Perry – Happy Birthday! Loads of love from Dad xxxxx

Perry gave a little sniffle. I hunched up beside him, and we looked up G for Guinea Pigs. The entry was quite encouraging. Guinea pigs originally came from South America, but had been kept in captivity for more than 3,000 years.

'That means kept in cages, right?' I asked Perry. 'So Daisy doesn't mind being in her cage, because all her great-great-great-great-great hundreds of times grandmothers have always been kept in cages,' I added eagerly.

'Maybe they all *hated* being in captivity. Think of battery hens. If you're caged with thousands of others with your beak cut and your wings clipped it doesn't necessarily help that your mother and grandmother suffered the same fate,' said Perry.

'Shut *up*!' I said. 'Why do you have to be so horribly gruesome?'

'I'm just stating a fact, that's all,' said Perry.

'So do you think it's a fact that it's cruel to keep Daisy in a cage?' I asked.

'Not if she's comfortable, and you remember to give her food and water and keep her clean,' said Perry.

'Anyway, I'm going to give Nigel a funeral whether you want me to or not,' I said, changing the subject.

Perry shrugged as if he wasn't remotely interested and went back to studying steam engines. I went outside. Sure enough, there was Becks up in the tree beside the house, though she shinned down quickly when she saw me staring.

'What are you *doing*? I didn't know you could climb trees!' I gasped.

'I didn't know I could either!' said Becks.

'Is this your new hobby now?' I asked.

Becks looked round quickly, making sure Mum wasn't nearby. 'No, it's my way of getting to go out with Jake,' she said, grinning.

'What? How does climbing a tree help?' I asked, baffled.

'Honestly, isn't it obvious?' said Becks, exasperated.

It wasn't at all obvious to me. It was upsetting being thought stupid by both my siblings in the space of five minutes.

'Mum isn't ever going to let me go out with Jake, is she?' said Becks. 'So I've got to sneak out. Here's the plan. I make out I'm tired and go up to bed really early. Then I climb out of the window, down the tree and sneak off!'

'But it'll be getting dark, won't it?'

'Aha!' Becks fished her mobile out of her pocket. 'I can still light my way even without a signal.'

'It'll be even darker getting back. And then what will you do? How will you get back in?' I asked, frowning.

'The same way I got out, silly. Up the tree and through the window. Which means you'll have to keep the window wide open, obviously,' said Becks.

'I'm not sure I want to,' I said. 'What if birds fly in? Or a *bat*?'

'Don't be silly, of course they won't,' said Becks, though she didn't sound too sure.

'Couldn't you just tap on the window when you're back up the tree and then I'll open it for you?' I said.

'Oh yes, you'll be fast asleep snoring your little head off and I'll be up the tree tap-tap-tapping half the night! No way! You're to keep the window open. And when I've sneaked out, stuff some of my clothes in my half of the bed to make it look as if I'm in it, just in case Mum decides to check on us,' said Becks.

'You've been reading too many of those Enid Blyton boarding school books,' I said loftily.

'Oh, ha ha! But *will* you help me?' Becks asked, in a wheedling tone.

'I shouldn't. You could easily fall out of the tree and break your neck, and then I'll feel it's all my fault for not telling on you.

And I'll get in the most awful trouble with Mum. She'll positively hate me,' I said.

'No she won't, you banana,' said Becks. 'Oh, go on, Phoebes, say you will. Please!'

'Well, will you help me give Nigel a lovely funeral?' I asked.

'What? Oh, Phoebe! If I must. I'll be the pall-bearer or whatever you call them.'

'And you'll take it all seriously and not get the giggles?' I asked.

'Promise!' said Becks, though her lips were twitching.

'You'll do it now, right this minute?'

'Yes, I'll play with you now if *you* promise to help me out tonight,' said Becks.

'Conducting a funeral isn't *playing*,' I said sternly, but we both shook on our promises.

We went to look at the abandoned aquarium to inspect the deceased. I was a bit wary, not wanting to look at Nigel too closely, but he looked reasonably OK, just a bit dried out. I extracted him from the tank and inspected him.

'He's rather lovely, in his own way,' I said softly. 'He's all different colours if you look carefully. He's orangey in parts and there are little blue bits too.'

'Ew! I'm not sure you should actually be handling him, not if he's starting to decay,' said Becks.

'I don't think it's mould – it's just the natural colour of his scales. It's a shame his tail didn't have time to grow back, but never mind. Now we need a shroud.'

I still had Mr Thomas Brown's handkerchief tucked in my pocket, but I didn't want to donate that because I needed to get it

washed and ironed and returned to him. I used several pieces of loo roll instead, wrapping them round Nigel tenderly.

'There! He looks rather sweet, like a tiny swaddled baby. Now, what can we use for a coffin?' I wondered.

'Why do we have to bother with a coffin? Can't we just dig a little hole and shove him in the ground?' Becks asked.

'He needs a proper coffin. It shows we care about him. Let's see if we can find something suitable in the kitchen,' I suggested. 'A cardboard box would be perfect.'

We poked about in the things Mum had bought at the supermarket. I hoped to find a big box of matches, but couldn't see one. The only cardboard box was a cornflakes packet, but obviously that was much too big. The only suitable container was a plastic box of easy-to-spread butter – but of course that was full to the brim *with* the butter.

I peered in the cupboards at the crockery.

'Aha! I've found a butter *dish*!' I said.

I scraped all the butter out of the plastic into the china dish, and then set Becks the task of washing the container thoroughly so it wasn't unpleasantly greasy. I fetched my drawing book and crayons and sellotape meanwhile.

'Are you going to colour? Have you got fed up with playing funerals already?' Becks asked indignantly.

'This is part of the funeral process. I'm putting an appropriate

inscription on the coffin,' I insisted.

I wrote in purple crayon: *Here lies Nigel Newt, dearly beloved companion of Perry Robinson. May he Rest in Peace.*

I drew a little picture of Nigel underneath, colouring it very carefully, and then found some kitchen scissors in a drawer. I cut it all out and stuck it to the butter lid.

'I wonder if there's any way we can make the plastic look more like wood,' I said, irritated by its garish colours and slogan.

'Oh, for goodness' sake, Phoebe. It's fine the way it is. You've done a lovely inscription,' said Becks. I don't think she really meant it. She just wanted to get the funeral done and dusted.

'We've got to look the part too. Could we cut up some of your black tights?' I asked.

'We could not!' said Becks firmly.

In the end she let me have one slightly torn pair, enough to make three black bands to tie round our left arms. Grandma, Mum's mum, had had a very posh funeral with all the mourners wearing black bands. I hadn't been too upset, if I'm honest. She was a very prickly gran who said she believed in telling it like it is. That meant she told me I was getting too lumpy, she told Perry he was downright spoilt – even though Dad tried to explain how he was just made differently – and she told Becks she was far too vain. She told our dad he was a useless piece of work! She didn't even have a kind word to say to Mum, who was her own daughter.

It was very difficult to imagine her Resting in Peace. I felt sorry for the people buried either side of her.

'Now we need a hymn book,' I said, and dashed upstairs.

Daisy's cage was balanced on the white bookcase in our bedroom. Most of the books were old and leather-bound, some of them falling to bits. I couldn't find a hymn book, but there was a big black Bible with a clasp. That would have to do. It certainly looked very impressive. I opened it up, wondering if Nina had left pressed flowers within its thousands of thin pages. She hadn't done that. She'd had a much better idea. There *were* flowers every so often, but they were delicate watercolours painted on the actual pages: pale pink wild roses, daisies, bluebells, cowslips . . .

'Oh, Nina, it's your special Bible! I hope you don't mind if I borrow it, just for half an hour or so?' I whispered.

I looked in some of the other books, hoping she might have painted on their pages too, but they were all plain print, very small and close together. They were classics by the Brontë sisters and Jane Austen and Charles Dickens. Dad said I'd love them all when I was a little bit older. I wasn't so sure. They looked very hard to read.

I opened one last book – and it actually had illustrations, hundreds of them! They were in black and white, but more than half had been carefully painted. There was a man in a funny furry costume, and lots of animals, and some beach scenes. Something

clicked in my mind! I turned to the title page. It was *Robinson Crusoe*, the original book by Daniel Defoe! Underneath the title there was a birthday message, just like the one Dad had written to Perry. *To little Nina, Happy Birthday, with love from Mother and Father.*

I clasped the big book, my arms prickling with excitement, momentarily forgetting all about the funeral. It seemed the most amazing magical coincidence that Nina's childhood book was *Robinson Crusoe*, Dad's initial inspiration. I wanted to rush downstairs to show Becks, though she probably wouldn't be that interested. Perry wouldn't be bothered about it either. And Mum would shake her head and sigh, because she disapproved strongly of colouring the illustrations in reading books. She'd been extremely cross when she caught me crayoning in an old nursery rhyme book, telling me I'd spoiled a really expensive book.

I tucked *Robinson Crusoe* back on the shelf, giving its worn leather spine a stroke. I would keep it just for me. It would be another way of being with Dad, sharing his special book. And when he came back we'd cuddle up on the sofa together and I'd look at all the carefully coloured pictures while he read me the story.

I sighed deeply, picked up the Bible, and went to fetch the chief mourner, who was back in his cupboard muttering to himself.

'What are you doing, Perry?' I said. 'Have you got an imaginary friend or something?'

'No, I'm reciting the names and numbers of trains, and being in the dark helps me concentrate,' he said. 'I've decided I'm quite definitely going to become a train driver on the Primrose Railway.'

'I think you'd be better off becoming a vampire and then you could lurk in the dark all day long. Anyway, we're all ready for the funeral now. Come downstairs,' I said.

'Do I have to? I don't like funerals. They make me sad,' said Perry.

'That's the whole point. You can have a good weep over Nigel and then you'll feel better,' I insisted.

'No I won't,' said Perry. 'I shall feel worse.'

'Oh, please come, Perry. I've tried so hard to make it a lovely funeral. Just wait till you see Nigel's coffin. He's got a shroud and everything.'

'All right, I'm coming,' said Perry, and he reluctantly followed me downstairs.

Becks was in the middle of experimenting with a new hairstyle, tying it up in a topknot. '*There* you are! I thought you'd gone off to play somewhere and forgotten all about the funeral. Now, do you think I look older with my hair up like this?' she asked.

'Maybe. Yes. But it looks a lot prettier when it's hanging loose,' I said.

'Really?' Becks pouted, and let her hair cascade down again. 'Pretty's better than older, isn't it?'

'*I* don't know. I don't care. Look, I've got a Bible. And Perry. We're all set,' I said. 'Would you like to view the deceased first, Perry?'

'Oh, for goodness' sake!' said Becks. 'Can't we just get on with it? I think I'm going to wash my hair now the water's heating up.'

'Yes, I would like to see its body,' said Perry. 'Is it decomposing?'

'Not at all!' I promised.

He seemed disappointed when I unwrapped the shroud, but managed to give Nigel a little stroke with his forefinger. Actually it was more of a poke, but thankfully the newt stayed intact. I wrapped Nigel up again carefully, reinserted him into the plastic container and put the lid on him. Then I tied our mourning bands round our arms, gave the coffin to the chief pall-bearer, and held the Bible solemnly like a platter.

'We may proceed,' I said.

The procession paused beside a tumbledown garden shed, where I found a rusty trowel amongst a pile of flowerpots, and then we went over to the far corner, behind the empty chicken coop.

'There, this is a nice quiet spot,' I said. 'Now, dearly beloved—'

'You say that at weddings, not funerals,' said Becks.

'I can say it if I want to. Dearly beloved, we are gathered here to mark the short but special life of Nigel Newt,' I said, in as deep and solemn a voice as I could manage. 'Now, let us sing a hymn

for him.' I thought quickly. I didn't know many hymns. '"Glad that I live, am I".'

'You don't sing that at a funeral!' said Becks.

'Oh, all right then. I'll say a prayer instead, and then we can start the actual burial,' I said. 'Our Father, which Art in Heaven, we commit this little creature to your care, ashes to ashes, dust to dust. Amen.'

Neither Becks nor Perry looked appropriately solemn. Becks was rolling her eyes and Perry seemed puzzled, but I didn't want to spoil the moment by snapping at them. I picked up the trowel and started digging a hole.

It was beginning to feel too real, as if it was a proper funeral. I started to panic. How would I ever cope when Dad died? What if Dad died soon? Was *that* the real reason he'd left us? Had he discovered he was terribly ill and had gone away to die?

'Phoebe? Are you crying because Perry's *newt* died?' Becks asked.

'*I'm* not crying,' said Perry.

'You did cry – you positively howled when you discovered he was dead yesterday, when we got here,' I said. 'And anyway, I'm not crying because of Nigel, I'm crying because of Dad. What if *he's* died?'

'Oh, Phoebe,' said Becks, kneeling down beside me. 'Of course

Dad hasn't died. Where do you get these ideas from? You always catastrophise.'

'No I don't! And anyway, what does that mean? It isn't a proper word,' I retorted.

'Yes it is. It means always thinking the worst is going to happen,' said Becks.

'I knew that. And that's absolutely the way Phoebe thinks,' said Perry.

'Well, the worst thing often *does* happen,' I said. 'Like Dad disappearing.'

'Yes, all right, but it doesn't mean anyone else will disappear,' said Becks.

'I wish Mum would sometimes,' I muttered.

'No you don't!'

'Well, I bet she wishes *I* would,' I said, digging so savagely I hurt my wrist.

'Mum's been gone a long time, hasn't she?' said Perry. 'You don't think she really has disappeared too, do you?'

'Oh, for goodness' sake, you're as bad as each other! Mum's just gone for a little walk like she said. It's her way of calming down. She was really irritated by that Mo lady,' said Becks.

'But she's lovely,' I said.

'I know. We've met some lovely people since coming here. Mo and your Mr Thomas Brown and . . .' Becks paused coyly.

'And your Jake Brown,' I said.

Becks flashed me a look, not wanting me to say any more in front of Perry. She needn't have bothered.

'And we discovered the Primrose Railway,' said Perry in awed tones, as if we'd found the Holy Grail. 'That's the best thing ever. I don't mind so much about my newt experiment now.'

'Let's finish the funeral. You two take a turn digging, it's making my whole arm ache,' I said.

When the hole was deep enough we gently lowered the coffin into it.

'Rest in peace, Nigel,' I said in my holy voice. Then I picked a few buttercups, sprinkled them into the grave and started trowelling the earth over it. Soon there was just a little mound in the garden to show that Nigel had ever lived.

'We could hold a little wake now,' I suggested as we went back indoors. 'With refreshments.'

'Phoebe, we're absolutely stuffed!' said Becks.

'I don't think I ever feel *totally* full,' I said sadly. 'And it happens to be way past lunchtime now.'

'*Lunch?*' said Mum, walking in the back door.

'Oh, Mum, you're OK!' I said, rushing to her and giving her a hug. I'd been so scared something might really have happened to her because I'd said I wished she'd disappeared.

'Hey hey, I've only been gone forty minutes or so! I had a

lovely explore,' said Mum. 'I think we should all go out and enjoy the countryside. I don't think we really need lunch right now, Phoebe, but perhaps we could have a little picnic tea?'

'Oh, yes please!' I said eagerly, pleased that she'd come back from her walk in such a good mood. She hugged me back, playing with my plaits the way Dad always did. Her own hair was immaculate as always, long and shiny, but her make-up was a little smudged, especially round her eyes. Had she been crying, to make her mascara run like that?

'I think it's an absolutely ace idea to go out exploring,' said Perry. 'I vote we go to the Primrose Railway and then get out at that little station Forest Lake!'

'Well, we could drive there,' said Mum. 'We can't go on the railway twice in one day, Perry!'

'Why not?' said Perry.

'Because it costs quite a lot of money, for a start,' said Mum.

'But you've *got* lots of money, Mum. And a credit card,' said Perry.

'Well, we'll maybe go on the train again tomorrow,' said Mum. 'Car ride today. And I think Forest Lake is a good idea. Let's hope there's a real forest *and* a lake.'

It turned out there was quite a big forest, twenty times the size of our little wood by the field. We parked the car in the special car

park along with a lot of other families. They were mostly mums *and* dads, but I tried not to let it get me down.

It was easy for us to find the lake, because every family seemed to be going that way. The forest cleared and there it was, very blue and beautiful, with swans gliding tranquilly across the still water, and little children paddling at the edge.

'Can we paddle, Mum?' I asked.

I expected her to say no, because it was likely we'd end up getting soaking wet, but she just shrugged.

'If you want to, darling.'

I certainly wanted to, and Perry came in too, looking for tiny water creatures. Becks sat on the grass beside Mum for a while, sitting with her chin up, her hair tossed back, one knee up, one knee down, as if she were posing for a photograph. Nobody was taking any notice of her and it was surprisingly hot, so in the end she rolled up her jeans as far as they would go and went in paddling too. Mum even joined in, and she just laughed when Perry dared splash her.

She seemed to have turned into a storybook mum, determined that we all have fun. We found an old ball on the footpath by the lake and had a game of catch, all four of us, and when we wandered further round the water where you could hire a canoe, she paid for two double-seaters. She took Perry on one, and Becks and I had the other.

It took us a while to get the knack of raising the paddles in unison, but Mum and Perry were surprisingly good at it straight away, and sped off impressively.

'Mum's in such a good mood that maybe I'll simply ask her outright if I can go to Orlington with Jake tonight,' said Becks.

'I think that would be pushing it,' I said.

'Yeah, you're right,' she said. 'Still, it's great that Mum's cheered up. That walk must have done her good. She's really enjoying herself.'

We watched her chatting to Perry, then laughing at something he was saying. She threw back her head, her mouth open wide.

'I think she's just pretending,' I said. 'She's trying too hard.'

'Well, good for her,' said Becks. 'She's just trying to make us happy.'

'She's trying to be a fun parent like Dad, but she'll never take his place,' I said.

'Honestly, she can't win. Poor Mum,' said Becks.

'And none of us *should* be happy, not without Dad. Aren't you missing him terribly?' I asked.

'Yes, of course I am. But I'm angry with him too, for leaving us in the lurch. He must have known how devastated we'd be. Especially you, because you idolize him so much,' said Becks.

'Well, why shouldn't I? He's the best dad in the whole world,' I insisted.

'Is he? I used to think so too, because he played with us so much and let us do whatever we wanted and made such a fuss of us—'

'Exactly!' I interrupted.

'But he always left Mum to tell us off for not doing our homework or leaving our rooms in a mess or for being careless and breaking something. He's always wanted her to be the strict parent so he can be the fun one,' said Becks. 'And actually I'm starting to find all his fun-and-games a bit embarrassing, especially when he starts pulling silly faces or pretending stuff in public.'

'Stop it! Dad's incredibly funny! He has us all in stitches,' I said.

'Only you,' said Becks.

'And think of all the wonderful games he's made up for us!' I said. 'The pirate game, and the treasure hunts, and the time we were all cavemen and we made up the grunt language – that was hilarious!'

'It was OK when we were all little. But it's kind of weird now. It's like he's a big kid himself, instead of a dad,' Becks went on relentlessly. 'It's as if he actually believes some of this stuff. And he's always convinced that his old Robinson things are going to come back into fashion and be huge brands like Harry Potter or Paddington when it's obvious to everyone that they're so *over*!'

'Shut up! I won't listen to another word!' I spat, and I put my hands over my ears.

I'd forgotten all about my paddle. It fell into the water. I reached out, trying to grab hold of it, making the canoe rock violently, almost capsizing us.

'Oh no!' said Becks furiously. 'Keep still!' She paddled hard herself, until we'd caught up with it. 'Now, lean out *carefully*, still sitting, and see if you can get a hold of it.'

I struggled, touched it with my fingertips, and then somehow curled my fingers right round it.

'Hang onto it now! Haul it nearer, and then try to lift it right up out of the water,' said Becks.

I did my best, but I was at such an awkward angle that I let it slip again.

'Oh, Phoebes!' said Becks. 'Here, you take my paddle and I'll get it.' She thrust her paddle at me and then reached out into the water for mine. I tried hard to manoeuvre the canoe into a better position – a little *too* hard. The canoe rocked violently and Becks lost her balance and fell headlong into the water.

'Becks! Oh, I'm so sorry! Help, someone! My sister's in the water!' I screamed.

Becks surfaced, her hair streaming, a little bit of pondweed hanging over her eyes.

'You poor thing! Here, catch my hand! Don't drown, oh please don't drown!' I begged.

'Shut *up*!' Becks spluttered. 'The water only comes up to my

waist! Yuck, it's all muddy on the bottom! How *could* you! Did you
do it on *purpose*?'

'No! I swear I didn't! It's all right though, some boys are
coming! They'll rescue us,' I gabbled.

'Oh God!' said Becks, frantically combing her hair with her
fingers and discovering the pondweed. 'Ew! Disgusting!'

'Hey, don't worry, we'll pull you out!' one of the boys called,
paddling furiously towards us. They started snorting with laughter
as they got nearer to us.

'I will kill you for this,' Becks muttered to me, trying to climb
back into the canoe. She still had hold of my paddle and thrust it

at me, digging me in the tummy. She had one leg over the side of the canoe and the other still in the water by the time the boys reached us. It wasn't the most dignified position.

'Don't worry, we'll help you,' said one.

'We'll just give you a little shove,' said the other, his hand in the air, hovering over Becks's bottom.

'I'm fine, I'm absolutely fine!' Becks insisted, scrambling desperately and landing in a heap in our canoe.

'You don't look very fine!' said the first one, and they both cackled helplessly.

'Start paddling!' Becks hissed at me, somehow managing to straighten up. Then she addressed the two boys. 'We really don't need your help. Goodbye.' She said it with icy dignity, even though she was dripping wet and still had pondweed in her hair.

We paddled away as fast as we could, while they laughed in our wake.

'We're going the wrong way,' said Becks. 'Oh God, how do we turn the wretched thing *round*?'

We discovered after a lot of trial and error, mostly error, that we simply had to paddle one side only, and then we made it back to the landing stage as quickly as possible.

'We're actually getting quite good at it now,' I risked saying.

'Shut up,' said Becks grimly.

Other canoeists were pointing and smiling at her. When we

got back the elderly man in charge of the canoes shook his head at her. 'Did you come a cropper?' he asked unnecessarily.

Becks didn't even bother to answer him. She stalked off towards a clump of trees. I hurried after her.

'Becks! Where are you going? We've got to wait for Mum and Perry!' I said.

'I'm not sitting by that landing stage where everyone can see me,' said Becks. 'I'll wait here.'

'You don't look too bad, honestly. Just a bit wet,' I said, picking another strand of pondweed out of her hair.

'It's so not fair! It's all your stupid fault!' Becks said furiously.

'No, it's not. *I* didn't make you fall in,' I said. 'Don't you dare blame me.'

'You're the most clumsy, useless sister in the whole world. The entire universe!' Becks snapped, crouching down, trying to make herself less visible.

I smarted, feeling miserable. I waited two minutes, rehearsing retorts in my head – and then thought of a better way to get my revenge.

'Oh, look, it's Jake Brown! He's waving! He's coming over here!' I said.

'*What?*' said Becks, in a panic. '*Where?*'

'Over there, beside the lake. Oh no, I don't think it is him after all. Mistake! Sorry,' I said airily.

'You absolute pig!' said Becks.

'Oink oink,' I retorted.

We didn't say anything further. Mum and Perry were another twenty whole minutes. They climbed out of their canoe, smiling, still pristine. Mum looked all around, then spotted us.

'That was great fun, wasn't it, girls?' she said, coming over to us. Then she got a proper look at Becks. 'Oh no! You poor thing! Are you all right, darling?'

'Do I look all right?' Becks asked witheringly.

'You look dreadful!' said Perry, as if she'd asked a serious question. 'You've taken a dunking!' He repeated it in a silly sing-song voice, getting louder and louder.

Becks glared at him furiously. Her teeth were chattering now, even though it was a warm day.

'Come on, darling, let's get you back to the car,' said Mum, putting her arm round her.

Becks had to endure many more people pointing at her as we made our way back through the forest to the car park. She sank down low when she got into the car, her eyes shut.

'Poor Becks,' Mum said softly.

'I have never felt so humiliated in my entire life,' Becks muttered.

Mum glanced at me as if she agreed it was my fault. 'What a shame, when we were all having so much fun,' she said.

'Yes, but we can't *really* have fun any more, not without Dad.'
I'd thought I'd muttered it to myself, but Mum heard me. Her face
crumpled, as if she was going to cry, and I felt terrible. 'I didn't
mean it like that,' I said.

'I know what you meant, Phoebe,' said Mum. She took a deep
breath. 'Right. Let's go home.'

Perry hadn't been listening properly, moving his arms round
and round as if he were still canoeing. But now his head jerked.
'We're going *home*?' he said.

'Back to the cottage,' said Mum.

'Oh. I thought you meant *home* home,' he said.

'I thought you were all so keen on the cottage now,' Mum said.
'And you can go to the Primrose Railway, Perry.'

'Yes. Great. But . . .'

'But what?'

'We are going home *eventually*, aren't we?' he asked.

I looked at Mum too. So did Becks.

'Of course we're going home eventually,' said Mum – but she
didn't sound one hundred per cent certain.

Becks used up all the hot water having a bath and washing her hair all over again. Then she spent ages drying her hair and styling it, fussing with hair tongs and twiddling it this way and that. She was clearly still planning the big escape tonight!

She put her dressing gown on when we went downstairs to have the picnic tea. Mum had set it all out on the kitchen table, arranging it prettily on Nina's green plates. There was a circle of cheese rolls with tiny red tomatoes in the middle, chipolata sausages in a pattern, a bowl of hummus with carrot sticks, crisps, chocolate brownies and big strawberries arranged in a heart.

'Oh, wow! This looks incredibly yummy!' I said.

Becks didn't eat much and didn't talk much either. I guessed she was getting really excited about going out with Jake. Perry talked a great deal, mostly with his mouth full, telling us all the

new facts he'd learned about engines, words like *steam pressure* and *pistons* and *cylinders* and *connecting rods* and *flywheels* streaming out of his mouth along with a lot of crumbs.

He started every sentence with: 'I bet you can't guess this!' Of course we couldn't – this was Perry's new special interest, not ours.

'I wonder if they make a Trivial Pursuit type game about steam railways?' said Mum. 'If they do, then that's your next birthday present sorted!'

We used to play our own version of Trivial Pursuit with Dad. He made up all the questions and wrote them out carefully on little cards. Sometimes they were General Knowledge, but often they were personal to us, like: *What was Phoebe's favourite activity at nursery school?* And: *How old was Perry when he learned to whistle?* And: *Which is Becks's favourite shop?* There were also a lot of Robinson-based questions too, where there weren't really any right answers – we just had to make it up. *What's Robinson's favourite food? What does Robinson dream about? Did Robinson have a wife and children?*

Maybe Mum was thinking about Dad's games too, because when we'd cleared up the picnic she produced a couple of packs of playing cards.

'Look, I found these in one of the cupboards. Let's play snap,' she said.

We sat round the kitchen table and played. They were very old cards, rather limp and creased, but they had an attractive rose

design on the back, a big flower, deep velvety red on a dark green background. They were very much like the paintings in the cottage. I peered at the box, and in tiny letters at the edge it said: *Designed by Nina Cresswell*.

Nina's own cards! How lovely! She'd clearly used them a lot herself. Did she play solitaire every night, all by herself, or did she invite a friend to come and play gin rummy or beggar my neighbour? I was so taken up by imagining it that I didn't concentrate on the numbers and was easily out first at snap. Repeatedly. Neither Becks nor Mum seemed to be paying much attention either, so Perry kept winning.

He was triumphant at first, punching the air as if he'd just scored a goal, but lost interest after a while.

'This is a boring game because you're all hopeless at it,' he said.

'Then let's play blackjack,' said Mum.

'With money?' Perry asked eagerly.

'I haven't got enough change, but we could play with matches,' Mum suggested.

'Um, you always say we're not allowed to play with matches,' I said, joking. Everybody groaned.

We played blackjack. Perry kept winning again, accumulating enough matches to light a bonfire. Becks looked at the grandfather clock and started yawning. Yawning and yawning. It was so

catching that I started yawning too, though I wasn't the slightest
bit tired.

'You're not getting sleepy already, are you, Becks?' Mum
asked. 'It's only just gone eight.'

'Actually I am,' said Becks, yawning again. 'Do you mind if I
go up to bed already? I can hardly keep my eyes open.'

'Oh well, I suppose it's all the fresh air affecting you – and
your unexpected dip in the lake! Off you go then, darling. Night-
night,' said Mum.

'I'm ever so tired too,' I said, attempting such a big yawn it's a
wonder I didn't break my jaw.

'Phoebe, for goodness' sake, put your hand over your mouth
when you yawn!' said Mum. 'All right, night-night to you too.'

'Ha!' said Perry scornfully. 'I'm not the slightest bit tired.' He
was shuffling the cards eagerly. 'Let's play poker, Mum.'

'Just the two of us? I don't think you can,' she said.

'Yes you can. You have five cards each, just the same as real
poker. Dad played it with me once. For real money!' said Perry. 'I
won heaps!'

'Well, if you're playing with me we're going to stick to matches,'
said Mum firmly.

'Then let's calculate how many matches are in each box so we
get the price of an individual match and then we can add them up
at the end and see exactly how much the winner has made in

pounds and pence,' said Perry.

'I don't think you're going to be an engine driver when you grow up. You'll be a professional gambler in Vegas and you'll come to a sticky end,' said Becks.

Perry looked thrilled at the idea.

'I wonder what Perry really will do when he grows up?' I asked, as we went up the stairs. 'He's so brainy – but it's about all sorts of different things.'

'Well, he'll have more choices than someone who's not brainy, like you,' said Becks. 'Oh, don't look so tragic! I didn't mean it!'

'I come *nearly* top sometimes at school. Amelie always copies me when we have tests,' I said.

It felt so odd saying Amelie's name. I'd only seen her last Thursday and yet already she seemed like a stranger. She'd definitely become Kate's best friend now I wasn't going to be at school and away for all the summer holidays. I wondered how I'd ever get a new best friend now. Everyone had paired up or went round in little gangs. I didn't really *mind* going round on my own – I always had lots of things to think about and I was good at playing imaginary games inside my head – but you looked pathetic. The other children shunned you and called you Billy-no-mates, and you looked left out when you were told to pair up with someone in class.

Perry didn't have a best friend at school, but he didn't care.

He said all the boys in his class were boring and the girls were silly. Perhaps he'd get a best friend when he went to secondary school.

Becks had plenty of friends. Everyone liked her because she was pretty and fun and they wanted to hang out with her. I watched, fascinated, as she sat down at the little dressing table in our bedroom and started on her make-up. I wasn't interested in putting make-up on myself, though I liked face paints because they could transform you into a butterfly or a tiger or a green witch. Still, the whole process was so elaborate and painstaking, all the rubbing on of the foundation and the eye stuff and blusher and lipstick. I wasn't sure it really made Becks look older, but it certainly made her look different.

She pouted at herself in the mirror, tossing her newly styled hair about, as if she were posing for a selfie.

'You're so *vain*, Becks,' I sniffed.

She stuck her tongue out at me, and then went to the wardrobe and rummaged right at the back, where she'd hidden her new outfit. It looked as if it had shrunk while it had been hanging there. She wriggled into the tiny top and tight shorts.

'Oh, Becks! Are you *really* going to go out in them here?' I asked, though I was secretly a bit jealous at how grown-up she looked.

'You are funny – you sound like Gran!' said Becks. She was

eyeing her flat midriff in the mirror. 'Does my stomach stick out in these shorts?'

'Yes, terribly,' I said, rolling my eyes. 'No, of course it doesn't. It's flat as a pancake.'

Becks craned round, trying to adjust the tiny legs of her shorts. 'You can't actually see my knickers, can you?' she asked.

'Yes!'

'You can't really, can you?' She sounded worried. 'Like, I really like Jake, but I don't want him to see my knickers!'

'Well, they *nearly* show,' I said.

'But not actually?'

'For goodness' sake!' I said, getting Daisy out of her cage. 'I'm never going to let *you* wear short shorts, young lady,' I murmured into her soft fur.

Becks stuffed her feet into the silver high heels, sticking out one leg and then the other. 'They look incredible, don't they?' she said.

'Yes. But they're so high! Won't they hurt your feet?'

'I don't care, just as long as they look good,' said Becks, glancing at her watch. 'Jesus, it's quarter to nine already, and I've got to scramble across the field and make my way through that little wood. I hope Jake waits for me. Now, put my dressing gown and some other clothes on my side of the bed, and pull the covers right up, as if I'm hunching down inside. If Mum comes up to say goodnight, just go shush and tell her we're both asleep.'

'But she'll know *I'm* not asleep if I say that,' I said, letting Daisy have a little run across the floorboards.

'Well, just . . . improvise! And keep the window open. Promise?' Becks wheedled.

'OK, so long as you promise to be careful. Don't fall over crossing the field, and don't stay out too late or we could both get into awful trouble,' I said.

'Stop worrying about me!' said Becks. 'I'll be fine. It's not like he's a boyfriend.' She took hold of my hands. Hers were icy cold. 'You're a pal for covering for me.'

'You're freezing. Put your jacket on!' I said.

'It'll look dreadful with my shorts. I'll be fine,' said Becks, but I could see she was shivering already. Or maybe she was just nervous. This was a pretty crazy thing to do, even for Becks.

She opened the window wide, took a deep breath, and then swung one leg out. She thrust an arm out too, and managed to get hold of the nearest branch.

'Bye then!' she whispered.

'Bye, Becks. Do be careful!' I begged her.

She gave me an anxious grin and then hauled herself right out of the window and onto the tree. I hung out and watched her descending rapidly, down and down and down until she jumped to the ground. She wobbled then, nearly falling over in her new heels, but she stood upright, waved at me, and then scurried away.

I watched out of the window, though I couldn't see her any more. It was getting dark already, and much cooler. My throat went dry just thinking of her wobbling across that big tussocky field. How would she manage in those shoes? Perhaps she'd take them off and carry them? But then she had to find her way through the wood. It should be easy enough in the dusk, but what about when it was pitch black later on? It was so terrifyingly dark in the countryside. She could light her way using her mobile, but what if it ran out of charge? What if she dropped it? What if, what if, what if?

'Stop it!' I told myself fiercely. 'Becks will be fine. You know she will. She's *Becks*.' I took several deep breaths, trying to convince myself.

It was cold with the window wide open. I knew fresh air was good for you, but I didn't like it quite as fresh as that. I could hear birds still singing in the evening air. What if one *did* fly in the window? I wasn't exactly scared of birds. I liked them when they were outside – but I wasn't sure I could cope if one was flying round wildly in a panic in my bedroom. A bat would be even worse because they had such scary little faces and big teeth.

I got undressed and into my pyjamas double-quick and jumped into bed. I tried to arrange Becks's dressing gown convincingly and then pulled the sheets over my head. I wished I

had Wiffle to comfort me. Becks must be crazy, trekking across the field and into the woods by herself. She didn't even know Jake properly. Maybe he'd drive off with her in his car and she'd never, ever come back.

Should I tell Mum? While there was time to go after her? But then she'd go berserk. She'd be mad at me as well as Becks. And then if Becks came back safe and sound she'd be grounded for weeks, and she'd hate me. But if something terrible happened to her then it was partly my fault for not telling. I'd be known as the girl who didn't save her sister, and *everyone* would hate me. Maybe even Dad.

What should I do, Dad?

I poked my head out of the bedcovers in case he was answering me. I strained my ears, but just heard an odd thrumming that might have been my own blood pulsing away.

I lay there, my fists clenched, hoping Mum would come to check on us and find Becks missing so the decision was out of my hands. I hadn't heard Perry stomping up the stairs to his cupboard yet. I seemed to have lost all sense of time. How long had Becks been gone now? Ten minutes? An hour? Had I fallen asleep without realizing?

I leaned up on one elbow so I could see the window. It still wasn't totally dark. If anything the dusk made everything look even eerier out there. I wanted to read to distract myself, but

I didn't dare switch the light on. It would be like a beacon flashing a message: this way, scary winged ones, swoop through the window!

I could hear them flapping now. Or were they scuffling? The leaves were rustling just outside the window. Something was climbing the tree! I could hear it panting! Was it some kind of wildcat, about to leap in and attack me?

I scurried out of bed and rushed to the window to slam it shut – and a face leered in at me!

I screamed.

'Shut *up*!'

'Oh, Becks, it's you!' I said, weak with relief.

'Who else would it be?' Becks hissed furiously. 'Help me!'

I seized hold of her shoulders and pulled. Becks shot into the room and landed on the floor, her legs sprawled. One of the heels of her wicked silver shoes had snapped right off. She had mascara smears all down her cheeks.

'What's *happened*? What did Jake *do*?' I asked, trying to help her up.

'He didn't do anything,' she said, pulling away from me and hunching up on the bed.

'I'm going to get Mum,' I said.

'No you're not! Don't you dare! Look, I didn't even *see* Jake,' Becks cried.

'Did he stand you up?' I asked indignantly. 'How dare he! I'll tell Mr Thomas Brown!'

'No! You mustn't ever say a word! It's so embarrassing! I never even got there! I knew I was a little bit late so I started to run, and that field is impossible, so bumpy—'

'And you fell over in your high heels!'

'No! I just twisted my ankle in a rabbit hole and then tripped on a bramble and went flying,' Becks wailed.

'Oh no!' I said.

'Oh yes! I landed with such a thump, and my hands are all grazed, and look at the state of my knees! My heel snapped off and I couldn't find it in the dark. I tried staggering on even so, and then I realized my phone was missing! I'd been using it as a torch. I searched and searched, but I couldn't see it anywhere. I think it went right in the brambles and it's lost for *ever*,' Becks howled.

'Oh, you poor thing! So did Jake help you look for it?' I asked.

'I told you, I never even met him. I couldn't let him see me all bleeding and dirty and crying. I came back here, but it took ages, walking all lopsided, and I hurt everywhere!' Becks held out her sore hands and dabbed at her bloody knees ineffectually.

'So *you* stood *him* up?' I said.

'Well, what else could I do?' Becks demanded.

'Couldn't you have let him know? He'll be feeling dreadful,' I said, picturing Jake in his car getting more and more anxious.

'How on earth could I let him know? I lost my phone – and there's no wretched signal anyway,' said Becks, kicking off her other shoe. 'Oh God, I'm going to look a total idiot with scabs all over my knees!'

'Stop making such a fuss,' I said. 'I've scraped my knees far worse than that! Look, you could have called out to Jake, shouted at the top of your voice. Sound carries in the country. He might have heard you.'

'Yes, and Mum might have heard me too, and just imagine what she'd say!' Becks paused. 'She hasn't been upstairs, has she?'

'No, not yet. Becks, what if poor Jake's *still* waiting there?' I asked.

'He'll have gone ages ago. If he even bothered to turn up. It was just a casual kind of arrangement. It wasn't like it was a real date,' said Becks, mournfully examining her knees.

'Why don't you put your dressing gown on over your clothes, just in case Mum does come up? She'll have a fit if she sees you like this,' I said. 'But we ought to check whether Jake's there. He'll think you stood him up on purpose,' I said.

'I know!' Becks sniffed miserably. 'But I won't ever have to see him again, will I?'

'Don't be daft, of course you will. Perry will want to go to the railway every day, you know what he's like,' I said.

'Well, I'll just have to stay here at the cottage. I should die of

embarrassment if I ever saw Jake now,' Becks declared, wrapping herself in her dressing gown.

I went to the window. 'I'm so sorry, Jake. Becks fell over in the field and had to come back here! She didn't mean to stand you up. She likes you ever so much,' I whispered.

I knew there wasn't the remotest chance that Jake would hear me. But I still hoped the whisper would float in the wind, over the field, through the trees, penetrate his car window right into his ear.

Becks had her hands over her own ears. She got into bed and ducked down under the covers.

'Night-night then,' I said, but she didn't answer.

I thought she'd gone to sleep, but a lot later I heard her crying.

'Are you all right, Becks?' I whispered.

'No,' she murmured.

'Do you want a cuddle?'

'No,' she said again, and turned her back on me.

Mum opened our door much later on, came over to our bed and gave us both a little stroke on the shoulder. She would have realized if she'd just been stroking a dressing gown, so maybe it was just as well Becks never got to meet Jake.

I slept deeply and had weird dreams about being at a disco myself. It was hot and noisy and embarrassing, with everyone from my school laughing and pointing at me because I was such a useless

dancer. But then Dad popped up out of nowhere, and we danced and danced together. We danced right out of the building and down the lane, shimmying up steps and whirling round lampposts, while the moon shone on us like our own private glitter ball.

When I woke up sunlight was pouring through the open window, and Dad wasn't there. I lay on my back, closing my eyes again, struggling to get back into my dream. Then I heard a little whirl through the air and I opened my eyes, startled.

The worst thing had happened. There was a bird in the room! It was only a little bird, a blue tit, flying this way and that, trapped inside the four walls. He tried flying up out of the way and brushed his wings on all the seagulls on the ceiling. I wondered if he recognized them as birds, or whether they were simply streaks of white paint to him.

I got out of bed and tried to point the way to the window. He flew fast in the other direction at first, but then whirled round, as deftly as if he were dancing in my dream, and suddenly shot out of the window.

I waved goodbye to him.

'What are you *doing*?' Becks mumbled.

'I'm just helping a little bird get out of our bedroom,' I said proudly.

'*What?*' Becks ducked under her bedcovers again.

'There's no need to be frightened. It was a harmless little blue

tit. And anyway, he's gone now,' I said, pulling the window shut. I felt totally thrilled with myself.

She didn't answer.

'You haven't gone back to sleep, have you? You do realize I managed to get the bird out of our room all by myself? Come on, wake up. It's a lovely day. Look, bright sunshine,' I said.

I tried to ease the bedclothes away from her head but she hung on tightly.

'You're not still worrying about last night, are you?' I said. 'All you have to do is explain to Jake. He'll understand.'

'I don't want to see Jake ever again. So will you just shut up and let me go back to sleep?' Becks hissed.

I decided I wasn't going to let her spoil my mood. 'You're just embarrassed because you made a clown of yourself,' I said, in a know-it-all manner.

I made a fuss of Daisy and told her I was going to bring her yet more dandelions for her breakfast. I pulled on a T-shirt and shorts, stuck my feet into my sandals and skipped out of the bedroom.

I listened outside the cupboard and heard Perry mumbling in his sleep. He was probably computing train facts. Mum wasn't up yet either. I had an early breakfast of chipolata sausages and a chocolate brownie, left over from the picnic, and then went out to the field.

It seemed so safe and sunny and peaceful in daylight. I wandered around, peering hard around the brambles at the edge, looking for Becks's phone and the snapped silver heel, but couldn't see either anywhere. I gave up after ten minutes and sat still by a burrow, hoping a rabbit or two might pop out for a snack of grass, but they all seemed to be asleep.

I rolled over onto my tummy and pressed my face into a little patch of daisies.

'Are you there, Dad?' I whispered.

I waited. Nothing happened. I waited some more. And then at long last I heard him, far away but still distinct.

I'm always there for you, Phoebe, no matter what!

Mum and Perry were in the kitchen having breakfast when I got back.

'There you are, Phoebe! I was just going to send Perry out to search for you. Have you been in the field again?' said Mum.

'It's so lovely,' I said, sitting down and reaching for a slice of toast.

'No, you can't have that, it's my second slice,' said Perry.

'But I haven't had any!' I said.

'I'm making more. Just wait a minute, Phoebe. I really don't get why you like that old field so much. There's nothing there!' said Mum. She paused. 'You didn't go out there last night, did you?'

I stiffened.

'Out in the field? Last night?' I repeated idiotically, trying to give myself time to think.

'I thought I heard someone stumbling about outside,' said Mum. 'I went and peered out of the door and couldn't *see* anyone. I was worried, obviously. We're very isolated here.'

'Oh, Mum!' I said, laughing uneasily. 'You mean you thought we had burglars?'

'That would be silly, because there's nothing here to burgle,' said Perry, munching his second slice double-fast in case I snatched it from him. He swallowed, and gestured to a corner of the kitchen. 'But if there *were* I'd bash them over the head with that broom. I want to look after you now that Dad's not here.'

'Oh Perry, that's very touching,' said Mum.

'But Dad's going to be here again soon, you wait and see. He's coming straight back when he's done his filming on the island, isn't he, Mum?' I asked, staring her straight in the eyes.

'Yes, of course,' she said, though she didn't sound especially convincing. She was scrutinizing me too. 'You're *sure* you weren't out in the field, Phoebe?'

'I absolutely swear I wasn't,' I said honestly.

'Oh well. What would you like for breakfast? Scrambled eggs? Perhaps I could heat up some of those chipolata sausages too,' said Mum, looking in the old-fashioned pantry. 'Funny! I could have sworn there were some left over from last night's picnic.'

I must have looked guilty this time, because Mum shook her

head at me and sighed. 'I think you were a Labrador in a former life, Phoebe,' she said.

'I'd have liked to be a Labrador,' I said. 'They're beautiful loyal, faithful dogs.'

'They slobber,' said Perry, licking his jammy fingers.

'So do you,' I retorted.

'Oh, Phoebe, don't start!' said Mum, whipping up some eggs. 'Go and give Becks a shake. I think she's still fast asleep.'

I stomped upstairs and into our bedroom.

'Becks!' I hissed at the huddle under the bedclothes. 'Breakfast time!'

She didn't respond, but Daisy started squeaking eagerly.

'Yes, I picked you some more fresh-from-the-field dandelions, Daisy, and some tufts of extra-juicy grass. Yummy yummy!' I said, tucking them inside her hutch. She started nibbling with enthusiasm.

'*Becks!* Do wake up! Hey, we had a lucky escape. Mum said she heard someone outside last night! She even went out to look, but she obviously didn't see you. She seemed to think it was me, but I swore it wasn't,' I said.

Becks stuck her flushed face out of the bedcovers. 'Did you tell Mum it was me out there?' she demanded.

'Of course not! I'm not a snitch,' I said. 'Come on, get up. Breakfast's ready.'

'I don't want any breakfast. I'm going back to sleep,' said Becks, and she disappeared inside the covers again.

I waited, but she didn't come out again. I went back to the kitchen.

'She says she doesn't want any breakfast – she wants to go back to sleep,' I reported.

'Teenagers!' said Mum. 'I expect she's still brooding over that catastrophe yesterday.'

'The catastrophe?' I said anxiously.

'When she fell in the lake,' said Mum, dishing up a lovely fluffy mound of scrambled eggs on toast for me.

'Oh. *That* catastrophe!' I said.

'She looked so silly,' said Perry, grinning.

'Don't be unkind,' said Mum. 'Wait till you're a teenager. I'm sure you'll do your fair share of agonizing.'

I tried to imagine Perry much older and taller, with a deep voice and cool haircut. It was impossible. Perry was smaller than me even though he was eighteen months older, his voice was high-pitched, and his fine hair stuck up all over the place because he was forever running his hands through it.

To be fair, I couldn't imagine me being a teenager either. When I was little I was silly enough to think that I'd start to look like Becks one day. I was old enough now to realize that wasn't going to happen.

I once told Dad that I wished I was pretty like Becks.

'But you're pretty like Phoebe,' he said, and he gave me a hug. He always knew exactly the right thing to say.

'Can we go to the Primrose Railway today, Mum?' Perry asked. 'I was thinking – we could get a season ticket and save a lot of money. Oh, Mum, *please* can we go? There's so much I need to find out. Phoebe, you want to go too, don't you?'

'Yes!' I agreed happily.

'And Becks will want to go too. She liked that ticket collector,' said Perry.

Becks was horrified at the idea of going back to the Primrose Railway.

'But then you can explain to Jake,' I said, back in our bedroom after breakfast.

'I told you, I don't want to see him again – ever, ever, ever. Or explain. He'll think me a total ninny,' said Becks. 'I'm staying in bed.'

'Well, you're acting like a total ninny now. You can't stay in bed for ever,' I protested.

'Watch me,' said Becks, and turned her back on me.

Mum came upstairs with a cup of tea for Becks and tried to reason with her.

'I don't feel very well, Mum. I think I'm getting a cold,' she

mumbled. Her voice was still a bit hoarse from all the crying last night.

'Oh dear. Perhaps you've got a chill from falling in the lake,' said Mum. 'I think you'd better have a morning in bed. That's a pity though. Perry's desperate to go back to the railway. It means so much to him.'

'He can go to the wretched railway. And you and Phoebe. I'll be fine here. I just want to sleep,' said Becks.

'I can't leave you here on your own. Especially if you're not feeling well,' Mum said.

'Of course you can leave me here. I'm nearly fifteen! Fifty years ago, girls my age were going out to work. What on earth's going to happen to me if I'm just staying in bed,' said Becks.

'You might start to feel worse,' said Mum.

'I'll feel way, way worse being jolted around on that train,' Becks insisted. 'Please. Just go!'

Mum felt Becks's forehead. 'I don't think you've got a temperature. Maybe a little lie-in will help. But we won't be back till lunchtime – that's ages.'

'I don't mind,' said Becks. She sensed Mum weakening. '*Dad* let me have a lie-in sometimes, when I was feeling like this.'

'What, he let you stay off school?' Mum said, sounding shocked.

'Just occasionally. When I have a cold or a heavy period.

Nearly everyone stays off then,' said Becks, fibbing.

'Really? I've never stayed off work for trivial things like that!' said Mum. 'Dad's much too soft with you.'

'Yet *you're* letting us miss three weeks of school now,' I pointed out, annoyed that she was criticizing Dad.

That unsettled her. She sighed deeply and then shrugged her shoulders. 'All right then, Becks. But don't wander off anywhere if you start to feel better,' she said.

'As if!' said Becks, and then rolled over and closed her eyes.

I marvelled at her acting ability. Mum told me to brush my hair properly and then went off to the bathroom.

'You don't half tell whopping lies!' I whispered to Becks.

'Phoebe, you won't say anything at all to Jake if he's on the train?' she whispered back. 'If he asks anything, pretend you don't know what he's talking about. You absolutely promise?'

'Promise!' I said.

I can tell lies too.

When we got to the Primrose Railway the car park was already crowded, and to my great delight there was another special Pullman excursion, for an eighty-year-old gentleman who'd had a lifetime passion for trains. He had a vast family celebrating with him, and lots of elderly friends, all dressed up for the occasion in proper suits and white shirts with stiff collars that must have dug into their wrinkled necks. They all wore ridiculous novelty ties

with *Happy Birthday* splashed across the front.

'Oh, Mum, can *I* have a birthday party on the Pullman train?' Perry begged.

Mum smiled at him. 'Maybe,' she said.

I frowned. It had been *my* idea! 'But how can he, Mum? Perry's birthday's in October. We won't be here then, will we?'

'What? Well, maybe we'll have to bring Perry's birthday forward,' Mum said vaguely.

'And I can have a birthday party on the train too?' I asked. I started to make a whirlwind list inside my head: Dad, of course, if he was back; and Amelie – she'd be sooo impressed. I'd definitely *not* ask Kate. Then I'd invite Mr Thomas Brown as a guest, even though it was his own railway, and Mo, and Mum would just jolly well have to be nice to her. Plus Jake, if he still wanted to be friends with our family. I couldn't think of anyone else, which was a bit depressing, but perhaps I'd have made more friends by the end of the summer.

Mr Thomas Brown was greeting all the birthday guests. He seemed to know most of them already. One of them tried to make him wear one of the fun ties, but he said he couldn't, not when he was wearing his uniform. Still, when a small jazz band of elderly men came marching along the platform to give the special birthday boy a rousing send-off, Mr Thomas Brown actually did a funny little dance, jumping and stamping to the beat in his brightly

polished shoes. He was surprisingly good at it and everyone cheered and clapped.

I wanted to have a go at dancing too because the music was so jolly, but Mum gave me a look. We watched the proceedings until they'd all boarded the Pullman. I peeped through the windows and saw the crisp tablecloths and the white gold-rimmed china and the glass flutes and silver ice buckets, ready for the champagne. There were ladies in black dresses with old-fashioned white caps and aprons standing in each carriage, all set to be waitresses. One of them was Mo. I waved at her and she winked at me and gave me a thumbs-up sign.

Perry went rushing over to say hello to Mr Thomas Brown, though Mum told him he was busy. But Mr Thomas Brown seemed delighted to see us.

'How splendid of you to come back already!' he said in a jolly fashion.

'We're going to keep on coming back, Mr Thomas Brown!' said Perry. 'Mum's going to get us a family season ticket, like you suggested.'

'This young man is a true railway enthusiast already,' Mr Thomas Brown told the birthday party, while Perry glowed proudly.

Mum actually *did* buy a season ticket. It was meant to be for two adults and two children, whereas we were one adult and three

children, but the man at the booking office said it didn't matter at all, and gave us twenty per cent off into the bargain.

I was starting to agree with Perry that this was the loveliest place ever. The next train wasn't due to depart for another hour so I rather hoped Mum might let us go to the Junction Cafe for another breakfast, but she said that was pushing it. Perry wanted to charge up and down the platforms anyway, asking questions and taking copious notes. He had converted his newt experiment exercise book into a Steam Railway Journal, neatly divided into sections: General Notes; Specific Facts; Train Categories; and Accounts of Journeys.

After the Pullman departed, with the jazz band on board playing 'Chattanooga Choo Choo', Mr Thomas Brown asked Perry if he'd like to see the big workshop where they renovated the trains.

'Oh, yes *please*!' said Perry.

'Please may I too?' I asked, not wanting to be left out.

Mum said Mr Thomas Brown was very kind, and let us both go with him while she sat on one of the old-fashioned benches and looked at stuff on her mobile. It seemed strange that this railway station, which was more than a hundred years old, was one of the only places round here where you could get a proper signal.

I thought the workshop would be like a glorified garden shed with an old man tinkering with a few nuts and bolts. I was totally wrong. It was huge – more like a factory: big enough to include

whole train carriages; and there were men in overalls everywhere, cleaning and painting and polishing. Mr Thomas Brown took us all round, introducing us to everyone as if we were serious visiting grown-ups rather than children. Most of the men seemed happy to chat.

I felt shy because I didn't really know anything at all about old trains. But Perry made enough pertinent comments and asked so many questions I couldn't have made myself heard if I'd wanted. They all seemed totally impressed with Perry. I was too.

They didn't seem to mind at all when he asked heaps of questions. In fact, these men seemed happy to give him their time, explaining this and that, treating him as if he was a welcome new member of their club.

I felt pleased for him – and tried not to mind that I was being totally ignored. Mr Thomas Brown was very kind to me, and suggested that the man with the pot of green paint might let me have a go at painting a small patch myself.

'Oh yes, please!' I said eagerly, though the painting man himself didn't look particularly keen on the idea.

I took the brush, dipped it carefully in the pot and painted a smooth shining stripe of green that blended in perfectly.

'That's the ticket!' said Mr Thomas Brown.

'Yes, not bad,' said the painter, nodding approvingly.

He let Perry have a go too, but he loaded his paintbrush too

full and his stripe went all blobby and had to be wiped off. He managed to get splodges of paint on his T-shirt too.

'Oh dear, your mother's going to be cross with me!' said Mr Thomas Brown. 'I'd better get you both back to her anyway. You don't want to miss your train!' he said.

Perry looked a little anxious.

'Don't worry, Perry. I'm the stationmaster. My chaps can blow their whistles and wave their flags, but each train stays put until I give the final nod,' said Mr Thomas Brown proudly.

'Will Jake be the ticket collector on our train?' I asked.

'Yes, he's on the eleven o'clock and the one-thirty sandwich special and the three-thirty fun ride for the little kiddies. He's not quite got the finesse needed for the Pullman yet, but he's a quick lad – he'll learn,' he said.

'Am I a quick lad, Mr Thomas Brown?' Perry asked.

'Quick as a wink, my boy,' said Mr Thomas Brown.

'Quick as a wink,' Perry repeated, smiling. 'Do you think I could have a few lessons on how to drive a train?'

'Little lads aren't allowed to drive the train, I'm afraid – but I'm sure you'd pick it up in no time. Tell you what – once we get to know each other properly and I'm satisfied you won't get up to any silly tricks, I'll make sure you get a special ride in the cabin. If Alf takes a shine to you I daresay he'll let you pull the whistle,' said Mr Thomas Brown.

'That would be awesome,' said Perry. 'And *I* daresay I'll grow a great deal during the winter so if we come to stay here *next* summer I'll be able to drive the train then.'

'Well, you can always keep hoping,' said Mr Thomas Brown. 'Come on now, there's your mum looking stressed.'

Mum was frowning over her phone, holding her head with her left hand as if she had a terrible headache.

'Here we are!' said Mr Thomas Brown brightly. 'I'm very impressed with your children, Mrs Robinson.'

Mum switched her phone off quickly and focused on us.

'Mr Thomas Brown says we're quick as a wink. At least, *I* am,' said Perry.

'Hey, hey, don't boast, darling,' said Mum. 'What's that you've got on your T-shirt?'

'Just a little splash of paint, I'm afraid. My fault for giving them a hands-on experience,' said Mr Thomas Brown.

'Oh well, never mind. You've obviously given the children a lovely time, so thank you very much,' said Mum. She rubbed her forehead as if she were trying to smooth away all her worries.

When we got ourselves seated at last, Perry insisting on choosing the perfect carriage, I gave Mum's arm a little tug.

'Mum, what is it? Did someone send you a nasty text message?' I asked.

'What? No, of course not,' said Mum, still frowning.

'It's not bad news, is it?' I asked urgently. 'Is Dad all right?' I clutched my mouth.

'Don't do that, Phoebe, it makes you look as if you're going to be sick,' said Mum. 'No, it's not bad news, it's not Dad – it's nothing. Goodness, you and your imagination! Now let's sit back and enjoy the journey.'

Perry had no problem enjoying the journey, though he was incapable of sitting back. He kept dashing into the corridor and back again, viewing the scenery from both sides, and every time he heard the whistle blow he gave a piercing imitation of it, which made the people in the surrounding carriages laugh.

Mum was behaving as if she were enjoying herself too, but I could tell she was only acting. One time when she followed Perry right down the corridor she left her handbag beside me. Her phone was tucked inside. I wondered if I dared whip it out to see what she'd been peering at so anxiously. I knew her password. It was the date Mum and Dad got married.

I'd seen all the wedding photographs. They didn't have a big elaborate affair. Mum wore a cream suit and high heels and carried a small posy of cream and pink rosebuds. Dad wore a grey suit in the photos and didn't look like himself at all. He had a neat haircut and looked very smart. He looked very happy though, smiling down at Mum. He clearly loved her so much.

I realized it was the suit he wore the last time I saw him. Mum

and Dad *couldn't* be getting a divorce. Dad would never leave Mum. Or if he did, he'd take us with him. At least one of us. The one who loved him with all her heart.

He was on his desert island. I had to keep believing it. And I needed to check he was all right. I slipped my hand into Mum's handbag and quickly tapped in the password. It jigged up and down,

not letting me in. I tried again and again – but Mum had obviously changed her password. She was hiding something from us.

I thrust the phone back into Mum's bag just as Jake walked into the carriage.

'Hello, Phoebe,' he said.

'Oh, hi!' I said, feeling my face flushing. I so hoped he hadn't seen what I was doing.

'I've just seen your mum and your brother further down the train,' said Jake.

'Right,' I said.

'And now here you are. So where's your sister?' Jake asked. He was red in the face too.

'Becks stayed at home today,' I said.

'Oh, I see,' said Jake, looking down-hearted.

'Please don't look like that,' I said. 'Oh dear, I feel dreadful. This is so embarrassing.'

'It's all right. I suppose Rebecca just changed her mind about meeting me. It's no big deal,' said Jake, trying to act as if he didn't care.

He couldn't fool me. I knew I'd promised Becks to keep quiet, but I couldn't leave him feeling so miserable.

'You don't understand. Becks was desperate to meet you, honestly. She actually climbed out of our bedroom window to shin down a tree to get to you,' I said.

'She did *what*?' Jake asked.

'So Mum wouldn't know she'd gone out,' I explained.

'Isn't she allowed to go out at night?' Jake looked surprised. 'She's sixteen, isn't she?'

'Well, not actually. She'll kill me for telling you, but she's only fourteen really,' I told him.

'Oh goodness – I didn't realize. Though she did *say* she was sixteen,' said Jake.

'Yes, well, that was because she wanted to impress you,' I said.

'Did she?' said Jake eagerly. 'Oh dear, though. I guess I am a bit old for her.'

'She's *nearly* fifteen,' I said.

'And I'm only just eighteen,' said Jake. 'So what made her change her mind about coming then? Did your mum see her climbing out of the window?'

'No, Becks just had a little mishap,' I said.

'Oh God, she didn't fall, did she?'

'No, well, not out of the tree. But she tripped over in the field and she broke the heel off her shoe and dropped her phone in the brambles and scraped her knees,' I said.

'Oh no! *Poor* Rebecca,' said Jake. 'I should have insisted on coming to the cottage to collect her.'

'Well, you couldn't, could you, because of Mum. And Becks wouldn't come today because she's so embarrassed. I think she's

scared you'd laugh at her if you knew the truth,' I said. 'I wouldn't blame you. It is a bit funny.'

'No, it's not!' said Jake. 'I feel very sorry for her. And touched, that she'd actually risk climbing out of a window to come to meet me! I was just sure she'd had second thoughts. I mean, I look a bit ridiculous in this weird uniform, with the cap and everything, but it means so much to my grandad that I'm here at the railway.'

'I think your grandad's lovely. I wish *I* had a grandad,' I said. 'I don't really have many relatives.'

'Is it just you and Rebecca and your brother and your mother?' Jake asked.

'And my dad! But – but he's away at the moment,' I said awkwardly.

'Oh!' Jake was polite enough not to enquire further. 'Well, I suppose I'd better get on with my ticket-punching. But when we get to Orlington I'll come and find you, and then maybe you'd like to hop up into the engine again?'

I wasn't actually that bothered, to be truthful, but I said it was very kind of him.

'And could you tell Rebecca when you get home that it was a shame she couldn't come last night, but maybe she'd like to meet up with me some other time? Perhaps not the Cat and Dog, if she's underage. We could have a meal somewhere, or just a coffee, whatever?' he suggested.

'I'll tell her,' I said. 'I think she's very lucky you're being so nice and understanding. Don't get upset if she won't go, though. And *don't* let her know I told you about her falling over. She can be a bit weird and moody sometimes. *I'd* go like a shot.'

He grinned at me. 'OK then, *we'll* go out on a date, you and me, Phoebe,' he said.

I knew he was just joking, but I couldn't help being thrilled.

He kept his word at Orlington, and asked Alf the driver if I could have a turn in the engine first.

'Phoebe?' Perry asked. 'But she's not particularly interested! *I'm* the one who wants to learn everything I possibly can about steam engines. She's just my sister!'

'Well, maybe she's *getting* interested then,' said Ann the firewoman. 'Just your sister, indeed. We have several very knowledgeable ladies working at the Primrose Railway, I'll have you know, lad. My pal Vera was one of our drivers for years, till her cataracts got bad.'

'Yes, you two made a grand team,' said Alf. 'So better keep that lip of yours zipped, buddy!'

I looked anxiously at Perry. He hated being told off like that. He would either argue back, getting more and more worked up, or dissolve into floods of tears. But amazingly he simply nodded, and mimed zipping his mouth.

I climbed on the footplate and chatted to Alf and Ann,

nodding at everything they told me, though I didn't really take much of it in. Alf let me balance his big cap on top of my head while Mum took a photo.

Then Perry had his turn. He wasn't bothered about wearing the cap, and he pulled a face when Mum asked him if she could snap him too, because he absolutely hates having his photo taken. But it was clear he absolutely loved everything to do with steam engines. When he climbed down again he had oil and soot on his T-shirt as well as green paint, but he was beaming so happily Mum couldn't be cross with him.

'Will you send the photo of me wearing Alf's cap to Dad?' I asked Mum, as casually as I could.

It was a test question to find out if she really did know where Dad was.

'You know I can't do that, darling. He hasn't got his phone with him,' said Mum.

If they were getting a divorce then Dad *would* still have his phone. He wouldn't go anywhere without a phone – so he absolutely had to be on that desert island, making his own Robinson film.

When we were getting off the train to get home Jake came running after us.

'No running, boy, not in uniform!' Mr Thomas Brown called, shaking his finger at him.

'Sorry, Grandad. But Phoebe left something behind,' Jake said, and he pressed a Primrose Railway pamphlet into my hand.

I opened my mouth to say it wasn't mine, but when I glanced at it I saw someone had written a message on it. It started: *Dear Rebecca . . .*

'Plenty more pamphlets in the rack over there,' said Mr Thomas Brown.

'Yes, but I'd made some special notes on this one. Thanks ever so much, Jake,' I said quickly.

He mouthed, 'You're a star!' at me.

'What notes?' Mum asked in the car.

'Oh, just jottings about the railway,' I said, still glowing. I loved Jake calling me a star.

'Goodness, are you getting as obsessed about the railway as Perry?' said Mum.

'Sort of,' I said.

'So do *you* want to be an engine driver too when you grow up?' Mum asked.

'I wouldn't mind working as a volunteer, painting the trains,' I said. 'But I'd much sooner paint pictures. Maybe I could be an artist like Nina Cresswell.'

'Well, I'm not sure you'll be able to make a living out of it,' said Mum. 'It's clear old Nina hasn't made her fortune, from the state of her cottage.'

'It's a lovely cottage!' I said fiercely. 'I like it being so old-fashioned. I'm going to have a cottage exactly like it when I'm grown-up. It'll be like living in a fairy tale.'

'What if you don't sell any paintings?' Mum asked.

'I won't mind. I shall hang them on my own walls and look at them every day,' I said.

'And what will you eat? Thin air? And what will you do about the leaky roof? Patch it with your own hair?' Mum persisted.

'Why are you being so mean to me?' I asked indignantly. 'You're spoiling my dream.'

'I'm not really being mean, darling. I just want to try to make you a bit more practical, that's all. You're so inclined to live in this imaginary world of yours. I don't want you to get too carried away,' said Mum.

'I'm being extremely practical,' I retorted. 'I could always do the illustrations in children's books too. You'll see! You might very well end up publishing them yourself!'

Mum did laugh at that, and concentrated on her driving as we went up and down the hills towards home. I stuck my tongue out at her back. She was unfortunately looking in her driving mirror, but she just tutted and didn't say any more.

'I do hope Becks feels a bit better now,' she said, as we tramped across the field. 'I'm worried this might be one of her really heavy colds.'

She was practically running by the time we got to the cottage.

'Becks?' she called. 'Where are you, darling?'

She wasn't anywhere downstairs.

'Oh God, if she's still in bed she must be feeling really groggy,' said Mum, rushing up the little staircase. 'I feel really bad now. We shouldn't have left her all alone.'

I followed her, while Perry made further notes in his railway book, totally unconcerned. Becks was still rolled up in the bedclothes. She didn't look as if she'd moved since we left. Mum anxiously uncovered her face.

'Becks, darling? How are you feeling now?' she asked.

'Rubbish,' Becks mumbled.

She certainly *looked* rubbish, her face very pale, her eyes red, her hair in a tangle.

'Oh, you poor sweetheart,' said Mum, sitting on the bed beside her and smoothing her hair. 'You feel quite hot. I wonder if you've got a temperature? I think I've got some paracetamol in my handbag. I'll make you some soup too.'

'I'm not really hungry, Mum,' said Becks, in a little wan voice.

'But you need to eat. You didn't have any breakfast. And you need a lot of liquids,' Mum fussed. 'I'll be back with a tray in two ticks.' She hurried out of the room purposefully.

'How do you really feel?' I asked.

'Like I said. Rubbish,' said Becks.

'Well, this might make you feel better,' I said, taking the Primrose Railway pamphlet out of my pocket.

'Railway information?' Becks muttered, raising an eyebrow.

'It's a note. From you-know-who,' I said.

Becks sat up properly and snatched it from me. She read it quickly, nibbling her lip. Then she relaxed and read it again, more slowly. Then she tucked it under her pillow, lay back and stretched like a cat. She didn't offer to show me the message. It didn't matter; I'd already had a peep at it when I was in the back of the car.

It went something like:

Dear Rebecca, I'm so sorry we couldn't meet last night. Your sister said you weren't very well. I waited for ages by the telephone box, but of course you had no way of letting me know. I do hope you get better soon. I'll be at the railway every day, looking out for you. I really hope we can go out together. Jake x

He didn't put *love* but there was a kiss. Becks was smiling.

'You feel better already, don't you?' I said.

'You didn't tell him anything about me falling over and getting in a state?' Becks said.

'As if I'd do that!' I said.

'And what exactly did he say?' Becks demanded.

'That he was worried and hoped you were all right,' I said.

'Not in front of *Mum*?'

'No, she was with Perry. He absolutely loved it at the railway. Mr Thomas Brown took us to see the workshop and Perry showed off like anything, impressing all these old men. I actually helped paint an engine, and they were quite impressed with me too,' I added casually.

Becks had stopped listening. She was reading her note again, still smiling.

We all had soup for lunch. It was just tinned tomato soup and yesterday's bread, but Mum put a swirl of cream on the soup

and toasted the bread into buttery triangles. She made it look pretty – but it wasn't like a proper Sunday roast.

Dad's Sunday lunches were wonderful. I used to help him. He'd tell me to peel the potatoes and wash the veg and take a turn at beating the Yorkshire pudding mixture. I'd say, 'Yes, Chef!' each time, and he'd slip me a handful of raisins or a couple of walnuts in return. He always made sure I had an extra roast potato on my plate, sometimes two, and Dad's roast potatoes were the best in the world, golden and crunchy. If we had chicken he always made sure I got the wishbone. He'd pull it with me, and somehow I always managed to get the longest bit of bone.

I remembered all the things I'd wished for: a box of paints, a pair of roller skates, a ukulele, a green rabbit china ornament, a Manchester United T-shirt . . . I'd whispered the wishes, and yet Dad always made them come true. The box of paints was messy and mostly used up now, so I was only left with boring colours like Umber and Burnt Sienna.

The roller skates were scarcely used. I wasn't any good at playing the ukulele either, even though I strummed until my fingers got blisters. And although I'd loved the green rabbit and kept him on the windowsill, one morning I'd yanked the curtains open without thinking and he'd gone flying. He'd broken both his ears and lost his nose, and even though Dad did his best to glue

him together again he was never the same.

The Manchester United T-shirt was still going strong, thank goodness.

Becks got washed and dressed after lunch and said she felt much better now.

'So what would you like to do this afternoon, all three of us?' Mum asked.

'Easy-peasy! Go to the railway!' said Perry.

'Oh, for goodness' sake! We can't possibly go twice in one day!' said Mum.

'Why not? It won't even cost any more because you've got the season ticket for us now,' said Perry.

'Yes, and that cost a small fortune!' said Mum.

'So we must go heaps and heaps of times to get our money's worth,' said Perry.

'I take your point, but it's not really fair on the girls, is it?' said Mum.

'I don't mind going, seeing as I missed out on the trip there this morning,' said Becks casually.

'Oh, darling, that's sweet of you, but we really can't put Perry's interests first *all* the time,' said Mum, misunderstanding.

We ended up going for another drive, exploring. The countryside was lovely, the fields full of big daisies and poppies, and I liked seeing the sheep and cows placidly eating grass all day

long. When we were high up a hill we saw a big puff of white smoke in the valley below.

'It's one of the trains!' Perry shouted, and he wound his window down and hung out of the car, peering at it. 'I think it might be Sir Thomas Browning on an afternoon trip!'

He wanted Mum to drive as near to the track as she could, but the roads were too far away, thank goodness. The trains were interesting, but no one except Perry could possibly find long strips of railway sleepers and the odd signal box fascinating.

We stopped in a little village called Long Barrow for an ice cream, and the man in the shop told us that there was a real long barrow burial mound up the lane. So Mum parked the car and we walked up the lane eating our choc ices. Mum ate hers daintily in little bites, Becks nibbled most of the chocolate off first, Perry sucked and slurped, and I gobbled mine up quickly and finished first.

We would have had time to eat ten choc ices each by the time we reached the long barrow. We'd thought 'up the lane' meant a five-minute saunter, but it took us over half an hour and it was uphill too. We started squabbling, Becks sure we'd taken the wrong lane, Perry desperate to get back in the car to see if we could find the railway track again, but I wanted to keep on trudging just a little bit longer because I'd never seen a long barrow and didn't want to miss this chance.

We'd done a project about the Stone Age at school and we all had to do some kind of visual display using plasticine. Most of the class did hunting, with little men wearing wisps of cotton wool chasing toy zoo animals with matchstick spears. Amelie made a village with neat little huts with grass-clipping roofs, but I thought that a bit lame. I made a long barrow burial chamber, with pink plasticine people cast down upon the painted plaster grass, weeping, while a very dead-looking man with a spear sticking out of his tummy and red paint all over him was lying stiffly on a stretcher, waiting to be inserted into the mound of the long barrow. Mrs Morrison gave me top marks for originality but said it was a little morbid.

I told Dad and he laughed and called me Little Morbid for a while, like a pet name. I got a big lump in my throat remembering, and my eyes started stinging. I blinked hard, and ran ahead so no one could see I was having a little weep – and then saw a sign saying 'Long Barrow'. It was in a field, much bigger and longer than I'd imagined.

'Is this all it is?' said Becks, unimpressed. 'Just a big mound?'

Perry started spouting about the Neolithic Age, because he'd done the same project and had retained an awful lot of information. I didn't bother listening. I walked reverently round the barrow, imagining all the dead people lying inside.

'Phoebe?' Mum caught me up. 'Phoebe, are you crying?'

'I'm feeling sorry for the people buried there,' I sniffed.

'You're the oddest child,' said Mum, but she put her arm round me. She swallowed. 'I do understand how much you're missing your dad. It's extra hard for you because you've always been so close to him.'

I nodded, the tears running faster now. 'He will come back, won't he?' I whispered.

'Yes,' said Mum.

'You promise?'

'Yes,' she repeated.

'But you don't know when?'

'No, I truly don't,' said Mum.

'And he really, really, really is on this island, doing a Robinson film?' I asked.

'Well . . .' she began.

'He *is*,' I insisted, then I started running all the way round the long barrow, repeating it again and again and again.

When we got back to the cottage I went to find the *Robinson Crusoe* book, determined to read it all and find out what it would be like for Dad stuck on an island all by himself. I propped up the pillows on my bed and made myself comfortable, the book on my lap.

I stared at the title page for a long time.

The Life and Adventures of Robinson Crusoe
by Daniel Defoe
Embellished by *Three Hundred Engravings*
After designs by J. J. Grandville

Nina had painted the lettering in different colours to make it look pretty. She'd selected interesting shades of sage and emerald and jade for the leaves on the trees and the grass and plants, and a watered-down Prussian blue for the stream. Robinson himself was all in brown: brown clothes, brown sandals, brown hat, brown basket, brown parasol and a long brown beard. It was all painted very carefully, but I was interested to see she'd gone over the line slightly once or twice, and there was a smudge at the edge of the page. She didn't colour much better than me. Well, maybe just a little bit better, but not much.

Robinson's long beard was disconcerting. Would Dad grow a beard too? I wasn't sure it would suit him. I hoped he might shave it off when he came back, though if he was giving television interviews he might want to keep it to look the part. I hoped it wouldn't tickle too much when he kissed me.

There were two small coloured-in pictures on the first page of the story: one of a parrot, and another of a big sailing ship. This seemed promising. It looked as if the exciting part of the story was starting straight away. I peered at the very small print. It started

with Robinson's *birth*, hundreds of years ago. He said he was born of a good family.

Dad wasn't really born into a good family at all. *His* dad was mean and nasty and drank too much, and his mum was ill a lot, and was often away in hospital. I always felt so sorry for little boy Dad, but he insisted his childhood wasn't as dreadful as I thought.

'Half the time I wasn't *me* anyway. I was Charlie in the chocolate factory, I was James in the giant peach, I was Danny and champion of the world, and I didn't live in our flat, I lived up the Faraway Tree or in Narnia or on a desert island,' he always said cheerily.

'But you still didn't have a happy family,' I said.

'You're my family now,' he'd say, meaning Mum and Becks and Perry and me.

I suppose we had been a happy family, but how could we be that now without Dad? I read several rather dull pages of *Robinson Crusoe*, having to concentrate hard, and then at last came to a picture of a young Robinson without a beard, in fancy clothes, clinging to the rail of a ship with huge waves rising up all around him. At last, the shipwreck! But it wasn't; it was just the start of Robinson's sea adventures, and I wasn't really interested. I just wanted to get to the island part.

I flipped through the dense yellowed pages. Nina didn't seem to think much of them either, because she hadn't bothered to

colour any of these pictures. I was about to give up on the book altogether, when I saw the words 'THE JOURNAL', and then there was a flurry of short entries, each with their own carefully painted picture. At last, the story was starting properly.

September 30, 1659. – I, poor, miserable Robinson Crusoe, being shipwrecked, during a dreadful storm in the offing, came on shore on this dismal unfortunate island, which I called the Island of Despair; all the rest of the ship's company being drowned, and myself almost dead. All the rest of the day I spent in afflicting myself at the dismal circumstances I was brought to namely, I had neither food, house, clothes, weapon, nor place to fly to, and in despair of any relief, saw nothing but death before me, either that I should be devoured by wild beasts, murdered by savages, or starved to death for want of food. At the approach of night I slept in a tree, for fear of wild creatures, but slept soundly, though it rained all night.

I was shaken to the core. The Island of Despair! I'd pictured Dad's island as a beautiful sunny haven with white sands and turquoise sea, like a travel advert on the television. His own made-up Robinson Island had been as colourful and cosy as Noddy's Toytown. If he'd wanted to mirror the real Robinson Crusoe's experience then maybe he was on a bleak and dismal island now, in fear of his life.

What about these wild beasts? Dad's creatures were wild, but

friendly and endearing, even the woolly mammoth. I looked at the little pictures fearfully. In one of the pictures Robinson was crouching on the top of a rock with a shotgun. There were two indistinct animals way below him, coloured a yellowy brown. Hyenas? Wolves? Jaguars?

In the morning, I went out into the island with my gun, to seek for some food, and discover the country; when I killed a she-goat, and her kid followed me home, which I afterwards killed also, because it would not feed.

What? Robinson killed a goat *and her baby?* I didn't actually like goats very much, because one had eaten half the sleeve of my cardigan when I was at a petting zoo, but I hated the idea of *killing* one. And killing a baby goat was totally barbaric. Dad would never, ever do that. He didn't have a gun anyway.

So how was he going to get food? What if there weren't even any coconut trees? Would he have to catch and cook his food like this Robinson? Perhaps he'd wade into the sea and try to catch a fish? But Dad wasn't very good at catching anything, not even a ball. And he was too kind and gentle to want to kill any living thing.

The next entry had a weird shape painted pale green, with a black cloud above it. It was clearly still raining on the Island of Despair, but Robinson could stay dry!

I set up my tent under a rock, and lay there for the first night, making it as large as I could, with stakes driven in to swing my hammock upon.

A tent! We'd been camping in Wales one holiday, Dad and Becks and Perry and I, when Mum was off at some publishing conference in Italy. It had rained then, a great deal, but Dad made it all fun, even when our sleeping bags got soaked. A hammock was a great idea! Dad might be able to make himself one out of plaited reeds. It would be much comfier than sleeping in a tree.

If only Dad had taken me to the island with him! It wouldn't be the Island of Despair if we were together, even if it poured with rain, and we were attacked by wild goats. We'd forage for food together, nuts and berries. I was always good at filling my basket at a Pick-Your-Own farm. And perhaps Dad had taken some packets of seeds with him so we could grow some vegetables.

I closed the book carefully and looked out of the window for inspiration. I saw the old chicken coop. There might well be wild fowl on the island. I thought about Kentucky Fried Chicken. No, we wouldn't kill them, but we could help ourselves to their eggs.

Dad and I would get lean and fit. We'd have races along the beach and go swimming every day and then warm ourselves up with a fire.

We'd make ourselves a vegetable stew on the fire, and maybe

we'd have grown potatoes by now so we could bake them. We'd eat our supper and then we'd have a sing-song and our pet parrot would start squawking along with us, making us laugh. When we were starting to get sleepy Dad would tell me a story – or if he got sleepy first I'd tell *him* a story. Then we'd go to our cave and Dad would get into his big hammock and I'd get into my little one, and we'd swing ourselves to sleep.

If Dad and I were together it would be the Island of Delight, no matter what. If only he'd taken me, if only, if only . . .

I needed to go out in the field! I rushed out of the bedroom and nearly tripped over Perry, who was lying on his tummy outside his cupboard, writing down lists of numbers in his notebook: 2-4-2, 2-4-0, 0-4-2 endlessly all down the page.

'Are you practising your maths?' I asked. 'You can do much harder sums than that.'

Perry sighed. 'They are the wheel formations of the various types of steam engines. I'm testing myself. See, the Stirling express engines are 4-4-0s, and Adams Jubilees are 0-4-2s—'

I stopped listening and bolted downstairs. Mum and Becks were huddled together on the sofa. Becks's head was on Mum's shoulder, while Mum was holding her close.

'I'm so glad you're feeling better now, poppet,' Mum murmured.

Mum and I never sat cuddling like that. I don't think Mum

had ever called me 'poppet'. She called me 'darling' occasionally, but she said that to lots of people, sometimes when she couldn't remember their name. I never particularly minded, because I had cuddles every single day with Dad. Until now.

I crept out through the back door without them even noticing me. I went past the dank lavatory and the chicken coop to the field. I trudged round the brambles until I got to the special magic place, and then I lay flat in the long grass, cradling my head with my arm.

'Dad!' I called urgently into the earth. 'Dad, are you there?'

I waited and waited. I heard little rustles around me in the grass. Perhaps rabbits were peeping out of their burrow and watching me. Rooks were cawing indignantly because I'd dared

invade their field. There were softer sounds of wood pigeons and blackbirds and maybe a skylark high above me, singing in the sky. Then at last there was a husky whisper in my ear.

I'm here, Phoebes. I'm always here for you.

'Oh, Dad, why didn't you take me with you to your island?'

I have to look after my girl. It's not safe for you here.

'Then it's not safe for you either, Dad! Come home! Please, please, just come home!' I begged.

I can't, my love. Not yet. Not for a while. One day.

'I can't manage without you any more, Dad! This is only the fourth day and yet it seems four *years* have gone by since I saw you! It's not fair! Becks has got Mum, and Perry doesn't seem to really need anybody, but I need *you*!'

I need you too, Phoebes. I think about you all the time. I talk to you in my head whenever I can.

'Are you very lonely, Dad?' I said. 'I've been reading about the real Robinson Crusoe on the Island of Despair and I can't bear it. It must be so awful for you. It's awful for *me* just imagining it.'

I'm so sorry. I don't want you to mind so much. Forget about your silly dad for a while. How's Daisy? Is she keeping you company?

'She is – she's adorable, the best guinea pig ever, but I worry about her too, because she's just stuck in her cage all the time, and yet I daren't let her out because she might run away,' I explained.

Dad was quiet for a while, and I thought he'd drifted away.

Have a good look at the chicken run.

He said it very softly. Perhaps it was my own thought. I couldn't quite tell the difference, but it didn't matter. The chicken run was a great idea!

'Thank you, Dad!' I said, in case he was still there, and then I scrambled to my feet.

I saw a flash of silver in the long grass. It was the snapped heel off Becks's shoe! I tunnelled my hand through the grass and grabbed it. Maybe she could stick it back on somehow. And if her shoe was here, maybe her phone was nearby too.

It took me twenty minutes of serious searching, scrambling around on my hands and knees, scratching myself on brambles and stinging myself in a nettle patch, but when I gave up and got to my feet I suddenly spotted a gleam of pink. Becks had customized her phone with candy-coloured beads. I darted forward and grasped it with a yell of triumph.

I went dashing back to the cottage. Becks was still with Mum, making a cheesy pasta bake for supper. I had to wait for ages till I could get her on her own, though I was absolutely bursting to produce her phone and heel from my jeans pocket. I went to examine the chicken run to distract myself. It had been a good idea, but there were holes in the wire netting and part of the wooden frame had rotted away. It definitely wasn't sound enough

to keep Daisy in and any foxes out. If only Dad were here he'd be able to fix it, no problem, but he *wasn't* here, and none of us would have a clue what to do.

I went to console Daisy, convinced now she was fretting for a little freedom. I made sure the bedroom door was tightly shut, lifted her out of her cage and then let her have a little run round on the floor. I was determined to keep an eye on her all the time, but she immediately darted under the bed, which made things difficult. I knelt down but couldn't see her. I called to her but she didn't come trotting up to me. She stayed resolutely hidden.

We were both going to get covered in fluff again. I lay flat on the floor and squirmed right under the bed until I felt Daisy's tiny feet pattering past my arm. I tried to stroke her, not wanting to grab hold of her in case I frightened her. This wasn't a great policy. Daisy played Hide and Seek with me for several minutes and then darted out again into the daylight. By the time I'd wriggled out myself she'd disappeared again.

I crept round the room looking for her, kicking my shoes off because I was terrified of stepping on her by accident. I couldn't see her anywhere. Then I heard Perry stomping along the landing, muttering train information to himself.

'Phoebe!' he said, and I heard him approach my door.

'Don't come in!' I said urgently.

'Why? What are you doing in there?' he said. He rattled the doorknob, giggling.

'Stop it!' I hissed. 'Daisy's got out! If you open the door she'll dash out and then I'll never, ever find her!'

'How did she get out?' Perry asked. 'Did she just burst out of her cage like SuperPig?'

'Well, obviously, *I* let her out, just for a little exercise—' I said.

'Well, if you let her out, you have to catch her,' said Perry, and walked off whistling.

I sighed. 'Daisy, please, please, come to me!' I begged her. I waited, crawling around on my hands and knees now, and eventually I heard more footsteps.

'Go *away*, Perry!' I said.

'I'm not Perry,' said Becks, opening the door before I could stop her.

'*Shut the door!*' I screeched.

Becks did so, but only after she'd come into the room.

'What on earth have you been doing? You've got grey fluff all over you!' she said.

'It's Daisy. I just let her out for a minute and now she's disappeared!' I wailed.

Becks sighed, rolling her eyes.

'There's no need to look like that. Especially as I've done you

a favour!' I said, feeling in my jeans pocket. I produced the silver heel with a flourish. 'I thought you could glue it back on,' I said.

'Oh, my heel! Clever you! But it's not really much use now. I think it will snap straight off the moment I start walking on it again,' said Becks. 'But thanks for finding it.'

'Want to thank me even more?' I said, fumbling in my other pocket. 'Ta-da!'

'Oh my God, you've found my phone!' Becks shrieked. She started tapping out her password. 'And it's still working!'

'But you still haven't got any signal, so I don't suppose it's much use either,' I said.

'Not here in the middle of nowhere! But there's a signal at the station! Oh, Phoebes, you're brilliant! Did you just spot it when you were in the field?' Becks asked, cradling her phone.

'No, I searched for ages and ages, and got all scratched getting it out of the brambles,' I said.

'Thanks sooo much!' said Becks. 'I am so in your debt!'

'Then help me find Daisy!' I said.

'What? Well, that's easy-peasy. She's in one of your shoes,' said Becks, laughing.

I looked – and saw that Daisy had climbed inside my right canvas boot and was nestling down as if she'd found the best bed in the world.

'Oh, how sweet! Just look at her, Becks! I think she's going to

sleep. I can't disturb her, can I? But I can't leave her in case she jumps out and gets lost all over again,' I said.

'Well, you can't just stand here dithering. Your pasta will be getting stone cold – *and* mine!' said Becks.

I ended up putting my boot inside the cage with Daisy still tucked up inside it.

'Well, where shall we go today?' Mum asked at breakfast the next morning.

'The railway!' we shouted in unison.

'We sound like a pantomime,' said Mum. 'Still, it suits me. I've got a few calls to make. I need to phone the office and catch up with what's happening – they'll have to send me so much work! Then I really should get in touch with your schools. Perhaps they'll want to send *you* some homework.'

'That's a very bad idea, Mum!' I said.

'We don't do much stuff the last two weeks of term anyway,' said Becks.

'And I'll probably know it all already,' said Perry. 'Plus going to the railway is *educational*! We're learning exactly how a steam engine works so it's physics. We can calculate how fast it can go

and how many tons of coal are required, so it's maths too. And the Primrose Railway has been so cleverly restored, it's a perfect example of an Edwardian station – so it's history. We can trace the track and take note of the terrain and so it's geography. We can look at all the flora and fauna on the way, so it's biology. Becks will flirt with the ticket collector and act silly, so it's drama. And I daresay Phoebe will start making up one of her soppy stories, and drawing lots of pictures, and the story will all be set in Edwardian times and so it's English and art too,' Perry gabbled, toast crumbs spraying out of his mouth.

'I don't act silly!' Becks said.

'And my stories aren't soppy!' I said. 'And how would you know anyway? They're totally private and I keep them locked up and hide the key!'

I obviously didn't hide them successfully. They weren't *totally* private, because I could never resist showing them to Dad. He always read every word straight away, and told me they were wonderful. He said I was a much better writer than him already. He gave Mum a couple of my best efforts. She read them suspiciously quickly.

'They're very imaginative, darling,' she'd said. 'And your spelling is very imaginative too. Don't they teach spelling at school nowadays?'

I'd woken up with an idea for a story that very morning. It just

happened to be set in Edwardian times too. Everything seemed so much nicer and safer then, according to the storybook world. Mothers and fathers stayed together and there weren't any worrying secrets and children didn't tease each other all the time. When there were iced buns for tea you could eat as many as you liked and no one said you were taking more than your fair share.

Mr Thomas Brown greeted us like an old friend, nodding and smiling.

'Well well, my favourite family!' he said.

'Good morning, Mr Thomas Brown. Where's your special train? And where are all the passengers this morning?' I asked.

'It's Monday, my dear, and the school holidays haven't started yet. We're a bit quiet during the week, and there's very few Pullman specials, but wait till the weekend! And after July we're chock-a-block. If you're still here then you'll have to book ahead and reserve your seats. That's if you're still keen to come. I expect you'll find trains boring by then,' he said, winking.

'As if!' said Perry, taking him seriously. 'Steam trains are my whole life now!'

'Well, I'm glad to hear it, son. I got hooked around your age and I've been obsessed ever since.' He ushered Perry and me into the waiting room – Becks didn't come with us; she was peering around, obviously hoping to catch sight of Jake. And Mum was

going into the Junction Cafe, her phone and charger at the ready. 'The history of the line is fascinating too. Look at this,' said Mr Thomas Brown.

There were enlarged black-and-white photos in frames all over the walls. They started with a blurry old picture of the railway station with bunting and flags and people cheering. The men all wore hats and the ladies long skirts. The boys' trousers looked very odd and the girls all had pinafores over their dresses.

'Opening day, 1906,' he said. 'Everyone had been waiting a long time for the railway to reach these parts. See how happy they all were!'

I peered at the photograph. There was one little boy with rather prominent eyebrows. He was grinning from ear to ear and waving a big flag in each hand.

'Was that you, Mr Thomas Brown?' I asked, pointing.

'Me? I might be very old, but I'm not *that* old, my dear! That photo was taken forty years before I was born!' he said, chuckling.

'Honestly, Phoebe!' said Perry.

'I just got a bit muddled, that's all,' I said, blushing.

Mr Thomas Brown showed us photos of the station in the 1920s. The men's hats were different and the ladies had surprisingly short skirts. The hats became trilbies and the skirts stretched to calf-length during the 1930s. The men wore army caps and the ladies knee-length skirts during the war years. There were no hats

at all during the 1950s, and the skirts were flared and puffy with petticoats. The last photograph was the saddest. There were no passers-by or potential passengers. A line of men in railway uniform stood sadly to attention outside the station, looking as if they were at a funeral.

'That was taken the day the Primrose Railway was closed down,' said Mr Thomas Brown, shaking his head. 'July the second, 1964, one of the worst days of my life. That Dr Beeching – the Chairman of British Railways – closed down thousands of stations and branch railways in the 1960s. *Thousands!* He closed this station and all the others on the line and left them to moulder!' He sighed. 'I *was* there then. See if you can pick me out, Phoebe.'

I glanced up and down the row of men in the black-and-white photograph. You couldn't see much of their faces underneath their peaked caps. I looked at the most senior upstanding man in the middle first, in the stationmaster's uniform – but the age wasn't right again. I looked at a tall young man at the end of the line, standing with his fists clenched. His cap was balanced at the back of his head, because he had an impressive quiff of hair flopping onto his forehead. His eyebrows were barely visible, but looked familiar.

'Is that you, Mr Thomas Brown?' I asked, pointing.

'It is, lass! Well done. Goodness knows why they let me get away with that ridiculous hairstyle! *I'd* have insisted I had a short

back and sides! I'd only been working a year or so, and I was younger than my Jake. I was proud as punch when I started working for the railway, determined to work my way up – and then they closed us down. After, I was always so sad when I passed the station and saw it getting more and more dilapidated, with grass growing over the tracks. The wood rotted, and some of the track disappeared altogether. There were no trains any more round these parts. All the steam engines were shunted off and forgotten about. End of an era. But *was* it?' Mr Thomas Brown paused theatrically.

Perry and I shook our heads.

'That's right! A group of us train enthusiasts got together in the 1980s and devised this plan to rescue the line and make it a working railway again. Folks thought we were off our rockers, of course, and I daresay we were, but we did it! It took us many years, and I can't tell you the number of setbacks we've suffered, but we got backing from the local businesses and now we're up and running again! We're all volunteers, most of us past retiring age, but this is the sort of work that goes on for ever.' Mr Thomas Brown's face shone with pride. 'It's the grandest job of all.'

'Good for you, Mr Thomas Brown!' I said.

Perry had been getting a little fidgety during his speech. He wasn't much interested in the history; he was far more concerned with facts and figures. He started talking about the different types of railway engines and their wheel formation, showing off his new

knowledge. I got bored and drifted off down the platform.

I suddenly spotted Jake coming out of the private staffroom. Becks was standing a little way along, peering around. He saw her. She saw him. He adjusted his cap self-consciously. She looked down at her feet, pretending she hadn't seen him. I heard him calling her name. She looked up, brushing her hair out of her face. She was trying to act cool, but she'd gone red. She's so lucky – when she blushes, she just turns a soft rose colour that makes her look even prettier. I've peered in the mirror when I'm blushing to see if *I* look prettier and I always look like a tomato.

Jake hurried towards her. She smiled nervously and started saying something. He interrupted, said something else. She laughed a little. He did too. Then he talked some more and she joined in. I went nearer, to see if I could catch what they were saying. They didn't seem to see me. The station could have caught on fire and they wouldn't have noticed.

It wasn't as if they were saying anything special. They both kept saying they were sorry, and I heard Becks telling Jake how she'd staggered about the field in one shoe and kept on falling over, turning it into a funny story, though she'd begged me never to tell him. She *didn't* tell him how old she was though, and he didn't tell her that he knew she was nowhere near sixteen. It didn't seem to matter anyway. They hardly knew each other and yet they already seemed to belong together.

I sighed and went to the cafe. There was very little chance of having another breakfast this morning but I just wanted to breathe in that lovely smell. Mo was behind the counter. She waved at me.

'Enjoying your holiday, lovie?' she said.

'You bet!' I said.

Mum was having a cup of coffee, peering at her plugged-in phone, nibbling at the knuckles on her left hand.

'Mum? Have you heard from Dad?' I asked, running to her table.

She jumped at the sound of my voice. 'What? Oh Phoebe, I've *told* you that your father can't contact us,' she snapped.

I didn't like the way she said *your father*. It was as if he wasn't also her husband. 'There's no need to bite my head off,' I said. 'I was just asking, that's all. You look worried.'

'Well, I can't seem to access my office emails. I don't know what's going on. I'll have to phone,' Mum said, sighing. She took a sip of coffee, and then sighed again. Tried another extension number. It went to voicemail – I could hear it. 'Oh, for goodness' sake!' She looked at her watch. 'Don't say they're *all* in a meeting?'

I was looking at Mum's watch too. 'Mum, we've got to get on our train. It's ten to eleven!'

'I know! But I've got to get this sorted out, darling. There are a hundred and one things I've got to arrange – and number one is access to my own wretched email account!'

'Can't you do all that while we're on the train?'

'No, I can't! It's too noisy to have a proper conversation, and the signal keeps fading,' said Mum.

'Well, you'll have to wait till we come back then. I'm sure it doesn't really matter,' I said.

'Of course it matters! I've got to find out what's going on!' Mum said furiously. She rang reception and asked to be put through to Geoff Campbell, the head of the company. She waited. And waited.

Perry and Mr Thomas Brown came into the cafe.

'Here's the boy wonder, raring to go on another train ride!' said Mr Thomas Brown.

'Quick, Mum!' Perry commanded.

'Oh, Perry!' Mum said. 'I'm so sorry, but I've got to get something sorted out first. We'll have to get the next train.'

'But we need to go on the eleven o'clock, like yesterday and the day before,' said Perry. He always likes to do things in a particular order. It upsets him terribly if he has to change his routine. His face set in a very familiar expression, his eyes screwed up, his jaw clenched.

'Oh, Perry, I'm so sorry,' Mum groaned. 'I know this is difficult for you, but we'll go on the next train, I promise.'

As Perry began to rev up, making a high-pitched groaning sound, Jake came into the cafe, Becks beside him, glowing.

'Two minutes to go! Please can you take your seats?' Jake said politely.

'What?' said Mum. She wasn't talking to Jake; she was talking to the receptionist. 'If he's not answering his phone, could you please go and find him? I need to speak to him urgently.'

Perry wrapped his arms round himself, and started shaking his head. Becks and I watched him anxiously.

'I can take Perry on the train, Mum,' Becks said quickly. 'You stay here and make all your calls. We'll come and find you when we get back.'

'Really? Are you sure you can cope?' Mum said.

'I'm so sorry, but no unaccompanied children under the age of sixteen are allowed on any of our trains,' said Mr Thomas Brown regretfully.

'So Rebecca's old enough,' said Jake, though he knew perfectly well now she wasn't. 'And I'll keep an eye on them, Grandad, so don't worry. We'd better hurry!'

He rounded us up. I waved goodbye to Mum and the three of us ran out of the cafe, along the platform, over the bridge and onto the train. Jake jumped on too. The whistle went and we were off.

Perry consulted his watch. 'Exactly on time, to the very second,' he said, in his normal voice.

I knew Perry couldn't *help* fussing about things and getting upset – but it was still so annoying that he always seemed to get his

own way! When I was little I often copied him, determined to get *my* own way, but it infuriated Mum. I suppose it must have been embarrassing having not one but *two* children kicking off in Waitrose or Wagamama, with Becks cringing in the background.

'Why can't you behave yourself like your sister?' Mum would hiss.

Even Dad got impatient with me sometimes, knowing I was doing it on purpose.

'Come on, Phoebes, stop that yelling. If you keep it up you'll get mistaken for a howler monkey and people will put you in a zoo,' he'd say. I suppose it was to make me laugh. It nearly always worked.

'Perry, can I ask you something?' I said, when he'd eventually settled on his carriage of choice, after charging up and down the train. Becks and Jake were out in the corridor, deep in conversation.

'Well, be quick, because I'm taking notes,' said Perry, whipping out his notebook.

'You know when you start to get upset, like just now, when you thought we weren't going to go on the eleven o'clock train?' I started.

'Yes,' said Perry warily. He absolutely hates any conversation like this.

'Well, what does it feel like inside your head?'

Perry thought for a moment. 'It feels hot and red like a fire,' he said. 'It hurts.'

'Like a headache?' I wondered.

'No. That's a different pain, caused by blood vessel spasms or dilation,' said Perry the Professor.

'Can you help it? Could you actually stop having a meltdown if you wanted?' I persisted, fiddling with the leather strap under the window to get it open.

'No, of course I can't help it. If I suddenly slammed that window down on your hand you couldn't help shrieking, could you?' said Perry. 'Now do shut up, Phoebes, I'm looking out for signals along the route.' He began to scribble in his notebook in his tight little backwards writing.

I was stuck with Perry most of the journey, while Becks and Jake stood gazing into each other's eyes in the corridor. Jake eventually had to justify his uniform by going up and down the train punching tickets. He grinned at me when he did mine.

'Thank you!' he murmured.

'Does this mean Becks is going to be climbing in and out of our bedroom window again?' I asked.

'No, absolutely not. I shall come and call for her properly, picking her up at the door,' said Jake.

'Well, it'll be a wasted journey, because Mum won't let her go out with you. She says she's too young to go out on proper dates,' I said.

'It's not a date. We're just going to hang out with some of my

friends,' said Jake.

'Then can I come too?' I asked.

'Well – maybe,' said Jake, taken aback.

'Thank you!' I said hurriedly. Becks would be furious when she found out. She was still in the corridor, peering out of the window, carefully posing with her selfie smile. I thought she looked an idiot, but Jake obviously thought her amazing.

I enjoyed the train ride even more this time, because it was starting to become familiar: the fields, the woods, the tunnel, Forest Lake station – and this time I caught a glimpse of blue through the trees. Then some little quaint cottages, some pink, some white, like marshmallows. Proper houses now, streets, shops, and then we were at Orlington.

Perry charged out of the train and dashed up to the engine. It was a different driver this time – one not quite so friendly as Alf – but Jake sweet-talked him into letting Perry climb up and ask a hundred and one questions. I stayed on the platform with Becks.

'Jake's asked me out again!' she said excitedly. 'They have this thing called Monday Funday at a club here in Orlington.'

'Oh, right,' I said, nodding. Maybe I didn't want to go to an actual *club*. I wasn't stupid. I was pretty certain a club wouldn't let me past the door. I wasn't even sure they'd let Becks in.

'Don't you have to be eighteen to go to a club?' I asked.

'It's for under-eighteens,' said Becks. 'But not for little kids.'

I smarted. 'I suppose you're going to get all dressed up again?'

'Maybe,' said Becks. 'Though Jake says it's very casual, so I'll probably wear jeans. I can't wait to see what *he* looks like out of that weird uniform. I'll take a selfie with him tonight. Wait till I send it to Jas and Emily! They'll be sooo jealous!'

I was actually so jealous too – jealous of how Becks still had her friends at home. I was pretty sure Amelie would be Kate's best friend for ever now I wasn't there.

I felt a bit glum on the train journey back. Becks was out in the corridor with Jake again, and Perry burbled train facts. The only one that stuck in my mind was that if you pulled the communication cord in the carriage it made a wheel go round in front of the guard and set a bell ringing to tell him it was an emergency.

I couldn't help eyeing that cord now, wondering if just one little tug would make the train screech to a halt. I wished there was an emergency cord for life itself, so that as soon as you felt something awful was about to happen you could pull it hard and stop it. Then maybe I'd have stopped Dad leaving us.

There seemed to be another emergency when we got back to the station. Mum was sitting at the corner table where we'd left her. She was staring into space, biting the corner of her lip, so her face looked lopsided. Her hair was unusually ruffled, as if she'd been running her hands through it.

'Mum?'

She jumped, blinking at me for a second as if she didn't even know who I was. Then she tried to force a smile. 'Hello, darling,' she said hoarsely. 'Did you have a nice trip? Where are the others?'

'Becks is saying goodbye to Jake and Perry is on his hands and knees peering at the wheels on the train,' I said. 'Mum, what's *wrong*? You look terrible!'

'Thank you for being so blunt,' said Mum. She fished a powder compact out of her bag and had a quick peer at herself. She started fussing with her hair.

'Not your hair, Mum, *you*! What's happened?'

'Keep your voice down!' said Mum, glancing over at Mo behind the counter.

'You *must* tell me, whatever it is, or I'll imagine it even worse!' I declared. 'It's Dad, isn't it?'

'No, it's not. I've told you, will you stop asking me all the time about your wretched father!' Mum hissed.

'Don't call him *wretched*. How dare you! That's horrid,' I said.

Mum was gathering up her things. 'Come along, Phoebe. You're making a spectacle of us. Outside, this minute!'

She took hold of me by the wrist and pulled me with her. On the platform, she

hurried up to Becks and Jake. 'Becks, we're going back to the cottage now. Where's Perry?' she asked.

'Up near the engine, bending down and peering,' said Becks, rolling her eyes.

'Well,' Mum said. 'We have to go. Phoebe, go and fetch Perry.'

'I wonder, Mrs Robinson. I'd love to take Rebecca to this little youth club tonight, so she can meet some of my friends,' Jake said to Mum politely.

'And me,' I said. 'You said you'd take me.'

Becks looked appalled.

'Certainly you could come too, though I think you'd probably find it a bit boring,' Jake said to me.

It was obvious he didn't want me to go either. I felt crushed.

'Well . . .' Mum said vaguely, barely concentrating. 'Phoebe, what did I just ask you to do? Get Perry!'

'Thanks, Mum!' said Becks, though Mum hadn't actually said she could go. 'I'll get Perry.'

She ran to fetch him. It didn't look like he was listening. Then he came over, looking mutinous.

'I want to stay! I want to have lunch here and then go for another ride!' Perry started wailing.

'Not today. I need to go home. I don't feel very well,' said Mum. She was very white, and there were little beads of sweat on her forehead.

'Shall I walk you to your car?' Jake offered his arm. 'And maybe I could drive you back if you feel dreadful? I'll go and tell Grandad.'

'Thank you, but I just feel a little faint, that's all. I'll be fine in a minute,' Mum muttered.

She was looking so ill that even Perry could see there was no point protesting any further.

'Take *my* arm, Mum,' he said.

'Well, I'll call for Rebecca around half seven then?' Jake persisted.

'I'm not sure, I'll have to think it over,' Mum murmured.

'Half past seven!' Becks said firmly, and she took hold of Mum's other arm, steering her. 'Come on, Mum. There's some water in the car – and mints. They'll make you feel better.'

'But come back and find me or Grandad if not,' said Jake.

'You're very kind,' Mum whispered.

She let Becks and Perry take her to the car, with me scurrying after them, wishing I could be useful in some way. When we were all in the car Mum suddenly put her head on the steering wheel.

'Mum?'

'Mum, what's up?'

'I think she's fainted!'

'No I haven't,' Mum said, her voice muffled. 'I just feel a bit woozy, that's all.'

'I'm going to fetch Jake,' said Becks.

'No! Don't! Oh God, this is so embarrassing. I'll be fine in a minute. I *am* fine,' Mum said determinedly. She sat up, sipped at some Evian water, and put a mint in her mouth. 'There!' she said. 'I feel much better already.'

She started the car and we set off – but halfway back, going up one of the hills, she suddenly drew in to the side of the road.

'Mum, you can't park here, it's not safe,' said Perry.

Mum took no notice. She put the brake on, undid her seat belt, opened her door, staggered out purposefully and was violently sick.

'Oh, poor Mum!' said Becks. 'Do you think it's something she's eaten?'

'It's weird to think we've got all that vomity stuff sloshing around inside our stomachs all the time,' I said, starting to feel sick myself.

'It's just partly digested food mixed up with acid,' said Perry.

'Shut up, you two ghouls,' said Becks. She grabbed the tissue box and water and got out of the car too. She helped Mum mop herself. Mum was crying. Becks put her arm round her, as if she was the mother.

Then they both got back in the car. Mum started up the car again and we drove off. She smelled a little bit but it would have been horrid to point this out. She didn't say anything and neither

did we. We parked by the telephone box and then Becks helped Mum through the trees, across the field, and into the cottage. Perry didn't offer his arm this time. He's as squeamish as me about sick, even though he tries to take a scientific approach.

When we got in Mum went upstairs to wash and change. She was gone a long while.

'I'd better see if she's all right,' said Becks. She came back almost immediately. 'She's lying on her bed, fast asleep,' she said.

'You're sure she's just asleep and not fainted?' I asked.

'Yes! It's probably some bug or something and she needs to sleep it off,' said Becks.

'So will she be able to take us back to the railway after lunch?' Perry asked. 'We could have toast and jam,' he added – but he'd finished the last of the bread at breakfast.

I inspected the contents of the cupboard. 'There's cornflakes and some chocolate. I could make chocolate crispy cakes!' I said, pleased with myself.

'*I'll* make a proper lunch,' said Becks, reaching over my shoulder for a packet of pasta.

She cooked it and served it with pesto. It was actually quite tasty, though I'd have preferred chocolate crispy cakes. But none of us ate with enthusiasm, worrying about Mum upstairs. What were we going to do if she was really ill?

It was a hot sunny afternoon but we didn't feel we could go out for a walk anywhere. We needed to keep an eye on Mum. Becks checked on her every so often. She'd woken up but said she had a splitting headache now and just wanted to stay in bed. Becks acted like a little nurse, closing the curtains to darken the room, bringing Mum water and paracetamol, even a cold flannel to put on her forehead. I heard Mum murmur that she was her lovely girl.

'I think she's got a migraine,' said Perry.

'What's that?' I asked anxiously.

'It's a sick headache – and she's been sick and her head aches.'

'Is it serious?' Becks asked.

'I don't think so. But it makes you feel awful at the time. Sometimes you get weird dazzling lights too,' said Perry.

'How do you *know* all this?' I said.

'One of the boys in my class has a mum who gets migraines. She couldn't come to the concert once,' said Perry.

'Our mum hardly ever came to concerts because she was always working late,' I said. 'But Dad came. Always.'

'Oh, do shut up, Phoebes. Mum couldn't help not coming. Mum's always been the main wage earner. And why would she suddenly get a migraine out of the blue?' Becks snapped. She sounded exactly *like* Mum now.

'You can sometimes trigger a migraine if you eat chocolate or spicy food,' said Perry.

'Mum doesn't ever eat chocolate,' said Becks. 'And we haven't had a spicy meal for ages.'

'Or it could be stress,' Perry added.

'Then that's it! Mum looked dreadful when we came back to the station, like she'd had the most awful news. It *might* be about Dad, you know,' I persisted.

But it turned out it wasn't about Dad at all. Mum came downstairs about five o'clock. She looked almost herself, though she was still very pale.

'I feel a lot better, darlings,' she said. 'I'm sorry to have been so pathetic.'

'You're not the slightest bit pathetic, Mum,' said Becks. 'Sit down. I'll make you a cup of tea.'

'Bless you, sweetheart,' said Mum.

'You're really all right, Mum?' I asked, still anxious that my wishing might have felled her. 'You promise you haven't had a stroke?'

'You and your morbid imagination, Phoebe!' said Mum.

'Becks thought that, not me!' I said.

'But it was a migraine, wasn't it, Mum?' said Perry.

'Yes, I think it was,' said Mum.

'Brought on by stress?' I said.

Mum sighed. 'Probably.'

'So what *was* it? You were in such a fuss when we got the train because you couldn't get into your email account. Wouldn't it work at all? Couldn't you get everything sorted out at your office?' I said.

'Phoebe, please! I've still got a bit of a headache. You're like a woodpecker going *tap-tap-tap* all the time,' said Mum.

'Only because you won't ever tell us stuff! That's why I imagine things worse than they are,' I said.

'All right! I'll tell you,' said Mum, her chin up. She sat down at the kitchen table. 'Just let me have my cup of tea first.'

Becks made us all tea, and we all sat, sipping, silent, waiting. I started to wish I hadn't badgered Mum so much. Did I really want to know? What if things really were worse than I feared? What if . . .

I found I had my hands over my ears. The tea was sour in my

mouth. I pulled a face. Becks gave me a nudge.

Mum took a deep breath. 'Well, if you must know, I've stopped working,' she said.

We stared at her. Mum always worked. She went to the office early and stayed late, often bringing work home. She was supposed to have the weekends off, but on Sundays she was usually busy catching up with manuscripts.

'You've stopped *working*, Mum?' I asked.

'You mean just for the summer, while we're here?' Becks said. 'Well, that's good. You always work so hard. It's about time you had a proper long holiday.'

'Did they make you redundant, Mum?' Perry said.

'Perry!' said Becks. 'Don't be silly. Mum's the boss of the whole department.'

'Well, I'm not the boss of the entire firm. And as a matter of fact, Perry's right. They've got rid of me,' said Mum. She said it very calmly, but her hands shook and she spilt some of her tea. She mopped at the little puddle with a tissue, her head bent.

'That's ridiculous, Mum!' said Becks. 'You're so well thought-of! You even won that publishing award. Why on earth would they do that? What are they thinking?'

'Surely they can't sack you just like that?' Perry said.

'Well, they're paying me till the end of the summer – but I can't go back, not even to collect my things,' said Mum. 'Lizzie –

my PA – has sent them to the house, but of course I'm not there. Maybe the delivery firm will leave them with Mrs Sutton.' She started running her hand through her hair and then stopped abruptly. 'I don't really care.'

'So what happens after the summer, Mum, when they've stopped paying you?' said Perry.

'Yes, what happens?' said Mum. 'I really don't know, Perry.'

'I do,' I said. 'Dad will come back by then, and his film will get edited and then it'll be on television, and he'll make lots of money for all of us. His Robinson programmes will all get shown again, and his books will come back into print, and he'll be even more famous than he used to be, you wait and see.'

'Yes. We'll wait and see,' said Mum, but with an edge to her voice, as if she thought it would never, ever happen in a million years. I didn't like the way she was looking at me. As if she was tempted to say something else.

'Well, never you mind, Mum,' Becks said quickly. 'You'll get another *better* job, easy-peasy.'

'I don't think so,' said Mum. 'Not in publishing.'

'You could start a whole new career,' said Becks.

'I've left it too late. I don't know about anything else, only books,' said Mum.

'*You* could write a book,' I said.

'Don't be silly, Phoebe,' Mum said.

'I'm not *being* silly! You know heaps and heaps about writing books, and you tell other people how to write them – you even told Dad how to write his Robinson books, so you could easily write one yourself,' I said. 'I could let you use my idea about an Edwardian family if you like. I've thought of all sorts of twists in the plot.'

'Oh, Phoebe!' said Mum, shaking her head, but she said it softly this time. Her eyes weren't properly focused, as if she were seriously thinking it over.

'Hey! That's a great idea, Phoebes!' said Becks. 'Mum, you're really good at making up stories! Remember those lovely stories you made up at bedtime when I was little.'

'That was Dad!' I said, thinking she'd got mixed up all of a sudden. 'It was Dad who always told us bedtime stories.'

'No, before that. Before you were born. And maybe even before Perry. I'm sure it was just Mum and me,' said Becks.

'That's right, darling. I managed to get home much earlier then – or maybe you went to bed later! Fancy you remembering. You were only about three or four,' said Mum.

'You made up stories about a green-eyed princess,' Becks said, smiling. *She* has green eyes. 'She was called Princess Emerald!'

'Oh, Mum, why didn't you ever make up a story about a brown-eyed princess for me?' I said.

'And what would she be called? Princess Mud? Princess Beer?

Princess Dungheap?' said Perry, and went into paroxysms of laughter at his own feeble jokes.

'Perry, stop the nonsense!' said Mum, but she was trying not to laugh.

'Shut up, Perry. Mum, please, write about a princess,' I said. 'One who can make wishes come true.'

'I'm not sure princess stories are very fashionable nowadays,' said Mum. 'But maybe I *will* try and write something!'

'Write about someone like me, Mum. A boy genius who knows absolutely everything about trains,' said Perry.

'A boy show-off!' I added.

'Will you really write a story, Mum?' Becks asked.

'I think I might. This summer, while I'm still getting paid. Starting tomorrow!' said Mum. Then she reached across the table and took hold of my hand. 'Thanks for the idea, Phoebe.'

That cheered me up a lot. And supper cheered me up even more. There was hardly anything left in the pantry.

'I could make more pasta – but actually I don't think there's enough to go round,' said Becks.

'Oh God, I was going to do a proper big shop! What sort of a mother am I?' said Mum.

'Let's get a takeaway,' I suggested, though I knew Mum didn't approve of that sort of food.

'I don't think there's anywhere to get a takeaway *from*,' said

Mum. 'And how can we call one when we haven't got a signal?'

'We could go out in the car looking for an Indian restaurant or a pizza place,' Perry said.

'I'm not sure there is one anywhere round here – and I'm not sure I could sit in one anyway. I still feel a bit queasy. What are we going to do?'

Dad's never, ever forgotten to get food for us! I yelled it inside my head but knew I couldn't say it, not with Mum so pale and upset already.

Then, as if by magic, there was a knock at the back door.

'Cooeee! It's only me!' Mo put her head round the door. 'There you are!' she said to Mum. 'How are you feeling? You

didn't look too clever when you were at the Junction, and young Jake said you were a bit wobbly walking to the car. I just thought I'd check up on you.'

'It's very kind of you, but I'm fine now,' Mum murmured.

'You're still white as a sheet, dear. I've made you a flask of my chicken soup. It always works wonders if any of my family feel dicky. And here's a fish pie out of my freezer, nicely defrosted now, for the kiddies, and some of my chocolate brownies for their pud, in case you didn't feel up to cooking,' said Mo, putting them all down on the table.

'How lovely,' said Mum. She paused. 'Would you like to join us?'

'Bless you, dear, I've got to cook for my lot now. Thanks for asking though. Take care now! Bye-eee!' She vanished out of the door, just like a fairy godmother.

'Oh, wow!' I said, having the tiniest nibble of one of the chocolate brownies. 'This is delicious!'

'The chocolate brownies won't give you another migraine, will they, Mum?' Perry asked.

'Bless you, darling. I don't think so. But you three share them out between you – *after* the fish pie. I'll try a little of her soup. It's incredibly kind of her.'

'Are you and Mo friends now?' I asked.

'Well. I'm very grateful to her,' said Mum, putting the fish pie in the oven to warm through.

It was delicious – actually even better than Dad's, though I didn't like to admit it. The brownies were marvellous. Mum finished up every spoonful of her soup.

'Is it good, Mum?' Perry asked. 'Do you feel less dicky now?'

'It's very good – only I'd sooner you didn't say dicky, darling.'

'Is it a swear word?'

'No, it's just . . .'

'An icky word,' I said, giggling. 'Icky dicky! Oh, I do hope Mo gives us some more of her food while we're staying here!'

'Let's hope we won't ever need it. There must be a farmer's shop round here somewhere, so we can get some really good fruit and vegetables, and I'm going to make sure I do a regular big shop at the supermarket,' Mum said firmly.

'While we're on the railway,' said Perry. 'All day long.'

'For one return trip. Then you'd better have a really long walk for a bit of exercise,' said Mum.

'Can we walk beside the track?' Perry asked.

'Maybe. As long as it's not *on* the track. I don't want the three of you getting squished by a train,' said Mum. 'Becks, where are you off to?'

'I'm just going to get ready,' she said.

'What for?'

'Oh, Mum! Jake's coming to take me to the club,' said Becks. 'Remember?'

'Vaguely. But I didn't say yes. I'm not really happy about you going off on your own with Jake. He seems very sweet, but we don't really know him,' said Mum.

'Well, I do! We've talked and talked and talked,' said Becks.

'And we know his grandfather ever so well too,' I said. 'You can't possibly object to Mr Thomas Brown's own grandson!'

'I'm sure they're a lovely family, but Becks is too young to go out to a club,' said Mum.

'It's not that sort of club, Mum. It's like a youth club, you know, table tennis and all that stuff,' said Becks. 'And it's not a *date* sort of thing; I'm just going to meet his friends.'

'And I could go too, so I can be there to keep an eye on her,' I said.

Mum and Becks agreed that this was a ridiculous idea, and they wouldn't let me go too, even though I begged and begged. I tried to get Perry to join in too, but he shuddered at the thought of table tennis.

'But I can go, Mum, can't I?' Becks said, smiling at Mum. 'You did *say* I could!' Her green eyes were big and pleading. She was even fluttering her long eyelashes.

'I suppose so,' said Mum.

'Thank you so, so much, loveliest mum in the world,' said Becks, and she rushed upstairs to get changed.

She didn't wear Saturday's tiny top and shorts. She wore her

best jeans and a pink T-shirt. She'd outlined her eyes so they looked bigger and greener than ever. She'd styled her hair artfully into long loose curls. She looked really pretty.

Jake knocked at the door at exactly half past seven. He was carrying a hurricane lamp in either hand, one for him, one for Becks. He looked different out of his Primrose railway uniform. His hair was longer than I'd expected, and flopped forward in an endearing manner. He wore jeans and a T-shirt too, and bright white trainers that looked brand new.

He looked dazzled when he saw Becks, but he waved at Perry and me too, and shook hands with Mum.

'I do hope you're feeling better now, Mrs Robinson. And I hope it's still OK for Rebecca to come to the youth club with me? What time would you like her to be back?' he asked.

How could Mum resist him? They set off together. Mum stayed at the back door, watching them. I went to join her. It was still light, so they didn't really need the hurricane lamps crossing the field – but we saw Jake light them as they went into the wood.

'Well, he really does seem a nice caring sort of boy,' said Mum. She sighed and murmured, 'I do hope she'll be all right.'

'Of course she will,' I said.

'You'll be going out with boys too before I know it!' said Mum.

'No I won't,' I said fiercely, but I was secretly pleased.

'I'm not ever going out with anyone, boys or girls,' said Perry behind us. 'Too much hassle.'

We had quite a peaceful evening, the three of us. Perry made notes in his railway book. Mum started making notes herself, gazing into space a lot of the time, sometimes biting her lip, often sighing. She was clearly trying to get ideas for her story. She kept making herself cups of coffee, and even nibbled a corner of a chocolate brownie. She let me eat the rest of it for her.

I wrote and wrote in my own notebook. It was a bright red one that Dad had bought me a while ago. It had several babyish poems and an old story that meandered along for ten or twelve pages, my writing getting bigger and bigger as I ran out of ideas. I wondered about tearing all the used part out as it was annoying me, but the notebook might disintegrate altogether. I just left several blank pages and then started making notes about my Edwardian story.

It would be about a father and a mother and three children. The father was wonderfully distinguished and charming and talented. He wrote the most amazing books. The mother didn't go out to work, because ladies didn't in those days. She had servants to look after the house, and a nanny to look after the children. The nanny loved all the children, but the youngest, Philomena, was quite definitely her favourite. Her older sister, Rowena, was a kind enough girl, but rather plain. Her older brother, Peregrine, tried hard at lessons, but he wasn't very clever. Philomena was

breathtakingly beautiful and brilliant at her schoolwork. She was also incredibly talented, especially at art. Several of her paintings already hung in the National Gallery, but she was a very modest girl and never showed off about it.

I drew the whole family on a blank page. I spent a long time on Philomena, because I wanted her to look just right. She had long wavy hair all the way to her waist, and the biggest eyes ever.

The family lived in a big house in London at the start of the story, but then they moved to a remote part of the country. They lived in a mansion in the middle of a field.

The opening of a railway station was going to be a major part of my story. The entire family would be special guests of the railway company, sitting in style in a Pullman carriage for the very first journey. I started to draw a big picture of the grand event. I could illustrate Philomena and her family easily enough, and I could just about draw a station, with bunting, but I really needed to attempt the train too, and I wasn't very good at drawing trains.

I borrowed one of Perry's railway books and tried to copy from a photograph of a Pullman train but found it very difficult. I drew it much too small at first, so the family would have to crouch in their carriage with their heads pressed against the ceiling. I tried again, drawing a train that filled the entire page, but the only way I could include Philomena and all her family (plus the

servants too, because I didn't want them to miss out on the celebrations) was to make them all little mouse-people, which looked ridiculous.

'Good heavens, Phoebe, you've written lots and done some wonderful drawings!' said Mum. 'I haven't even got my main idea or characters yet. Maybe you'll be the one to produce a wonderful picture book and get it published and make our fortune.'

For one glorious second I thought she was being serious. Then I realized she was joking.

'Ha ha,' I said dryly.

'I wish you two would pipe down,' said Perry. 'I'm trying to concentrate and the print is very small and I can hardly see it.' He was squinting in the dim light, his eyes screwed up.

'Wear your glasses then,' I said.

'I told you, I'm experimenting without them. There's a theory that glasses make your eyes weaker,' said Perry.

'I think you don't like wearing them because that horrid boy in your class called you Specky at school,' I said. 'I've been called far worse,' I added.

'What do they call you?' Mum asked indignantly.

'One of the boys in my class called me Fatty Bum-bum,' I said.

Perry snorted with laughter.

'You shut up! I don't laugh when people call *you* names!' I said.

'Yes, don't be so infantile, Perry,' said Mum, taking my side. 'It's very rude and hurtful to make unkind comments about people's appearances. I'll have a word with your teacher!' Then she paused. 'Well, I would have done, but I suppose there's no point now you've left Blatchford.'

'What do you mean, "left"?' I said. 'This is just an extra little summer holiday, isn't it? I will be going back in September, won't I?'

'Perhaps. I'm not sure yet. We'll just have to wait and see,' said Mum.

'Wait and see what?' Perry demanded. 'I'm starting at the Manor school in September, aren't I? I have to!'

It was a very academic private secondary school, especially good at teaching maths and science. Perry had sat their entrance exam and been awarded a special scholarship. Mum had been so thrilled she burst into tears when she heard.

'Yes, of course you are, Perry,' she said quickly, but she didn't sound certain. 'Or you might get a scholarship to an even better school somewhere,' she added.

'There isn't a better school – everyone says so,' said Perry, starting to get worked up. 'I'm the first boy at Blatchford to get in there.'

'I think it's time to end your glasses experiment anyway, Perry,' said Mum. 'You're getting permanent little frown lines on your forehead.'

'They're just there because I think such a lot,' said Perry. 'And my glasses are pretty useless, seriously. They make everything look blurry.'

'That's possibly because they need a jolly good clean,' said Mum. 'Anyway, it's time to put those railway books away and go up to bed. Are you *sure* you still want to sleep in that funny little cupboard? It must be so uncomfortable.'

'I like it there. It's so dark it makes me feel safe,' said Perry.

Mum looked stricken. 'Don't you always feel safe then, Perry?' she asked.

'No,' said Perry.

'What is it that's worrying you, darling?'

Perry shrugged. He wouldn't say.

'I expect it's Dad not being here,' I said for him. 'It worries me. Dreadfully.'

'Well, I daresay it does, but there's nothing I can do about it,' said Mum. 'Now, up to bed, both of you.' She looked anxiously at her watch. It was gone ten o'clock and Jake had promised to bring Becks back by half past ten, but I wasn't sure he would. Mum didn't look sure either.

I went up to bed with Perry. When I went to the bathroom I

bumped into Perry on the landing, in his pyjamas. I held up my torch. His frown was making his whole forehead wrinkle.

'It *is* Dad, isn't it?' I said softly. 'It's so weird him not being here. Are you missing him terribly too?'

Perry didn't answer but his eyes screwed up even more. I wished I could put my arm round him but he would only shy away.

'Night, Perry,' I said instead. 'Sleep well.'

He nodded and went into his cupboard. I wondered if he went to sleep straight away or whether he lay awake for ages, staring into the pitch darkness.

I was still wide awake myself when I heard the back door opening downstairs. I peered at my old alarm clock. It was half past ten exactly! Mum would be so relieved. I heard the murmur of voices for five minutes or so, and then the sound of the door again. I ran to the window – and there was Jake below me, a little ghostly as he held his hurricane lamp high. I watched him walk past the chicken coop and out into the field.

Becks came into the bedroom and stood beside me at the window.

'Ah!' she said. 'Doesn't Jake look sweet, trudging along in the dark. Oh, Phoebe, he's so lovely.'

'So you had a great time then?'

'Yes. Well. Sort of,' she said.

'Only sort of?'

'It turns out this Monday club of his really *is* a youth club. It's in a church hall and it's actually got table tennis, just like I said, only I was just making it up. We were practically the oldest ones there. Still, it didn't really matter, because Jake's such fun to be with. Ever so popular with everyone too. A lot of the girls clearly fancy him. There's this one girl, Yvonne, who kept looking daggers at me.'

'I think she's Mo's daughter. What was she like?' I asked.

'Oh, quite pretty, I suppose,' said Becks, a little smugly, because this Yvonne obviously wasn't as pretty as Becks herself. 'She wears an awful lot of make-up.'

'So do you!' I said.

'Yes, but I go for a more natural look,' said Becks.

'So I guess you didn't make friends with her?'

'She didn't want to be friends. Jake introduced me to some of the people there, but we didn't really mix much with them. It was mostly just him and me.' She sighed. 'I really, really like him, Phoebes.'

'So what did you do all evening? Did you actually play table tennis?'

'We did for a bit. I was rubbish at it at first, but then I got better. Not as good as Jake though. And then we had these refreshments – sandwiches and biscuits, plus cans of Coke – no alcohol! Then there was this disco type thing, and some of the

girls danced together. There weren't many boys there, and they didn't seem interested in dancing anyway,' Becks said.

'Did you and Jake dance?'

'Yes, we did – and he's great at dancing, thank God. Everyone was watching us,' said Becks proudly. 'I could have danced all night – ha, like that old song!'

'But you must have left early to get back here dead on time,' I said.

'Well, the club closed at ten, actually. Ten! I thought Jake would suggest we go for a proper drink in a pub somewhere, but he insisted we drive back so we wouldn't be late,' said Becks.

'He *is* lovely,' I said.

'Well. Almost too lovely, actually. He was so . . . considerate. Kind of gentlemanly,' said Becks, wrinkling her nose.

'Did he kiss you goodnight?'

'Yes, he did, but it was a very *polite* kiss on the cheek,' said Becks. 'He was treating me as if I'm so young and innocent.'

'Well, you are, aren't you?'

'Yes, but he doesn't *know* that. He thinks I'm sixteen,' said Becks.

'Mm. He might have guessed you're younger,' I said, trying to sound casual. Not casual enough.

'Oh God, you didn't tell him, did you?' Becks said, seizing me by the shoulders. 'You *did*! You sneaky pig!' But she wasn't really

angry. In fact, she started laughing. 'I get it now! And yet he still wants to go out with me! He asked if he could take me out for a meal sometime this week, and Mum's said yes! Oh, Phoebe, I'm so happy.' Becks let me go and started dancing round the room. 'Happy, happy, happy!'

'How can you possibly be happy when Dad is away and we don't even know where he is?' I said sourly.

'Look, you're not the only one who's worried about Dad – but there's nothing we can do about it, so we might as well be happy while we can,' said Becks.

I wondered if she was right. I didn't think so. I couldn't imagine ever being properly happy until Dad was back, safe and sound.

I still thought about Dad constantly. I pored over the pictures in *Robinson Crusoe* and imagined Dad with a long beard and strange clothes of fur, though I knew he'd hardly had time to grow stubble, and his own jumper and jeans would still be perfectly wearable. I saw Dad fishing in the shallows, picking fruit, even hunting for a wild pig. I could see him cooking on a camp fire, and sleeping in a wooden hut. He filmed himself and then etched a cross on his home-made wall, marking off each day. He woke early every morning and lay on the sandy beach and called to me. And each morning I woke up early too and ran out into the field and called back to him, though it was a struggle making my way through the long grass because it was growing so fast.

All my T-shirts had grass stains now, even my special Manchester United one, though Mum scrubbed them hard.

'Have you been playing roly-poly in the grass, young Phoebe?' Mr Thomas Brown asked, on our daily visit to the station.

'She goes to the field before breakfast and then she just lies there for ages,' said Perry. 'I spy on her sometimes.'

'That's not a very gentlemanly thing to do, spying on your sister,' said Mr Thomas Brown.

'That's typical Perry,' I said. I nodded over at Jake and Becks, who were standing by the excursion Pullman, chatting to each other. 'My sister says your Jake is very gentlemanly, Mr Thomas Brown.'

'I'm pleased to hear it,' he said. 'He's a good lad, our Jake. He and Rebecca seem very smitten, don't they?'

Perry wrinkled up his nose. 'They're all lovey-dovey. Yuck!' he declared, and dashed off to see Alf and Ann.

We already knew everybody who worked at the station, and they greeted us like old friends. Most of the men seemed especially pleased to see Perry. Mum tried to keep an eye on him, but without much success. Apart from when she went shopping, she stayed having endless coffees in the Junction Cafe while she made phone calls, sent emails and worked on her children's book. When it was Mo's shift they often just sat chatting together. They seemed good friends now, even though Mum had been so frosty at first.

Mr Thomas Brown was *my* friend, and we had our little chats together too.

'So what are you up to when you're lying in the field, Phoebe, apart from mucking up all your T-shirts?' he asked. 'Are you rabbit spotting? Peering at all the insect life? Or simply daydreaming?'

I wriggled, wondering what to tell him. I found myself suddenly blurting out the truth. 'I'm talking to my dad,' I said.

Mr Thomas Brown looked puzzled. 'On your mum's mobile?' he said. 'Can you get any signal out in that field?'

'No. I don't mean *really* talking to him,' I said. 'Though it feels real. Well, it *is*. He talks back to me.' I felt myself blushing. 'I know it sounds impossible, but I truly hear him if I listen hard enough.'

'Oh, I get you now,' said Mr Thomas Brown, patting my shoulder. 'I still sometimes have a little chat with Alice. She was my Mrs Brown, but she passed away five years ago. She tells me to make myself a proper tea and she reminds me I'll need to iron a clean shirt for the morning and she often watches telly with me. Tells me I'm watching a load of rubbish sometimes!'

'My dad hasn't passed away, Mr Thomas Brown!' I lowered my voice. 'He's just not able to be with us. He's on this island, see, but it's a secret.'

'Ah!' said Mr Thomas Brown. I don't think he *did* see, but he nodded all the same.

'I hear Dad best if I lie flat on the ground, only you can barely *see* the ground now because the grass is getting so long. Well, it's

not really *grass* grass, the sort you get in parks. It's got all kinds of other stuff mixed up in it, wild stuff that reaches right up past my knees. It's getting hard to wade through it, and I can't watch out for all the anthills and rabbit burrows,' I said, sighing.

'Isn't there a path all the way round the edge of the field?' he asked.

'Yes, but my special place is right in the middle,' I said.

'Oh, I see,' said Mr Thomas Brown. 'Well, that won't do. You'll put your foot in a burrow and break your ankle if you don't watch out. Perhaps I'd better come out to this field and make you a little path to the middle of the field.'

'Could you really do that? I think the grass is much too long for a lawn mower,' I said.

'I have my ways and means,' said Mr Thomas Brown, winking.

His ways and means proved to be a large strimmer machine, fully charged up, with a spare battery. He brought it with him late that afternoon, when the station closed.

Mum was taken aback, as I hadn't told her about our conversation. I got tremendously worried she might tell him to go away, because she hates it if she thinks we've been pestering anyone to do us a favour.

'I didn't ask Mr Thomas Brown, honestly!' I said hurriedly.

'Young Phoebe here was telling me she likes to play in the very

middle of the field, so I thought I'd strim her a special secret path,' he said.

'Well, it's very kind of you, Mr Brown,' said Mum. 'I feel so embarrassed. You're always so good with the children at the station – and now you're even giving up your spare time to help us out!'

'It's a pleasure, Mrs Robinson. I've got very fond of your children. This is just like the old days. I used to pop round here donkey's years ago and do odd jobs for Miss Cresswell. I like it when I can make myself useful,' he said. 'Right then. You come with me, Phoebe, and show me just where you'd like this little path.'

'Could you make me a path too, Mr Thomas Brown?' Perry asked.

'We can't have too many paths, Perry, or it'll look like a giant's scribbled all over the field. But tell you what – *you* can help me with the strimming, seeing as you're such a sensible lad.' He nodded at Mum. 'Don't worry, I'll bring him back with the same number of hands and feet.'

We went out into the field together, Mr Thomas Brown, Perry and me. I pointed out my special place, and by the time we came back to the cottage there was a little path all the way to the middle of the field, only you couldn't see where it was because the grass was so tall.

'It's secret!' I said happily. 'Just for me!'

Mrs Alice Brown didn't have to tell her husband what to eat

that evening. He had spaghetti Bolognese with us and then strawberries and cream for pudding. He finished up every mouthful, and then gave a great sigh.

'That was the best supper I've had in years,' he said. 'Thank you very much indeed, Mrs Robinson.'

'Thank *you*, Mr Brown,' said Mum. 'You've been so lovely to the children.'

'You're like family, Mr Thomas Brown,' I said. He was like a *grandad*.

I got up very early the next morning and went straight to the field, when the clouds were still tinted pink by the sunrise. The feathery tips of the grass wavered in the breeze. I couldn't see a trace of the new path until I was actually standing at its start. I skipped along it, butterflies dancing ahead of me, a little grey rabbit suddenly scooting across the new track.

I got to the secret place and lay down in delight. The grass was wet with dew and I could feel damp seeping through my T-shirt and shorts, but I didn't care.

'Are you there, Dad?' I whispered into the earth. 'Or are you still asleep? It's a lovely morning here. My friend Mr Thomas Brown has made me a special secret path and I can get to you so easily now. I wish I could *really* get to you. I'd give anything in the world to give you the biggest hug ever!'

And I'd give you the biggest hug back, my best-ever girl.

'Oh, Dad, you *are* there! It's so wonderful to hear you. Perry made the path with Mr Thomas Brown. Well, he held the strimmer sometimes, but Mr Thomas Brown held it too and guided it for him. Anyway, if Perry comes will you talk to him too? I think he's missing you heaps.'

I waited for Dad's reply. I wanted him to say yes, because I was pretty sure it would mean a great deal to Perry. But I also wanted him to say no, because I wanted this secret place to be just for us, Dad and me. Dad seemed to be in agreement.

I'll find another way to talk to Perry – and Becks too.

It was a perfect answer. When I got back indoors I wondered if I should have mentioned Mum as well, but perhaps they were already secretly talking. I still couldn't make Mum out. What did she mean, '*Your* wretched *father*'?

It was so early that Mum was still fast asleep when I opened her bedroom door and peered inside. I wanted to see if she was hugging Dad's jumper again, but I couldn't see it. Mum lay on her back, snoring very softly – but then she started and gave a little moan. She seemed to be having a bad dream. Her face was all contorted now. She turned on her side, one hand over her head as if she were protecting herself.

'Mum?' I whispered, going to her bed. 'Mum, are you all right?'

Mum opened her eyes and blinked at me. 'Phoebe? What is it? Have you had a bad dream?' she asked.

'No, I think you're the one having a weird dream. Oh, Mum, you scared me!'

'What? Don't be silly, darling. Go back to bed now, it's still very early,' she murmured, and then went straight back to sleep.

I waited for a couple of minutes but she seemed peaceful now. I was shivering, so I got back into bed with Becks to warm up.

'Phoebe, you're icy cold!' Becks protested. 'And *soaking*! Oh my God, you haven't wet yourself, have you?'

'No I haven't! I'm not a baby! I'm just a bit damp because I've been in the field,' I explained.

'You and your field,' said Becks, sounding exasperated, but she put her arm round me.

'Mr Thomas Brown's made me such a lovely path,' I said.

'He's very kind,' Becks agreed.

'He's like our grandad,' I said.

'Well, thank goodness he isn't a real grandad,' said Becks. 'Because Jake is his grandson, and that would mean Jake and I would be cousins, or even brother and sister, and that would be awful because we couldn't go out together.'

'Are you two boyfriend and girlfriend now?' I asked.

'I suppose,' said Becks.

I couldn't see her face but I could tell she was smiling.

'Did you like it when he kissed you?'

'Of course I did,' said Becks, giggling.

I decided to inject a little romance into my Edwardian story. I'd have my oldest girl Rowena meeting a young man and falling in love. When I was warmed up and Becks had gone back to sleep I got out of bed again, found my notebook and pen, and started scribbling away. I felt that Edwardian teenagers wouldn't just meet casually and hook up, so I had to find a way of bringing them together.

Daisy squeaked in her cage, reminding me that it was nearly her breakfast time.

'Aha! Thank you, Daisy!' I said. I whizzed downstairs, chopped up a little kale and broccoli and carrot, sprinkled with her special guinea-pig nuggets, and gave them to her. Then I jumped back into bed and wrote several pages about Rowena's new brown-and-white puppy, Daisy, and how she slipped her lead when she took her for a walk in the park, and a kind young man caught hold of her – the puppy, not Rowena – and so they became friends. I drew a picture of the puppy in the margin.

I was very pleased with myself by the time I went back downstairs for my own breakfast. 'I've done three and a half more pages of my story this morning,' I told Mum proudly. '*And* an illustration. How's your own story getting on?'

'Not very well,' said Mum, busy making toast.

'I seem to make things up, just like that,' I said. 'I think I must take after Dad.'

'Don't say that,' Mum said quickly, and then bit her lip.

'Why? I want to take after Dad!'

'I just meant it's better to be yourself,' said Mum.

'But I don't really like being myself,' I said.

Mum sighed. 'Don't be silly,' she said. 'Call Becks and Perry and tell them breakfast's nearly ready. Dear goodness, we've nearly finished the strawberry jam already. Perry must be eating it by the spoonful.'

I'd actually been sticking my finger in the jam every now and then for a secret treat, so I was happy to drop the argument and go to fetch my brother and sister.

Perry was scrunched up in his dark cupboard, reading his train books by torchlight.

'Perry, do you like being yourself?' I asked him.

He wrinkled up his nose. 'What?'

'Do you like being Perry? Or would you like to be some other boy entirely? Or a girl? Or would you like to be a dog, say, or a jungle king like a lion?' I persisted.

'I'd like to be me, but without a pesky little sister asking stupid questions,' said Perry.

Mr Thomas Brown nodded and winked as normal when we got to the railway station, but when Perry ran off to bombard Alf with further questions and Becks was chatting to Jake and Mum was in

the Junction Cafe ordering her first coffee from Mo, he turned to me.

'Have you been to the field this morning, pet?' he asked.

'Yes, I have! It was wonderful running along the secret path. I'm so pleased with it, Mr Thomas Brown. You're ever so kind,' I said.

'Nonsense, nonsense. I like doing a spot of strimming.' He paused, then lowered his voice. 'Did you manage to have a little chat with your dad?'

'I did!'

'There now. I'm so pleased,' said Mr Thomas Brown. 'Now listen, young Phoebe. I couldn't help being a bit taken aback about the state of the grounds. It's all gone to rack and ruin. I wonder, do you think your mum would mind if I came round occasionally and did a bit of tidying up? Mo keeps the house relatively shipshape, but you'd never call her a gardener. I know you're only renting the place for the summer, but it's not too late to plant a few flowers and get some veg started.'

'I think Mum would be thrilled,' I said. 'I know I would. And this is an awful cheek, but do you think you could possibly mend the chicken run? It's all falling to bits at the moment.'

'Are you planning to keep chickens then?' Mr Thomas Brown asked, looking amused.

'Not really,' I said. I wasn't too keen on chickens. I didn't like

the look of their beady eyes and their fierce beaks. 'Actually, I was thinking of Daisy, my guinea pig. I worry she's a bit cramped in her cage. I think she'd love to have a little run in the grass.'

'Excellent idea!' said Mr Thomas Brown.

He had a word with Mum. She fussed at first, saying that he was too kind, and we mustn't take advantage. Honestly, why on earth couldn't she say *Yes please!* straight away? But eventually she gave in and Mr Thomas Brown came round to our cottage a few days later, with some wood and chicken wire and his tool kit. Jake came too, but he wasn't much use, because he sloped off to talk to Becks.

'Love's young dream,' Mr Thomas Brown said, when Mum brought him a cup of tea.

'Rebecca's rather young for boyfriends,' Mum replied, frowning. 'There's nearly four years' age difference between her and Jake. Don't you think they're seeing rather too much of each other?'

'I'm sure it's all very innocent,' said Mr Thomas Brown. 'You've no need to feel anxious about my Jake. He's a lovely gentle lad.'

'I daresay he is – but Rebecca's only fourteen, Mr Brown. She should be concentrating on her schoolwork,' said Mum.

'Oh, Mum, how can you say that! You've taken us all *out* of school!' I said.

Mum flushed. 'That's enough, Phoebe,' she said, in a tone that meant she was going to give me a right telling-off later on.

She went back indoors.

'I wish Mum wasn't so stuck up and strict,' I mumbled.

'Now now,' said Mr Thomas Brown. 'Don't take that tone about your mother. She means well. All mothers worry about their daughters. She'll be just as protective of you when you're a bit older and wanting to go out with boys.'

'That's never going to happen,' I said firmly.

'You're a character, young Phoebe. I think you'll change your mind. Though maybe not. Nina Cresswell was perfectly happy being single. She could be sociable, mind. When she was young she used to give these parties for all her friends from London – one party lasted all night and the next day too, with music and all kinds of dancing and fireworks. It was the talk of the village for weeks!' He shook his head wistfully. 'She really could give a good party.'

'Did you go to them, Mr Thomas Brown?' I asked eagerly.

'Me? No! She did invite me once, though. She knew I liked a dance.' He stopped hammering nails and gazed straight ahead, remembering.

'So why didn't you go?' I asked.

'I'd have been a fish out of water with all those arty types. I didn't want to seem a total country bumpkin. Mind you, I was considered a sharp dresser in those days. It sounds as if I'm

boasting, but I could have had the pick of the girls round here,' said Mr Thomas Brown proudly.

'Like Jake?'

'I suppose so! Looks like he's really fallen for your sister. But your mother's right, they're very young,' he said.

'How old were you when you went out with your Alice?'

'Well, I suppose I was Jake's age. Maybe even younger,' he said, shaking his head. 'But it was different then. I left school at fifteen, mind, to do an apprenticeship.'

'And she was *your* true love,' I said.

'Yes, it turned out she was. Though I didn't deserve her,' he said, tutting at himself. 'Right then! Let's get this chicken run properly sorted. Guinea-pig run, I should say.'

Perry had been wandering up and down with a train book, testing himself on all the different types of locomotive. Now Mr Thomas Brown was concentrating on work, Perry became very interested. Mr Thomas Brown showed him what to do, and even let him have a go at hammering.

'Though watch what you're doing, lad, or I'll be in deep trouble with your mum,' he said.

Perry bent a couple of nails at first, but soon got the hang of it. He helped Mr Thomas Brown fix the chicken wire into place, and they rehung the door together so it clicked shut in a safe and satisfactory manner.

'There! I've made a chicken run!' Perry said proudly. 'We could build all sorts of things together, couldn't we, Mr Thomas Brown? Maybe even a little shed? It could be my den, couldn't it?'

'It could indeed, lad. And what about you, Phoebe? Do you fancy a playhouse?'

I'd always adored the playhouse in Reception class, but I felt I was really too old for one now. 'Perhaps I could have a little shed too, where I can write and draw?' I suggested.

'Perhaps you could!' said Mr Thomas Brown. 'Well, we'll have to see what your mum says.' He checked the chicken run carefully. 'We've done a good job, Perry. Little Daisy should be safe in here. Don't leave her out at night though, Phoebe. You never know what those pesky foxes can get up to. Tuck her up in her cage safe and sound.'

'Shall I run and fetch her now?' I asked eagerly.

'Good idea!'

The house smelled warm and savoury. I breathed in deeply. 'Shepherd's pie!' I said. 'Is Mr Thomas Brown invited to supper again, Mum? And Jake?'

'Well, I've made a really big shepherd's pie, so there's plenty to go round,' said Mum. 'But if Mr Brown's going to come round here on a regular basis doing all these odd jobs I'll have to pay him. He must just be living on his pension now – they're nearly all volunteers at the railway.'

I wasn't really concentrating on what she was saying. I carefully lifted Daisy out of her cage, held her close to my chest to soothe her, and then took her downstairs. Mr Thomas Brown gave her a careful stroke with one finger.

'She's a dear little thing,' he said.

'My dad gave her to me,' I said. 'She's the best pet ever.'

'Dad gave me an aquarium for my newt,' said Perry. 'It wasn't a pet, it was an experiment. But it went wrong. I've only got the aquarium now. It's a very splendid one.'

'Daisy's got a very splendid hutch. And *now* she's got a very splendid garden,' I said, lowering her slowly into the chicken run.

She huddled into a ball, quivering.

'Oh dear, she looks frightened,' I said.

'It's probably the first time she's ever felt grass and earth under her feet. Give her a few minutes,' said Mr Thomas Brown.

He squatted on his haunches and Perry and I sat cross-legged, all of us watching. Daisy slowly relaxed. She lifted her head, her nose twitching, smelling the air. She took one step forward. We held our breath. Then she suddenly scampered the whole length of the run. She paused at a little weedy patch and discovered a dandelion. She nibbled it joyfully.

'That's right, Daisy. This is your very own garden, and you can eat breakfast whenever you fancy,' I whispered. 'Thanks so much, Mr Thomas Brown! You've made us both so happy.'

'It's a pleasure, Phoebe,' said Mr Thomas Brown, going red in the face.

'Do you like shepherd's pie? Mum's making it for supper. She's made a specially big one tonight so you and Jake can have some too. I do hope you'll stay,' I said.

'I'd be delighted, and I'm sure young Jake will be too,' said Mr Thomas Brown.

Perry and I had to use the canvas beach chairs at the table for supper. Our chins were practically on the table, but we managed. I had Mr Thomas Brown on the other side of me. Mum was at the top of the table, serving, and Becks and Jake sat opposite us. Jake was being very polite, talking to Mum about his holiday job at the railway, and then his plans for university. Becks was looking thrilled.

Perry often found visitors difficult, and either showed off or went completely silent, but he seemed relaxed now, chatting trains with Mr Thomas Brown. It was as if we were one big family – only of course we couldn't be a real family without Dad.

But then Mum spoilt it. When Mr Thomas Brown and Jake were going home she fumbled in her handbag and then tried to press some twenty-pound notes into Mr Thomas Brown's hand.

'What's this?' he said, staring at the money.

'Well, you've been so marvellous, first of all doing all the strimming, and now making the run for Phoebe's guinea pig. You must take some payment for all your trouble,' said Mum.

'I never dreamed of asking for payment,' said Mr Thomas Brown. He looked incredibly wounded.

Mum saw she'd made a big mistake. 'No, of course not, but please take it all the same. Use it to take your wife out one evening,' she blustered.

'I haven't got a wife now,' said Mr Thomas Brown. 'And I really don't need your money, Mrs Robinson. I just wanted to make myself useful, that's all. As a friend.'

He put the notes on the table.

'I'll be off then,' he said.

'Grandad!' said Jake. He looked agonized.

Mr Thomas Brown took no notice. He walked straight out of the back door.

'I'll have to go after him,' he said to Mum, standing up.

'I didn't mean to offend your grandfather,' said Mum, bewildered. 'I just wanted to reward him for everything he's done for us.'

'I know. But I think you hurt his feelings,' said Jake. 'He's a very proud man.' He reached out and held Becks's hand. 'Sorry,' he said softly. Then he went too.

'I'm going after them,' I said, nearly in tears.

'No you're not. Sit down!' said Mum.

'But Mum, I have to! I can't bear it! Mr Thomas Brown's so upset!' I wailed.

'I didn't mean to upset him. For goodness' sake, I just wanted to show him how grateful we all are,' said Mum. 'If anyone comes and does a splendid job for us I always offer them some money and they're pleased!'

'You're talking about proper workmen. Mr Thomas Brown's our *friend*. Only now he won't want to be our friend any more. You've spoilt it all,' I said, the tears starting to drip down my cheeks.

'Stop getting in such a silly state, Phoebe,' Mum said sharply.

'Mr Thomas Brown has to be our friend. He's in charge of the railway,' said Perry. 'We go there every day.'

'And we'll still go. I know it's part of your routine while we're here, Perry. But remember that other children go only once, for a holiday treat. You've been incredibly lucky so far,' said Mum. 'We'll do something else tomorrow. And the next day. And the next.'

'But I have to see Jake!' said Becks.

'Yes, well, I think he's a nice enough boy, but he's a bit too old for you. You're not ready for a serious boyfriend,' said Mum.

'How would you know?' said Becks. 'I really care about Jake.'

'Becks, you've only known him five minutes! You're being really silly. You don't have to see him every day,' Mum said firmly.

'How can you be so *mean*?' Becks cried. 'I think you're jealous! Now Dad's walked out you're lonely and you can't stand to watch Jake and me being happy together.'

'Stop it!' said Mum. She put her hand up, shielding her eyes as if she couldn't bear to see us, and stumbled out of the room. We heard her going upstairs. The creak of her bed as she threw herself on it. Then silence.

We all looked at each other.

'Oh God,' said Becks, breathing out. 'I didn't really mean to say that.'

'Dad hasn't walked out,' I said. 'He's acting out Robinson on a desert island. You know that. And it's a secret, but those horrid men who came to our door at home had found out somehow, and wanted to put it in the papers.'

'You're so stupid, Phoebe. I don't think they were reporters at all. I think they were debt collectors. Dad's hopeless with money, you know that. I bet he's maxed out all his credit cards and now he's stuck,' said Becks. 'He's done a runner. But he can't stay running for ever. He'll probably end up going to prison for debt!'

'I'm not listening,' I said, putting my hands over my ears. 'La la la, I can't hear a word you're saying, and it's all wicked lies anyway.'

Perry started rocking very fast on his chair, forwards and backwards.

'Oh no!' I said. 'Don't listen to Becks, Perry, she's just talking wicked rubbish.'

'I have to go to the railway every day,' said Perry. 'I have to go to the railway every day. I have to. I have to.'

'Oh, do shut up. Is that all you care about, those stupid trains?' I said.

'Steam trains aren't stupid. They were one of the most exciting inventions ever,' said Perry, rocking harder.

'I care about Jake!' said Becks. 'I'm going to see him, and Mum can't stop me.'

'Well, I'm going to see Mr Thomas Brown and Mum can't stop me either,' I said.

'I'm going to the railway and Mum can't stop me,' Perry mumbled.

We looked at each other and all nodded determinedly.

I woke up very early again but I didn't slip out to the field. I sat up in bed, hugging my knees, thinking things over. Then I gave Becks a nudge.

'Mm? What? Is it breakfast time?' Becks murmured, her head in the pillow.

'I've had an idea!' I whispered.

'You're always having ideas,' Becks said, wriggling away from me.

'Yes, but this is a good one. Do you want to go to the railway today or not?'

'Of course I do,' said Becks.

'Then let's get up now. And Perry too, because he'll go nuts if we leave him behind. We'll creep out before Mum's awake so she can't stop us,' I explained.

'Don't whisper right in my ear, it tickles!' said Becks.

'But don't you *like* my idea?' I said.

'Well, it's stupid. We can't drive the car, can we?' Becks said, exasperated.

'No, but we could walk,' I said.

'It's miles and miles away!'

'No it's not. Well, five miles maybe. I was thinking, it's probably much quicker if we go across the fields, because the roads bend all over the place. Say you'll come, Becks! Please!' I begged.

'I think it's more than five miles. And then we'd have to trudge all the way back,' said Becks, but she sounded more awake now.

'We'd have had the train ride in between, for a rest. We could do the walk easy-peasy. In Edwardian times people like us walked everywhere,' I said.

'No they didn't, they had horses and carts,' said Becks.

'The children walked to school, and their boots were hard leather, not soft bouncy Converse ones. Oh, do say you'll give it a go, Becks. If it seems too far we can just turn back. But it will be such fun. And won't it just show Mum she can't boss us around and stop us seeing our friends?' I said.

'I suppose,' said Becks. 'But she'll go frantic when she wakes up and finds we're gone.'

'We'll leave her a note, telling her not to worry.'

I wrote it quickly, tearing a page out of my exercise book, after we'd both got dressed.

Dear Mum,

Do not worry. We have gone for a very long walk. We won't be back till this afternoon. Sorry!

Love from Phoebe, Becks and Perry

'But you haven't told her where we're going,' said Becks, brushing her hair.

'Well, duh! Then she'd come straight after us in the car, wouldn't she?' I said.

'She'll do that anyway.'

'Not if we try going the field way,' I said.

'I bet she'll be waiting for us when we eventually get to the station, and she'll be so furious,' said Becks.

'Don't be such a wuss. She won't tell us off too much, not in front of everyone,' I said. 'And *we're* furious with *her*, right? She drags us off here away from all our friends, and yet she doesn't like it one bit that we've made lovely new friends. She's so mean.'

'She's not *really*,' said Becks uncomfortably.

'Yes, she is! She doesn't want you to see Jake any more,' I said.

'But that's just because she worries about me,' said Becks. 'I didn't really mean that stuff I said last night.'

'All right, you go to sleep. I don't care. I'll just go with Perry.

And if he won't come I'll go all by myself,' I said fiercely.

'You can't go by yourself. You're far too young. You know perfectly well I'm going to have to come with you,' said Becks. She started fiddling with her make-up bag, getting out all her eye stuff.

'For goodness' sake, don't bother with mascara! You don't need make-up! We've got to be quick before Mum's alarm goes off!' I said.

'But I have to look good if I'm seeing Jake,' said Becks.

'You always look good – and you know it,' I said. 'Come *on!*'

I grabbed her hand and pulled her out of the bedroom. We stood still and listened on the landing. There was still no sound from Mum's room. We tiptoed along to Perry's cupboard – and he suddenly jumped out at us, like a jack-in-a-box! We both started violently but managed not to scream.

'What are you playing at?' I whispered.

'I was just coming to get you,' said Perry. 'I've had a brilliant idea. We can walk to the station all by ourselves!'

'That's *my* idea!' I said.

'Great minds think alike. Now shut up, both of you. Come downstairs!' Becks hissed.

We crept down and helped ourselves to hunks of bread and jam and glasses of milk.

'But I need my special bread and I have to make my toast,'

said Perry.

'I know it's different,' said Becks, 'but it's still bread and jam and if you make toast Mum might wake up and stop you going to the railway. So come on, eat up!'

We ate – Perry was cautious, but managed one slice without looking too worried. We drank the milk, we opened the back door slowly and cautiously – and then we were off! We kept quiet while we were going across the field because Mum might just hear us – but when we were in the wood I suddenly let out a whoop.

'We've done it!' I yelled.

'We're going to the railway!' Perry cried.

'I'm going to see Jake!' Becks sang, and she jumped up, hooked her hands over a low branch, and swung herself to and fro. She was just like the old Becks from long ago, who played all our games and was great fun.

We got to the abandoned telephone box and saw some crumpled paper inside, on the floor. I opened the door and breathed in a weird smell of dust and stale air and tobacco. I picked up the paper gingerly, wondering if it was some kind of secret message, but it was just someone's old fish and chips paper, greasy and disgusting. I dropped it quickly.

'How did they use these old phones?' I asked, feeling the shape where the phone had been.

'You lifted the phone receiver, dialled a number and put your

pennies in a slot,' said Perry. 'If the person you were phoning replied, you pressed button A and started talking to them. If they didn't reply then you pressed button B and got your money back.'

'Seriously?' said Becks, wrinkling her nose.

'Yes. Like this.' Perry mimed picking up the phone and dialling. He held an imaginary penny at the ready. 'Come on, Dad. I want to talk to you,' he said. Becks and I looked at each other, startled.

Perry made phone noises under his breath. *'Brr brr! Brr brr! Brr brr!'* He looked like he was going to stay ringing a very long time.

'I don't think Dad's in,' Becks said gently.

'OK,' said Perry. 'I'll press button B. There! I've got my penny back.'

He pretended to put them in the pocket of his shorts and started walking up the narrow footpath, placing one foot in front of

the other and holding his arms out for balance as if he were on a tightrope.

'Oh!' I mouthed at Becks.

'Bless!' she whispered back.

I wondered if Perry often tried talking to Dad. Perhaps Becks did too. I imagined her peering in the mirror, asking Dad if he liked her new hairstyle or the black lines she painted round her eyes.

I thought of Mum holding Dad's jumper tight in bed . . .

'Come on, you guys! Let's stop at the top of the hill and try to work out the best way to get to the station,' I said.

There was no traffic at all so we could spread out across the road. I hoped when we got to the top and peered all around we could catch a glimpse of the station or a stretch of railway track, but there was just field after field right up to the sky everywhere we looked.

'Oh well, we know we turn left when we get to the crossroads, so let's walk across the fields on our left, OK?' I said. 'Does that make sense?'

Becks shrugged and Perry looked uncertain.

'Oh, come on, let's give it a go,' I said, and I clambered over a gate and started running down the grassy slope.

It was so steep my feet didn't have to do any work. I was just propelled downwards so quickly it felt like I was flying. I stuck

my arms out and threw my head back, wondering if I was going to rise right up into the blue sky above – and ran right into a bramble bush.

'Oh God, Phoebes, are you all right?' Becks cried, stopping beside me.

'Just a bit scratched, that's all,' I said breathlessly. 'I'm fine, honestly.'

I *was* fine too, still joyful, and the scratches were only little ones. I ran on down to the flat grass at the bottom, but Perry barged past me.

'I'm first, I'm first!' he yelled, punching the air as if he'd won an Olympic race.

We walked on together, singing 'We Are the Champions', thrilled at the novelty of being out on our own. Well, it would have been even better with Dad, but it was pretty good just us.

We strode out, the sun warm on our backs, but there was a little breeze too, so it was ideal walking weather. There were a lot of wild flowers in the fields. The primroses were over, but there were still yellow buttercups and cowslips and enough dandelions to feed a million guinea pigs. Birds sang above and butterflies fluttered everywhere, brown and white and bright blue. The lambs in the first field were quite big and boisterous, playing in little gangs while the adult sheep grazed, but the calves in the second field were still sticking close to their mothers, nuzzling up to them trustingly.

'Oh, I just love, love, love the countryside!' I said. 'We should walk to the railway every day. Who needs a boring old car ride? This is much more fun.'

The fun lasted for a long while, but then I started to get really tired. Becks flung herself down and took off her trainers, rubbing her toes.

'I thought so! I'm getting a blister,' she said.

'This is taking ages and ages. It's so much quicker going to the station in the car,' Perry said.

'Yes, but there wouldn't be any point getting there too early, because the first train doesn't go till ten o'clock,' I said.

'There would have been heaps of points, because I could talk to Mr Thomas Brown and Alf and Ann and Jack the painter and all the others, and I could look at the trains still in the siding and I could go in the signal box and I could see the water tank and I could look out for *real* points which are the moveable rails that taper to points so a train can travel from one set of rails to another—'

I interrupted him. 'Come on, you two, let's keep walking. We must be nearly there. The station's probably just over that next hill.'

'My toe's practically bleeding,' Becks whined.

'Look, I'm all over scratches and I'm not complaining,' I said. I dug into the back pocket of my jeans. 'Here, use my tissue for a bandage.'

'Yuck, you've used it, it's all crumpled up!' said Becks.

'Well, it's only going on your grubby sweaty foot so what does it matter?' I said.

Becks padded her sore toe and put her trainer back on. She walked a few steps experimentally. 'Actually that is a bit better. Thanks, Phoebes,' she said.

Perry started doing his tuneless whistling, playing a counting game on his fingers.

'What are you doing now, Perry?' Becks asked.

'I know what he's doing!' I said. 'He's counting wheels on engines in his head.'

'Correct!' said Perry.

'Weird,' Becks muttered fondly.

I took a deep breath. I had my second wind now. 'Shall we have a race to see who can get to the top of the hill first?'

It was far harder running up rather than down, especially when we'd already walked such a long way, but we staggered along as best we could. By the time I'd actually got to the top my head was throbbing and my eyes so blurred I could hardly see. I blinked hopefully, looking for the railway station.

There were a couple of streets of grey flint cottages and a little church down in the valley, but they didn't look at all like the red- brick houses of Primrose village, and there was no sign of the station.

'Oh dear,' I said weakly.

'We should have stuck to the road way. Now look at us! We've walked about a thousand miles already and we're totally lost,' said Becks. 'Honestly, Phoebe!'

'I want to go to the railway!' said Perry. Then, as if we hadn't understood, '*I want to go to the railway!*'

'I know! Will you please stop stating the obvious. And it's mean to pick on me. I'm the youngest!' I said.

'But it was all your idea. I should have realized right from the start that it was a totally rubbish idea too. A Phoebe fantasy!' said Becks.

'Don't be so horrid!' I said. 'At least I *have* ideas! Your head's just full of mush about Jake and clothes and hairstyles and Perry's head is bunged up to the brim with so many facts. I *imagine* things!'

'Yes, you do,' said Becks. 'I know you meant well. Don't cry.'

'I am *not* crying!' I said fiercely. 'My eyes are just watering, that's all.'

'I'd give you your tissue back, but it'll be all manky after being wrapped round my sore toe,' said Becks. 'Sorry, Phoebes. Come on, let's go down to the village. It'll be easy going downwards.'

'But I want to go to the railway!' Perry continued, clearly building up to a meltdown.

'Yes. We know that. So we'll go down to this village and see if anyone can give us directions, right?' said Becks, looking straight

into his eyes. 'We're going to go to the railway. Someone will tell us the way.'

'I want to go to the railway,' Perry mumbled.

'Yes, and when we're there we'll see lots of trains and you can tell us what kinds they are and what sort of wheels they have,' I said. 'What about the Sir Thomas Browning Pullman? What sort of wheel formation does it have?'

'Easy-peasy! Four-six-two!' said Perry, and he started striding down to the village, chanting names of trains and the numbers of their wheels. It grew incredibly tedious, but we were pleased we'd distracted him and stopped him getting too upset. He was like a little train himself and I'd levered him onto another set of rails.

When we got much nearer to the houses, we could see there was one cottage at the end which looked slightly different. It had bigger windows and some sort of sign outside.

'It's an ice cream sign!' I said. 'Oh, I'd die for an ice cream now. But we haven't got any money!'

'Haven't we?' said Becks, and she felt in her jeans pocket. She didn't bring out a crumpled tissue. She produced a crisp twenty-pound note!

'Oh, Becks!' I marvelled.

'Mum gave it to me the first time I went out with Jake, just in case I needed to get a taxi home,' she said.

'We're just going to give up and get a taxi home?' I said, agonized.

'Well, we *could*, though I'm not sure it would be enough. But it might be enough to get us to the station, if the shop people will call one for us.'

'Or we could all have ice creams and then walk there!' I said.

It turned out we really could. The nice man in the shop reckoned it was only a mile or so more to the station.

'We could walk that, easy-peasy, and treat ourselves to ice cream now!' I said.

'But we're all exhausted. I think it would be more sensible to call a taxi. Would you mind terribly if we asked you to call us a taxi on your land line?' Becks asked the man.

'I'll call you one with pleasure, dear, but I doubt they'll have one free. You have to book ahead in these parts,' the man explained. 'They'll be taking old folk backwards and forwards to the shops and the doctors at this time, and then they'll start the lunch run. They *might* be able to squeeze you in before they fetch the kiddies from school . . .'

'But we want to go to the railway now!' said Perry.

'And we're so hot and tired and thirsty,' I said.

So Becks gave in and bought us ice creams. She had a raspberry ice cream, Perry had an ice lolly, and I had a big ice cream cornet. They were bliss.

'Can you tell us exactly how to get to the station, please?' Becks asked.

'Turn right out of here, and basically just follow your noses. You'll spot the track before too long. Don't you try walking on it, mind. That would be highly dangerous!' he said.

We promised we wouldn't, and set off, refreshed. I was a little bit anxious that we might get lost again, but it wasn't long before Perry yelped and darted forward like a terrier chasing a rabbit.

'Perry?' we shouted, running after him.

'The track, the track!' Perry cried.

He squatted down when he got to it.

'Don't touch it!' Becks shouted.

'I'm not touching it! I'm just looking.'

'What on earth are you peering at?' I said, kneeling beside him, hoping he'd spotted an interesting insect or a little mouse.

'The rail, silly!' said Perry. 'The wooden planks are the sleepers, and the long steel bit is obviously the rail. See there's a gap between the ends of the rails, joined by this fishplate thingy, bolted into place.'

'Oh. Right,' I said, starting to wish I hadn't asked.

'And look, *this* bit is the chair, it's bolted to the sleeper. That means it's a bull-head rail. If it was held by a spring spike it would be a flat-bottom rail,' said Perry.

'It's actually quite interesting,' said Becks. I stared at her.

Becks wasn't remotely interested in anything technical. 'Jake was explaining how it all works the other day,' she went on.

I rolled my eyes.

'Let's follow the rail and see if we can spot a mile post – they're at quarter-mile intervals,' said Perry.

'But we mustn't walk on the track, right?' Becks said, in a bossy older sister way.

It was actually terribly tempting. 'It would be such fun to jump from sleeper to sleeper,' I said wistfully.

'Oh yes, great fun to be leaping about, not paying attention, and then a train comes whizzing along and squashes you flat,' said Becks.

'It couldn't actually take me by surprise, because the trains all make such a noise and the driver would see me and blow his whistle,' I argued, just for the sake of it.

'If it was my friend Alf driving the train he'd be very angry with you and probably ban all of us from ever going near the railway again,' said Perry. 'You have to stick to the rules, Phoebe.'

It was infuriating being lectured by Perry, who always seemed to make up his own rules about everything he did. I wasn't being serious anyway.

'I shall do what I like,' I said nevertheless – and I kept *pretending* I was going to jump on the track.

'Cut it out,' Becks said sharply. 'Come on. We should have

tried phoning the taxi service. They *might* have been able to take us to the station straight away. We all wanted ice creams, but now they're gone – and we're just as hot and tired and thirsty. More so. And I can't see the station anywhere yet. I don't recognize a single thing.'

'I do!' said Perry suddenly, squinting into the distance.

'Where? You can see the station? I can see much better than you, but *I* can't see it. There's just grassy banks either side of us and fields beyond them, and then there's a humpy sort of bridge in front of us,' I said. Then I blinked. 'Oh!'

'You recognize the humpy bridge, don't you?' said Perry.

'I don't!' said Becks. 'What are you two on about?'

'It's where the tunnel starts,' I said. 'It *is*, isn't it, Perry. The one before you get to Forest Lake. *That's* the station the ice-cream man meant. We've walked even further than we thought. We've missed Primrose station altogether!'

'I don't believe it,' said Becks, and she flung herself down in the grass. 'We're such *idiots*.' She took off her shoe and examined her foot. The tissue was a little bit red. 'Look! How on earth can I walk all the way back when I'm pouring blood!' She glared at me. 'Whose hare-brained idea was this?'

'Stop being horrible to me. You both thought it was an ace idea to walk to Primrose station. And we don't have to walk all the way back there! We just need to keep following the track and we'll

get to Forest Lake. We can wait for our train there. Simple. So you're the one who's dim, not me,' I retorted.

'But when we've been to Orlington and gone back again to Primrose we'll have to trail all the way home to the cottage,' Becks said. 'I'll be walking in a puddle of blood by then.'

'No you won't, because I think we'll be on Jake's train and he's got a car, hasn't he, so he could give us a quick lift home,' I said.

Becks perked up a bit then. 'I suppose,' she conceded. 'But we've still got to get to Forest Lake station. We've got to climb up that steep bank and go all the way round the top to avoid the tunnel, and I think I'm getting a blister on my *other* foot now.' She took that shoe off and examined her toes. '*Two* more!'

'We don't have to go all round the top. We could go *through* the tunnel,' I said.

I didn't really mean it. I knew perfectly well that no one sane would ever go through a tunnel on a railway line. I just said it to sound incredibly daring.

'We could certainly look inside it now we're so near,' said Perry, taking me seriously. 'I want to see what it's like!'

'Stop it, both of you. You're just winding me up,' said Becks, rubbing her feet and wincing.

'Are we?' I said, and I started running beside the track towards the tunnel.

'Stop it! You can't!' Becks cried. 'It's far too dangerous. You could be *killed*!'

'We can, we can!' I shouted over my shoulder. 'You can go round the long way and meet us at the other side!'

'*No!*' Becks grabbed her shoes and started running after us barefoot, but she must have stepped on a thistle because she screamed and started hopping.

'Can't catch us!' I yelled.

'Can't catch us!' Perry said. 'Can't catch us, can't catch us, can't catch us!' He sounded like a little steam engine himself, puffing along.

He was a faster runner than me, though uncoordinated, his arms flapping, his legs sticking out sideways. He reached the mouth of the tunnel and pelted headlong inside.

'No, Perry! Stop! It's just a game to tease Becks! We mustn't *really* go into the tunnel!' I shouted after him, terrified.

He didn't stop. I heard him further on, in the pitch dark. 'Can't catch us, can't catch us!'

'Oh, Perry. Come *back*! *Please!*' I begged.

He took no notice. I started sobbing. Becks came stumbling closer.

'I know you're just pretending! Perry's hiding, isn't he? Can't fool me!' she panted, but when she caught me up she saw my face.

'Oh God, Phoebes, Perry hasn't really gone in the tunnel, has he?' she gasped.

'I didn't mean him to. He didn't understand. He was so excited. Oh, Becks, I'm going to have to go after him!'

'No, you mustn't!' Becks took a deep breath, and then screamed into the tunnel at the top of her voice, 'Perry Robinson, come back here this instant!'

We listened. We heard the echo of Becks's voice in the dark, eerily loud at first and then gradually getting fainter. But we couldn't hear Perry at all.

'Perhaps we should run round to the other end and just wait for him?' said Becks.

'He could have stumbled in the dark. You run round but I'll go in after him. It's all my fault. If a train comes and he's fallen across the line I'll have *murdered* him!' I wept. 'I'm going in!'

'No, I will. I'm the oldest! Let me!' said Becks, trying to elbow me out the way.

'I have to,' I said.

'Then I have to too,' said Becks.

We went into the horrible dark tunnel together, me first, then Becks gripping the back of my T-shirt, so we couldn't possibly get separated. We shuffled forward, both of us shaking as the dark closed over us. The tunnel smelled dank and the

brick wall felt cold and slimy. Trickles of water dripped on our heads and splashed on the floor.

'It's so wet!' Becks said. 'Ugh, it's like the worst puddle in the world. And I haven't got any shoes on!'

Then there was a scuttle, and a squeak.

'A rat! Oh God, a rat!' Becks screamed, and she jumped forward.

'Keep back against the wall! A train might come at any minute!' I cried.

And as I said it there was a far distant rumble and the rails started vibrating.

'Oh no, oh no, oh no!' said Becks. '*Run!*'

'Perry, run! There's a train coming!' I screamed, running so fast I kept banging into the wall. Becks ran behind me, stumbling too.

I kept hoping it was my imagination, and that it wasn't really a train, just a trick of the wind, but I could hear it properly now, and smell the smoke.

'Run faster!' I shouted into the pitch dark.

Then something grabbed hold of me and thrust me to one side. It grabbed hold of Becks too, and did the same to her. We both screamed our heads off.

'Shut up, you're deafening me!' It was Perry, standing in some kind of alcove in the wall. 'Isn't this *fantastic*!' he shouted.

'For God's sake, Perry!' Becks yelled. 'Don't move an inch! Phoebe, press right back against the wall!'

I was already pressing so hard I was practically going through the bricks. The huge hot monstrous train roared right past us. If I'd been stupid enough to reach out I think I could have touched it. My eyes watered and I choked with the smell and the smoke.

The three of us clung together until at last it was gone. We were left in the middle of the tunnel, in the pitch black again, with no sound but the drumming in our own ears.

Becks and I collapsed together, shaking, but Perry was still rigid with excitement.

'I never thought I'd get that close to a train going at full speed! It was so magnificent, wasn't it?' he breathed.

'It was the most terrifying experience of my whole life,' said Becks.

I still couldn't even speak. I opened and closed my mouth like a goldfish but no sound came out.

'But we weren't in any danger!' said Perry. 'Isn't the tunnel cleverly constructed with these little alcoves, so anyone working on the line can tuck themselves away when they hear a train approaching?'

'It . . . was . . . so . . . so . . . scary!' I said, my teeth chattering.

'But it was all your idea! You said we should go in the tunnel.

We ran so Becks couldn't catch us,' said Perry.

I didn't have the breath to try to explain. It would have been pointless anyway.

'Anyway, the train's gone,' said Perry. 'So there's nothing to be scared of now.'

'Perry, we're in the middle of the darkest tunnel ever and it's damp and smelly and I'm sloshing through slimy water in my bare feet and there are rats running around – I just know there are!' said Becks.

'No worries,' said Perry. 'Come on. Follow me. We'll be out the other side in no time.'

He strode forward, whistling cheerily. Becks and I stumbled behind him, shivering. I shuddered whenever a drip from the tunnel roof landed on my head. Becks yelled whenever she heard something scuttling. By the time we got to the end of the tunnel we were totally exhausted.

We stepped out into the sun, blinking, unable to believe we were actually safely back in the daylight, with the grassy banks and fields and meadows all around us.

'We made it!' I said, whirling around in triumph. 'We've really walked all the way through the hateful tunnel!'

'Look at us! We're all in such a state! And oh my God, I've dropped one of my shoes somewhere! I can't believe it. Why do I keep losing my shoes?' said Becks.

Becks was right: we did look a terrible sight. We were covered in sooty smuts and our clothes were stained green from brushing against the slimy wall. Becks tried wiping her face and cleaning her T-shirt but she only made it worse.

Perry didn't care in the slightest. His hair was all over the place and the smuts were as thick as freckles on his face, but his eyes shone with joy.

'I think that was quite possibly the best experience of my life,' he said.

But it was almost the worst experience of our lives when we boarded the next train at Forest Lake station. Alf was driving it, and he actually got out of his cabin to come to our carriage.

'So there you are, you dreadful children!' he said sternly. 'Your poor mother's back at Primrose, in a terrible state, ready to call the police! They're organizing a search party! I thought you were sensible kids, especially you, Perry – and yet it's obvious you've been playing hide-and-seek in the tunnel, risking your lives!'

He actually locked us in our carriage in case we decided to make a bolt for it at the station.

'I wish he hadn't done that,' I said, as he went back to the cabin and started driving the train. 'I'm absolutely desperate to go to the loo now! Do you think Jake might be on this train? He'd let us out.'

'I hope he isn't! I couldn't bear him to see me in this state,' said Becks.

'I thought Alf was my friend,' Perry wailed, his face crumpling.

It was even worse when we got back to Primrose at last. I'd thought Mr Thomas Brown was my friend, but he gave us such a stern telling-off that we cowered like whipped dogs. Mo came out of the Junction Cafe to stare at us, but she didn't smile; she just shook her head at us.

'Look at the state your poor mum is in!' she said.

Mum was paper-white, her eyes red. 'Thank God,' she said, when she saw us and she gave us a frantic hug.

But when we were in the car she started shouting at us.

'How could you? You've worried everyone dreadfully. It was so awful! I'll tell you this – you're not going near that railway ever again!'

We didn't actually think Mum was serious. We thought she'd stay furious with us for the rest of the day but be over it by the next morning. It was a shock when she stuck to her word.

'No. Absolutely not. You'll have to find some other way to amuse yourselves,' Mum said sternly at breakfast.

'But I can go to the station just to meet up with Jake, can't I, Mum?' Becks said softly, her eyes big and pleading.

'No you can't,' said Mum.

'But I have to see him, Mum, just to explain,' Becks said.

'And I have to see Mr Thomas Brown and say sorry. I can't bear it if he won't be my friend any more,' I said.

'And I have to go to the railway. I have to. I *have* to,' said Perry. He was red in the face, his eyes squeezed shut.

Becks and I glanced at each other hopefully. Perry was

on the verge of a meltdown.

Mum looked worried, but stayed resolute. 'I know it's especially hard for you, Perry,' she said. 'But I can't let you go to the railway now. It's your own fault.'

'But it's not my fault! It was all Phoebe's idea!' Perry blurted.

'Perry!' said Becks. We had a rule that we never told tales on each other – but Perry couldn't always be relied on.

'Even if it was, I'm sure she didn't frogmarch you to go along with her,' said Mum. She turned to Becks. 'I'm very disappointed in you, Rebecca. You're not a silly little girl any more. You're the oldest. How could you *possibly* have let these two go through a tunnel! Don't you realize how highly dangerous that could be? It's a wonder you weren't all three killed.'

Becks looked anguished.

'She tried to stop us. Perry's right. This is all my fault and I feel absolutely terrible about it. Look, I'll stay at home as a punishment, but let them go to the station, please,' I said.

'Oh please, will you stop acting the martyr and being such a drama queen, Phoebe!' Mum snapped.

I was truly hurt. I was simply trying to be fair and noble.

'Why are you always extra-horrible to me, Mum?' I demanded.

'Don't be ridiculous,' said Mum. 'I treat you all the same. None of you are going anywhere today. You're all staying right here in this cottage.'

'But I can go to the field, can't I?' I asked. I was longing to run through the long grass up to my special spot and talk to Dad. I needed him badly.

'No, you can't go to the field,' said Mum. 'Do you think I was born yesterday? You'll try to run off again!'

'No, I won't – I swear I won't. I just need to go in the *field*,' I said.

'And I just need to talk to Jake for ten minutes, to explain,' said Becks.

'And I have to go to the railway. *I have to go to the railway!* I HAVE TO GO TO THE RAILWAY!' Perry roared, thumping his fist on the table so that all the crockery clattered.

'Oh God,' said Mum.

Perry slid to the floor and started screaming. Mum sat beside him. She tried saying all the right soothing things, and she sent me to get Perry's earphones and his Thomas duvet, but they didn't help much.

Eventually he stopped, though he still sobbed every few seconds. He put his arm up over his face, embarrassed. Mum crept quietly away, holding her head.

'I – I—' he said.

'I know,' said Becks. 'You want to go to the railway. We all do.'

'But we can't, because we've got the meanest mother in the whole world,' I declared.

'Keep your voice down, Phoebes! She might hear you!' Becks warned.

'I don't care,' I said. 'Oh, if *only* Dad were here!'

'Well, we wouldn't be here either then, and we wouldn't even know about the railway,' said Becks.

'I want to go there so much,' said Perry, but in a small sad voice now, his head drooping.

He trailed upstairs and went and shut himself in his cupboard.

'Oh dear,' said Becks.

'Do you think we should go up to Mum and say sorry?' Becks asked.

'Do you think it might make her change her mind?'

'No.'

'Well then, what's the point? Because I'm not sorry. Well, I'm sorry that it was my idea to go to the railway yesterday, and I'm sorry that it was actually my idea about the tunnel too, and I'm sorry that we can't see all our friends there, and I'm sorry Perry's so upset, but I'm *not* sorry that I've been rude to Mum, because she's not being *fair*. And if you're right that Dad's just walked out on her, though I absolutely don't think he'd ever do that, and he wouldn't leave *us*, but if he *did* I wouldn't blame him,' I said in a great rush.

'Oh, Phoebe,' said Becks, sighing. She patted my shoulder and went to the stairs.

'You're *not* going to say sorry, are you?' I asked.

'No, I'm going to our room. I might as well practise my new routine for TikTok – or I could try to invent another,' she said.

'But you can't post it from here.'

'I said *practise*. When we eventually get to go to the railway I'll send it from there – or smuggle my phone to Jake so he can send it for me from his home,' Becks said.

'You don't mind him reading all your drippy texts?' I asked.

'Well, he won't know my password, will he?' said Becks.

'It's easy-peasy to work out, seeing it's the year you were born, and now he knows exactly how old you are,' I said.

'How do *you* know that's my password?' Becks demanded.

'It was the first one I tried!' I said, honestly enough.

'You sneaky nosy little pig!' said Becks, but she didn't say it with any real venom.

Neither of us wanted to have another row. And besides, she didn't really have any juicy secrets. She just texted her friends about nothing much, though she added loads of exclamation marks and emojis.

She trailed upstairs and I sat in the kitchen by myself. It was very quiet and still in the room. I wondered what Mum was doing upstairs. Was she crying? I *wasn't* sorry, though I was starting to feel very uncomfortable.

I distracted myself by sticking my finger in the butter, coating

it with sugar, and then licking it clean. It tasted so good I did it several times. Then I cleared the breakfast things and washed them all up carefully, just for something to do.

I looked at all Nina's lovely paintings in the kitchen – the birds, butterflies, sheep, cows and flowers – and then I went into the living room and admired the jug, apple tree, bowl of fruit and the rabbit. But no people, apart from the young couple upstairs dancing through time, his feet flashing, her skirts whirling.

I did a little twirl around the room myself, remembering all the times Dad and I did our crazy dance together. Then I fingered the bare canvases stacked in the corner, stared at the pastels in the box.

I was better at people than sunrises. I propped a canvas on the easel, picked up a peach chalk and made a faint oval shape near the top. It was the sort of squiggle a three-year-old might make – and yet as I peered at it I saw Dad's face tilting to one side, smiling at me.

I took a deep breath and settled into my picture. I lost sense of time altogether. There was no sound from Mum and Becks in their rooms or Perry in his dark cupboard. There was just the steady tick and tock of the grandfather clock, and the faint sound of my breathing as I drew and shaded and smudged.

There was Dad on the canvas, the sleeves of his old navy jumper rolled up, one hand pumping the air, the other clasping

mine as he whirled me around. I was half the size of Dad, my red Manchester United T-shirt too big for me, my feet in my old furry slippers, the same turquoise as Wiffle. I was grinning, gazing up at Dad, imitating his moves.

I'd slightly misjudged the placing of the figures, Dad's head too near the top, so that our feet were too high up the canvas, dancing in thin air – but it made us look as if we were flying.

'Oh, Phoebe!' said Mum.

I'd been so absorbed I hadn't heard her come into the room. I jumped guiltily, clutching the chalk so fiercely that it snapped in two.

'I didn't think Nina would mind,' I stammered.

'You've done that picture so carefully. I didn't know you could draw like that.'

'Neither did I,' I said.

'It's exactly right, you and your dad dancing away.' Mum reached out and touched the navy wool of Dad's jumper with the tip of her finger, careful not to smudge it.

'It's the jumper you've got here, isn't it?' I said.

Mum nodded, looking embarrassed. 'I just wanted a little bit of him with me,' she murmured.

'You do still love him, don't you?' I asked.

'I can't help it,' said Mum. 'In spite of everything.'

'In spite of . . . what?' I asked.

Mum sighed deeply and then shook her head. 'Just everything,' she said, shrugging.

'Do you still love me too, even though I got us all into trouble?' I whispered.

'Of course I do – though I'm very angry at the same time,' said Mum. 'Come here!' She held out her arms and I ran to her for a hug.

I held onto her tightly. When we stepped apart I saw I'd got pastel smudges on her shirt. Mum saw them too.

'I'm so sorry – I didn't mean to,' I said. 'I'm just so hopeless.'

'It's all right. It'll wash out,' said Mum. She sat down on the old velvet sofa and sighed. 'I'm the one who's being hopeless,' she said.

'No you're not,' I said, going to sit beside her.

'I'm pretty useless at looking after you three,' Mum said. 'Not a patch on your dad, eh?'

I tried to think of something tactful to say. 'Well, he's *Dad*,' I said. 'He's the one who looks after us. Usually. You're the one who goes out to work.' I stopped abruptly. That wasn't tactful at all.

'Not any more,' said Mum.

'I think they're horribly mean, taking your job away like that. Can't you just get another job in publishing?'

'I wish it was as simple as that,' said Mum. 'I don't think I *can*. And anyway, someone's got to look after you, even though I'm making a pig's ear of this, aren't I? Is Perry all right now? He's in

the cupboard, isn't he? I didn't want to look in on him in case I set him off again.'

'He'll be fine,' I said. 'You know how he sometimes sleeps after he's kicked off.'

'He was in such a state,' said Mum.

'Yes, but that often happens. He kicks off with Dad too – you know he does,' I said.

'I did look in on Becks, but she was in the middle of acting something,' said Mum.

'Oh well, Becks. She's practising her new routine for TikTok,' I said. 'You know.'

'I *don't* know. That's the trouble,' said Mum. 'Becks is so different now. Like how she's getting really serious about Jake.'

'I suppose,' I said. 'Don't you like him then, Mum?'

'Well, yes, he's a really sweet boy, but I do hope they just stay friends,' said Mum.

'Oh, Mum, you are funny,' I said. 'How's your story getting along?'

'It's not,' said Mum. 'I've been struggling all morning. It just won't come right. I can't do it.'

'Yes you can,' I said.

Mum shook her head. 'I feel so stupid. I've spent years telling all my authors how they should write their books, and yet I can't do it myself.'

'What do you tell them?'

'Well, just the usual sort of stuff. Make it fun, make it dramatic, make it current. Write about what you know. Only it turns out I don't know anything about children,' said Mum.

'You know about us,' I said.

'Not really,' said Mum. But then she smiled. 'I do know quite a lot about you, actually, Phoebes. You're wondering what we're going to have for lunch. And hoping like anything that I've changed my mind and I'm going to take the three of you to the railway this afternoon!'

'Are you?' I asked.

'No, not today. You're still officially in disgrace,' Mum said firmly.

'But maybe tomorrow?' I wheedled.

'Maybe,' said Mum.

We might have been in disgrace, but she let us have pizzas for lunch, adding her own extra toppings of cheese and veg and tomatoes. Perry was still rather pale and quiet and only ate half his, but I was very appreciative.

Then Mo came round late afternoon with a home-made lemon drizzle cake and a bottle of damson gin.

'It smells lovely,' I said, unscrewing the top and sniffing it.

'It's not for you lot, it's for your poor mum,' said Mo. 'I make it myself, and it's got a good kick to it. I think she needs a stiff

drink after the fright you all gave us yesterday.'

'It's very kind of you, Mo,' said Mum. She sounded as if she genuinely meant it this time. 'Shall we have a little drink now?'

'That sounds like a good plan!' said Mo.

Mum made a pot of tea too. We had juice, although Mum let Becks have a sip of damson gin using one of the little crimson glasses in the cupboard, perfect for the dark red gin.

'Oh, I like it,' Becks said.

'That's not fair! Can't we have just a little sip too?' I begged.

So Mo gave me a sip of hers. It didn't taste lovely, and it burned when I swallowed. Becks had to be fibbing. Mo offered her glass to Perry too.

'Count me out,' he said. 'I've seen a photograph of a diseased liver in my science book at home. I'm never drinking alcohol.'

'Cheery little soul, aren't you?' said Mo. 'Aren't these pretty glasses? Old Nina had some lovely things. I think they call it Bohemian glass. Nina was a Bohemian too by all accounts. Liked to party.'

'Mr Thomas Brown told me that,' I said eagerly.

'Was she very pretty?' Becks asked.

'I didn't know her till she was well past middle-age, and I wouldn't say she was a pretty woman then. Striking though, with long dark hair, and she wore strange colourful clothes, very bright

and arty. But I saw her just before she had her fall and got carted off to the nursing home, and she looked a sad old soul then, bent and shrunk, and her hair stark white. Not that I can talk – I get through umpteen bottles of hair dye nowadays,' Mo said, patting her bright blonde hair into place.

'Do you visit her in the nursing home?' I asked.

'Well, I didn't really know her that well, dear. She kept herself to herself for years. I think she'd lost touch with all her wild friends,' she said.

'Wasn't she lonely?' I asked.

'Maybe. Though I think she was happy enough staying here, painting away. It's a shame she never made a proper name for herself. She could have done with some more home comforts! Imagine, no telly, no internet!'

'I know,' said Becks, with feeling.

'I don't know how you lot can bear it,' Mo said. 'Don't you want to stay in a proper holiday let?'

'This suits us very well,' Mum said hurriedly. 'Let's all have a slice of your cake. It looks delicious.'

It really tasted delicious too and we were all enthusiastic.

'The Junction mostly sells cakes from a catering firm, but I bring in one of my home bakes every now and then, and they're always popular, especially the lemon drizzle,' said Mo. 'We missed you there today, Mrs R, tapping away on your computer. And it

goes without saying that you kids were missed too,' she said, winking at us.

'We're in disgrace,' said Perry.

'Well, I should think so too, scaring everyone half to death yesterday. I'd have shut you up in a cupboard for a week if you'd been my little boy,' said Mo.

'Mum shuts me up in a cupboard every night,' said Perry.

Mo blinked at him. 'I think you're telling stories!' she said.

'No I'm not,' said Perry.

'He *likes* being in a cupboard,' I said quickly.

'Phoebe's right, he really does like it,' Mum said. 'I mean, he doesn't have to stay there all night, I could make him up his own bed anywhere, but he likes the dark.'

'That's why he didn't mind going into that tunnel,' I explained, trying to make it less embarrassing for Mum.

It was the wrong thing to say.

'You went into the *railway* tunnel?' said Mo, choking on her own damson gin. 'We all thought you'd just gone off exploring by yourself and worrying your poor mum. I can't believe you went in the tunnel! You mustn't ever do that! It's the most dangerous thing to do. When my youngest, Yvonne, was a little girl two boys in her class went into the tunnel for a bet and the train came along and was going too fast for them to get away in time. It was such a tragedy! The railway almost got closed down too. Tommy Brown

and all his pals nearly had their hearts broken.'

'We won't ever do it again, I promise,' I said.

'I've tried to explain to them it was totally irresponsible, how they could have been *killed*,' Mum said. She rubbed her forehead. 'You must think I'm the worst mother in the world, not looking after them properly.'

'Nonsense! You've been doing a grand job, it's clear as day. They're all lovely kids. We can see you're doing your very best for them, and working your socks off too. You're running yourself ragged. Look at you – I've seen more meat on a butcher's pencil! You're not eating properly, are you? Just living on your black coffees, and there's no nourishment in that. Here, have another slice of cake!' said Mo.

I looked at Mum. She'd always been very slim, but I realized she had got thinner over the last few weeks. Her face was pinched and her wrists sticking out of her shirt sleeves looked as if they'd snap right off any minute.

Mum smiled wanly. 'I'm fine,' she said, ducking her head because we were all looking at her.

'You're not ill, are you?' Mo said, lowering her voice, though we all heard.

'No, no! I'm just a bit tired, that's all,' Mum said.

'Well, you need a good rest, clearly. Why don't you bring the kids over to my place sometime? I work a couple of days at the

railway, but I babysit my little grandson at home most of the time. I'd be glad of the company. I brought up five kids of my own and I miss the noise and the banter now.'

'Oh, can we, Mum?' I asked.

I didn't think Mum would say yes in a million years. I thought she'd just smile politely and make some excuse. But to my astonishment she said she'd think about it. Then she hesitated, and said, 'Actually, I wonder if you might be free this Thursday? I need to go to London and I wasn't sure what to do about the children. I was thinking of leaving them with Rebecca in charge, but now I don't think I can trust them to be sensible.'

'Oh, Mum, I'd be sensible, I promise!' said Becks, looking very upset.

'I would too!' I said.

'Could we go to the railway if we swear not to go in the tunnel?' said Perry.

'No, young man, you'll come to me, and if you behave yourself you can help my Barry service his old motorbike. You'll like that,' said Mo.

Perry blinked slowly, pondering, and then nodded.

'And you can hang out with Yvonne,' Mo said to Becks.

Becks looked much less keen, but nodded too.

'And *you* might like to help me with my baking,' said Mo, winking at me.

'Oh, yes *please*,' I said.

'There! Sorted!' said Mo.

'I might have to drop them off really early. Would that be all right?' Mum asked humbly.

'Of course. Maya drops little Taylor off at half seven. That suit you?' Mo said.

'That would be perfect,' said Mum. Mo gave her the address and when she went she patted Mum's hand. 'You have a lovely time up in town, dear.'

'Are you going shopping, Mum?' Becks asked, when Mo was out of the door. 'Couldn't I come with you? I don't think Yvonne likes me. Perry and Phoebes will be fine at Mo's, but I'd really love a day out with you.'

'It's not really a day out, darling. It's . . . business,' said Mum.

'Are you going to try to get your job back, Mum?' I asked.

'I don't think there's any chance of that,' said Mum.

'So are you looking for a new job?' Becks wondered.

'Something like that,' said Mum. 'I've got to go on my own anyway. Maybe we can have a proper day out together later in the summer.' She looked at me. 'And Phoebe too.'

'But not me! I hate shopping,' said Perry. 'I might like motorbikes.'

'Hey, you're not going off railways already, are you?' I asked.

'As if!' said Perry scornfully. 'But I can like motorbikes too, can't I, Mum?'

'Of course you can,' said Mum. 'Only you're not allowed to ride on them, do you hear me? I'm going to instigate a few rules around here. Number one is not to do anything dangerous at all, understand?'

'So I'm not allowed to drink this bottle of bleach?' said Perry, pointing underneath the kitchen sink. 'And I'm not allowed to hit myself hard on the head with this broom? And I'm not allowed to run upstairs and hurl myself out of the window? But am I allowed to climb out of the window and down a tree, like Becks?'

'Shut *up*, Perry,' said Becks, but luckily Mum had stopped listening.

'How did he *know* I did that?' Becks asked me when we were going to bed. She looked at me suspiciously. 'You didn't tell him, did you?'

'No, I didn't. I swear I didn't, on Dad's life,' I said. It was my most sacred swear ever and Becks knew I was always telling the truth if I said that.

'Then how else could he possibly know when he was shut up in his cupboard?' Becks demanded, getting under the covers.

'I don't know. I sometimes think he's got secret superpowers.' I didn't really believe that, of course, and yet it did seem to explain an awful lot of things about Perry. 'I wish I had a superpower,'

I said. 'Do you think it could be being good at art, Becks?'

'Maybe,' said Becks. 'You're very good at it, anyway. That picture you did today of you and Dad was great.'

'Really?' I said, delighted. 'Mum seemed to like it too. So what's your superpower, Becks?'

'Haven't got one,' said Becks, thumping her pillow.

'Yes you have. It's getting people to like you. Jake acts like he's totally nuts about you,' I said.

Becks giggled.

'Has he said he loves you yet?'

'No! Stop it, Phoebes!'

'He likes you very much, anyway,' I persisted.

'Still, getting one boy to like me doesn't mean I've got superpowers.'

'Loads and loads of people like you. Look how many friends you have at school,' I said.

'I do miss them ever so,' said Becks. 'They think I've vanished into thin air. I'm starting to be scared that we're going to be stuck here in the middle of nowhere for ever.'

'But it's lovely here. If only Dad could be here too then I'd *want* to live here for ever,' I declared.

It seemed very strange going to Mo's house on Thursday. She lived on a neat estate the other side of Orlington, in a modern three-bedroomed red-brick house. Their car and a motorbike – minus its wheels – were on the front drive.

Mo came to the door in a lilac T-shirt and tight jeans, with a large baby in dungarees riding on her hip. It was a very jolly-looking baby with a lot of curls, red cheeks and a huge grin.

'Hey, folks! Here's little Taylor. Wave hello to the nice lady and her children, Taylor!' Mo commanded. She took Taylor's pudgy fist and waved it up and down for him, while he giggled and drooled a little down his chin.

'Hello, Taylor,' said Mum, and gingerly took his tiny hand.

'Sorry he's a bit slobbery. He's teething,' Mo explained.

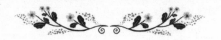

'You're sure you don't mind looking after the children?' Mum asked.

'I told you, my love, it will be a treat to have them,' said Mo. 'Would you like to pop in for a quick cup of tea before you go? I've just made a fresh pot.'

'No thanks, I'd better be off.' Mum turned to us and lowered her voice. 'You'll behave yourselves, won't you? Play nicely?'

Becks looked indignant. '*Mum!* I don't *play!*' she protested.

Perry looked appalled. 'I won't have to play with the baby, will I?'

I'd brought along my drawing book and Nina's box of chalks. 'I could maybe draw the baby,' I said. 'As well as making cakes?' I added hopefully.

Mo heard the last part and laughed. Taylor laughed too, copying her.

'Off you go then, Mrs R,' she said.

'Please. It's Petra. Thank you *so* much,' said Mum. She gave us a quick anxious smile and then rushed back to the car.

We called goodbye after her.

'And good luck!' I said. I didn't really know why. She just looked like she needed it.

Mo ushered us inside, into the kitchen. It smelled gloriously of bacon and toast. Mo's husband Barry was sitting at the head of the table, reading his paper, though he looked up and gave us a cheery

nod. I was taken aback. He was wearing Dad's jumper! Well, not Dad's actual jumper, but an identical navy woollen sweater, slightly bobbly, with a couple of oil smears down the front. I wanted to pull it right off him because he didn't suit it in the slightest. He didn't look remotely like Dad – Barry was practically bald, and much older and larger.

I looked at Becks and Perry but they didn't seem to recognize the jumper themselves. Becks was glancing warily at the girl at the table. She had to be Yvonne, their youngest daughter. She looked very grown up to me, and her tight ponytail made her face look very sharp. She was wearing a skimpy top that showed her bare waist and ripped jeans. She had a ring in her belly button. I couldn't help staring at it.

'Say hello to our guests, Yvonne,' said Mo.

Yvonne didn't react in any way.

I wondered if Mo would seize *her* hand and wave it up and down, but she didn't force her.

'She's a bit shy,' she said.

Yvonne didn't look the slightest bit shy, just hostile.

'Aren't you going to school?' I asked her, because her outfit clearly wasn't official uniform.

'Finished,' said Yvonne.

'She's taken all her GCSEs so her year are off school early,' said Mo. 'She don't know what to do with herself, do you, Yvonne?'

'Yeah, I do. I want to go round my mate's,' she said.

'Yes, well, you can't, because we've got guests,' said Mo. She rolled her eyes.

'It's OK, I'm fine,' Becks said hurriedly. 'You don't have to stay on my account.'

Yvonne pulled a face, sticking her tongue between her teeth.

'You two've met already, haven't you?' said Mo. 'Down at the club?'

'Is that the club where you went with Jake?' I asked Becks.

'Jake!' Yvonne muttered. 'Surprised he wasn't still wearing his lame uniform for the little kiddie railway!'

'It's a proper working vintage steam railway,' said Perry. 'It's not *little kiddie*!'

'Whatever,' said Yvonne.

'Don't you talk about the railway like that, Yvonne!' said Mo. 'You used to love going there!'

'When I was a *kid*,' said Yvonne. 'I think it's pathetic now. All them old codgers playing at trains. Plus Jake. What a loser!'

'They're not *playing*,' said Perry. 'They're a team of expert enthusiasts. They've resurrected steam locomotives rusting away in scrapyards and now they're in incredible condition, so you can just shut up!'

'Perry! You can't say shut up when you're a guest,' said Becks, though she looked as if she'd like to say far worse things to Yvonne.

'He can say whatever he likes, bless him,' said Mo. 'It's my Yvonne who should watch herself. She's implying *I'm* an old codger because I take my turn in the cafe and serve on the Pullman specials. Did you hear what your daughter just said, Barry?'

Barry turned over the page of his paper, and took a bite of his bacon sandwich. 'Cheeky mare,' he said to Yvonne, but fondly. 'And what's all this about young Jake? I thought you girls treated him like a pop star. Didn't you use to want to go out with him?'

'*No!*' said Yvonne, going red.

'Looks like Jake's got a girlfriend already,' said Mo.

Becks blushed this time, but looked smug. Yvonne flounced out of the room.

'Sorry about that. She's a bit moody today. But she'll come round, just you wait and see,' said Mo.

I thought it highly unlikely but didn't care, and Becks looked positively relieved she'd gone.

'Are you really going to let me help you with your motorbike?' Perry asked Barry.

'Depends what you know about motorbikes, lad,' he replied.

'Not a lot just yet, but I want to. I'm a quick learner,' said Perry.

Barry put his bacon sandwich down. 'Then let's get cracking,' he said, smiling. 'I like your attitude. So, what sort of bike have you got? A Suzuki GSX-R600? Or are you a Honda man? Maybe the CBR900RR Fireblade?'

Perry rarely detected a joke. He looked anxious. 'I haven't exactly got my own motorbike yet,' he said.

'Barry!' Mo said sharply. 'Stop plaguing the boy with your silly nonsense. Now, you have had breakfast at home, haven't you, dears?'

'Yes,' I said reluctantly.

'What did you have, eh?'

'Cornflakes,' I said.

'And I had toast and strawberry jam. I always do,' said Perry, relaxing a little.

'That sounds lovely,' Mo said tactfully. 'But would you like a little bit extra? A bacon sandwich?'

'Oh, what a brilliant idea!' I said.

Becks wasn't too keen, pretending she wasn't hungry, and Perry repeated the only breakfast he ever ate was toast and jam.

'But this isn't breakfast, sweetheart. It's *snack* time. And if you're going to be messing about outside with Barry's motorbike all morning you'll need a bit of sustenance,' said Mo, getting a new pack of bacon out of her fridge and going to her frying pan.

Mum would never make us bacon sandwiches because she said they weren't healthy. Mo made the most wonderful bacon sandwiches, and I certainly *felt* healthy afterwards. I helped her clear the table and put everything in the dishwasher when we'd finished.

It was so strange being in a normal house again. It seemed magical to have piping hot water at the turn of a tap. I visited the shiny pink bathroom several times just for the joy of sitting on a proper toilet rather than an old manky one with a chain that wouldn't pull properly.

'Have you got a bit of tummy trouble, poppet?' Mo whispered to me.

'No, it's just so great to use a proper bathroom again,' I said.

'Oh, bless!' said Mo. 'You could have a bath too if you like! I keep forgetting how basic it is at Nina's cottage.'

'We do keep clean though,' Becks said quickly.

'But the water is never really hot enough and you can't lie down in that hip bath thing,' I said.

'Well, you're very welcome to pop upstairs and have a good long soak,' said Mo, laughing.

'You won't start making the cakes without me, will you?' I begged.

'Not so much as a rock bun, dear,' Mo promised.

Becks and I tried to encourage Perry to have a bath too, but he looked appalled at the idea.

'You don't have a bath when you're visiting someone's house,' he said.

'Not usually, Perry, but this is different,' said Becks.

'*I'm* not different!' said Perry, wrapping his arms firmly round

himself, as if he thought we were going to pull his clothes off there and then.

'Leave the lad alone,' said Barry. 'He'll get all oily anyway, if he's mucking about with my motorbike with me. Come on, son.'

'I'm not your son,' said Perry, but he looked eager, and trotted off with Barry happily enough.

Becks and I went off to share the bathroom together. There was a big shiny bath *and* a proper walk-in shower. I lay back in the piping hot bath, submerged up to my chin, like the happiest hippo ever. Becks had a long shower, shampooing her hair so vigorously it looked as if she was wearing a white bubbly hat. Mo had given us clean fluffy towels.

'Mm, they smell so good,' I said, snuffling into mine.

'*I* smell so good!' said Becks, who had helped herself liberally to all kinds of conditioners and lotions.

Our clothes were clean so it didn't feel odd putting them back on again. Since we'd arrived, Mum had washed all our clothes herself by hand, even our jeans, and hung them to dry outside. She used an ancient iron to smooth out all the creases, but even I could see we still looked a bit scruffy round the edges.

'I wish I'd brought my make-up with me,' Becks moaned.

'I'm sure Yvonne will let you use hers,' Mo called, from outside the bathroom.

Yvonne wasn't at all keen at first, but Mo suggested she might

like to do Becks's make-up for her. 'She's learned all these beauty tricks from YouTube,' said Mo. 'She does my make-up now when I'm going on a night out, and does a really great job. She wants to be a make-up artist.'

Becks didn't look too keen either. Yvonne might take the opportunity to make her look like Fungus the Bogeyman. But in actual fact she did it properly, making Becks sit in front of her dressing table with another towel round her neck, as if she were in a proper beauty salon. It took *ages*. Then Yvonne started blow-drying Becks's hair, styling it this way and that. I amused myself peering round her bedroom. Barry had painted it purple for her, and she had a lilac satin duvet and all kinds of spotlights so that it looked really glamorous and grown-up.

But she still had some little girly things in her room too. Sylvanian Families animals paraded along her windowsill and a little pile of fluffy toys sat squashed up in a swivel chair. One teddy had googly eyes like Wiffle, and I gave it a furtive stroke. She still had a few children's books on her shelves, and an old set of Disney DVDs.

I started humming 'Let it Go' from *Frozen* and Yvonne surprisingly started singing the words. Becks joined in, and soon we were all belting it out, doing all the gestures, and ended up practically crying with laughter. Becks dabbed at her eyes carefully, not wanting to muck up her eyeliner.

'You do look different,' I said.

'I know!' said Becks. 'Thanks, Yvonne!'

I wasn't so sure it was a *good* different, but Becks seemed thrilled.

'I'll give you a makeover too, if you like,' said Yvonne, nodding at me.

I wavered. I didn't fancy all that black stuff round my eyes, and I knew I'd rub it and end up looking like a panda. But I did like the idea of proper lipstick.

'Hey, dreamy? Make-up? Hair?' said Yvonne.

I let her put lipstick on me, even outlining it with a lip pencil and then adding a bit of gloss. I wasn't sure if it made me look good or not. It certainly tasted really odd.

'Don't lick it, silly!' said Yvonne.

I found the temptation so great I had to keep my mouth open, which didn't improve my looks at all. Yvonne did my hair too, piling it up on top of my head. I rather liked this new look. I hoped it made me look much older. I sucked in my cheeks and peered at myself in the mirror, turning from side to side.

Becks fell about laughing and Yvonne sniggered. I flounced off downstairs to find Mo. She was on her hands and knees playing peek-a-boo with little Taylor. He was sitting up but every time he reached forward to grab his grandma's hands he wobbled precariously, which only made him chuckle more.

'Oh my, look at Her Ladyship!' said Mo. 'We'd better make sure we wash all that lipstick away and give your hair a good brush before your mum comes to collect you.'

'I wonder where she's actually going today?' I said, kneeling down to play with Taylor too. 'Did she tell you, Mo?'

'No, dear. Your mum isn't one for confiding, bless her. It would maybe do her good. She's looking very stressed – and you lot disappearing into thin air the other day didn't help!' said Mo.

'I know,' I said guiltily. 'But we've promised never to do that again.'

'I should think so too. It got us all in a state. You should have seen dear old Tommy Brown. He's got such a soft spot for all you lot, especially you, Phoebe,' said Mo.

'Really?' I said, thrilled to the core.

'Now, let's start baking, eh? We'll pop Taylor into his highchair and he can watch the proceedings. I thought we'd start with a fruit cake. It's my Barry's favourite. It always gets him in a good mood when he has fruit cake with a knob of cheese for his tea. Still, he's feeling pretty perked up anyway, with young Perry helping him with the bike. He used to spend ages out there with our Ryan and misses him something chronic now he's living up north. None of our girls have been interested. You can't imagine Yvonne in oily old dungarees messing about with a spanner, can you?'

Mo kept up a cheery chatter all the time we were weighing out

ingredients. I couldn't stop myself slipping the odd sultana or glacé cherry into my mouth, but she didn't seem to mind at all. When we got to the mixing stage she let me have a turn with the wooden spoon too. I was very pleased, though it made my arm ache dreadfully.

'That's the ticket,' said Mo. 'You're a great little baker, Phoebe. Do you help Mum make cakes at home?'

'Mum doesn't ever make cakes when we're at *home* home because she's too busy at work. Dad makes birthday cakes for us, but we put everything in the mixer and just whizz it all up. I help him write our names on the top with icing sugar but it goes a bit splodgy sometimes. Dad doesn't care though, he just laughs,' I said. I had to screw up my face to stop myself crying because I suddenly missed him so much.

'There's one bonus when you hand-mix a cake,' Mo said quickly. 'You get to make a wish.'

'Really?' I said.

'Yep. I think you've done the most mixing so you get the first wish,' she said.

I closed my eyes and wished with all my might. *I wish I get to see Dad soon, soon, soon!*

'Do the wishes come true?' I asked.

'Ah!' said Mo. 'Some of mine have certainly come true.'

'So will mine?'

'Well, I'll wish that your wish comes true, and then it'll be a double wish,' she said. 'Much more powerful.'

She took the spoon from me, closed her own eyes, and wished too.

'Thank you, Mo!' I said.

When the fruit cake was baking in the oven we put little Taylor down for a nap because he'd gone a bit grizzly and kept rubbing his eyes. He protested furiously for two minutes and then suddenly went fast asleep.

'Funny little lamb,' Mo said fondly. 'Now then, Phoebe. Are you still in the mood for baking? Would you like to make a rhubarb pie?'

'Oh, yes please! I love rhubarb,' I said happily.

We picked the rhubarb in the back garden first. It was a lovely garden, with lots of flowers and a proper fruit and vegetable patch at the bottom. There were chickens too, pecking about in their run. I watched them, fascinated. I hoped Daisy wasn't feeling too lonely in her own run.

'Do you want to hold one?' Mo asked.

I wasn't sure. They had very beady eyes and pointed beaks. I thought they might object strongly.

'This one's my favourite, Snowdrop,' said Mo, picking up a small white one. She handed her to me. She was much softer than I'd imagined, her body very little under all her feathers.

'Oh, she's lovely,' I said, stroking her. 'Nina Cresswell used to keep hens. Mr Thomas Brown turned her chicken run into a special playground for my guinea pig Daisy.'

'Did he now? He's a good soul, Tommy.'

'Yes he is. And you're a good soul too, Mo,' I said.

She laughed, and gently pinched my cheek.

I put Snowdrop back with the other chickens and helped pick the rhubarb. I tried nibbling a tiny bit but it tasted so sour I had to spit it straight out.

'It has to be cooked first, with a lot of sugar!' Mo laughed.

I had to take her word for it, though I wasn't so sure I liked her kind of rhubarb. But when I had a slice of pie with creamy custard at lunchtime I decided it was the best fruit I'd ever tasted, and I wanted to eat rhubarb pie and custard for pudding every day of my life.

We had cheese omelettes first, Mo standing at the stove whisking up plate after plate of them, six in all. Taylor had a runny boiled egg and soldiers and a little portion of custard in his Peter Rabbit dish.

Perry picked at his food cautiously, always unnerved by anything different. Becks ate hers slowly and daintily, not wanting to smudge her lipstick. I ate enthusiastically and Mo gave me one of her winks.

'That's what I like to see – a child with a healthy appetite,' she said.

After lunch Perry went back to the motorbike with Barry, and Becks went upstairs with Yvonne to look at their favourite influencers on Yvonne's mobile.

Mo and I loaded the dishwasher together and put Taylor down for another nap in his cot.

'What shall we do now, eh?' she said. She nodded at the drawing book and pastel box I'd brought with me. 'Are you going to do some colouring, pet?'

I nodded.

'In that case I'll watch a bit of telly,' said Mo, sinking down on the sofa.

I sat opposite her and half watched television too, while I started sketching. It felt odd being back in a house where you could amuse yourself just by pressing a button or two. I mostly stared at Mo, taking in the shape of her head and the comfortable slump of her body.

She glanced over at me. 'You're not drawing *me*, are you?' she said.

'You don't mind, do you?' I asked.

'Well, when our Yvonne used to draw me she gave me a huge head with my arms coming out each side instead of ears. Not very flattering!' Mo laughed. 'I hope you're a bit more artistic like.'

I wanted to tell her that even Mum thought I was good at drawing, but worried that it might sound like boasting. I just

smiled instead, and carried on. After a while Mo's head nodded and she slumped a little more. She was having a nap like Taylor.

I'd already drawn her eyes open, but it was easy to smudge things differently with Nina's pastels. I closed her eyes and lowered her chin and drew her fast asleep. When I felt I'd got her whole shape right, taking up all the page, I started doing the colouring part, the best bit. It didn't really matter if I didn't get the colours the exact shade.

Mo was still fast asleep when I'd finished her portrait, twenty minutes later. I didn't really want to start another picture. It was an awful lot of effort just doing one. The television was a bit boring now, and I wanted to flick through the channels to see if there was anything more interesting, but Mo had hold of the remote, and I didn't think it fair to wake her up.

There was a pile of magazines on a little table beside my chair. I turned the pages idly, but it was mostly about the Royal family and celebrities I hadn't even heard of. I was tempted to scribble moustaches and beards on all the silly ladies, but I couldn't spoil Mo's magazine. I flipped through and then stopped, surprised. There was someone I recognized! She was much older than all the other ladies featured, but she still wore a lot of make-up, and she had mad pink hair. She was holding up a picture book with a dog on the cover. I recognized that snubby little face and those bulgy eyes too. It was silly old Puggy-Wuggy and Melissa Harris, the

writer Dad used to work for. And there was Dad's name too, in bold black print: Michael Robinson!

I gave a little squeak and started reading the article.

Melissa Harris welcomed me into her beautiful eclectically furnished apartment, and settled me on an ornate velvet sofa with a cup of tea in rose-patterned fine china. She didn't spill a drop, but I noticed that her many-ringed hands were shaking. She's still a very sprightly charming lady in spite of her seventy-nine summers, but her fine skin was very pale and her blue eyes were troubled.

'I shall never get over it,' she said softly, still clearly utterly stricken. 'I took Robbie into my home. I treated him like my own son. I trusted him utterly. And this is the way he repaid me!' She dabbed at a tear with her long silk scarf. 'How could he steal all my money?'

What! How could that terrible old woman say such a thing about my dad! He'd never stolen a penny in his life!

I wanted to strangle her with her silk scarf! How could they write such wicked lies?

'*You had no inkling that he was systematically pocketing your own earnings from your wonderful Puggy-Wuggy books, Miss Harris?*'

'*None whatsoever! I cheerfully admit that I should have paid more attention to my bank statements, but I don't get along with modern technology. Oh, for the days of cheques and little conversations over the bank counter! That's partly the reason I employed Robbie – to take care of such things. I am a creative! I need to live in my own little fantasy world.*'

'*I understand entirely, Miss Harris. But even so, did it never occur to you that it was a little risky to give Robinson so much responsibility?*'

'*Oh my lord, you sound like that terrible defence lawyer, hounding me as if* I *were the criminal!*'

She shed several more tears and I felt truly terrible. I apologized profusely and did my utmost to reassure her. She shook her head helplessly, and spread her hands in the air in an expressive gesture.

'*There there, dear heart. I'm the one who should be apologizing for being such a foolish soul. But I must explain that I wouldn't have taken on anyone out of the blue. Robbie is married to the head of children's books at my publishing house! I'd met him at little soirées. He is a creative himself, for goodness' sake!*'

(Michael Robinson used to write the Robinson stories and scripts, a minor hit a few years ago.)

They weren't minor! The first Robinson book was *massive,* top

of the children's charts! And the Robinson series on television had hundreds of thousands of viewers. How *dare* this horrible fawning journalist write such nonsense.

I asked Miss Harris if this whole shocking state of affairs had affected her creativity in any way. At this she sat up straight and gave me a dazzling smile, suddenly reminding me that she'd been a famous spirited beauty back in the days of Swinging London – and, in fact, was still a beautiful woman now.

'Not at all! Well, I can no longer bear to write about Puggy-Wuggy, because all this ugliness comes flooding back to me. But I am not a woman to give in and go under. I have laid that poor little dog to rest, but now I have another dear little chap in my life. His name is Noodle-Poodle, a tiny teacup poodle who is totally adorable. I already have a television contract, and the first book about him will be published late autumn, ready for Christmas. My new publishers and I are so excited!'

Noodle-Poodle! He sounded even more ridiculous than Puggy-Wuggy. How could these sickening books be successful when Dad's wonderful Robinson stories were already out of print, and the television series almost forgotten!

I congratulated Miss Harris, and asked her how she felt about Michael Robinson, now he was languishing in jail.

In jail! In jail, in jail, in jail! I could barely believe it! How could they put Dad in prison when it was clear as anything that it was all wicked lies! Someone else must have pocketed Miss Harris's money and now poor Dad was being blamed! What was the matter

with Mum? Why hadn't she hired the best lawyers in the land to prove Dad's case? How could she let them send Dad to *prison*?

Miss Harris sighed softly. 'Do you know something? Even after what he's done, I can't find it in my heart to hate him. In fact, I feel sorry for the poor man. If he'd only asked me for a loan of money I'd have given it to him gladly. I know he needs to be taught a lesson, and heaven forbid he ever preys on any other gullible artiste, but I'm sad he was given a prison sentence. Still, I understand nine months is pretty lenient. I hope he uses his time in confinement purposefully. You never know, perhaps he might even write another of his little Robinson stories.' Miss Harris gave a tinkling laugh. 'Poor Robbie-Wobbie!'

Tears spurted down my cheeks. Nine months! Oh, my poor dad! He wasn't exploring his island, constructing his shelter, gathering berries, fishing for food, building his fire, filming every day for his Robinson book. Of course he wasn't. I'd made it up so vividly that it had become real, but deep, deep down, perhaps I'd known all along that it couldn't possibly be true.

But this couldn't possibly be all true either! Dad must be in prison if the magazine said so, but it was obviously the most terrible wicked mistake. Mum had to hire a private investigator to work on his case, interrogate Melissa Harris, demand the bank statements, look at Dad's, *prove* that he was totally innocent.

That was why those hateful men had been lurking at our gate at home, asking questions, trying to take photographs. Why didn't Mum march up to them and tell them that they'd got the story all

wrong, and that Dad was utterly innocent? Why didn't *she* give a long tearful interview to this magazine journalist explaining that it was all a total mistake? How could she have run away with us here, without saying a word?

I pictured Dad in a dank cell, his head in his hands, wondering why he hadn't heard from us, thinking we'd all abandoned him.

I thought of people back at home opening up this magazine and reading about my dad, thinking he was a criminal. I thought of Amelie reading it and then whispering about it to Kate. Maybe she'd got wind of it already and that was why they seemed so secretive. Well, it wasn't a secret now. The whole class would know, the whole school, even all the teachers.

I thought of people here reading it. Mr Thomas Brown and all our friends at the railway station. Mo herself. Or had she read it already? The magazine felt smooth and shiny, with no turned-down corners or rumpled pages. Perhaps she hadn't got round to reading it yet.

I glanced at her. Her eyes were still shut and she was snoring softly. I heard Becks and Yvonne laughing upstairs. I heard Barry explaining something to Perry outside. I took hold of the magazine and ripped out the entire article, crumpled it up into a tight little ball and stuffed it into my jeans pocket.

I put the magazine back on the pile and then wrapped my arms round myself, my hands hanging onto my elbows, and

rocked slowly backwards and forwards. I mustn't shout or scream or cry. I had to hold it all in until Mum came for us and we were back in the cottage.

It was so hard. I sat while the television talked on and on about escaping to the country. Mum had tried to do just that. We had escaped to the middle of nowhere, but it didn't make any difference. There was no escape, no matter where we lived. I couldn't pretend anything about Dad now. I had to face it. He was in prison, my poor lovely wonderful dad.

'I know where you've been, Mum!' I said, the minute we were in the car.

'Barry and I fixed his motorbike, Mum, and he says I make a grand mechanic!' Perry interrupted.

'Mum, guess what, Yvonne and I are kind of friends now. She did my make-up. Don't you think it suits me, doing it like this?' Becks said simultaneously.

'Shut up!' I shouted. 'Mum, listen! I *know*!'

'Phoebe, please! Don't bellow like that. I've got a splitting headache. Could you all please be quiet so I can concentrate on my driving,' Mum said sternly.

'*I know what's happened to Dad!*' I insisted.

Perry looked at me, wrinkling his nose. Becks craned round from the front seat, peering at me. Mum stared straight ahead at

the road. She was holding the steering wheel so tightly her knuckles were white.

'Not . . . another . . . word!' she said, in her scariest voice.

So I bit my lip and said nothing further, though I felt I might burst. Perry kept staring at me. Becks turned again and mouthed, 'What?' I nodded at Mum and shook my head, because I knew she could see me in her driving mirror.

The journey felt like it took for ever. It seemed to get hotter and stuffier in the car, even though the windows were open. I felt the blood beating in my head. The screwed-up article from the magazine dug into my back uncomfortably. It was as if all the hateful words were scratching and biting. Sickly phrases kept repeating endlessly inside my head.

The moment Mum parked the car by the telephone box I blurted it out: 'Dad's in prison!'

Becks and Perry stared at me as if I'd lost the plot. But Mum didn't argue. She got out of the car and leaned against it, as if her legs were about to give way. She took a deep breath. Then she looked around at the quiet road and the silent wood. There were two hikers making their way up the hill, knapsacks on their back.

'Wait till we're indoors,' said Mum. Then she walked ahead, weaving in and out of the trees.

'You're crazy! Dad's not in prison!' said Perry.

'I know I said he might end up there, Phoebes, but I didn't really *mean* it,' said Becks.

'*Come along!*' Mum called.

'See! I'm right! She's not even trying to deny it!' I hissed. I wished she *would*. I wanted her to say that it was all a huge mistake. Of course Dad wasn't in prison. The magazine had got it all wrong. It was another Michael Robinson altogether. The Puggy-Wuggy woman was deluded and needed psychiatric treatment. Or maybe I did? I'd imagined the whole thing. If I looked at the piece of paper in my pocket I'd see that it was about another man, another woman, nothing at all to do with Dad and Melissa Harris . . .

Mum could make up anything she wanted, and I'd believe her, because anything was better than that truth. But when we'd trekked across the field and were in the cottage, Mum drank a glass of water and then faced us.

'Sit down,' she said, gesturing at the kitchen table. 'All right, Phoebe. You're right. How did you find out?' She poured herself more water with shaking hands. 'Did Mo tell you?'

'It was in one of her magazines. She doesn't know I've read it. I tore it out. Look!' I fished it from my pocket, and smoothed it out. My hands were trembling too, and I tore part of it. 'It's not true, Mum, is it? Melissa Harris is telling wicked lies. We have to get Dad out of prison. It's absolutely ludicrous, isn't it? We need to

clear Dad's name. He's totally innocent, isn't he?' I said.

'What do you mean? What's Dad supposed to have done? Is he *really* in prison?' Becks said, shaking her head.

Perry said nothing at all. He stood up and made for the stairs.

'Perry? Where are you going?' said Mum.

'I don't want to listen,' he said, blinking rapidly. 'I don't want to listen, I don't want to listen.'

'I'm sorry, Perry, but just this once you have to listen,' said Mum. 'Come back and sit down, please.'

He put his hands over his ears, trying to block everything out.

'Will you just *tell* me exactly what's happened,' said Becks, crying in frustration.

'That awful Puggy-Wuggy woman says that Dad stole all her money, and now he's in prison,' I said.

'But that's ridiculous! Dad would never steal anything! He's *Dad*!' said Becks.

'Yes!' I said. I wanted to hug her. 'Of course Dad would never, ever do such a thing. Would he, Mum?'

Mum put her glass down on the table. She looked at the three of us. 'He did do it,' she said.

'No, he didn't! He couldn't have,' I said automatically. 'I won't listen to you if you're going to say such stupid wicked things.'

'Please, Phoebe. Perry. Becks. I've tried so hard to hide it from you. I knew it would be terribly upsetting for you. Dad has been

desperate to keep it all a secret. He's so ashamed,' said Mum.

'No he's not! He hasn't *done* anything. He's on his island, making his film,' I insisted. I tried with all my heart to conjure up the old images – but they stayed as flat as the drawings Nina Cresswell had painted in her old book of *Robinson Crusoe*.

'Phoebe, I think it's time to stop pretending. You have to understand,' said Mum. She tried to take hold of my hand.

I snatched it away. 'I *do* understand. Dad would never, ever do anything wrong. He especially wouldn't steal. He's not a thief!' I cried.

'Mum, there must be some mistake. Dad would never take money off anyone,' said Becks.

'Never, never, never,' said Perry, his hands still pressing hard over his ears.

'Dad says he was just *borrowing* the money,' said Mum. 'He knew it was wrong, but he was desperate for someone to finance his film. The animation company for the Puggy-Wuggy books seemed very interested in adapting Robinson too. They actually had a pot of money for it from some pop star enthusiast whose children had loved the books. But not enough. Melissa Harris let Dad take over all her financial affairs – she was always hopeless with money matters. Her books are enormously popular, and I know it sounds incredible but she was making millions. So Dad was tempted to use her money to finance his own film and get it

into production. He got carried away. You know what he's like. He hoped he'd make enough money to pay it all back without her even knowing.'

'That's nonsense,' I said.

'It *is* nonsense. He just wasn't thinking straight. He was so desperate to reboot his career. He hated not making any money for the family. He couldn't stand it that I had to pay all the bills. Which is ironic, because now I haven't got a job and *I* can't pay the bills,' said Mum.

'Because of Dad?' said Becks.

'There was a suggestion from the prosecuting lawyer at the trial that I might have been involved too. I'm not sure anyone actually believed it, but my boss still felt that under the circumstances it would be better if I handed in my notice,' said Mum. 'It didn't help that Melissa Harris has now gone to another publisher, so we've lost our bestselling author.'

'Oh, Mum,' said Becks, and she stood up and gave Mum a big hug. 'Poor, poor Mum. Why didn't you tell us all this before?'

'How could I? I didn't want to break your hearts. I know you all think highly of Dad. Especially Phoebe,' said Mum. 'That's why I took you all here. It would have been a nightmare at home, with so many people knowing us.'

'So are we going to stay here then?' Becks asked.

'I don't know what we're going to do, to be totally honest. I'm

not sure what we can afford,' said Mum. She paused. 'I've even had to put our house up for sale.'

'*What?*'

'I know, it's a terrible shock, but part of the reason Dad got such a light sentence was the fact that he's determined to pay all the money back. A lot of it had gone already, when he was trying to develop the animation. We have to sell the house and find somewhere smaller,' said Mum.

'It's not a *light* sentence – the magazine said it was nine whole months!' I said.

'Dad will probably get out earlier for good behaviour. He's trying his hardest in prison. He's even helping some of the guys there with their reading and writing,' said Mum.

'How do you know?' I said. 'You kept saying you didn't know where Dad was and you couldn't be in touch, and yet you must have been lying all along!'

'Phoebes, don't get angry with *Mum*! She's had to be heroic,' said Becks.

'I was trying to protect you, darling,' Mum said. 'And I wasn't really lying anyway. I saw him today for the first time. It was so awful.'

'Dad isn't awful,' said Perry, putting his head on the table, with his arms crossed over it.

'I didn't mean *Dad's* awful, Perry. Of course he's not. It's

just seeing him in prison is so upsetting. It's awful *for* him,' Mum said.

'You've really been to see Dad in prison?' Becks asked.

'Yes. The whole process is so difficult, because I had to apply for a visiting order, and it's a nightmare without the internet or a phone signal,' said Mum. 'But it's all sorted now, and as you all know about the situation I'll apply for a family visit too. If you'd come?'

'Of course we'll come,' said Becks.

'I need to see Dad,' Perry muttered, his voice muffled by his arms.

'And you'll come too, Phoebe, obviously?' Mum said.

Obviously, obviously, obviously. But in this new terrifying topsy-turvy life it wasn't obvious at all. Did I want to see Dad in prison? I imagined a bleak, grey building with strict warders in uniform and scary criminals shuffling around in ugly prison clothing. I pictured Dad amongst them, cringing. He wasn't *my* dad, my big wonderful brave dad.

I thought of that last evening, when he'd bought us all presents – with Mum's card. I'd sat with him up in the attic, when he was looking at the Robinson game. Why hadn't he told me then, if he loved me so much? Why hadn't he explained? How could he have walked off the next morning without telling us that he wouldn't be coming back for months and months?

How could he have been so cowardly? How could he have taken Melissa Harris's money? She was horrible and stupid and ridiculous, but it was still *stealing*. And pointless stealing too, because the Robinson animation had never been made.

I thought of that dusty plastic toy island up in the attic. I remembered the old Robinson programme I'd seen on YouTube with a younger, thinner Dad chatting self-consciously to the camera, giving Robinson and all his animal friends different silly voices. I thought of the books I knew by heart and the words themselves seemed so silly now. There was no chance they'd ever be turned into a successful animation. If Dad had actually made a real desert island film nobody would want to watch it. My dad was a nobody himself. My own dad.

'I don't want to see him,' I said.

Mum and Becks and Perry stared at me.

'I don't want to see him!' I repeated.

'It's all right, Phoebe. I know what you must be feeling,' Mum said gently.

'You don't know what I'm feeling at all!' I said.

'Phoebes!' said Becks.

'I know you can't help feeling scared, Phoebe,' said Mum, doing her best to be reassuring. 'I can't pretend prison is the most welcoming place, though I suppose they do their best in the circumstances. The visiting hall is a bit bleak, and it's all so public.

I hope in a little while they'll let us have a proper extended family visit, in a room all by ourselves. But for now you'll be able to sit at a table and chat to Dad. He won't be behind bars; he'll be there right in front of you. *I* was scared, and I think poor Dad was scared too, so at first we hardly knew what to say to each other, but after five minutes or so it became more normal, and we managed to forget all the other people and just be us.'

'I don't want to be us,' I said, tears dripping down my face. 'There isn't any "us" any more. Dad's spoilt it all. I don't want to see him in prison. I don't want to see him ever again.'

I ran out of the kitchen, out of the house, past the mended chicken run, past Nigel's grave, out into the field. I rushed up the newly-strimmed path to the special place where Dad spoke to me and threw myself down on the grass.

'How could you do it, Dad? How could you be so stupid and mean and spoil everything? Tell me!'

I held my breath, choking back my tears, pressing my ear to the ground. I waited and waited. Dad didn't say anything. Dad wasn't there. That Dad wasn't real. Maybe he never had been. Perhaps I'd just made him up.

After a long time Mum came and sat beside me.

'Oh, Phoebe,' she said softly. She started stroking my back. 'I'm so sorry.'

'You're not the one who should feel sorry,' I muttered.

'I felt exactly the same way when I found out,' said Mum.

'He's spoilt everything,' I wept.

'I know. But Phoebe, he's still *Dad*.'

'No he's not. I don't want anything to do with him now,' I said, clenching my fist and thumping the grass.

'It's only natural to feel angry, but you'll calm down soon,' said Mum.

'No I *won't*!' I insisted. I was angry at Mum too. I was angry at everyone.

I stayed out in the field long after Mum went back indoors. The sky darkened. The clouds gathered overhead. It looked as if it was going to rain. I didn't care. I wanted thunder to crash and the whole sky to burn with sheet lightning. But there were just a few drops of rain, not enough to soak me, though I felt uncomfortably damp.

I wriggled round, staring through the swaying grass. Some kind of rodent with a long tail suddenly dashed past my nose. Beetles crawled all around me, small but menacing. A bird of prey hovered high above the field. The brambles seemed unusually thick and close, creeping nearer.

I curled into a tight little ball. I could feel my heart thumping inside me. I always called Dad when I was frightened, but he wasn't there any more. I was trapped in the middle of nowhere without anyone at all.

Then I heard someone tramping along the path, whistling tunelessly. Perry. I sat up, wiping my eyes with the back of my hand. Perry's own eyes were red.

'Here you are,' he said, and he squatted down beside me.

'Have you had one of your turns?' I asked.

'Nope,' said Perry. 'I just cried a bit in the cupboard, that's all.'

'Are you angry too?'

Perry wrinkled his nose, wondering. 'I don't think so.'

'So what are you feeling?' I said, sniffing.

Perry considered. 'I'm feeling sad,' he said eventually.

'I can't believe this is all happening, can you? It's the worst thing ever, isn't it?' I said.

Perry thought for a while. 'But we've still got the railway and all the trains. And I've got motorbikes now too,' he said.

'You're hopeless, Perry. You only ever seem to care about *things*,' I said. 'Maybe you'd like a robot for a dad.'

'I *like* robots,' said Perry. 'If they're carefully programmed they can't surprise you. Maybe I'd like to be a robot too.' He straightened up. 'I am a robot! I am a robot! I am a robot!' he chanted.

'Go and be a robot somewhere else,' I said.

'I have been sent with a message,' he said, still in his robot voice. 'Mum says it's teatime. Come in for tea.'

'I'm not the slightest bit hungry,' I said. I realized this was actually true. The thought of putting anything in my mouth made

me want to heave. Perhaps I was never going to eat again. I'd soon be as thin as Becks. Thinner. 'I've given up eating,' I announced.

'As if! You're always hungry,' said Perry. 'And anyway, how would that help anything?'

'Oh, go back to the cottage and leave me in peace!'

'All right. I am a robot and I do as you command,' he said and walked off stiffly.

I could hear him chanting *I am a robot* as he made his way through the field. I waited for Becks to be sent to persuade me, but she didn't come. Mum didn't come back either. I wasn't sure how

long I was waiting, but it seemed an extraordinary age. They were clearly having tea without me.

I decided I didn't care. I truly wasn't hungry, but I was starting to worry about Daisy. What about *her* tea? Would Becks remember? I hadn't even checked on Daisy yet and she'd been left on her own all day long. She'd be wondering what on earth had happened to me.

I thought of her bumbling around her hutch, her little nose quivering, and after a while it got too much. I picked myself up and started trailing back to the cottage, limping a little because I'd given myself pins and needles.

I stood outside the back door a while, feeling embarrassed, not wanting them all to stare at me when I came back indoors. I listened, wondering if they were talking about me. I could hear a murmur of voices but couldn't make out what they were saying. They all sounded quite normal, which made me feel indignant. Perhaps they'd forgotten all about me. Maybe they'd have left me all by myself in the field the whole evening? All *night*?

I automatically thought of Dad for comfort, knowing he'd always come and get me and make me feel better. But he wasn't here: he'd spoilt everything – he wasn't *Dad* any more. He was a thief.

I used to count cherry stones with Amelie to see who we were going to marry. *Tinker, tailor, soldier, sailor, rich man, poor man, beggar*

man, thief. Thief was always the worst. I remembered the pictures in my old Nursery Rhyme book. The thief was climbing furtively through a window, with a horrible greedy leer on his face, clutching a sack marked *Swag*.

I hated that picture when I was little. I couldn't help imagining the thief climbing through *my* window, wanting to steal all my toys, maybe wanting to steal *me*. I had nightmares about him.

I never dreamed that there was a real thief hiding inside my dad. He hated thieves. He was hardly ever cross with any of us, but he always made a fuss if we stole something. He was horrified when Becks started secondary school and he spotted a blue nail varnish at the bottom of her school bag. When he asked her where she'd got it from she confessed that she'd stolen it from Boots when she met up with some new friends.

'I didn't *want* to steal it, Dad! But we all have to steal something to be in this little gang, and so I had to do it. Please don't be cross with me!' she begged.

Dad gave her this long lecture that it was always very wrong to steal, for whatever reason, and he was very disappointed in her. He actually made her cry.

Perry tried to steal a little screwdriver in B&Q once and Dad was cross with him too, and then Perry had a bit of a meltdown, and Dad had to stand there for an hour while he calmed down, with everyone staring at us.

The only thing *I* ever stole was a strawberry out of a punnet in Morrisons, *one* strawberry, but Dad saw and gave me a big lecture too, even going on about it again when he came to kiss me goodnight.

'I know it seems a little thing to you, Phoebe, but think what would happen if *everyone* stole from the supermarket. It's wrong, and you mustn't ever do it again,' Dad said solemnly.

He made me feel like I was a terrible person – for taking one strawberry worth ten pence. He was the biggest hypocrite in the whole world, because now I knew he had stolen hundreds of thousands of pounds from one old lady. He was a liar too, pretending everything was all right when it was terribly wrong.

My dad was a liar and a hypocrite and a thief and I never wanted to see him again ever, especially not in prison.

I didn't know why I was hesitating outside the cottage, when *I* hadn't done anything wrong. I marched inside, my head held high.

Mum and Becks and Perry were all sitting at the table, eating cheese on toast and tomato salad, as if it was an ordinary supper time and nothing at all had happened.

'There you are, Phoebe,' said Mum. 'Come and sit down, darling. I'll make you a fresh cheese toastie.'

'No, thank you,' I said. It was no sacrifice. The smell of grilled cheese suddenly made my stomach turn. The thought of putting

a big wodge of it in my mouth made me retch.

'What can I get you then? How about a bowl of cornflakes?' Mum suggested.

'I'm not the slightest bit hungry,' I declared grandly. I gave her a withering stare and stomped up the stairs. How could they sit there munching as if nothing had happened? I didn't want anything more to do with any of them.

I went into my bedroom and rushed to Daisy. She squeaked excitedly at the sound of my footsteps.

'You poor little darling,' I said. But I saw someone else had already given her dandelions and lettuce leaves, replenished her food bowl with nuggets and filled her drinking bottle. She bobbed her head at me, and then carried on nibbling. I badly wanted to take her out of her cage and cuddle her, but it would be mean to interrupt her meal.

I sat down on the bed, shivering. I realized my clothes were really wet now, but I decided not to care. I *wanted* to get a chill. I stared up at the seagulls on the ceiling. I could hear their sad cries inside my head. When I was grown-up, I wanted to be like Nina, and live all by myself. I'd never bother to see anyone. I'd never, ever let myself love anyone ever again. I'd just have animals: a loyal dog, a little cat, and several soft little guinea pigs. Charlie the cockapoo, Selina the Siamese – and Rosie, Bluebell and Buttercup to be Daisy's friends.

I'd been so thrilled when Dad gave me Daisy. I'd said he was the best dad ever, the most wonderful dad in the world. He'd looked so pleased – and yet he must have known he was going to court the next day. He knew he was going to prison – but he didn't *tell* me.

I picked up my drawing of Dad and me, dancing in the air. I reached for the box of pastels, took a black one, and started fiercely scribbling over our faces.

'What are you doing?' said Becks, coming into the room. 'Oh, Phoebe, don't! Stop it! You're ruining your lovely picture!'

She grabbed hold of my hand but I wrenched it free and started stabbing at the canvas instead. I was so violent I made holes in it.

'Everything's ruined!' I panted, carrying on until there was nothing left of Dad and me, just a black pock-marked mess.

As if in confirmation there was a sudden flash of lightning, a clap of thunder, and the drizzle of rain suddenly became a downpour.

The rain had stopped by the morning, but everywhere was still soaked. My feet got really wet picking dandelions for Daisy. It was hot and humid, and my head ached.

Mum said she was taking us to the railway, trying to act as if nothing had happened.

'Do you think Mo knows about Dad?' Becks asked. 'That article was in her magazine.'

'I don't know,' said Mum. 'Maybe she read it and didn't connect it with us. I'd sooner you didn't mention it to her, anyway.'

'As if I would,' said Becks.

'Are you going to tell Jake?' Mum asked her.

Becks shook her head. 'No, I'm not telling *anyone*, not even Jake. It's private family stuff.'

'Yes, it is,' said Mum. 'Do you understand that, Perry?

I don't want you to tell any of your friends at the railway about Dad.'

'We don't talk about private stuff, we talk about the railway,' said Perry.

'That's good,' said Mum. She turned to me. 'You're not going to tell anyone, are you, Phoebe?'

I shook my head.

'She's not talking to anyone, not even us,' said Perry.

That was true. I'd gone into my own silent world. I didn't want to care about anyone any more. They just let you down and broke your heart.

'Oh, Phoebes,' said Becks, and she put her arm round me. I didn't cuddle in to her. I just stood there, not reacting.

'I do wish you'd cheer up a bit,' Becks said. 'It's not the end of the world. I mean, it's awful, and terribly sad, and it looks like we're going to be really poor for a bit, but Dad isn't going to be in prison for ever.'

'That's right, Becks,' said Mum, looking at her gratefully.

Becks had been crying last night in bed, but she was trying so hard to make the best of things now. Even Perry was making a big effort. He might have acted like a robot yesterday, as if he didn't care that much, but I'd heard him muttering in his cupboard alone in the dark last night: *No Dad, no Dad, no Dad, no Dad.* He sounded heartbroken.

I was the one who had loved Dad most, yet I'd decided I wasn't going to care at all. I didn't care about *anything* any more. Mum tried gently persuading me to have breakfast, but I kept shaking my head, my lips pressed together. I eventually tried to push the wretched plate of toast away and knocked over my cup of tea instead.

'For God's sake, stop acting like a sulky toddler!' Mum snapped, unable to stop herself.

I didn't react. I just sat there scowling, staring straight through her.

'Go without then,' said Mum. 'Come on, everyone, let's clear up and get going.'

I made no attempt to help. I just sat there.

'Now listen to me, Phoebe,' said Mum. 'We're going to the railway, right?'

I shook my head. I didn't want to go anywhere, least of all to the railway.

'You'll feel better there. It'll be a bit more normal. And you'll like seeing Mr Brown,' said Mum.

I shook my head again.

Mum took a deep breath. I could see a little pulse beating on her forehead. 'I can't leave you here, not all by yourself. Do you really want us all to stay at home too? It would be so unfair to Becks and Perry. And to me too, because I've got to apply for the

prison visit and work on my story and both my phone and my computer need charging. So will you please stir yourself and come too?'

I decided I couldn't be bothered to argue. I got ready and sat in the car with the others and went to the Primrose Railway, but it didn't feel as if I was really there. I was floating above myself, not attached to anyone.

Mr Thomas Brown was standing there in the entrance. 'Hello, hello, here's my favourite family,' he said. He looked at Mum. 'Sorry I was so huffy the other evening, my dear. My Jake's given me a good talking-to. I do hope we can let bygones be bygones?'

'Of course, Mr Brown! I was being incredibly tactless,' said Mum.

They smiled at each other awkwardly. The old me wanted to run to him and throw my arms round his waist – but I was the new me now. I didn't even smile at him. Becks greeted him warmly and Perry grabbed hold of his hand, though he usually hates touching anyone. He started talking at the top of his voice. He'd been reading his history of the Primrose Railway and wanted to know what the strange trolley in one of the old photographs was used for.

'I thought it might be for transporting luggage?' he asked.

'Good guess, lad, but it's actually for the plate-layers. They used to be employed by the company to make sure the track was

kept in good working order. They used the big handles to propel themselves up and down the line on the trolley. I think there might still be one in a corner of the workshop.' He consulted his watch. 'There's time to show you before the eleven o'clock. Come with me,' he said. He put his head to one side and looked at Mum. 'If that's all right, Mrs Robinson?'

'Of course it is. It's very kind of you,' Mum said gratefully.

I felt as if I'd been punched in the stomach. Mr Thomas Brown was *my* special friend, and yet here he was, going off with Perry. I glared at his back. Then he turned round and beckoned to Becks and me.

'Coming, girls?'

'I think I'll go and find Jake,' said Becks.

Mr Thomas Brown looked at me. 'Phoebe?' he asked, smiling.

I shook my head.

His eyebrows went up, but he just shrugged, and went off with Perry. I felt my eyes stinging. I bit my lip furiously. What was the matter with me? I was new me and didn't care a jot about anything.

'Why don't you go with them, darling?' Mum said.

I shook my head again.

'Oh well, I can't make you,' said Mum, sighing.

Becks spotted Jake on the other side of the track and went rushing over the bridge to see him.

'Come on, let's go and have a cup of tea in the Junction,' said

Mum. 'Tell you what: I'll treat you to a fry-up as you didn't have any breakfast.'

I went with her because I didn't want to be left standing on the platform by myself like a lemon. Thank goodness it wasn't one of the days that Mo volunteered there, so I didn't have to respond to her chat. The lady behind the counter was equally friendly, but I just hung my head and didn't respond.

'Bit shy, is she?' she said to Mum.

Mum sighed. 'You could call it that,' she said. 'Two teas please. And one full breakfast.'

I shook my head, but Mum took no notice. I was forced into speech. 'I don't *want* it, Mum!' I mumbled.

'Well, I've ordered it now,' said Mum. 'I think you'll get your appetite back when you see it.'

The plateful looked beautiful: the egg bright yellow, the bacon crispy, the tomatoes not too soggy, the sausage very slightly burnt, just the way I like everything. It smelled so good too, making me feel suddenly faint. But I was determined not to eat even one small mouthful.

I had to drink the tea though, because my throat ached so.

'That's a good girl,' said Mum. 'Now, how about a bite of sausage?'

'No thanks. I told you I didn't want it,' I said.

'Phoebe, I know you're very unhappy, and I understand. *I'm*

unhappy too. I wish you hadn't found out about Dad. Dear God, I wish he'd never been fool enough to take the money. I wish I still had my job. But we've just got to get on with things and cope the best we can. You being difficult and starving yourself isn't going to help anyone, least of all yourself,' Mum said.

I didn't *want* to be difficult, but I just couldn't seem to help it. I sat there letting the fried breakfast go completely cold. The lady behind the counter looked anxious.

'Is there something wrong with it?' she called to Mum.

'No, it looks delicious,' Mum said, embarrassed.

'Would she like some sauce? Brown or tomato?' the lady offered.

'No thank you. I think she just suddenly doesn't feel very well,' Mum said.

'Oh dear. Well, you've wasted your money then, haven't you?' she said.

'Yes, I have,' said Mum, sighing.

However, Perry ate the sausage and the bacon when he came back from his trip to the workshop.

'It's not breakfast, is it, Mum? It's brunch. Mr Thomas Brown showed me the trolley. He even let me have a go on it. He's the kindest man ever, isn't he?' said Perry, picking up my second slice of bacon.

'Don't eat with your fingers, darling. And it must be stone cold

by now. Yes, Mr Brown is very kind and very patient with you.' Mum hesitated. 'Though wouldn't you normally say *Dad* is the kindest man ever?'

Perry stopped chewing. 'Yes, but he took that lady's money, didn't he?'

'Keep your voice down! Yes, I know he did a very bad thing, but he's still a good man too, and he loves you very much and he's missing you all terribly,' said Mum. 'And we're missing him, aren't we?'

'Yes,' said Perry. He looked down at the floor. 'I love Dad, but I don't want to think about him now because it makes me unhappy.'

'*I* don't love him any more,' I muttered.

'Of course you do, Phoebe. That's why you're behaving like this,' said Mum.

'No it's not. And I *don't*, so there,' I said.

'Hey, hey! That's not the way to talk to your mother,' said Mr Thomas Brown, coming into the Junction.

'It's all right, Mr Brown. She's . . . upset,' said Mum.

'Oh dear,' said Mr Thomas Brown. 'Well, I've just come to tell you the eleven o'clock train's going in three minutes. Chop chop!'

'Have a lovely trip,' said Mum. 'And remember – Becks and Jake are in charge. And remember your promise too: don't do anything *dangerous*!' She plugged in her computer and opened it up.

'Still hard at work? Why don't you have a little ride too?' said

Mr Thomas Brown. 'You'll give yourself a headache crouching over that computer all the time.'

'*I've* got a headache,' I mumbled.

'I think it's the weather. Did you see the sheet lightning last night?' said Mr Thomas Brown.

'Sheet lightning? When? Oh, why didn't you get me out of my cupboard?' Perry wailed. 'I've never seen sheet lightning. It's the most amazing phenomenon. I've read all about it. Do you know why some lightning is forked and some is sheet?'

I didn't know and I didn't care, but Perry burbled about it for ages, long after we'd got on the train, leaving Mum still in the Junction. Becks was trailing around after Jake as he punched everyone's tickets. I sat staring out of the window, watching the damp fields and soggy meadows.

When we were getting near the terminus at Orlington, Perry went into the corridor and craned his head out of the window. So dangerous!

'Get back, Perry,' I muttered irritably.

'I'm looking for the plate-layers' hut where they had their lunch and had a rest. Mr Thomas Brown said they've still got one standing. It's like a little wooden house,' said Perry, leaning out even further.

'For goodness' sake, get back!' I shouted, and I tugged hard at his waist.

He came hurtling backwards, right on top of me. We scrabbled about on the floor, both protesting bitterly.

'Get *off* me! Why did you do that? I bet I've missed it now!' said Perry.

'Oh, excuse me for saving your life, Perry Robinson! And getting squashed to death into the bargain!' I said.

'Hey, hey, what are you two doing, rolling around on the floor?' Jake called along the corridor, smart in his ticket collector's uniform, but minus his peaked cap. Becks was wearing it, smirking behind him, though she frowned when she saw us.

'Stop it, you two! Rolling around like that! Mum would be mortified if she could see you,' Becks remonstrated.

'She'd be mortified if she could see *you*, larking around wearing Jake's cap. And I bet your grandad would have a thing or two to say to you too, Jake Brown, for flirting with my sister rather than doing your job properly,' I retorted, heaving myself to my feet. '*And* I just happened to stop Perry flinging himself out of the window.'

'You shut your face, Miss Bossy Knickers,' said Becks, but she gave me a quick hug. 'Are you OK now?' she whispered into my ear.

She was only being friendly, but I glared at her. What was the matter with her? Of course I wasn't OK! There she was, acting the fool with Jake, when we'd found out that our dad was in prison for committing a horrible sneaky shameful crime! What was the

matter with Perry, obsessing about the railway again, putting Dad right out of his mind?

There was an announcement over the train's intercom:

'Ladies and gentlemen, girls and boys, we will have a thirty-minute break at the terminus, so please feel free to stretch your legs, wander up and down the platform and make use of the refreshment room!'

Jake chanted along with it, word for word.

'Would you kids like a Coke or an ice cream?' he asked Perry and me.

'No, thank you,' I said.

'No, thank you,' said Perry, surprisingly.

'Suit yourselves,' said Becks. 'I'd love an ice cream, Jake.'

'So would I,' said Jake, smiling at her.

It made my stomach turn, seeing the way they looked at each other. I don't think Perry liked it either, because he wrinkled his nose up and looked the other way.

So Becks and Jake went off together at the terminus.

'See you right here, in plenty of time to get the train back,' said Becks.

'Yes, don't you dare be late, because the train will go without you,' said Jake. He drew himself up to his full height and imitated his grandad. *'The Primrose Railway takes great pride in running on time.'*

Perry and I rolled our eyes.

'Come on then,' said Perry, when they'd gone into the refreshment room.

'Come on where?'

'We'll nip back and have a proper look at the plate-layers' hut!' said Perry impatiently.

'What? On the tracks?' I swallowed, remembering the tunnel. 'Is it safe?'

'Yes, silly. It's *beside* the tracks. There's a little footpath,' said Perry.

'There isn't time!' I protested.

'There's heaps and heaps of time. It's only about a quarter of a mile away. Probably much less than that. We can walk there and back in thirty minutes, easy-peasy,' he said.

'I don't think so,' I said doubtfully.

'Yes, we can. If we get a move on and stop bumbling about,' said Perry. He sniggered stupidly and repeated the word *bumbling* several times with pleasure.

'Stop saying that! If we go we might miss the train back,' I said.

'So. We'll wait for the next one, right?' said Perry.

I thought about it. What did I care if we got into trouble again for missing the train? I didn't care about anything now, did I? 'All right then,' I said, though I had no desire whatsoever to see some old hut.

We walked up to the end of the platform and then turned round to see if anyone was watching.

'It's OK. No one's looking at us. They're just bumbling about. Bumbling, bumbling, bumbling . . .'

'Do shut *up!*' I said, but he ignored me.

We both jumped off the platform into the rough grass at the side of the tracks. It was muddy from last night's rain so it was hard to walk briskly. Perry was always fussy about his shoes, wanting the strip between the canvas and the sole to stay brilliantly white. He hopped from one sparse dry patch to another, giving little moans whenever he misjudged and got spattered in mud.

'Look, do you want to see this little hut thingy or not?' I said.

'Yes! But my shoes are getting spoilt!' said Perry.

'Then why don't you take them off and go barefoot? You can clean your feet much more easily,' I said.

I wasn't *serious*, but Perry bent down and started tugging at a shoelace.

'For goodness' sake, Perry, I was joking! You won't be able to get back on the train with totally muddy feet,' I said. 'Don't take your shoes off.'

'Why do you keep changing your mind?' Perry asked. 'You're confusing me.'

'I know,' I said, feeling guilty. 'Sorry. But do hurry all the same.'

'Phoebes, you do still like me, don't you?' Perry asked.

Perry never, ever asked that sort of question. It really worried me.

'Yes, of course I like you. I love you, you nutcase, because you're my brother,' I said.

'Yes, but Dad's your father and you've stopped loving him,' said Perry.

'That's different,' I said shortly.

'I know. You don't like him now because he stole that money. So if I told you I stole a penknife from Marcus White at school because I liked it so much and Mum and Dad won't let me have one – would that make you stop liking me?' Perry asked.

'Oh, Perry. That's *entirely* different, don't you see? I don't care if you stole a stupid old penknife from Marcus White.'

'It wasn't a stupid old penknife – it was a Swiss army knife with twenty-six functions. I wanted to see what they were and try to invent my own knife with twenty-seven. I thought you could have a little gadget with a soft rubbery bit on the end, which would be very useful for picking your nose,' Perry said seriously.

I burst out laughing in spite of myself.

'Oh, Perry, that's so typical of you!' I said. 'So, have you still got this Swiss army penknife hidden away?'

'No, Marcus guessed it was me who took it out of his desk, and

he and his mates found me in the playground and snatched it back,' said Perry.

'Oh dear,' I said.

'But you really still like me?'

'*Yes.*'

'But not Dad?'

'I don't want to talk about him,' I said.

'*I* like Dad,' said Perry. 'He was just trying to borrow the money, not steal it for ever.'

'I said I don't want to talk about him,' I said, putting my hands over my ears. 'Now do hurry *up*, Perry, or we won't be back in time to get on the train.'

'I *am* hurrying,' said Perry.

We both were, but time seemed to be hurrying much more rapidly. I kept glancing anxiously at my watch.

'Look, I think we'll just have to turn back now,' I said. 'We've been walking for nearly ten minutes already and there's no sign of the hut.'

'Hang on, the track bends round to the left. Let's just run round so we can see properly!' said Perry.

'No!' I said, but he took no notice.

I had to run after him, round the bulge of the bank, where we could see down the track almost to Forest Lake.

'*There* it is, look! Let's keep running! We can't go back when

we're so close to it now!' Perry cried, pointing at a little brown lump far along at the side of the track.

He charged ahead, not bothering with the mud splatters now. I sighed and followed.

It was a total disappointment when we got to it. It was just a little log cabin affair, very basic, not interesting or exciting in any way. We peered through the murky window and saw it was completely empty inside.

'I hoped they'd still have all their machinery there,' said Perry, sighing. 'Or maybe a chair or two, and a few old mugs for their tea. But there's nothing!'

'So come on then, let's hurry back. Twelve minutes left. We should just about make it,' I said, pulling at him.

Then I turned my head, because there was a strange creaking noise above us. I looked up at the bank, at the row of trees above. I couldn't see anything at first glance. Then I saw a tree leaning forward weirdly, as if it was bowing to us.

I wondered if I was imagining it. No, it was really happening, the tree was sliding forward, slowly at first, but then gathering momentum, rushing right down the muddy bank towards us.

'Run!' I screamed to Perry, grabbing his hand and pulling him.

We both pelted headlong away from the bank – and then there was a crash behind us. The tree had fallen, its roots sticking up

oddly, its branches broken. It was lying right across the tracks!

We stared at it, stunned. Then Perry suddenly darted forward, towards the tree.

'No, Perry! Keep back! Look at all those other trees up there! They might fall too. Do you want to be squashed to death?' I cried out.

But Perry took no notice. He was at the tree now, yanking at the branches desperately.

'Help me, Phoebes! We've got to get it off the tracks! The train will be coming back from the terminus!' Perry shouted. 'It will get derailed!'

I looked at my watch. In ten and a half minutes' time!

I pulled at the branches too. We even tried lifting it, but we couldn't make it budge so much as an inch.

'We'll have to run back to the terminus. We *might* make it if we run like the wind. Come on!' I said.

So we ran, faster and faster, Perry soon pushing in front. I tried desperately to keep up, my heart pounding, my throat dry, a terrible stitch in my stomach – and then I slipped on a muddy patch and sat down hard on my bottom, so winded I couldn't move.

'Don't wait for me!' I gasped. '*You* run. You're the quickest runner. Go for it!'

Perry took a deep breath and then ran on, his arms pumping,

his legs kicking out sideways, but going really fast. He didn't stop to look out for the muddy parts. He charged forward, mud spattered up to his knees.

I picked myself up slowly and painfully and looked at my watch. Seven and a half minutes. I wasn't sure he could make it in time, even though he was running like the wind.

I hurried back to the fallen tree, and had one last feeble tug at it, even though I knew I couldn't possibly move it by myself. Still, Perry could surely wave frantically at the train if it had started on its return journey and shout a warning to Alf in the engine.

I tried to picture it in my head. The engine made a terrible roar and clatter and Alf wouldn't be able to hear Perry's high piping voice. Perry would be waving and gesturing frantically, but Alf would assume he was trying to stop the train to board it. Alf would be furious to think we were messing about on the tracks. He wouldn't slow the train down and stop for him.

So *I* had to stop it somehow. I walked back up the track. It was no use standing right by the fallen tree. I knew the train couldn't stop straight away. Alf had to have plenty of distance to put the brakes on safely.

I stood where I was, trying to work out what I had to do. If only I had some way of writing DANGER AHEAD on a huge placard. How on earth could I convince Alf? I needed a whistle but I didn't have one. I tried whistling loudly myself, but I just

dribbled down my chin, hardly making any noise.

How did you stop things? I thought of football matches. I needed a red flag! I didn't have one of course – but I was wearing my red Manchester United shirt! I whipped it off and grabbed one of the smaller branches torn off the tree. I stuck it through both sleeves of my shirt, ripping the seam so it would stay in place. I tried waving. It made a good flag, big and bold.

I looked at my watch. A minute to go! It was horrible waiting here by myself. If only Becks had come with us! I was so scared.

I had to hope Perry had reached the terminus in time. I pictured him rushing along the platform, screaming, 'Stop! Stop! Stop!' Alf would look out of his cabin and glare at him, thinking he was playing some silly prank. Perry would gasp that there was a tree on the line. Alf would realize he was telling the truth. He'd sweep him up into the cabin and pat him on the back. He'd tell him he was a total hero. There would be an announcement to all the passengers and Perry would be hoisted on their shoulders, the boy who saved everybody's lives.

What about the *girl*? Would I be waiting here for hours, until a team of railway volunteers came along to deal with the tree? A girl looking foolish in her vest, with a weird red flag lying beside the track.

I wouldn't wait. I'd march back as soon as I was sure Perry had stopped the train. He'd wave at me and say, 'Hey, everyone,

this is my sister Phoebe. She spotted the tree, *she* told me to run back to the station, *she* was prepared to stay behind and stop the train all by herself if I didn't make it in time. *She's* the hero! Three cheers for Phoebe!'

I closed my eyes and shook my head fiercely, trying to stop my thoughts. I imagined my brain bouncing around in my head like a ball. I felt giddy and there was a roaring in my ears and a strange whistling sound . . .

I opened my eyes. It was the train, gathering speed along the track, coming right towards me! Perry hadn't got there in time. There was just me and the train. I had to stop it.

I picked the flag up, held it high and jumped right onto the railway line. I started waving it frantically from side to side, shouting, 'Stop!'

The train didn't slow down. It got faster and faster. But I wouldn't give up. I had to stop it, no matter what.

'Dad! Help me!'

Get off the track!

'But I have to stop the train!'

And I have to stop you killing yourself! Get back! GET BACK, PHOEBES, GET BACK!

I jumped back and the train roared past, but it *was* slowing now, screeching, jolting, and all the passengers inside were staring at me and pointing, while I still waved my flag feebly until the

train came to a halt. Then Alf and Ann came running down the track, shouting at me. They started blurring. Everything whirled around me, making me feel sick.

Then I was tumbling downwards – but someone caught me and held me close and told me he loved me to the moon and back.

'Dad?'

There were strong arms holding me, carrying me along, but he didn't smell of books and woolly jumper and coffee. This man's chest smelled of coal dust and oil. I looked up and saw Alf. He had little drops of water on his face.

'Is it raining?' I asked idiotically.

'What? Bless you, girl, I'm sweating, because you gave me such a fright! I thought I was going to plough straight through you. There was no way I could get those brakes to work any faster. Thank the lord you stepped back at the very last moment!' he said, hugging me closer.

'It was the tree,' I said. 'I had to stop the train because of the tree. Oh, please believe me, Alf.'

'I do believe you, pet. I saw it myself. If it hadn't been for you

the whole train would have been derailed and I wouldn't be here talking to you now,' he said.

'Where are we going?' I wondered.

'Back to the terminus with everyone else,' said Alf.

I peered over his shoulder and saw a long line of passengers. Someone saw my head moving and called out, 'She's conscious! The little girl's all right!' Someone else said, 'Bless her!', and then they started *cheering*!

'They're not cheering *me*, are they?' I asked.

'Of course they are! You saved us all, you and your red flag. Though it was a very risky thing to do. I keep panicking, thinking about what might have happened!' he said, puffing.

'Do put me down. I'm a bit of a lump and it's ages back to the station. I feel fine now, honestly, just a bit woozy,' I said.

'I'm not letting go of you! You passed out for several minutes. You might have banged your head. I've called for a paramedic. We don't want to take any chances with you. You're our little hero,' said Alf.

My heart started thumping again. I couldn't believe it. *I* was a hero! I felt a pang for Perry. 'It was my brother too,' I said. 'He ran back to the terminus to tell you but he obviously didn't get there in time. I'm sure he tried his best though. He ran ever so fast.'

'Then he's a hero too,' said Alf.

Perry was jumping up and down on the platform when we got

back. He peered at me when Alf carried me into the waiting room.

'You stopped the train then?' he asked eagerly. 'It didn't derail? It's not damaged at all?'

'No, I made a flag out of my T-shirt and waved it,' I said.

'You look a bit weird just in your vest,' said Perry. 'OK, I want to go and see them taking the tree off the tracks. Becks is looking for you.'

He was off before we could stop him.

'Come back here, young Perry!' Alf shouted, but he pretended not to hear.

I laughed shakily. 'He was desperate to know if the train was all right, but he didn't ask if *I* was!'

Becks came running up then, her face chalk white. She burst into tears when she saw me. 'Oh, Phoebes, Perry told us about the fallen tree. I was so terrified you'd do something stupid and be killed trying to save the train. It's all my fault *again*. I should have been looking after you properly!' she said in a rush, weeping all over me.

'It's all *my* fault,' said Jake. He was very pale too, and his cap was askew. 'I promised Grandad to keep an eye on you. He'll kill me when he finds out I let the two of you wander off by yourselves.'

'It wasn't either of your faults. We just sneaked off to see this silly old plate-layers' hut and then saw the tree fall,' I said.

'It'll have been the storm, loosening the roots. We'll have to

get the team out to check the entire length of the track,' said Alf, putting me down very carefully on one of the chairs. 'There now, you sit still and wait till the paramedic gives you a proper going-over to make sure you're really all right, pet.'

I hung onto his hand for a moment. 'Alf, can I whisper something?' I asked.

He bent down.

'Did you tell me you loved me to the moon and back?' I whispered into his ear.

He looked surprised but touched. 'No, I didn't, dear. Perhaps you had a little dream when you passed out,' he said.

'Perhaps,' I said.

Someone gave me a cup of sugary tea and someone else wrapped me up in a blanket, even though it was a hot day, and lots of people kept putting their heads round the waiting-room door to thank me and see if I was really all right.

'It's like I'm famous!' I said.

Then the paramedic arrived and he took me into his van with Becks, and he measured my blood pressure and checked me carefully for any broken bones and even monitored my heart. Perry would have been very interested, but he was busy with some people who had a forklift truck. Poor Jake hurried off to find him, scared that he might have somehow injured himself too.

I wasn't actually hurt myself, and I'd stopped feeling dizzy.

It was quite enjoyable being looked after by the kind paramedic, with Becks holding my hand and making such a fuss of me.

They were laying on emergency buses to get all the passengers back to Primrose station. Jake had to stay behind to help reassure everyone and make sure they were all accounted for. We rather wanted to stay behind too, but one of the railway benefactors, who'd been on the train, lived in a huge house nearby and insisted on taking Becks, Perry and me back in his chauffeur-driven Rolls-Royce! He was a very grand man called Mr Frobisher-Smythe, which was a bit of a mouthful. We were a bit overawed at first, but he was very friendly, and tremendously grateful that we'd saved the locomotive. His chauffeur, Phil, was even nicer and chatted to us all the way.

He was amazed to hear we were staying at Nina Cresswell's cottage. 'The old artist lady who lived in a hut in the middle of nowhere?' he said incredulously.

'Well, it's not actually a hut,' I said. 'It's a cottage.'

'But without any facilities!' said Becks. 'Not even a proper bathroom!'

'And I sleep in a cupboard,' Perry said proudly.

'Good heavens,' said Mr Frobisher-Smythe. 'Perhaps you had better come and stay with me for a few days until you find somewhere more suitable.'

Becks looked quite keen, but Perry and I shook our heads firmly.

'It's very kind of you, but we like it at the cottage with all Nina's lovely paintings on the walls,' I said.

'And I like to have a good think in my cupboard,' said Perry.

'You're a funny lot,' said Phil. 'Still, I've a soft spot for old Nina myself. Before I got my permanent job with Mr Frobisher-Smythe I used to drive a taxi at Forest Lake and I often gave Nina a lift. I had to pick her up at the telephone box. She was a lovely old girl, very chatty, though a bit eccentric, especially the way she dressed. Long velvet dresses and bangles up to her elbows, that kind of thing. Shame she had to go into that nursing home at Orlington. I went to visit her there once, to see how she was doing.'

'*Did* you!' I said. 'So she can have visitors?'

'Yes, though I don't think she gets many. It was sad seeing her laid up like that, but she seemed pleased to see me. I think she was already going a bit ga-ga then, maybe getting me mixed up with someone else,' said Phil.

'Do you think I could go and visit her?' I said eagerly.

'Phoebes! We don't even know her!' said Becks.

'But I feel as if I do. We live in her cottage. And I want to tell her how much I love her paintings,' I said.

'Well, I think she'd like that. Though I'm not sure she'd be up to much chit-chat nowadays,' said Phil. 'I saw her quite a while ago.'

'I think you'd better ask your mother and father first,' said Mr Frobisher-Smythe.

'We could ask our mother,' said Perry. 'But our father is—'

'Perry!' Becks said, elbowing him sharply.

'I was just going to say he's away somewhere,' Perry said indignantly.

'Shut up!' Becks hissed.

Dad! I knew he was far away in prison – but I also knew he'd spoken to me. I'd heard him above the shriek of the train. He'd made me jump back in the nick of time. He'd caught me and cradled me in his arms. He'd told me he loved me to the moon and back.

I started crying.

'Are you all right, poppet?' said Phil, looking at me in his driving mirror.

'I expect she's still in shock,' said Mr Frobisher-Smythe.

Becks put her arm round me and held me tightly.

'She was bright as a button just a minute ago,' said Phil. 'Never you mind, sweetheart. Have a little weep if you want to. You've been such a clever brave girl, hasn't she, Mr F-S?'

'She has indeed. I think we should organize a little celebration to show how grateful we are. I'll have a word with Mr Brown. I daresay the press will want to be involved,' he said.

'Oh dear, I don't think our mother would like that,' Becks said quickly.

'Well, I'll have a word with her when we get back to Primrose village,' said Mr Frobisher-Smythe.

Mum would hate the idea of reporters and photographers. They'd ask so many questions. Maybe they'd find out about Dad.

'Do you think Mum will be really, really cross?' I whispered to Becks.

'She'll be cross with *me*,' said Becks. 'I was supposed to be looking after you.'

'You don't think she'll ban us from going to the railway all over again?' Perry asked, looking agonized.

There was a little crowd gathered outside Primrose Railway station. They'd heard the news of the blocked track and the near derailment, and started questioning us the moment we got out of the car.

Some people took photos on their mobiles, though Mr Frobisher-Smythe and Phil tried to stop them. They ushered us into the station and there were Mum and Mr Thomas Brown. He had his arm round her in a fatherly way.

'You children are going to be the death of me!' Mum said in a shaky voice, running to us. She opened her arms wide and hugged all three of us hard. 'Is it true what they've been saying? Did you really flag down the train, Phoebe?'

'Yes, Mum! But I wasn't on the track, truly, not when the train got really near,' I said hastily.

'And I ran all the way to the terminus to try to stop the train. I was only seconds too late, else *I'd* have saved the day,' said Perry.

'I just took my eye off them for a minute, not even that, but when I looked round they'd vanished,' said Becks.

'They were supposed to be in Jake's care,' said Mr Thomas Brown. He looked ashen. 'Where is he now?'

'He stayed behind to make sure everyone got on the replacement buses,' said Becks. 'You won't be too cross with him? He's so worried he's let you down.'

'He *has* let me down,' said Mr Thomas Brown. 'I'm so sorry, Mrs Robinson. You must hold me personally responsible.'

'But all's well that ends well,' said Mr Frobisher-Smythe, clapping Mr Thomas Brown on the back. 'These children have acted so quickly and courageously – saved a lot of lives! Three hearty cheers for little Phoebe!'

The railway volunteers joined in, shouting, 'Hurray!' and I went hot all over with embarrassment. I'd always longed to be the centre of attention but now I just wanted to hide myself away. I started shaking, and I couldn't focus properly.

'Your eyes have gone funny, Phoebes. I think you're going to faint again,' said Perry, with great interest.

'You're shivering, darling,' said Mum anxiously. 'Oh my God, what have you done with your shirt! You're just in your vest!'

'Let the child sit down. We need to bring her blood sugar up,' said Mr Frobisher-Smythe, in his lordly manner.

'I know just the thing, sir,' said Mr Thomas Brown.

He went to the Junction and brought back a whole plate of iced buns.

'No, thank you. I feel a bit sick,' I said weakly – but I tried one little nibble. I suddenly realized I was desperately hungry. I hadn't eaten any breakfast and it was now past lunchtime. I ate my way rapidly through one whole bun and then another. I'd never been allowed to eat two buns before, but Mum didn't try to stop me. We *all* had buns, with cups of tea, so it was almost like a party.

There was a local press photographer outside with a journalist clamouring to ask questions, but Mum wouldn't let him talk to me. They spoke to Mr Frobisher-Smythe instead. She did agree to let them take a few photos of Perry and me, though she buttoned me into her own cardigan first.

'Come on, love, give us a smile!' said the photographer.

I did my best, but I was still feeling a bit weird. Perhaps it hadn't been such a good idea to eat two whole iced buns.

'*Smile*, Phoebes,' Becks hissed.

'*I'm* smiling,' said Perry, though he always does a wide cartoon smile showing all his teeth.

I'm not sure whether I managed a proper smile or not, but as soon as the camera stopped flashing I ran to the ladies' toilet and

was sick. When I staggered out of the cubicle Mum washed my face and mopped me up. I'd got just a little bit of sick on her blue cardigan but she didn't tell me off. She gave me a hug.

'Oh, Mum, I'm sorry!' I said. 'I mean I'm sorry for everything, not just being sick.'

'It's all right, darling. I'm sorry for everything too,' said Mum.

'Are you being so lovely to me now because I'm a hero?' I asked, clinging to her.

'No, you banana! I'm just glad you're safe!'

'I've been horrible to you,' I wept.

'Well, you've just been so upset about Dad,' said Mum.

'He stopped me being run over by the train,' I mumbled into Mum's shirt.

'*Dad* stopped you?' Mum said.

'I heard his voice. I know it was him,' I said. 'He kept telling me to get off the track.'

'Well, if Dad had been there that's exactly what he would have done,' said Mum.

'Does he talk to you too?' I asked. 'You know, in your head.'

'Not really. But then the two of you have always been so close. He feels so devastated that he's let you down now. He'll hate me telling you this, but he cried when I went to visit him,' said Mum.

'He *cried*?' I'd never, ever seen Dad cry, not even when I accidentally whacked a ball right into his face when we were

playing French cricket in the garden at home. He had a nosebleed and then he had a black eye for a week, but he pretended it didn't even hurt.

'So he's really sorry he took that money?' I said.

'Of course he is! Dad's not a wicked man and he knows that what he did was very, very wrong. He was just so depressed that he wasn't earning any money for us, and he thought a Robinson film would fix everything. He convinced himself it would be a big success and that he'd be able to pay all the money back into Melissa Harris's account. He started believing it would really happen. Like you tried hard to believe Dad was on a desert island. You didn't *really* think that, did you, darling?' said Mum.

'Yes, I did! Well, sort of. I don't know. It *seemed* real,' I said.

'You're very good at making things up. Perhaps you'll be a writer yourself one day. I'm starting to realize I'm never going to be one. I keep pegging away at my story every day, and I've written thousands and thousands of words, and yet they don't *seem* real. I'll carry on till I've finished the wretched story but I think I'm going to have to find another way of making a living,' said Mum, sighing.

I gave her a hug back.

Then Becks came into the ladies', looking anxious.

'Phoebes? Are you OK? You've been gone ages! There's another photographer arrived, and someone from the local radio, and Mr Thomas Brown says some local television people have

phoned – they're filming at the tracks by the fallen tree and the train, but they want to come on here and interview you,' she said breathlessly.

'What do you want to do, Phoebe?' said Mum. 'I don't want to rob you of your big moment.'

'I just want to go back to our cottage,' I said.

'Then that's what we'll do,' said Mum.

She put her arm round me and led me out of the ladies' room. There seemed to be a crowd of people pressing all around us, everyone asking questions, but Mum batted them all away.

'I'm so sorry. My daughter's in shock. I need to get her home straight away,' she kept saying, steering me through the crowd.

She thanked Mr Frobisher-Smythe and said I needed to go home immediately to rest. He did his best to persuade us to stay for the television interview, but Mum stood firm.

'I'm afraid I must insist that I take Phoebe home now, Mr Frobisher-Smythe. She might be the hero of the hour but she's also only a little girl who's been through a very traumatic experience,' said Mum, and she refused to be dissuaded.

Becks was by our side, and Mr Thomas Brown stood close behind Perry, making sure he couldn't dash off anywhere.

'I think you're being very sensible, Mrs Robinson,' he said quietly.

'I don't think Mum's being very sensible at all, Mr Thomas Brown,' said Perry. 'I want to stay to see the television people. I want to tell them how I ran and ran and very nearly got to the terminus in time. And I want to go back there too and see exactly how they get the tree off the tracks and I want to—'

'And *I* want you to calm down, lad, and look after your mother and sisters,' said Mr Thomas Brown. 'But you're quite definitely a hero too, and I daresay you'll be getting a special award from the Primrose Railway Company in due course, along with young Phoebe.'

'And I won't be getting any award whatsoever because I wasn't looking after you properly,' Becks said miserably.

'You're still a child yourself, Rebecca. *You're* not to blame, my dear,' said Mr Thomas Brown. 'The two youngsters just sneaked off.'

'And if we *hadn't* sneaked off, the train would have rounded the bend and gone *splat* into the fallen tree and everyone would have been killed or at least horribly injured, and all three of us and Jake would have probably been killed too. Do you think the impact would have been so great that we'd have died immediately, or would we have been left all bloody and mangled and in tremendous pain?' Perry asked.

'I don't want to think about it!' said Mr Thomas Brown, shuddering.

'Yes, not another word, Perry Robinson!' said Mum. 'Let's get in the car and go home.'

When we got back to the cottage at last it was mid-afternoon.

Mum sent me upstairs to put a fresh T-shirt on. Daisy squeaked at me excitedly, certain it was *her* lunchtime. I took her out of her cage and sat with her on my lap, stroking her. She was so used to me now that she didn't scrabble to get away. She just curled up happily, her eyes slowly closing.

'You'll never guess all the things that happened this morning,' I whispered.

Daisy didn't seem particularly interested. I wondered what it was like to be a guinea pig. Did she ever miss her mother and her father and her brothers and sisters? I gave her as much attention as I could, but she must get very lonely at times. Maybe Dad thought we would comfort each other while he was gone?

I loved soft furry Daisy, but not the way I loved *Dad*. I'd loved him so much there was only a little bit left over for Mum and Becks and Perry. But I didn't love him like that any more, did I? So now there was this great aching gap in my life. Perry had been given a book about astronomy last birthday, and for a whole six months he had talked solidly about black holes. I didn't have a clue what they were and what caused them, but now I felt as if I had a black hole inside me. It was as if all the *me-ness* of me had been sucked out.

I didn't hate Dad any more. I wasn't angry. Maybe I did still love him, but not in the same way. How could he still be the best dad in the whole world when I couldn't look up to him now?

I couldn't even be properly happy any more, even on an amazing day like this when I had thought of a way to stop the train crashing and I'd maybe saved everyone's lives. I was a hero.

'Did you know that, Daisy?' I whispered into her little curled ear. 'I'm actually a hero. Me! Stupid old Phoebe. Who'd have thought it, eh?'

Daisy didn't look remotely impressed. She didn't bow her head or roll over and wiggle her little legs in the air. She didn't even squeak. She just sat placidly on my lap, twitching her small pink nose.

I kissed her and carried her carefully downstairs. I took Daisy out to her run and popped her down. There were several dandelion clumps growing inside it. She squeaked then, still overjoyed to find her breakfast, lunch, tea and supper literally growing out of the ground at her feet.

I went indoors and ate boiled eggs and toast cut into buttery strips: safe, comforting nursery food.

'I've never thought about it before, but I really love boiled eggs and soldiers,' I said.

'I do too,' said Becks. 'It's like being three years old again.'

'I suppose so,' said Perry. 'Though it's a bit of a waste having toast without strawberry jam.'

We didn't know quite what to do after we'd eaten. So much had happened in the morning that we were all still buzzing with it, and yet now we had all the rest of the afternoon and the evening to get through and we had nothing to do. We'd got so used to hanging out at the railway most of the day, but it would be closed now until they got the tree off the tracks and repaired any damage.

'Though it would be so fantastic to see exactly how they do it. They might even let me join in,' Perry said wistfully.

'Absolutely not,' said Mum. 'There might still be reporters there, and television people. And you'd only get in the way.'

'No I wouldn't! All my railway friends say I know more about doing their jobs than they do! And anyway, I'd *like* to be on television,' said Perry. 'Mum, do they let prisoners have televisions in their cells? Dad could watch it and he'd be so proud of me. Well, Phoebe too, I suppose.'

I felt my heart thump. I suddenly so wanted that to happen.

'No, I truly don't think that's a good idea,' said Mum.

'Yes it is!' said Perry, his voice rising.

We looked at him warily. He hadn't had a proper meltdown for a while.

'Perry. Please! Think of *another* idea,' Mum said quickly. 'Something you'd think really good fun.'

'All right,' said Perry, surprisingly. 'Let's go to Forest Lake and go boating. That was great fun, especially as we were best at it, and Becks looked hilarious sopping wet.'

'I am never going boating again,' said Becks. 'And that's final.'

'Yes, I think we've had enough excitement for one day,' said Mum. 'One of you has very nearly got run over by a train. I don't want another one of you very nearly drowning, thank you very much. Besides, Phoebe should take it very easy this afternoon. I don't want her fainting again.'

'She was so lucky! I'd give anything to know what it feels like to faint,' said Perry.

'I'm starting to feel a distinct lack of oxygen in *my* brain,' said Mum. 'Let's all play cards,' she suggested.

We took out Nina's lovely flowery playing cards and played pontoon, using little packs of raisins as betting money. I couldn't help nibbling mine, so I was always the loser. Perry won almost all the games, and crowed about it.

Afterwards, I took my sketchpad and started drawing. I copied Nina Cresswell's flower design, repeating it to make a pattern, but it went lopsided and I got disheartened. I couldn't be bothered to start all over again. My neck ached now from keeping my head bent over my drawing and I had to keep flexing my fingers to make them work properly. I sat up and stretched.

'I think I'll go and have a run round the field,' I said to Becks.

'Mm,' she said, peering in the mirror. She'd stopped doodling and was experimenting with her make-up, trying to do little flicks with her eyeliner. She lost concentration and got a blotch all over her eyelid.

'You look as if you've got a black eye, if you don't mind my saying,' I told her, and went out of the room.

Mum was in her own room. The door was half open. She was sitting on her bed, propped up with pillows, tapping on her computer. She kept stopping and sighing. Her story clearly wasn't going well.

Perry was back in his cupboard, judging from the torchlight underneath the door.

I looked at Nina's picture of the dancers – the man with his quiff, the woman with her ponytail. I tried mimicking their movements. Dad had said I was great at jiving. I wished I hadn't spoilt my picture of us now.

I went downstairs and out of the back door. I stopped to watch Daisy scurrying here and there while I loomed over her. Then I went into the field. I went up the strimmed path and stopped when I got to my special place. I lay on my tummy.

'Are you there, Dad?' I said out loud, the grass tickling my nose.

I couldn't hear anything but the rooks and the rustle of the trees in the wind.

'If you're listening I'd like to say thank you,' I whispered. 'Someone spoke to me and I'm certain it was you. I mean *really* you, not just me making you up.'

I didn't get any response.

'It seemed like I was stuck standing on the tracks, with the train getting nearer and nearer. I was so desperate to stop it I just kept waving and waving my shirt like an idiot. I might not have jumped back if you hadn't told me to. But you did, didn't you? And then you picked me up when I fainted, or maybe that was Alf, but it was your voice telling me you loved me to the moon and back, wasn't it?'

I listened and listened and listened.

'Dad, *please*. Talk to me now! Make me believe it! I really, really need to feel you're still there for me,' I begged him.

I'm here! I'm always here for you!

It was such a faraway husky whisper that I could hardly make out the words, but I knew it was Dad. And then I heard a trudge of footsteps through the grass. I sat up hurriedly, half-blinded by the sunlight.

'Dad! Oh, Dad!'

'Phoebe?'

It wasn't Dad. Of course it wasn't Dad. He was locked up in prison. It was Mr Thomas Brown.

'Are you all right, dear? Oh my goodness, did you faint again?' he asked, hurrying to me.

'No. No, I didn't,' I said, dazed. 'I was just lying down.'

'Tired out after all the excitement?' Mr Thomas Brown asked, sitting down beside me. He gave a little oomph groan as he did so.

'Are *you* all right?' I asked.

'Yes, just getting a bit creaky in my old age,' he said. 'Goodness, this grass is a bit damp, isn't it?'

'Is it? I didn't really notice,' I said.

'Oh, to be young!' said Mr Thomas Brown. 'I've brought your red football shirt back with me, though it's a bit the worse for wear

now. Your mum might be able to patch it up for you. I just popped over to see her, and apologize yet again. I've brought young Jake with me. He's hanging his head suitably, as well he might.'

'But honest, it wasn't Jake's fault, Mr Thomas Brown! Please, he mustn't feel he's in trouble. Or Becks. It was Perry and me. Well, mostly Perry, because he wanted to go and see this plate-layers' hut. You know what he's like,' I said.

'Yes, bless him. It's a joy to find a lad so keen and interested in everything Railway but sometimes I feel he's like a little woodpecker, tapping away at my head for information,' he said. 'However, Jake wasn't doing his job properly. Too taken up with your sister.'

'Well, Mum thinks Becks is still too young for a boyfriend,' I said. 'Though she does like Jake, honestly. We all like him.'

'Really?' said Mr Thomas Brown. 'I mean, *I* think he's a lovely lad, but then I'm his grandad. Maybe I've expected a bit too much of him. He's just a young boy when all's said and done. I'm just so proud of him. He'll be the first in the family to go to university. He's going to be studying engineering too! He'll likely be managing the whole railway in a few years. I think the world of him.'

'He thinks the world of you, Mr Thomas Brown. And so do we. I wish you were *my* grandad,' I said.

'Oh, bless you, dear,' he said, smiling at me. 'Well, if I had a granddaughter I'd be thrilled if she were like you. Our little Primrose Railway hero! Mr Frobisher-Smythe's tickled pink with

you. I'm supposed to keep quiet about it, but he's insisting you and all the family have a special celebration slap-up meal on him on the Pullman!'

'Really! Oh, can we have champagne?' I asked, thrilled.

'Well, I daresay you could have a little sip or two,' said Mr Thomas Brown. 'It won't be for a few days, so we can clear the track and check all the banks to make sure there's no more rogue trees about to fall. Is there any chance your dad could come along too?'

'Not really,' I said. I could feel my face going very red.

'Well, never mind,' said Mr Thomas Brown quickly. 'I daresay he's very busy at his work . . . or whatever.' He was far too tactful to pry further. 'He must be feeling so proud of you though,' he added.

I nodded silently.

'And I am too,' he went on. 'In fact, I'd like to give you a little present myself for being such a brave clever girl. Now, what would you like most of all?'

I thought hard. I knew Mr Thomas Brown was a pensioner and probably wouldn't have much money. What could I ask for that wouldn't cost him very much? I suddenly thought of something that wouldn't cost him anything at all!

'Could you possibly take me on a little trip, Mr Thomas Brown?' I asked.

He looked surprised. 'Well, certainly, so long as it's not *too* far, and your mother approves,' he said.

'It's to Orlington,' I said. 'Would that be all right?'

'Of course it would,' he said. 'So what do you want to look at in Orlington? I'm afraid it hasn't got any pet shops.'

'I don't want to do any shopping,' I said. 'I want to go to the nursing home.'

Mr Thomas Brown wrinkled his nose in astonishment. 'The nursing home?' he repeated. 'Why would you want to do that?'

'Can't you guess? I want to meet Nina Cresswell!' I announced.

'Oh my goodness!' said Mr Thomas Brown. 'Why do you want to meet her?'

'Because I love her cottage and all her artwork. She's *my* hero!' I said.

'That's lovely, dear, but don't forget, she's a very elderly lady now,' he said.

'Wouldn't I be allowed to see her?' I asked.

'I don't suppose anyone would mind. But I rather think you should ask your mother to take you instead,' said Mr Thomas Brown.

'Mum doesn't know her. *You* do!' I insisted.

'Yes, but I haven't seen her in donkey's years,' he said.

'Then isn't it time you went to see her if you used to be her friend?'

'I didn't say I was her friend, Phoebe. I used to do odd jobs for her,' said Mr Thomas Brown. 'She'd never have expected me to come and visit her.' He was biting his lip and looked anxious.

'Do you have a thing about nursing homes?' I asked gently. 'Like some people hate hospitals?'

'No, no, it's not that.' He sighed. 'I'm afraid I made a bit of a fool of myself with Nina long ago. I haven't seen her since.'

'What happened?' I asked.

'Never you mind,' said Mr Thomas Brown.

'Oh, do tell me! Did you try and fix something and then it broke again?' I guessed.

'Of course not! I never do a shoddy job!' said Mr Thomas Brown. 'No, it was more embarrassing than that. And inappropriate.'

'Really? What did you *do*?'

'If you must know, I used to have a bit of a crush on Nina Cresswell many years ago. She was older than me, of course, and very glamorous, though she never put on any airs and graces. We'd have a good chat while I was fixing things, and it turned out that we both liked dancing – you know, jiving to rock and roll, which was all the rage in those days.'

'You can jive, Mr Thomas Brown?' I said.

'Well, not nowadays – I'd get out of puff – but I was reckoned to be king of the dance hall when I was a youngster,' he said. 'I

suppose I was daft enough to boast about it to Nina, and she asked if I'd take her dancing some time. I don't think she was actually serious, but *I* took her seriously enough. So I made a date with her and she came along, and she even dressed up for the occasion. She tied her hair up in a ponytail and wore a flared skirt with a big frilly petticoat. I suppose it was just a game to her, but I was thrilled.' He shook his head, remembering.

'And what happened? Didn't you have a good time together?' I asked.

'It was the best night of my life,' said Mr Thomas Brown. 'Well, no, I don't mean that seriously. I mean, I had some grand times with my Alice, and the kids, and I was really chuffed when I was made stationmaster, but . . . it was *magic*, that time Nina and I went dancing. It was as if we'd been dancing together for years. We were even picked to be the couple in the spotlight on the stage.'

He stopped and started humming a funny tune. 'There was a song we were all mad about in those days, "The Brighton Rock".'

'"The Brighton *Rock*"?'

'I know – it had the daftest lyrics, but it was a big hit. They played it for our spotlight dance. Folk talked about our doing "The Brighton Rock" for years,' said Mr Thomas Brown.

I laughed because it sounded so funny, but he was looking sad.

'So didn't you ever do it together after that?' I asked.

'Nope. Never went dancing. In fact, I could never face her again,' said Mr Thomas Brown, sighing deeply. 'I made a total fool of myself. I was daft enough to think she was as thrilled to be with me as I was with her. I told her I loved her and tried to kiss her.'

'Oh!'

'It makes me cringe just thinking about it,' said Mr Thomas Brown, shaking his head. 'She was so nice about it too. Just told me gently that she liked me a lot, but not in that way. I stammered out some kind of apology and she told me to forget all about it, but obviously I couldn't. The next time she got in touch to ask me to fix something I made some excuse, saying I didn't do that sort of work any more. And that was it.'

'I'm so sorry,' I said. 'But that was ages and ages ago. I'm sure she's forgotten about it now.'

'Oh, I daresay. It probably meant nothing to her. Maybe she even told some of her arty friends and they all had a good laugh about it,' Mr Thomas Brown said bitterly.

'But now she's an old, old lady, and she's probably very lonely. Don't you think she'd like to see a dear friend from the past?' I said. 'Oh, please, Mr Thomas Brown, do take me to see her.'

'You're worse than your brother, you know. Peck peck peck at my poor head,' he said. 'Very well, I'll take you.'

'Tomorrow? First thing?'

'Tomorrow, in the afternoon, when it's proper visiting time,' said Mr Thomas Brown firmly.

'You absolutely promise?'

'We'll shake on it,' said Mr Thomas Brown, offering his hand.

I clasped it and we shook hands.

'You're my absolutely favourite man, Mr Thomas Brown,' I said.

I meant it for a moment. And then I felt dreadful.

'Well, apart from my dad,' I muttered.

'Of course,' said Mr Thomas Brown. 'Shall we go back to the cottage?'

'Good idea,' I mumbled, sniffing.

We walked in single file down the narrow path, and went through the gate into the cottage grounds.

'How's little Daisy liking her guinea pig run?' he asked.

'She loves it,' I said. I stopped to peer over it. Daisy was in a little huddle, happily snacking. I saw a flash of brown and white. No, she was dashing about, squeezing through a little tunnel I'd made her, her head poking out of the other end. But she was still busy eating dandelions. There were *two* Daisys!

'Oh my goodness!' I exclaimed.

'I thought she might like a little friend,' said Mr Thomas Brown. 'I was sure you'd ask for another guinea pig when I said I wanted to buy you a little present. I was going to pretend I had

magic powers, and then when we went back to the cottage you'd see there were two of them! I brought her over in a cardboard box. A pal of mine breeds guinea pigs. He's assured me she's another girl – we don't want a boy, because then you'll have a hundred and one guinea-pig babies in no time.'

'I'd rather like that,' I said.

'Yes, but I don't think your mother would,' he said. 'So what are you going to call this one?'

I looked at both guinea pigs. When I looked closely I could see the differences, even though they were the same size and were both brown-and-white. The new one had a little white pointy patch on her face.

'She's Star!' I said. 'Oh, Mr Thomas Brown, she's lovely. Look at them running round together now! I think Daisy likes Star. And so do I! She's a wonderful present!'

'So do we still have to go and see Nina in the nursing home?' he asked.

'Yes please!' I said.

He sighed. 'I wouldn't do it for anyone else – but I suppose I promised. Let's go and square it with your mother.'

Mum was very surprised, but agreed I could go tomorrow afternoon.

'I don't have to go too, do I?' Perry asked, sounding horrified.

'I can't say I really want to either,' said Becks. 'I mean, we

don't even know her, do we?'

'It's just me and Mr Thomas Brown. He's her old friend – and I want to be her new one,' I said. 'I like all her paintings so much – I like her whole cottage. I just know I'd like *her.*'

'Well, that's very sweet of you, Phoebe. Why don't you show her that lovely picture you did of you and Dad dancing?' Mum said.

I felt myself going red. Mum didn't know I'd scribbled all over it. But then I suddenly thought of *Nina's* picture of the dancing couple.

'Come with me a moment, Mr Thomas Brown,' I said, taking his hand.

I led him up the stairs and along the corridor.

'Look,' I said, pointing to the man. 'Is that *you?*'

He didn't really look at all like him, with his big coif of dark hair and his snake hips and his pointy shoes. Mr Thomas Brown had short grey hair and he was a lot larger and his shoes were polished brogues. But when I looked at the face of the man in the picture I saw he had Mr Thomas Brown's expressive eyebrows, his long nose, his smiley mouth.

'It *is* you!' I said.

'So it is,' he murmured. 'And that's Nina, all dressed up for dancing. So she actually drew a picture of us together and put it up on the wall!'

'And kept it up, all these years. It's the only picture of people too. You and her. So that night must have meant a lot to her too, don't you think?' I said.

'Maybe,' said Mr Thomas Brown. He stared at the picture for a very long time. His eyes were misty when he looked at me at last. 'Thank you for showing me, Phoebe.'

The next day I unhooked the picture from the wall, wrapped it up in a T-shirt for protection, and put it in Mum's shopping bag. I wanted to show it to Nina too. I also wrapped her copy of *Robinson Crusoe* in another T-shirt. I felt a pang as I looked at those carefully painted little pictures once more, and then shut the book firmly.

I was starting to feel a bit nervous now. I was still certain I'd like Nina – but what if she didn't like me? Mr Thomas Brown looked nervous too when he came to collect me. He was wearing a dark suit that was much too small for him, and a white shirt with a very rigid collar. He had to keep putting his finger inside to ease it.

'You look ever so smart, Mr Thomas Brown,' I said, though I actually thought he looked much nicer in his Primrose Railway uniform.

'So do you, Phoebe, so do you,' he said. 'Right, let's get this over!'

Mr Thomas Brown's car was parked by the telephone box. It

was quite old, but immaculately clean, inside and out. Our car was a clutter of discarded Wellies and old CDs and chocolate wrappers and crumpled maps.

I chatted away until we got to the outskirts of Orlington, and then I was suddenly quiet. Mr Thomas Brown was too. He turned into the driveway of a very big white house, practically a mansion.

'Is this it?' I asked.

He nodded, and switched the car engine off. We sat there, still and silent. I swallowed.

'Oh dear. I feel really nervous now,' I said.

'Me too,' said Mr Thomas Brown.

'Maybe this isn't such a good idea,' I said.

'We don't actually have to go inside,' he said. 'We could just drive off. No one would be any the wiser.'

'Yes, but that might be a bit . . . cowardly,' I said.

'That's true,' said Mr Thomas Brown. 'Come on then.' He took a box of chocolates out of the glove compartment, and I clutched the shopping bag.

We got out of the car and approached the front door. He rang the bell and we waited apprehensively. I expected a bustling matron figure in navy uniform, but a girl not much older than Becks came to the door. She wore a white apron, but she was wearing an ordinary T-shirt and jeans underneath.

'Hello, I'm Julie. Are you visitors?' she said. 'I don't think I've seen you before.'

'This is our first time,' said Mr Thomas Brown. 'We've come to see Miss Cresswell.'

'Nina? Oh, that's nice, she doesn't get visitors nowadays. Though I don't really think she'll recognize you,' Julie said.

'No, I daresay she won't. I'm a friend from long ago,' Mr Thomas Brown explained.

'And I haven't actually met her yet, though I want to very much,' I said. 'I want to ask her all sorts of questions.'

'Well, I'm afraid she's not very chatty,' said Julie awkwardly. 'Still, I'll sign you in, and then you can come and say hello. Nina doesn't like television very much, so we generally put her in the garden room after lunch.'

The garden room was very peaceful, with green chairs arranged in front of big picture windows. One gentleman was nodding over a newspaper, and two ladies were playing some kind of card game at a little table. One was wearing a pretty blue dress and I wondered if she might be Nina, but Mr Thomas Brown shook his head.

'I think that's Nina over there,' he whispered.

He nodded towards a little hunched-up woman in a wheelchair right in the corner. I knew Nina was old, but this lady seemed ancient. She had white hair, tangled past her shoulders, but it was

very sparse, so you could see glimpses of her pink scalp. She was wearing a very worn coat as if she were about to go out, but it was clear from her pallor that she stayed indoors most of the time. The coat was a dull brownish grey, but where it caught the sunlight it glowed purple with a sheen that showed it was velvet. She had beautiful rings on her fingers: a large milky opal and a purple amethyst, both embedded into her flesh, so it didn't look as if she could ever take them off. Her fingers were very misshapen and shook a little. It was clear her painting days were long over.

Mr Thomas Brown took my hand and we went up to her. She must have heard us approaching, but she didn't turn her head.

'Miss Cresswell?' Mr Thomas Brown murmured. Then, more loudly, 'Nina?'

She did turn a little then, so we could see her face properly. Her eyes were surprisingly blue, but blank. Her mouth hung open a little. She had no expression at all.

'Oh, Nina,' said Mr Thomas Brown. 'You look in a right pickle.'

Julie was hovering. 'She won't be parted from that coat of hers, or her rings, bless her. I brushed her hair this morning, but she won't wear an Alice band to keep it out of her eyes. She's got a will of her own, has Nina.'

'She always did,' said Mr Thomas Brown. 'Nina, I used to

work for you long ago, do you remember? I'm Thomas. Tommy, you called me.'

Nina didn't respond.

'And this young lady is Phoebe. She's actually living in your cottage at the moment, aren't you, dear?' Mr Thomas Brown continued valiantly.

'I do hope you don't mind,' I said. 'We love it there. It looks beautiful with all your pictures.'

Nina stared straight through me, without a flicker of interest.

'I'll go and fetch you all a cup of tea, shall I?' said Julie. She raised her voice. 'Isn't this a treat for you, Nina? Your own visitors?'

Nina looked as if she couldn't care less.

'Like I said, she doesn't really talk much,' said Julie.

Mr Thomas Brown turned away from Nina and whispered to Julie, 'Does she actually ever talk at all?'

'Well, not really, no. Apparently she did when she first came, but not since I've been working here. But we talk to her, and sometimes it seems like she understands,' said Julie. 'Right, I'll get cracking with your tea.'

She walked off purposefully. Mr Thomas Brown and I were left standing with Nina.

'Let's sit down,' he said, going over to fetch some stacking chairs.

'Mr Thomas Brown used to like you ever so much,' I said to

Nina. 'I know you don't talk now, but do you think you could give him a smile? It would mean a lot to him.'

Nina didn't seem to care.

'He's the stationmaster at the Primrose Railway. He looks lovely in his uniform,' I said. 'We go there nearly every day.'

Mr Thomas Brown came over with the chairs and we got settled either side of Nina.

'Were you talking about the railway, Phoebe? Let me tell you, Nina, young Phoebe here is quite the little hero. A tree fell on the line and it could have been totally disastrous but she flagged the train down just in time! There now! It was very dramatic!'

Nina was totally unimpressed.

Mr Thomas Brown went on talking bravely. After a couple of minutes Nina closed her eyes.

'I think she's gone to sleep,' I whispered.

'Well, maybe she can still hear us,' said Mr Thomas Brown. 'You chat to her for a bit, Phoebe. Tell her all about yourself.'

'Well . . .' I couldn't think of a thing to say.

And clearly Nina couldn't either. It was a relief when Julie came back with a tray. There were two teas in thick china cups, and another in the sort of beaker you give a toddler.

'And I thought you might like some biscuits,' said Julie.

There were six custard creams on a plate, probably my least favourite biscuit.

'Here you are, Nina, dear,' said Julie, giving her a gentle shake. She gave her the beaker in one hand and a biscuit in the other.

'That's very kind,' Mr Thomas Brown murmured. We both sipped our tea and nibbled at a custard cream. Nina sucked at her beaker. Neither of us liked to watch because it looked so undignified. She didn't keep a grip on her biscuit and it fell to the floor.

'Oh dear. Would you like another one?' said Mr Thomas Brown, offering her the plate.

Nina didn't look interested.

'I know what you might like,' said Mr Thomas Brown. He showed her the box of chocolates. 'They're for you. Shall I take the cellophane off for you? I remember you often used to have a fancy box of chocolates on the go. Try one of these.'

He took the box lid off and held them in front of her. Nina blinked her eyes. She focused on the chocolates and then pointed with her shaky finger.

'Ah, the one with the cherry on the top!' said Mr Thomas Brown. 'Good choice.'

Nina tried to take it out but her fingers were too scrabbly.

'Here, let me help.'

He took the cherry chocolate out and popped it in Nina's mouth. She sucked it, her blue eyes brighter, and then nodded, as if to say thank you. Mr Thomas Brown smiled. He offered me a chocolate too. I chose a nutty one. He had a coffee cream.

'Why don't you show Nina what you've got in your bag, Phoebe,' Mr Thomas Brown suggested.

I fished *Robinson Crusoe* out first and shyly held it out to Nina. She seemed to have lost interest in her beaker so I gently took it from her and put it on the tray so she wouldn't spill any tea out of the spout.

'This is your book, Nina,' I said. 'I think you might have had it when you were a little girl. *Robinson Crusoe*. You've painted the pictures ever so carefully. Shall I show you?'

I put the book on her lap and opened it up at a picture of Robinson walking along the beach, looking out to sea. The waves were coloured different shades of blue, with white flecks at the

crests. Nina reached out and slid her finger up and down the waves as if it was surfing. She touched Robinson, stroking his animal skins. She made little twitching motions with her finger and thumb at his long beard.

'You're tugging it, aren't you!' I said. 'You've made it look so real.'

She looked at me and for a moment I could see the proper Nina trapped inside this ancient old lady.

'I've looked at all the pictures and pretended they were real too,' I said. 'I love all your artwork – you've got so many pictures back at the cottage! I've brought one to show you.'

I took out the picture of the two dancers and held it in front of her. She stared at it intently. Then she pointed to the girl, touching her ponytail and her swirling skirt.

'I think that's you,' I said. 'I love the way your skirt sticks out.'

'Petticoats,' said Mr Thomas Brown. 'The girls used to soak them in sugar water so they stood out stiffly.'

Nina's finger touched the boy's quiff of hair.

'That's Mr Thomas Brown,' I said. 'Tommy. He was very good at dancing. And you were too.'

Nina looked at Mr Thomas Brown.

'It *is* me, though I look a sad old crock now,' he said. 'I had a fine head of hair in those days. I didn't know you'd done a

picture of us dancing, not till Phoebe showed it to me. I don't suppose you remember, but that was a wonderful evening for me. We did a grand jive to "The Brighton Rock". Daft song, but it didn't half have a bounce to it. *Rock, rock, oh let's do the Brighton Rock!'*

Nina nodded her head. She swallowed. Then she opened her mouth wider. 'Rock, rock,' she whispered.

'That's it! You do remember it, don't you?' he said.

'*Rock, rock, oh let's do the Brighton Rock!'* Nina quavered.

'Yes! Let's sing it together!' said Mr Thomas Brown. He took hold of her hands and they swayed together as they sang.

'Rock, rock, oh let's do the Brighton Rock
Pink and sweet and good to eat
Stamp your suedes and swirl your frock
Yeah, yeah, let's do the Brighton Rock.

Roll, roll, oh let's do the Bacon Roll
Crispy filling gets top billing
Faster faster, slow to a stroll
Yeah, yeah, let's do the Bacon Roll.'

They were both word-perfect, and burst out laughing at the end.

We all had another chocolate to celebrate, and stayed chatting to Nina for quite a while. She didn't actually chat back, but her eyes were bright and we could tell she was listening to every word.

When we said goodbye she smiled at us sleepily and murmured, 'Rock, rock!'

'You've been a real tonic for Nina,' said Julie. 'I do hope you can come back another day.'

'I'd like to come every week, if I may,' said Mr Thomas Brown.

'So would I!' I said. I still thought Nina magical, even though she was such a fragile old lady. I didn't want to make up stories any more. I wanted to be a proper artist like Nina.

'Is it possible for us to hang this in her room?' Mr Thomas Brown asked, holding out the portrait of the two of them.

'And I'd like to leave her this book because she likes to look at the pictures,' I said, clutching *Robinson Crusoe*.

Julie took us to see Nina's room. It was spotless, but very plain. The walls *were* painted blue, but a very pale wishy-washy shade.

'Do you think we could paint it a darker blue?' I asked.

'I'm not sure that would be allowed,' said Julie.

'But we can put the picture up? Several pictures? And maybe find a darker blue blanket for the bed? And drape a bright shawl over that chair? And put some ornaments on the windowsill, just to make it *more* like Nina's room,' I begged.

'I don't see why not,' said Julie.

When we got outside I held Mr Thomas Brown's hand again, this time triumphantly.

'I bet you're really pleased I made you come,' I said.

'Don't crow, you little baggage!' said Mr Thomas Brown. 'Yes, of course I'm pleased. Oh, Phoebe, she really did remember!'

'She was word-perfect on that funny song! Will you teach it to me? I love it!'

We sang it happily all the way home. Mr Thomas Brown came into the cottage with me, and stayed for supper. Mum made cheesy spinach pancakes with a salad, and Mr Thomas Brown said they were very tasty.

'Only if you like the taste of spinach, which I *don't*,' said Perry, opening his pancake up and removing every single speck of green. 'And it's been an absolutely horrid day because the railway's still closed. It would have been all right if Mr Thomas Brown had stayed here and we could have done stuff together. I don't see why he had to go off with Phoebe all afternoon to see some old lady she doesn't even know.'

'I do know her now!' I said.

'Perry, I think Nina Cresswell somehow means a lot to Phoebe,' said Mum.

'Yes, and it's pretty weird if you ask me, Phoebe being so desperate to see Nina Cresswell when she won't even go to see her

own father!' said Perry.

There was a sudden intake of breath. Even Perry looked startled, his hand over his mouth as if he wanted to stuff the words back inside him.

'Go upstairs, Perry,' said Mum.

Perry went straight away, without arguing.

'I'm so sorry,' Mum said to Mr Thomas Brown.

'That's all right, Mrs Robinson. I know young Perry can't help being a little blunt at times,' said Mr Thomas Brown.

He tactfully didn't ask about Dad, or why I wouldn't visit him. He talked about the railway instead, and all their special plans for the autumn, and the Santa Special rides in December.

'I bet you dress up as Santa, Mr Thomas Brown!' I said.

'It has been known,' he said, twinkling.

'Oh goodness, does Jake get to be one of your elves?' said Becks, giggling.

'He did when he was a little boy, bless him, but when he got into his teens he made it very clear that his elfin days were over,' said Mr Thomas Brown.

'You know it was just as much my fault as Jake's that Perry and Phoebe slipped away,' said Becks. 'In fact, probably *more* my fault. You won't stay cross with him for long, will you? And would you mind if we still saw each other? Like, tonight?'

'If he volunteers at the railway he has to take his duties seriously,'

said Mr Thomas Brown. 'But I think he's learned his lesson now. So if it's all right with your mother, it's all right with me.'

Mr Thomas Brown went after supper. Becks started getting ready to go out. Perry stayed upstairs in his cupboard. It was just Mum and me.

We did the dishes together and I chatted for a while about Nina. I even sang 'The Brighton Rock' to Mum.

'It was just like they were dancing it together again,' I said. I sighed, sad that I'd ruined my picture of Dad and me dancing. 'It seems so awful that Mr Thomas Brown steered clear of Nina for so many years when they'd been so close once,' I added. 'I think they loved each other!' Then I started crying because *everything* was sad.

'Oh, Phoebes,' said Mum, and she put her arms round me.

'Perhaps . . . perhaps I do want to go to see Dad after all,' I whispered.

We went up to London a few days later, Mum and Becks and Perry and me. I wore my washed and mended Manchester United football shirt. Perry wore a Primrose Railway whistle round his neck. Becks wore full make-up, but she kept rubbing her eyes and licking her lips nervously, so it was rather smudged by the time we got there.

Mum played CDs in the car, but we weren't in the mood for singing. We didn't even talk much, though Perry shouted excitedly when he saw a wisp of white smoke far away.

'It's a steam train! The railway's open again! Oh, Mum, can we go on the train when we get back?' he pleaded.

'If there's time,' she said.

We stared out of the windows as the lovely fields and sweeping hills gradually gave way to grey streets and rows of shops. After

a very long while they started to seem weirdly familiar.

'Mum? Isn't this near *home*?' Becks asked huskily.

'Yes. Well, a mile or two away,' Mum said.

'Can we go down our road? Oh, Mum, can we stop at our house so I can pick up some more of my clothes?' Becks begged.

'Maybe on the way back,' said Mum. 'We don't want to miss our visiting slot, and it will take us ages to find somewhere to park near the prison.'

We all winced when she said that word. I suddenly felt sick, even though I'd hardly eaten any breakfast. Perry looked a bit greenish too, his hair plastered to his forehead. Becks fussed about her clothes for a good ten minutes, as if it was the only thing in the world that mattered.

'Do shut *up*!' I said at last, poking her in the back.

'Ouch! That really hurt!' Becks turned round and tried to slap at me, but she couldn't reach.

'I have to get out of the car,' Perry announced.

'Oh, for God's sake!' said Mum. 'Stop it, all of you. I need to concentrate on my driving.'

'I *have* to get out of the car,' Perry repeated.

'We can't go home, darling, not now. There isn't time,' said Mum.

'I'm going to be *sick*!' said Perry, and he suddenly retched.

Mum managed to slam on the brakes and get Perry out of the

car before he threw up. It was revolting seeing him being sick into the gutter. My own stomach lurched ominously.

Mum bundled Perry back in the car and handed him a bottle of water and a pack of mints. 'You'll feel better now,' she said hopefully.

'Mum, I think *I* might be sick,' I said.

Mum took a deep breath. 'I think you're fine, Phoebe. You're just copying Perry.'

'That's monstrously unfair! I felt sick *first*!' I argued.

'Will you all shut up about being sick!' Becks complained. 'It's totally disgusting. What's the matter with you two? Throwing up like babies all the time!'

'It's all right for you sitting in the front. We have to squash up in the back. It's no wonder we feel sick,' I said.

Cars were hooting at Mum now. She did her best to move off into the traffic.

'I know you're all het up about seeing Dad. So am I. But for pity's sake, pipe down now,' Mum said, driving away. 'You've no idea how stressful it is, driving in London.'

We were silent until she'd parked the car up a little side road. I felt so wobbly I had to lean on the car when I climbed out. I rather hoped I might be sick just to show Mum. Perry was still pale green. Becks looked like a zombie, her eyes heavily ringed with smudged liner.

'Here.' Mum passed round the water and mints again and wiped Becks's eyes with a tissue. 'There, let's spruce you all up a bit,' she said.

We walked down the street, and then another and another. There was a grim grey-brown building dominating the skyline. It was obviously the prison. It looked even worse than I'd imagined.

'It must have been awful for you coming to see Dad the first time, all by yourself,' said Becks, tucking her arm through Mum's.

'I was very nervous. And worried. And a little bit angry too,' said Mum, looking at me. 'Very angry, in fact. But the moment I saw Dad that all melted away.'

'Will we see him in his actual cell?' I whispered.

'No, no, there's a visiting hall. But we have to go to the visiting centre first, to get checked in and searched,' said Mum.

'*Searched?*' said Becks. 'But *we* haven't done anything wrong!'

'Children don't get searched, do they?' I asked anxiously.

'I'm afraid so. But it only takes a minute,' said Mum. 'It's to make sure none of the visitors pass on anything they shouldn't to the prisoners.'

I imagined these other visitors would look incredibly tough and scary, but when we got to the visiting centre we saw they were mostly weary-looking mums with young children, some of them wailing babies in buggies.

'They won't search the *babies*, will they?' I asked.

But the female wardens picked each baby up and gave them a little pat down. They even had a quick look inside their nappies! One of wardens was big and looked rather fierce, but the other one was plump and smiley, chatting to everyone.

I prayed we'd get the smiley one, but we ended up with the fierce one. Mum showed her our visiting order, and took all our passports out of her handbag to prove our identities.

'Right, let's give you the once-over,' said the warden.

She patted Mum up and down with her blue plastic gloves, delving into her pockets, feeling everywhere. We all winced, watching our proud elegant mother being treated like a suspect.

'Now the kids,' said the warden. 'You first, young lad.'

'My son Perry is on the autistic spectrum and has issues with strangers touching him,' Mum said firmly.

'This means my brain is wired up a little differently to yours, and I don't always react like other people,' Perry said.

'Well, you've still got to be searched,' said the warden. 'We'd search the Queen herself if she came visiting.'

'I very much doubt that,' said Perry.

'Perry. Please. If you don't do as you're told we won't get to see Dad,' Mum said.

Perry was scowling and shaking his head. He looked as if he was about to kick off.

'It's the rule, Perry,' Becks said quickly. 'Like all the rules at the railway. Mr Thomas Brown is forever saying you have to stick to the rules.'

Perry *didn't* always stick to the railway rules – but mentioning Mr Thomas Brown did the trick.

'All right,' he muttered, and held his hands up high and let the warden search him. She did it as lightly as possible, though.

She searched Becks. Then she searched me. I didn't like it one bit, but I stayed still and silent, holding my breath.

We had to wait quite a while so that everyone could be assessed and searched. Most of the women stood there barely reacting, obviously used to the whole procedure. But one woman started objecting angrily, slapping the warden's hands away. She got escorted back to the entrance, even though she started screaming. We watched, round-eyed.

I started trembling. If they treated visitors like this, how on earth did they treat the prisoners? A little film clip ran in my head, over and over. Dad was wearing one of those awful old prison uniforms with arrows all over it. He was cowering away from huge wardens with rubber gloves who were beating and kicking him.

I wished I hadn't come. Dad would look so different now. I wasn't sure I could bear it. I wouldn't know what to say, what to do. This new Dad would seem like a stranger.

'Phoebe?' Mum pulled me close. 'There's no need to be scared, truly.'

I tried my hardest to believe her, but it was impossible. Even Becks was shivering now, so white that her blusher stood out like stripes on her cheeks. Perry was muttering, 'Rules, rules, rules are rules,' faster and faster.

Then a bell rang and everyone stood up. Mothers scooped their babies up in their arms, leaving their buggies behind. Our own mum gathered us close, Becks and me on either side, Perry in front of her with her hands on his shoulders.

'Here we go!' she said.

We were all ushered through a door, across a courtyard, and into a much larger building. I put my hand over my nose – I hated the sour institutional smell. We were herded into a large room a bit like a shabby church hall, with cheap tables and chairs set out in a pattern. There were a few toys in one corner and a bigger table at the side with a tea urn and various snacks. I think there might even have been iced buns, but I didn't give them a second glance.

There were men at the tables, all dressed in T-shirts and sweat pants. A few sat back taking it easy, as if they were lounging in their own homes, but most were sitting up straight and looking round eagerly at the visitors. And there was Dad, right in the middle, looking just as he always did, with his hair all over the

place and his T-shirt rumpled! He wasn't a stranger, he was still my own lovely dad.

'Dad! Oh Dad!' I ran to him and threw my arms round his neck.

'Phoebes!' Dad hugged me as if he would never let me go.

'Now, now, minimum contact, please. You know the rules,' said a male warden, pointing at us.

'Rules, rules, rules are rules,' said Perry, approaching shyly.

'It's so lovely to see you, Dad,' said Becks, crying, smudging her make-up all over again.

'There, darling, I told you the children were desperate to see you,' Mum said. 'So much has happened! Phoebe, tell Dad about the train, when you were the hero of the hour!'

'I was the hero too!' said Perry.

'It was partly because I was chatting to Jake. Did Mum tell you, Dad? I've got a *boyfriend* now,' said Becks.

'I know sooo many things about steam railways, Dad,' said Perry.

'Let Phoebe tell her bit first, Perry,' said Mum.

But it was a while before I could say anything but, 'I love you, Dad.'

And Dad clasped my hand and told me he loved me to the moon and back.

* * *

Well, it's not quite the end. Maybe you want to know what happened next?

Dad came out of prison before Christmas, let out early because of good behaviour. He really did behave well in prison, starting up his own special club for inmates who struggled with reading. He's very into prison reform now, and helping young offenders. He goes round secondary schools talking about it. And he's written another book! It's not about Robinson: it's about his own prison experiences, and it got to number eight on the bestseller lists. There's even going to be a television film of it, with a famous actor playing Dad! It's made almost enough money to pay Melissa Harris back.

Mum and Dad sold our London house and paid the rest back from the profit. We live permanently in the country now, near the Primrose Railway. We don't live in Nina's cottage though, because it would be too much of a squash. We've got our own cottage just outside Orlington. It's quite an old cottage, with a thatched roof and roses round the door – but it has a lovely modern bathroom and mobile reception and broadband.

Mum never finished her children's book. She runs a tea shop in Orlington, specializing in savoury and sweet pancakes. And Mo makes a fresh batch of scones for the shop every morning.

Becks isn't seeing Jake any more. He got a new girlfriend when he went to university. But it's all right, because Becks went dancing with Yvonne and has got herself a whole bunch of new friends. Becks and Yvonne are best friends now.

Perry hasn't yet made any special friends his own age at his new school, but he's palled up with an older boy who's totally into steam trains too.

I like *my* new school. I especially like Miss Rhapsody, our art teacher. I don't want to boast, but she says I'm very talented! I've made friends with a girl in my new class and you'll never guess what she's called. Amelie! She's much nicer than my old friend Amelie. Luckily there aren't any girls called Kate. But Mr Thomas Brown is still my *best* friend. We go to visit Nina every week. We've hung up all her paintings in her room and she loves looking at them. Sometimes she's in the mood for singing and sometimes she's not, but it doesn't really matter.

Mr Thomas Brown is my favourite friend, but he's not my favourite man. That's Dad, of course. He's not exactly a hero to me any more, because I know what he did was bad and silly. Still, I admire what he's doing now. I still love him more than anyone else in the whole world. And he loves me to the moon and back. That's all that matters.

And guess what! Mr Thomas Brown's friend was right about Star. She is a girl guinea pig. But it turns out Daisy is actually a

boy. Star's had a lot of babies now. They have a specially built big pen in our back garden. I'd love to be an artist like Nina when I grow up, or a writer like Dad, but if I don't succeed I'm sure I'll make an excellent guinea-pig breeder.

About the Author

JACQUELINE WILSON wrote her first novel when
she was nine years old, and she has been writing ever since.
She is now one of Britain's bestselling and most beloved
children's authors. She has written over 100 books and is the
creator of characters such as Tracy Beaker and Hetty Feather.
More than forty million copies of her books have been sold.

As well as winning many awards for her books, including
the Children's Book of the Year, Jacqueline is a former
Children's Laureate, and in 2008 she was appointed a Dame.

Jacqueline is also a great reader, and has amassed over twenty
thousand books, along with her famous collection of silver rings.

Find out more about Jacqueline and her books
at **www.penguin.co.uk/jacquelinewilson**

About the Illustrator

RACHAEL DEAN has illustrated numerous books including Aisha Bushby's 'Moonchild' series and 'B is for Ballet', a non-fiction picture book in collaboration with The American Ballet Theatre to mark their 80th anniversary.

Rachael works both digitally and traditionally in gouache to create vivid scenes and lively, engaging characters. She is inspired by the natural world, particularly when visiting the gorgeous national park and beach on her doorstep near Liverpool.

🌿 Dame Jacqueline Wilson, author of over 100 books for children and young people, is a huge fan of *The Railway Children* by E. Nesbit and is currently the President of the Edith Nesbit Society, which was set up in 1996 to celebrate the life and work of the author and her friends.

🌿 Edith Nesbit wrote many much-loved classic children's books including *The Story of the Treasure-Seekers*, *The Phoenix and the Carpet* and *Five Children and It*. She was a political activist and believed that property and wealth should be shared fairly. To help spread her message, she and her husband, Hubert Bland, founded the Fabian Society, a socialist organization that then became associated with the early Labour Party.

🌿 Have you read the original story of *The Railway Children*? It was first serialized in 1905 in a publication called *The London Magazine*. The instalments were so popular that in 1906 they were brought together as a complete book, and it has been in print ever since. Amazing!

🌿 In the original story, after their father is taken away unexpectedly Roberta (Bobbie), Phyllis, Peter and their mother move from their comfortable London house to a run-down cottage in the country near a railway line. Life is so different, but while their Mother writes stories to earn money to live on, the children soon make many new friends, including the porter, the stationmaster and the kindly 'Old Gentleman' who waves to them every morning from the 9.15 train. However, the mysterious disappearance of their father continues to haunt them. Maybe the Old Gentleman can help?

🌿 In 1970, the story of *The Railway Children* was turned into a film, which launched the highly successful acting careers of Jenny Agutter and Sally Thomsett. It also starred the much-loved English actor, Bernard Cribbins. Although it was made over fifty years ago, the film remains a firm family favourite.

🌿 In 2011, *The Railway Children* was adapted for the stage in a unique way – it was performed not in an ordinary theatre as you might expect, but inside York's National Railway Museum! With special sound effects and visual tricks, it was easy to imagine being right by the tracks of a real steam train. Two years later it was staged at London's Waterloo mainline station in a space created from the former Eurostar terminus where, again, it was a huge success with children and adults alike!

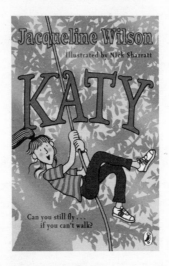

**Inspired by Susan Coolidge's classic *What Katy Did*,
read Jacqueline Wilson's modern day take
on the story about the feisty tomboy heroine.**

Katy Carr is a lively, daredevil oldest sister in a big family.

She loves messing around outdoors, climbing on the garage roof
or up a tree, cycling, skateboarding, swinging . . .

But her life changes in dramatic and unexpected ways
after a serious accident.

**A bestselling story of four children who discover
an extraordinary way to make wishes come true,
inspired by E Nesbit's classic, *Five Children and It*.**

Rosalind is the eldest sister.

Robbie is her younger brother.

Smash is their stepsister and she isn't too happy about it.

Maudie is the baby of the family.

Now you've met the four children.

But what is IT?

Have you read them all?

LAUGH OUT LOUD
THE STORY OF TRACY BEAKER
I DARE YOU, TRACY BEAKER
STARRING TRACY BEAKER
MY MUM TRACY BEAKER
WE ARE THE BEAKER GIRLS
THE WORST THING ABOUT MY SISTER
DOUBLE ACT
FOUR CHILDREN AND IT
THE BED AND BREAKFAST STAR

HISTORICAL HEROES
HETTY FEATHER
HETTY FEATHER'S CHRISTMAS
SAPPHIRE BATTERSEA
EMERALD STAR
DIAMOND
LITTLE STARS
CLOVER MOON
ROSE RIVERS
WAVE ME GOODBYE
OPAL PLUMSTEAD
QUEENIE
DANCING THE CHARLESTON
THE RUNAWAY GIRLS

LIFE LESSONS
THE BUTTERFLY CLUB
THE SUITCASE KID
KATY
BAD GIRLS
LITTLE DARLINGS
CLEAN BREAK
RENT A BRIDESMAID
CANDYFLOSS

THE LOTTIE PROJECT
THE LONGEST WHALE SONG
COOKIE
JACKY DAYDREAM
PAWS & WHISKERS

FAMILY DRAMAS
THE ILLUSTRATED MUM
MY SISTER JODIE
DIAMOND GIRLS
DUSTBIN BABY
VICKY ANGEL
SECRETS
MIDNIGHT
LOLA ROSE
LILY ALONE
MY SECRET DIARY

PLENTY OF MISCHIEF
SLEEPOVERS
THE WORRY WEBSITE
BEST FRIENDS
GLUBBSLYME
THE CAT MUMMY
LIZZIE ZIPMOUTH
THE MUM-MINDER
CLIFFHANGER
BURIED ALIVE!

FOR OLDER READERS
GIRLS IN LOVE
GIRLS UNDER PRESSURE
GIRLS OUT LATE
GIRLS IN TEARS
KISS
LOVE LESSONS
LOVE FRANKIE

r
6
b
4
v

F
s

"
I
N
R

'A
S

'A
o
o
D

'N
ar

Sunday Telegraph

'Practical and often hilarious guide'
You Magazine

'The Mary Poppins of the feline world'
Mail on Sunday

'Packed with anecdotes and tips, this is a must-have book for anyone who is moggy mad'
Sun

'This wise and entertaining book is a must have for all cat lovers'
My Weekly

Also by Vicky Halls

CAT CONFIDENTIAL
CAT DETECTIVE
CAT COUNSELLOR

and published by Bantam Books